Praise for

The Love Song of
JONNY VALENTINE

"Sad-funny, sometimes cutting . . . Mr. Wayne depicts Jonny as a complicated, searching boy, by turns innocent and sophisticated beyond his years, eager to please and deeply resentful, devoted to his unusual talent and aware of both its rewards and its costs. This is what makes *The Love Song* more than a scabrous sendup of American celebrity culture; it's also a poignant portrait of one young artist's coming of age."

—Michiko Kakutani, *The New York Times*

"The most authentic voice."

—NPR, "All Things Considered"

"Depicting the inner life of a protagonist who is not yet a full-fledged adult is no small feat, but author Teddy Wayne pulls it off masterfully."

—*The Daily Beast*

"Few novels with child narrators can truly appeal to adults in a complex way. Flannery O'Connor's *The Violent Bear It Away* and, of course, Harper Lee's *To Kill a Mockingbird* are obvious exceptions, and we can add this novel to the list."

—*BookReporter.com*

"Hilarious and heartbreaking. . . . An original, poignant, and captivating coming-of-age story . . . a breathtakingly fresh novel about the dark side of show business [that] includes one of the most complicated portrayals of the mother-son relationship since *Room*."

—*BookPage* Top 10 Best Books of the Year

"Switchblade-keen satirist Teddy Wayne . . . delves into the twisted world of celebrity culture with delicious, detailed insight. It's as if *People* magazine were written by Kurt Vonnegut, smart and fun and fanged . . . there are also great swaths of heart and pain and genuine compassion."

—*Tampa Bay Times*

"Wayne cleverly submerges readers into the distorted world of child celebrity. . . . Like a contemporary Oliver Twist or Holden Caulfield, Jonny is slowly grasping a world outside his insular one . . . a fresh and intriguing slice of life of today's celebrity culture."

—*St. Louis Post-Dispatch*

"Teddy Wayne has all the classic trappings of a rising novelist."

—*New York Observer*

"Deft and delightful . . . touching (and unexpectedly suspenseful) . . . so frank and engaging. . . . A sweeter, softer-edged satire of the pop-culture carnival."

—*Wall Street Journal*

"A showstopper. . . . The book's greatest triumph — and there are many — is Jonny's voice . . . a serious book that is way more fun than the life of a child star."

—*The Boston Globe*

"Surprisingly moving . . . heartbreaking. . . . A mix of preadolescent angst and industry cynicism that makes him sound like Holden Caulfield Jr. adrift in *Access Hollywood* hell."

—*Rolling Stone*

"A scathing portrayal of our culture's celebrity obsession . . . assured prose and captivating storytelling."

—*Oprah.com*, Book of the Week

"The best—and only—tween-pop novel you'll ever read."

—*Details*

"*The Love Song of Jonny Valentine*" is a fun, highly diverting read. . . . Wayne generates considerable sympathy for the eleven-year-old kid trapped at the center of the churning entertainment machine . . . . This is a portrait of the artist as a young brand."

— *San Francisco Chronicle*

"A deeply likeable and thoroughly heartbreaking character . . . air-tight satire . . . masterfully done. . . . A rollicking satire of America's obsession with fame and pop culture "

—*The Millions*

"Wayne brilliantly narrates from the perspective of Jonny's tweenage prison. . . . Reading about Jonny means rooting for him, even though there is a sense that he, like so many real stars who we will never know so well, is already long gone."

—*Boston Phoenix*

"Moving, funny, and strangely fascinating."

—*Arizona Republic*

"Laid out in a surprisingly poignant mix of cynicism and innocence, Wayne intertwines both Jonny and Jonathan's voices into a sublime plot, making it an unconventional coming-of-age story that digs beneath the glossy veneer of mainstream pop."

— *The National* (UAE)

"A scathingly funny look inside the tween-pop industrial complex . . . extremely clever, and alive."

—Standard Culture

"Masterfully executed . . . the real accomplishment is the unforgettable voice of Jonny. If this impressive novel, both entertaining and tragically insightful, were a song, it would have a Michael Jackson beat with Morrissey lyrics."

—*Publishers Weekly* (starred review)

"Provocative and bittersweet . . . Jonny is such an engaging, sympathetic character that his voice carries the novel. . . . A very funny novel when it isn't so sad, and vice versa."

—*Kirkus* (starred review)

"Satire with a heart, capturing the sadness, longing, and confusion beneath the celebrity veneer. . . . A top-of–the-charts tale."

—*Library Journal* (starred review)

"*The Love Song of Jonny Valentine* takes us deep into the dark arts and even darker heart of mass-market celebrity, twenty-first-century version. In the near-pubescent hitmaker of the title, Teddy Wayne delivers a wild ride through the upper echelons of the entertainment machine as it ingests human beings at one end and spews out dollars at the other. Jonny's like all the rest of us, he wants to love and be loved, and as this brilliant novel shows, that's a dangerous way to be when you're inside the machine."

—Ben Fountain, National Book Critics Circle Award-winning author of *Billy Lynn's Long Halftime Walk*

"I'd wanted to go slowly and read *The Love Song of Jonny Valentine* over the course of a week or two, but once Jonny's voice got into my head, I was hooked, and kept picking it back up, and so I ended up on the last page, reading that final, amazing sentence, at like three in the morning. . . . This novel is a serious accomplishment . . . America as we know it, with laughs on every page, but also a book that doesn't take one cheap shot. . . . And at the swirling core, you have an eleven-year-old boy trapped by his fame and trying to figure out how to move through the world, and who wants nothing more than to find his father. This is a book with a runaway narrative engine, tremendous ambitions, and an even bigger heart. I do not lie when I tell you: Teddy Wayne is as good a young writer as we have."

—Charles Bock, *New York Times* bestselling author of *Beautiful Children*

"What is most searing about Teddy Wayne's splendid new novel is not his trenchant social criticism, nor the itchy, unsettling way that he makes tragedy entertaining, but that in the bubble of celebrity which comprises little Jonny Valentine's whole world, at times the only differences between the savvy, drug-taking, lonely adults and the savvy, drug-taking, lonely kid himself are his outsized talent, and their avarice plus wrinkles."

—Helen Schulman, *New York Times* bestselling author of *This Beautiful Life*

"*The Love Song of Jonny Valentine* is a novel of ferocious wit and surprising poignancy. Teddy Wayne has written a pitch-perfect anthem for our surreal American Dream, a power ballad for the twenty-first-century unhappy family, an epic ode to the fleeting glory of fame. . . . Adored by his fans, enslaved by the music industry, Jonny Valentine navigates the high-stakes game of celebrity while secretly longing for the love of his missing dad. And we, in turn, long for him to hold on to his soulful spirit, his baby chub, his cri de coeur, his 'major vulnerabilities.' A deeply entertaining novel with humor and heart to spare."

—Amber Dermont, *New York Times* bestselling author of *The Starboard Sea*

"In Jonny Valentine, Teddy Wayne has created a vivid and achingly authentic portrait of an adolescent prodigy trying to make sense of a world from which he's been kept mostly separate. Wry, witty, and genuinely moving, this is a novel that delves into the private longings of a public figure, exposing the sometimes dark and often ridiculous inner workings of a life in show business. *The Love Song of Jonny Valentine* is absorbing and beautifully written—and also a ton of fun to read."

—Aryn Kyle, *New York Times* bestselling author of *The God of Animals*

"It speaks well of both Jonny and his creator that the result is this good, a moving, entertaining novel that is both poignant and pointed . . . his satirist's eye is impeccable . . . so limpidly does Wayne imitate the voice of a preteen celebrity, he risks making it look easy."

—Jess Walter, *The New York Times Book Review*
(cover review and Editors' Choice)

ALSO BY TEDDY WAYNE

Kapitoil

The **Love Song** of

To Nina

JONNY VALENTINE
A NOVEL

*Cowboy up!
Visit NYC again!*

Teddy Wayne

Teddy Wayne

SIMON & SCHUSTER PAPERBACKS
New York London Toronto Sydney New Delhi

Simon & Schuster Paperbacks
A Division of Simon & Schuster, Inc.
1230 Avenue of the Americas
New York, NY 10020

First Simon & Schuster trade paper edition February 2014

SIMON & SCHUSTER PAPERBACKS and colophon are trademarks of Simon & Schuster, Inc.

For information about special discounts for bulk purchases, please contact Simon & Schuster Special Sales at 1-866-506-1949 or business@simonandschuster.com.

The Simon & Schuster Speakers Bureau can bring authors to your live event. For more information or to book an event contact the Simon & Schuster Speakers Bureau at 1-866-248-3049 or visit our website at www.simonspeakers.com.

Book design by Ellen R. Sasahara

Manufactured in the United States of America

1   3   5   7   9   10   8   6   4   2

The Library of Congress has cataloged the hardcover edition as follows:

Wayne, Teddy.
The love song of Jonny Valentine: a novel / by Teddy Wayne. — 1st Free Press hardcover ed.
p. cm.
1. Child celebrities—Fiction. 2. Fame—Psychological aspects—Fiction. I. Title.
PS3623.A98L68 2013
813'.6—dc23
2012038331

ISBN 978-1-4767-0585-9
ISBN 978-1-4767-0586-6 (pbk)
ISBN 978-1-4767-0587-3 (ebook)

To my sister and brothers and parents

I want my world to be fun. No parents, no rules, no nothing. Like, no one can stop me. No one can stop me.

—Justin Bieber

Complete control, even over this song.

—The Clash, "Complete Control"

The Love Song of JONNY VALENTINE

CHAPTER 1

Las Vegas

I hit the remote control next to the bed and turned on the lights to play The Secret Land of Zenon. Normally the game helped me fall asleep after a show. But tonight I was too wired, so after a while on Level 63 I paused it and called Jane's room next door. Maybe talking to her would calm me down, or at least she could give me one of her zolpidems.

It rang six times before going to the hotel's voice mail. I tried her cell.

"Jonathan?" Jane said through loud background music.

"I thought you were staying in tonight," I said. From the song's bass line, I could tell it was Madonna's "Like a Virgin," which has a dance groove that closely mimics "Billie Jean," even though it's directly influenced by that old Motown song "I Can't Help Myself." But pretty much everyone rips off bass lines.

"The label asked me to meet a radio producer for a drink," she said. "And turn off the game."

Zenon still plays background music when it's paused, synthesized strings and light percussion, and I guess she could hear it over the Madonna. It's savvy audience-loyalty retention strategy, because it reminds you the world of Zenon is still there, always waiting for you to come back.

"I can't sleep. When are you coming home?"

"I'm not sure. Take a zolpidem."

"I finished all the ones you gave me. Can Walter or someone from concierge get the bottle from your room?"

"Absolutely not," she said. "I don't want anyone poking through my stuff. You'll have to fall asleep on your own."

I ran my hand over the puffy white comforter. Hotel beds are way too big, like the mattress and sheets are swallowing you up and you could disappear inside them if you aren't careful, and it can be harder to fall asleep in a luxury king than it used to be in a sleeping bag on the carpet at Michael Carns's house.

"Can you sing the lullaby, at least?" I asked. Sometimes it made me sleepier.

She waited a few seconds. Then she quietly sang the part of the lullaby that goes

> *Hush-a-bye, don't you cry*
> *Go to sleepy, little baby*
> *Go to sleepy, little baby*
> *When you wake, you shall have*
> *All the pretty little horses*
> *All the pretty little horses*

She doesn't have a great voice, but she sang it slow and low. "I'm sorry for snapping before, but try to go to sleep," she said. "We have an early start and a big day tomorrow."

"Good night, Jane."

"Good night, baby," she said, and hung up.

I put down the phone and stared at it. It was easy for her to say I should try to fall asleep when she wasn't the one who'd just performed for two hours in front of a capacity crowd of 17,157 fans and had to take a meeting with the label tomorrow back in L.A., who was probably going to voice their concerns that the new album hadn't meaningfully charted yet, which meant it never would, since sales momentum rarely reverses at this stage in the game unless there's a major publicity coup.

And now that I'd convinced myself zolpidem was the only way, I didn't have a chance without it.

Walter needed his shut-eye to be alert enough to protect me, and I wasn't supposed to call Nadine for nontutoring issues unless it was an emergency and she didn't like it when I took zolpidem, plus neither of them could get access to Jane's room anyway and they might tell her I'd asked them.

I had one other option, but I'd never tried anything like this on tour before. If it didn't work, I'd be in big trouble, but thinking about my schedule the next few days, a bad night's sleep might be worse. My body shook a little as I picked the phone up again and called the front desk.

"Hi," I said. "I'm in 2811. Can I get into 2810, belonging to Jane Valentine, under the name Jane Valentino?"

The woman who answered sounded black, but it's hard to locate accents in a city like Vegas, where everyone's from someplace else. She went, "I'm sorry, but we can't allow anyone access to guest rooms."

I told her I was Jane's son, Jonny, and it was okay. "Hold up," she said. "You're Jonny *Valentine?*"

I said yeah, and she laughed. "Uh-huh, right," she said. Her voice changed the way it does when people think I'm fooling them. "Even if you *were* Jonny Valentine, I don't know if I could do it."

I was probably checked in under James or Jason Valentino, so I told her that, and said, "If I could prove who I am, will you let me in?" and she said she'd believe it when she saw it, so I asked where she was working and what her name was.

Then my body *really* started shaking, except part of it was from setting the thermostat to sixty-four since colder temperatures make you burn more chub. I changed out of my pajamas and put on my sunglasses and Dodgers hat and stood on top of a chair to scope out the peephole for any child predators. If I ran into someone without Walter providing crowd buffer to prevent interference or trampling or abduction, I needed something to cover my face, so I grabbed the teen-demo glossy with my one-page write-up in it that the label had messengered over in the morning. It wasn't the smartest disguise, because there was a small photo of me in the top horizontal strip, which meant my plan was to cover my real face with a *picture* of my face. But, as usual, Tyler Beats owned the central real estate and commanded consumer attention, with a candid of him holding hands with a brunette actress and the headline TYLER'S NEW SQUEEZE!

I poked my head out to make sure the hall was clear. It might've been fun to do this with someone else, but on my own, it was way scarier than preshow butterflies at the MGM Grand Garden Arena.

I didn't have Walter with me getting clearance to use the freight elevator, so I inhaled down to my diaphragm and ran to the regular bank. If we'd had penthouse suites, I could've just taken a private elevator to the private concierge lounge, but the label didn't spring for them in every city this tour. They didn't want to do it *at all* at first, but Jane fought them to a compromise.

One was coming down, and the closer it got to the twenty-eighth floor, the more nervous it made me that I was going somewhere by myself. I didn't know what would be worse, encountering a child predator or Jane finding out I'd left my room alone.

So I imagined I was playing Level 63. Instead of being in Vegas, I was in The Secret Land of Zenon, and I wasn't trying to get the keycard to Jane's room, I was looking for the key to a locked castle door. The easiest part was pretending about experience points, since you get them in Zenon for exploring and experimenting with different actions you don't do in other games. Like if you reach a real locked castle door and don't have the key, you might get points for picking the lock, or breaking it down with your sword, or setting it on fire with a torch, or casting a spell to destroy all nearby wood. You don't know what gives you the most points until you do it, and when you get enough, a gem appears, which means you can fight the Emperor's minion on that level and advance to the next one. Most of the time, I don't even care much about getting to the next level. I just like doing whatever I want, seeing what gives me experience points, and wandering around wherever I want in Zenon, over the tall mountains and through the deep forests and into the dark dungeons.

The elevator opened with a gray-haired guy in a relaxed-fit suit and tie. He looked up from his phone at me for a couple seconds when the door slid open, but I think he was wondering what a random kid in sunglasses was doing by himself in a Vegas hotel elevator at ten o'clock on a Thursday night. That's the nice thing about flying business class, the business guys are too far out of my demo to visually ID me, unless they have daughters who are rabid fans. He seemed safe, but I sized him up like Walter would, since sometimes the guys who look the most normal are the biggest pervs of all.

I got in and held up the glossy over my face. Jane was pissed they'd pushed back the pub date to over two weeks into the tour, after we'd already finished the South and Southwest legs. At least we still had the heartland ahead of us, where I need to bulk up my presence so I don't project only a bicoastal identity, which is funny considering I'm from St. Louis, but St. Louis isn't high-tier enough for me to strongly connect with it. Geographic background is a tightrope you have to walk carefully.

I folded it over to my profile to read it. I'd been putting it off all day, because in the interior photo I wasn't wearing a track sweater and was slouched over and it looked like I had way more stomach chub than I actually did, and they didn't help me out with Photoshop.

Will He Be *Your* Valentine?
by Wendy Detay

Send an RSVP to your local arena: Jonny Valentine is cruising into your city! We caught up with the eleven-year-old heartthrob before he launched his cross-country *Valentine Days* tour on New Year's Eve, with shows in thirty cities over forty-six days, as he dished about what song made him want to be a pop star (Michael Jackson's "Billie Jean"), what his life goal is ("To share the music and the love"), and, of course . . . girls!

"I love spoiling girls with one-on-one face time," JV says, brushing his world-famous blond hair out of his eyes as his mother and manager, Jane, watches over him in their Los Angeles home. "Like, if a girl wants to see a movie, I'll surprise her and rent out the whole theater just for us, like the rest of the world doesn't exist, with all the popcorn and soda we want. It's awesome."

But the Angel of Pop swears there's no one in his life right now—he's focused on his supersonic career. And what he's most psyched about is his final show on the tour, on Valentine's Day at New York City's Madison Square Garden.

"It's every performer's dream to play the Garden, but I've only been to New York before on business trips," says the "Guys vs. Girls" singer in his crush-worthy voice. "And we're bundling it with an Internet live-stream for $19.95."

I was glad the writer hadn't asked why I'd never played the Garden before, because we always had gate-receipt conflicts with the bookers that Jane finally ironed out, but I was even gladder she'd put in the plug for the live-stream, which we were hoping would make it my exposure breakthrough in the untapped Asian market. The whole thing, the Garden debut plus the live-stream, could make this a brand-perception game changer, if we pulled it off.

The elevator stopped and a good-looking couple in their twenties got on in clubbing clothes, smelling like alcohol. *They* might be able to ID me. And if they did, and blabbed or Tweeted about it, it might end up in a tabloid or on the Internet, and it would eventually get back to Jane, and she'd enforce check-ins every half hour and not give me my own key-card, like on the first national tour. I held the glossy closer to my face like it was the most interesting article in the world, but I couldn't focus on it to read the rest.

In real life you might encounter a child predator who could molest or kidnap or kill you, or a tourist who could take a candid of you with his phone and post it and create a mini-scandal, but in Zenon you encounter enemies who can reduce your damage percentage. The lower it gets, the slower and weaker you are, and if your damage percentage or anyone else's hits zero percent, your ghost silently floats up into the air and the narrator's voice and the screen both say, "Everyone must depart the realm sometime." It's for the thirteen-and-up demo, but Jane let me get it anyway. The online version against real people is supposed to be different, but I haven't played it because who knows what kind of crazies I'd meet out there.

The business guy's finger pecked at his phone like a bird's beak until we hit the lobby. The younger guy told his girlfriend how everything that happened tonight was definitely going to stay in Vegas. People repeat everything they see in commercials. Yeah, what *they* did here, they'd keep private. Gossip about riding in an elevator with a celeb didn't count. My stomach kept tightening up every few seconds, especially when the guy got off-balance and put his hand on the wall near me for support, but they were so into themselves and drunk that they didn't notice me.

We got out, and with the blinking lights and sounds of the casino on the ground floor like an overproduced video and song, I blended in more easily and could've passed for being on vacation with my parents. I found the lobby desks and saw a black woman with gold glasses and the name tag ANGELA behind one. She was fit for her age, which I'd guess was thirty-seven or thirty-eight. I'm getting almost as good at the age game as Jane.

A few people were in line, so I waited to one side with my back turned and pretended to be reading the glossy. What would really kill my chances was if a tween girl spotted me. But I was the only kid around. When no one else was near, I walked over to Angela and lifted up my sunglasses for a second. "Is this enough proof?"

She put her hand over her mouth and was like, "Oh, my God, you weren't joking! Wait till I tell my girls about this, they play 'Guys and Girls' twenty-four-seven!"

Normally I'm only a little annoyed when adults act this crazy around me and forget I'm in the room with them, except Angela made me extra pissed since she could've sparked crowd interest and she called it "Guys *and* Girls," not "Guys vs. Girls." There'd been like a five-hour discussion with the label when we produced it about *vs.* or *and*.

But I acted like a consummate professional. "If it wasn't for my fans I wouldn't be here. Everything I do belongs to them," I said. Angela was still in shock and I don't think she really heard me, so I waited a few seconds, also to make it not sound like this was all I cared about. "So, do you think you can get me the key-card to my mother's room?"

"I don't know." She wasn't so starstruck that she wasn't worried she could get caught, the same way I was. "You're not authorized in the system."

"What if I give your kids an autograph and let you take a picture?"

She looked around to make sure no one was watching. No one was, and she pushed a hotel stationery pad and pen over the desk. "Write it to Ashley and Lucy," she said. Offering the autograph was like gaining thirty experience points in Zenon.

I grabbed the pad and wrote a "Songs, Smiles, and ♥ JV" autograph, which I basically do without thinking now like when Dr. Henson hits my knee with that little hammer. Angela took a photo of me with her phone and gave me a key-card and whispered, "Don't tell *anyone* about this, okay?" which relaxed my diaphragm because it meant she wasn't going to tell anyone, either, plus the photo could've been taken at any time so I didn't have to worry about it getting back to Jane. I waited until the elevator area was clear before going upstairs.

I got back to Jane's door without running into anyone else. The locked castle door. I knocked in case she'd gotten back, but no one answered. When I opened it, the lights were on and a bunch of dresses and thongs and shoes were scattered around one of Jane's open suitcases like a mage from Zenon had cast an explosion spell inside it. She throws a fit if there's any mess or dirt at home, but she's a slob in hotels.

One of her toiletry kits was between the two bathroom sinks, and the zolpidem bottle was inside. That was Level 63's gem, the zolpidem. I shook out one of the tiny rectangles. It's harder to wake up when you've had two.

I turned off the lights to save energy, but when I did there was still something blue glowing from the back of the room. Jane's computer was open on the desk, and it was on my Twitter account's sign-out screen. It's super-important to have a strong social media presence, and Jane's always going, When interviewers ask you about your Twitter, say you love reaching out directly to your fans, and I'm like, I don't even know *how* to use Twitter or what the password is because you disabled my laptop's wireless and only let me go on the Internet to do homework research or email Nadine assignments, and she says, I'm doing you a big favor, it's for nobodies who want to pretend like they're famous and for self-promoting hacks without PR machines, and adults act like teenagers passing notes and everyone's IQ drops thirty points on it. Jane hasn't set up her own Twitter since she doesn't have as much brand awareness.

I went over to the computer and Googled my name in a new window. It was the same stuff I always saw, tons of pictures and videos and fan sites and articles and blog posts and the "Jonny Valentine Legal Countdown Page" this gay guy set up that has a timer ticking down to my eighteenth birthday that Jane tried to take down but he has a legal right to keep up because he's not explicitly being a child predator. It was at 2,248 days, one hour, thirty-three minutes, and sixteen seconds. I watched it tick down a few more seconds.

There was too much to go through, and some of it I couldn't access anyway since Jane had a parental block on and it thought a lot of regular sites were porn sites, sort of like how normal-looking guys might be child predators.

I was about to close the browser and get out before she caught me, but I noticed a piece of paper sticking out of an envelope at the corner of the desk. It was one page, and there were a lot more underneath it in the envelope. The stationery address listed a law office in L.A. called Bergman Ellis Jacobson & Walsh and the top said

VIA OVERNIGHT MAIL AND EMAIL

Re: Albert Derrick Valentino

Jane always told me my father didn't have a middle name, so I almost didn't recognize his name at first. I tried reading it:

Per our telephone conversation on 1/12, until we are able to determine the identity of the individual(s) referred to in the letter dated 1/7, we cannot seek any judicial remedy. However, we recommend the following precautionary measures.

The rest of the page was all legal language, and I'm usually okay at understanding financial terms because Jane reviews my contracts with me, but I couldn't figure any of this out, and I was afraid to take out the other papers from the envelope in case I screwed up the order. I slipped the page back in where it had been and spun in the chair once around the room to make sure I was still alone and for fun.

Then, even though it was a high-risk decision, since if Jane caught me she wouldn't just enforce check-ins, she'd take away my game system, too, I double-checked that Jane's computer was preset for private browsing like it always is, and Googled "Albert Valentino."

All the usual info about him being my father and how nobody knows anything about him came up, like that he left our house when I was five or six, and even I don't know which it is or when they got divorced because Jane doesn't hardly ever talk about him. The times I've asked, she says something like, Jonathan, remember that your father left and the one person in this whole world who will always stick with you is me, everyone else will try to take from you, but people who love you will give to you.

Once in a million years, though, she'll slip and say something nice about him, like when we saw this war movie on TV two Christmases ago with a telegenic young Irish actor, the first time he came on-screen Jane whispered to herself, "God, Al," and at the end of the movie, when the Irish actor jumps in front of his general before a grenade goes off and he departs the realm, Jane cried a Jacuzzi, and it had to be because the actor looked like my father, since it was a mostly crap movie and he was the caliber of actor who you could tell was repeating someone else's words. I only have a couple memories of him and don't totally remember what he looked like, just brownish hair and that he smelled like cigarettes. If we ever had any pictures, Jane threw them out.

Then I Googled something I'd never Googled before: "Albert Derrick Valentino."

There weren't many hits, and they were all about people or things that weren't my father, but I went to the second page anyway, and when I did, something stopped me. His name showed up in a Jonny Valentine fan forum.

A bunch of comments from a message on December 24 were from haters, saying I was gay or sounded like a girl or they hope I'll get electrocuted onstage when I cry into my mike. When Jane sees this stuff she's like, It's not the Internet that makes people stupid and annoying, they were *always* stupid and annoying, now it's in our face. But at the bottom of the message, a commenter named "Albert Derrick Valentino" wrote, "If Jonny is reading this, he can contact me."

His email address was listed, but that was it. There were a lot of impostors pretending to be either me or Jane or sometimes my brother or sister who don't even exist and once in a while my father, but I never saw anyone use a middle name, and especially with our old last name, which only the rabid fans know about, not the lay fans, and *not* say he was my father. The media never pays them any attention because they know they're fakes, but I always guessed my real father never went to the media. Or maybe he did, but Jane shut it down by threatening a publicity freeze-out to whoever was going to break the story.

I Googled "Albert Derrick Valentino Jonny Valentine." A bunch of different fan sites came up, and he'd posted the same message in each of their forums, all on December 24, at different times over the whole day. So it probably wasn't a spam-bot. It was a real person. I just didn't know if it was actually my father.

My hand was shaking over the touch pad like it does sometimes holding the mike preshow, and I got worried Jane would come back and find me reading it. I scribbled the email address on a piece of hotel stationery in case the post got erased and made sure the letter was exactly where it had been and left her room with the lights on like it was before even though it's wasteful.

Back in my room next door I buried the stationery in the pocket of a pair of jeans in a suitcase. Was that message really from my father or an impostor? If it was an impostor, how did he know my father's middle name? And if it was my father, why didn't he say anything else besides telling me I could contact him, which was a weird way to say it?

I was thinking about it so much I got even more awake. I could have taken the zolpidem, but I was also excited to get back to Zenon now that I'd pretended to be playing it in real life.

So I loaded my saved game, and after a few minutes of traveling through a forest I encountered a horse. First I tried riding the horse, which didn't do anything. I reloaded and damaged the horse, and it jumped up on its back legs and kicked at me, but my two-handed sword was too powerful and I got it all bloody and its horse ghost floated up in the air, except that didn't give me any experience points, either. The second time I reloaded, I fed it a loaf of bread in my inventory. My experience points went up by seventeen, and a gem appeared on the ground.

I picked up the gem, and a few seconds later the Emperor's minion jumped out from behind a tree. He was a regular-looking soldier in chain-mail armor, with a curved sword and shield. We battled, and he reduced my damage to seven percent and I thought I was going to depart the realm, but I came back and knocked his shield away and hacked him down to zero percent, and the narrator's voice and screen said, "You have defeated the minion of Level Sixty-three and advanced to the next level of The Secret Land of Zenon. You must pass through thirty-seven additional levels until you encounter the Emperor."

That's the other cool thing, how you don't have a name in it. Other games, they'd give you a stupid name, like Kurgan or Dragonslayer or even just the Warrior. In Zenon you're only you.

Finishing a level always helped me feel less wound up. I turned off the game and popped the zolpidem. I'd be able to conquer sleep now, and sleep was the Emperor's minion. We had an early start and a big day tomorrow.

CHAPTER 2

Los Angeles (First Day)

Walter waited for the room service guy who'd delivered my breakfast to leave before tasting it first for me. He always makes some joke about how it's not poisoned but it might as well be, because it's a three-egg-white omelet with spinach, no hash browns or toast, which are straight carbs, and coffee, no dairy. Walter eats meat and fried food and ordered a salad like once in his life, since he's from Nashville, where he has three daughters he's on the child-support hook to his old lady for and where we'll play later in the tour and which still has a strong country base that's difficult for pure pop acts to penetrate. He's about 250 pounds, which is half muscle from lifting four days a week, but half fat because he says walking from a hotel or venue to the car service counts as cardio. He says chasing around his daughters used to keep his weight down. Now he just has to walk briskly by my side, but I'm not supposed to run indoors because of injury risk and I definitely shouldn't in public or it might spark crowd interest and trigger a stampede. I bet he was fun with his daughters, though.

I thought of asking him about the legal letter and telling him about the Internet fan-forum messages, but first of all, Walter never went on the Internet, and second, even though he wouldn't tell Jane, I didn't want to make it so he had to lie to her.

He left to eat in one of the hotel restaurants with the rest of the crew, and I sipped my drink and imagined the coffee beans were fighting the early onset dementia that Grandma Pat had maybe passed down to me and Jane, and they were using the paralyze spell from Zenon, which freezes your enemies for a few seconds. There should be an early onset dementia spell, too, which places your enemy in an old-age home.

After breakfast Walter came back to escort me down to the basement service exit, and I put on my sunglasses and a Detroit Tigers hat because I'd been wearing the Dodgers hat three days in a row. You never want to alienate fans in different markets, even though my following is all girls who think you score a touchdown in baseball. Jane is like, Let the paparazzi take your photo but make it look like you're not letting them take it, so the baseball hat and sunglasses are perfect for that. And plus the baseball hat is my trademark now. Jane once showed me a big website that's only candids of me in different hats.

In the bus parking lot, the star/talent bus was parked all the way past our five other buses and four eighteen-wheelers. Me and Walter boarded it and said hi to the driver, Kenny, and Jane weighed me on the scale near the front. Eighty-eight pounds. I'd started the tour eighteen days ago at eighty-six. You almost always *drop* weight when you're performing, no matter how bad you're eating, but I'd been raiding the minibars and gift-basket amenities more than normal, and now that I'd seen the number, I could tell I was getting beefier.

She didn't say anything about it, but she didn't have to. She just whipped out the hotel bill and said, "Three packages of candy. Thirty-two minutes on the bike, either now or later."

"I sang and danced for two hours last night."

"Are we going to argue about this every morning? That's only six hundred calories, and it's not sustained cardio that raises your metabolism," she said. "You want your next publicity photos to show you with a gut, too?"

I chose the bike now, because it's worse to have it waiting for you and I didn't like seeing eighty-eight any more than she did. Before I left the driver's section, Walter stepped on the scale. "I've gained six pounds," he said, and patted his belly. I wanted to laugh, but Jane was already in a bad mood.

I walked into the living room, over the wooden floors and past the tan leather couches and TV and kitchen and bar and the three rows of bucket seats, up to the door leading to me and Jane's bedrooms and the additional bunk beds. In front of the door was the mounted stationary bike. I strapped the seat-belt harness over me and programmed the bike on medium-intensity intervals. What would Jane say if I asked her about the letter in her room about my father? She'd probably pretend it was nothing, like about an impostor or something. She'd go even crazier if she found out I'd gone down to the lobby by myself to get the key-card for her room.

I biked and listened on my iPod to an album by a new British singer Jane downloaded for me, who's got decent phrasings but a flat upper range. When this one track had about a minute of white noise, I overheard Jane and Rog talking quietly two rows up in the bucket seats. "I can't believe I'll be forty in three weeks," she said. "The number *sounds* wrinkled."

"Nonsense," Rog said. "You look early thirties. If I were straight, I'd do you in a second."

She looks early thirties from a distance because she's short and how she dresses, and sometimes if she's turned around and I don't realize it's her, I think she's in her twenties. But when you have face time with her, if I had to play the age game, I'd guess forty-two or even -three.

"As if I'd *let* you, with your gray-haired balls," Jane said, and they laughed. Jane's going gray and is naturally mousy brown but dyes it blond, and Rog would be salt-and-pepper but he dyes it black. He says none of the queers in L.A. would even think about going for him if he didn't, even though he's a super-successful choreographer and voice coach who used to sing and dance on Broadway. He won't say his age but I saw on our payroll that he's fifty-three and makes $315,000 a year with bonuses for tours.

"Listen." Jane twisted the thick silver ring she wears on her right hand's middle finger. "When we go to Salt Lake City, the Mormons are gonna freak the fuck out if they see a gay working with Jonny."

"I can't wait," Rog said.

"I know, but this time, it might be best if you lay low at the hotel and don't come to the arena."

The white-noise track on my iPod started up with music, but I pressed pause. Jane had never told Rog not to come to the arena before. If it was cover for a business decision, it didn't make sense, because it was our album sales that were flat, not our ticket sales, which were still okay even if we weren't selling out every single show within three minutes like last time.

Rog said, "Jane, we're going to Salt Lake City *next week,* not in 1897."

"Still, I don't want to take the risk."

"Who's going to help him with his preshow tune-up?"

"I booked a woman for the night." She twisted her ring some more.

I couldn't see Rog's face, but I knew he wasn't happy. "I don't like the idea of someone else messing with his routine."

Jane got into her business-negotiations voice, which is like half an octave lower and she enunciates more clearly and with her diaphragm. "Rog, it's one night. Please don't make this difficult."

Rog's always asking Jane for salary advances, so he got quiet and said, "All right, I'll lay low."

I finished my workout and sang "Breathtaking" on the final stretch to simulate singing while I'm out of breath at the end of a concert and showered in me and Jane's bathroom and went into my bedroom for tutoring with Nadine. She asked what I wanted to start with, and I said language/reading, which I'm best at even though I don't do any pleasure reading, then science and history and math for last, which I used to be a numbskull at but I've gotten better from studying revenues and market breakdowns with Jane, and when it's a subject that affects you, you care about it more, and Nadine tells me I have to work hard at math since I don't want people cheating me out of my money when I'm older, except Jane shows me exactly how it's getting diversified and invested in our portfolio. We don't do Spanish till next year, so I can use it in interviews and maybe even sing a song in it to boost my Latin-market presence, but she teaches me a new word each session. *Yo soy un cantante de música pop.*

We finished our work early, so we did freewriting time at the end with a prompt from Nadine. Sometimes it's song ideas, only I'm not allowed to write my own songs until I'm older and until then we have to go through the normal process, where the label rents studios for two weeks and invites all these professional songwriters and producers to collaborate on an album. Each song costs about eighty thousand dollars to produce from songwriting to mixing and mastering, not including marketing, so we figured out that a twelve-song album costs almost a million. Marketing is where the money really goes. It's better to have a poorly produced album with a robust marketing budget than a top-shelf producer but weak marketing muscle.

Today, though, she said, "Jonny, write down all the feelings you had today."

I said, "What do you mean?"

"Tell me a feeling you had."

If I told her about the legal letter and the Internet message, she'd want to talk more about it and would probably mention it to Jane since she's as scared as anyone about child predators. So I decided I wouldn't tell anyone about it.

Finally I said, "When I heard the wake-up call, I was mad."

"Why were you mad?"

"Because I hate being woken up."

The bedroom door was open a few inches, and she got up and closed it. Her shirt rode up her back a few inches when she did it, and it showed her pale skin. She's five-three and won't tell me how many pounds but I'd guess 110 because she's not fat and is only twenty-six and a half, but she also never goes to the gym so it's not a toned 110. It's better to be a toned 120 than a flabby 110. Muscular marketing for mediocre content. "Why do you hate it?"

"I want to sleep."

"Why else, though?"

"Beats me." The name of Tyler's smash hit and album, but I bet Nadine didn't even know that. I've never heard of the bands she likes.

"I want you to think about this, Jonny." She squinted as the sun bounced through my window onto her eyes and turned them from blue to green. "The only way to understand yourself is by articulating your thoughts."

"Articulating is when you separate out the notes you're singing," I said. "You want me to sing my thoughts?"

"It also means figuring out what you want to say, and saying it. Using language to describe what you mean."

I articulated, "I get tired."

"You get tired in the mornings?"

"No, I mean I get tired of waking up early every day."

"When you're on tour, you mean?"

"No. Every day."

She wedged her pen behind her ear so it got lost in her black hair. "You've never said this before."

I shrugged, and she asked why I was saying this for the first time. I was about to say, "Because you asked," but Bill, the head crew guy, who was riding on our bus today because he had to confab with Jane and the label over crew changes when we got to L.A., knocked on the door and stuck his head in. He has a big beard he's always scratching and muscles on his arms like little rocks are poking out under his skin with tattoo sleeves on both of them. In a few years I can lift with Walter but not now because we want to keep me slim and boyish. I wonder if Albert Derrick Valentino lifts.

Bill said, "Three hours, guys, and the driver needs a break so we're stopping for grub."

So Nadine reminded me the next unit was on slavery and we were going to read some autobiographies of slaves, and she showed me a few and I said, "Nadine, can we get the kid versions of these?" and she said no, they cut out all the sad stuff and whitewashed what it really meant to be a slave, and it's important to hear from the victims of exploitation themselves since history is always written by the victors. I asked, "Why are all the guys who write history named Victor?" and she was like, "Ha-ha, very cute, Jonny," and messed up my hair, which Jane doesn't like people to do but I didn't have a show that night, and I don't mind when Nadine does it.

I asked Jane could I please get a vanilla shake, and she sized me up and pinched the side of my waist and got about half an inch of chub. It stung but she said yes, so long as I did seven additional minutes of cardio before we got to L.A., and I said, "I'll do a million minutes of high-intensity intervals." She let me get a small, and I drank it without stopping except when we passed a cemetery on the highway and I held my breath. Jane taught me that game on our first tour, but she doesn't play it herself.

Me and Rog went into my room for voice lessons. He recorded the start time and told me we'd logged 2,568 hours of practice together and had 7,432 to go. Jane read in a book you need to practice ten thousand hours at anything to become the best at it. Me and Nadine figured out last week when we were on fractions that at this rate I'll reach ten thousand hours in about eight and two-thirds years, so when I'm twenty and one-half years old, which is around the peak age for global presence in the music industry for girls because they get cellulite and wrinkles after that, but guys peak a little older. I asked Jane if I'll be as good as MJ after ten thousand hours, and she said, "No, you'll be *better* than MJ." Ronald says a more attainable goal is becoming the next Tyler Beats, and he's the head of the label so he knows. Jane spends a lot of time studying his career, and if she isn't sure about something, she asks people what Tyler would do. He started off in the teen demo, but evolved into broad-spectrum appeal.

First Rog was pissed that Jane let me have a shake since dairy is crap for the vocal cords. Then when I reminded him I'm allowed one dairy per day for the calcium and my voice sounded off on the word *calcium,* he was like, "Did your voice just crack?" and I had to say for the millionth time, "No, I'll let you know when I hit puberty," and I rolled up the sleeves of my T-shirt and said, "See, no hair?"

We did octaves warm-ups like we always do on "Oh, say can you see," since the first time I ever did octaves was when the music teacher Mrs. Vincent had all the second-graders sing that line the lowest we could and the highest, and now it's like my superstitious ritual. She'd gone through each of us in class and most of the kids didn't have hardly any range. Then she got to me. I hit my lowest octave and her face changed like, *What?* because it's way lower than my speaking voice, and she said, "Can you do that again?" and I did it again no problem. She asked me to do the highest I could, and I did it probably 2.5 octaves higher. I didn't have the 3.4 range I have now, which Rog thinks I'll get a clean four octaves eventually because I have a lean muscle aperture. Mrs. Vincent asked me to repeat both, so I did, and she told me to sing the whole song, which I knew from baseball games and was the main way I'd practiced singing before. I added some vibrato for the last line even though I didn't know the name of it then but I'd seen singers do it on reality shows. When I was finished she was very still and quiet and just said, "That's very nice, Jonathan, very nice."

That night Jane said Mrs. Vincent had called her and told her I had the best natural voice she ever heard, and Jane was crying when she hung up and said she always knew I was talented from the way I'd echo songs playing in the supermarket, when I'd wait behind the checkout aisle for her to finish her Schnucks shifts, and that this was the start of something big. I was only seven years old but I was like, "Okay, but why are you crying if you're happy, Mommy?" and Jane was hugging me and said, "Because you're my beautiful baby boy, Jonathan." My father had already left by then. I don't know what he would've said.

Me and Rog ended with an analysis session of Buddy Holly's "Everyday." He's been on a Buddy Holly kick lately, and he said to pay attention to the simplicity of the melody and instrumentation, the drummer just beating out the rhythm by slapping his knee, how it wouldn't work without Holly's vocal control and textural smoothness. He had me imitate his "a-hey" and the way he slows down and ranges up and down the scale within a word like his voice is going over a speed bump. I told him to pass on to whoever top-lines the next album that I wanted to do something like this in a song.

When we wrapped up, I said, "Don't worry, I won't let anyone mess with my routine in Salt Lake City."

"Thanks." He stopped putting his notes away and looked at me. "But after, let Jane know you prefer my techniques. We're in this together. Right?"

"Right."

"Good. You're going to have a long career if you stick with what I tell you."

As a voice coach, Rog is one of the best out there, but there are probably better choreographers. That's one reason he has me focus on my singing, even though he says it's since anyone can dance but no one can sing as naturally angelic as me.

The other reason is that he's the oldest person on our team. Definitely older than Walter. Up close his eyes crinkle into wrinkles like cat whiskers, and he's super-tan, but when he looked at me just then, I thought, Man, if I played the age game right now, I'd guess Rog is like sixty, which I don't usually think because he's still in good shape, but last week when we were finishing up the Southwest leg of the tour, he was teaching me a new eight-count move with a jump and a deep knee bend, and when he demoed it for me there was a loud *crack!* like his knees were going, Uh, thanks but no thanks for the ten *million* hours of dance practice, Rog, and he acted like it didn't hurt but he didn't do any more demos the rest of the day and iced it for half an hour later and popped a bunch of Vikes and told me not to tell Jane since she gets too nervous about other people's health, which isn't really true. She only gets nervous about mine and hers.

I said, "I know, Rog."

We had two nights in L.A. with a concert the second night, so all the backup singers and dancers and crew guys were excited about going home with a day off. But me and Jane didn't have it off, because the talent's work is never done, so we had the big strategy session with Ronald scheduled for lunch, which is why we had the early start. I was like, Jane, can't you go without me, I never have any creative input in these meetings anyway, but she said that Ronald specifically requested me to be present, and Ronald controls the purse strings so we have to pick our battles.

We finally got back into L.A. after a century on the highway. Our bus dropped me and Jane and Walter off at the Ivy. It's the main L.A. restaurant Jane knew about before we moved here, and the minute we signed for my advance from the label she took me there for dinner.

There were about ten paparazzi, which isn't that much. You could tell they were bottom-feeder paparazzi, not just because they were stuck working the daytime Ivy shift, but because they dressed really bad and stood out from the lunch crowd. My bus doesn't have any markings on it, so they didn't know who it was until we got out. Then they were all like, "Jonny, how's the tour?" or "Jane, looking hot, give us a smile," which I thought she might do since me and her got our teeth whitened by Dr. Kim pretour, but she didn't, and Walter barked in his policeman voice, "Guys, give 'em some air, you'll all get your nice pictures but you gotta back up!" I always let Jane do the talking and I just smile and once in a while dance if they ask but never sing. You have to save it for when people pay. They shouted for me to do my trademark spin move, but Jane shook her head at me. People must have asked MJ to do the moonwalk all the time, too.

We went up the stairs and through the patio and Julian at the front smiled at us and told us our table was ready. Jane likes the table right next to the fireplace, with her back to the wall. Walter stayed outside and Jane ordered a burger for him to go.

Ronald wasn't there yet, so Jane got an Ivy gimlet plus a Diet Coke for me and asked the waiter to take away the bowl of mixed nuts, even though he told her there weren't any peanuts. When he brought me my drink I said, "Thank you," and "Thank you" again when he set Jane's down since she never makes eye contact with waiters. Maybe it's because she used to be a waitress before Schnucks and before she was a secretary for a few months at a marketing firm, and she said it was the worst job she ever had, so that should make you friendlier to waiters, except we go to gourmet restaurants where they're paid pretty good, and she worked at a diner. But she's a generous tipper, and sometimes it shows up in the press that she gave a tip bigger than the meal, so people might think she does it for that, but it's really because she used to get stiffed by her customers all the time.

Jane worked on her phone while we waited. I straightened up in my seat to see. I wondered if she knew about the comments from Albert Derrick Valentino, too. But she wasn't on any fan sites or Twitter. She was browsing my mobile app and probably coming up with ideas for how to diversify it and attract more JV/Varsity Club memberships.

She has a lot of street cred in the industry for her innovation in the digital space, and she's an excellent multitasker and doesn't waste time when she's working. She says it's from years of packing grocery bags and dealing with screaming mothers and crying babies and her asshole supervisor and incompetent coworkers. Ronald calls her "the Architect" because right when she started she had an idea of how to build my career and insisted she would be my manager, even though the label strongly recommended an experienced manager, but she was always into movie stars and celebs and used to take old copies of *InStyle* and *Us Weekly* and *Star* home from Schnucks and read them for hours at night, except now they're tentative allies who could betray us any second and we've got to be careful.

Ronald was late, so Jane asked for another gimlet and Diet Coke. When he showed up in a few minutes he apologized for the delay, but Jane said, "That's fine, we just ordered our first drinks."

Ronald is only a couple inches taller than Jane and balding but he has a raspy voice that makes everyone pay attention and dresses in expensive suits so he seems taller. He'd brought a woman a few years younger than Jane that we'd never met before. She wore black-framed glasses that made her look smart, and she was thin without looking like she had to work out for it.

"This is Stacy Palter," he said. "She's our new EVP of creative."

Stacy smiled like an emoticon and said, "Jonny, I'm a huge fan of 'Guys vs. Girls' and just about everything else you've recorded. And, Jane, I'm really excited to be working with you."

Jane smiled back a little when she said hello. After they sat down, she asked, "So, Stacy, how long have you been in the industry? I only ask because you seem quite young to be head of creative." Jane was good at flipping someone's advantage into a weakness.

Stacy laughed once to herself and looked at Ronald for a second and said, "Well, I began as an intern while I was at Columbia—"

"Did you work with Dan Freedman there?" Jane asked.

"Which department is he in?"

"Creative."

"Oh!" Stacy laughed again. "I'm so sorry, I meant Columbia University, not Columbia Records. I interned for a few indie labels when I was a student there. Econ major."

Jane smiled but didn't say anything, so Stacy talked about how she'd gotten a job in the industry after she graduated and then became Ronald's assistant and worked in creative at another label before Ronald poached her.

Ronald grinned with his crooked old-person teeth like he was her father and they were used to joking around. "*Enticed,* Stacy, I *enticed* you back," he said. "Stacy's got a gimlet eye for spotting talent and knows how to position artists better than anyone else at the label." I was trying to figure out if *gimlet eye* meant the same thing as Jane's drink, but didn't want to interrupt Ronald, who added, "The opening group that's filling in for the rest of the tour, the Latchkeys? Stacy found them."

"I haven't had a chance to give them a listen yet," Jane said.

"They play edgy rock, literate lyrics. The front man, Zack Ford, dresses in a vintage suit," Stacy said. "Stones meets the early Strokes."

"Doesn't seem like a fit with Jonath—Jonny's sound," Jane said.

"It isn't, exactly, but they have a big teen-girl fan base, which loves Zack," Stacy said. "They'll catapult off and age up Jonny's listenership. And they'll certainly fill more seats in the Midwest than Mi$ter $mith."

Whenever Jane's studying the career longevity of pop stars, she's like, Thank God you're not black.

Jane sort of cleared her throat and took a sip of her gimlet. Ronald said, "Stacy also helped develop Tyler Beats—though, obviously, not for us," and Jane looked up and asked, "Really?" and Stacy told her how she saw videos of Tyler singing on YouTube before anyone knew who he was, the same way I was discovered, and she got her label to sign him right away, and Ronald said she was instrumental in packaging him, especially overseas.

So Stacy actually did have a gimlet eye for spotting talent, which was what made her different from the fakes on those reality shows that pick singers who have no originality, and made her *really* different from the people who watch those shows who have no clue what makes a good singer and vote mostly on personality and song selection. People who don't have any talent themselves always want to believe they can at least spot good talent, like that's a talent itself. But they usually can't except when someone's a singing and dancing freak, like with MJ. Or Tyler

Beats, though maybe it wasn't so obvious when Stacy signed him. My skills were raw before the label groomed me.

Stacy excused herself to the restroom. "Is she even thirty, Ronald?" Jane asked. Ronald sighed and said yes and that everyone in this industry is young and you know that, and Jane was like, "I've simply noticed you tend to promote a lot of young women who've worked for you, is all," and Ronald said she wouldn't have gotten the job if she weren't extremely qualified, and they had some fresh ideas they wanted to bring up with us and Jane would be well served to listen with an open mind. She picked up her menu even though she always gets the grilled salad.

When Stacy came back she asked me how the tour was going.

"It's good. A lot like the last one." I didn't mention I was seeing a few empty seats this time around. She'd already know anyway.

"Any fun stories?"

I was starving and tore off a piece of walnut-raisin bread. Jane wouldn't say anything in front of them about it. I repeated what she'd coached me to say if they asked about the tour: "No, we've been working super-hard, so we don't have much time for messing around. But the shows are hella fun."

Jane's been trying to get me to say *hella* more in interviews to make up for any conversational accent I have left from St. Louis, so I knew this would please her and make her forget about the bread.

Ronald laughed and put his hand on my shoulder and said, "Kid's got a work ethic like a Korean immigrant," and Jane laughed with him, but Stacy looked down at her drink and half smiled.

They gossiped about which musicians and execs were going to rehab or were out of rehab and whose careers were crashing or stalling or supernova-ing. When our food came, Ronald said, "So let's get down to brass tacks," and Stacy took a folder out of her bag whose cover page said

JONNY VALENTINE 2.0 BRAND-EXTENSION STRATEGY

Stacy said, "Peruse this at your leisure. It's a comprehensive overview of the market, Jonny's salability and performance strengths and stumbling blocks, and what directions we can go in. I'll touch on the main bullet points."

She discussed the record industry for a little while, but I tuned out and ate my lamb burger and drowned my fries in ketchup and thought of the opening lines to "Guys vs. Girls" the way I always do when I see a burger now, even a lamb burger from the Ivy: "Girls and guys, burgers and fries, all gets ruined with a coupla lies." It was the same stuff about shrinking sales and a contraction in concertgoers from the recession and media fragmentation and limited control over talent perception that Jane had been complaining about a lot the last few months.

Then Stacy said, "We think, after this tour, it's time to reassess Jonny's image and his music."

Jane's fingers gripped her fork tighter but she kept her voice calm. "What do you mean, reassess?"

"Ish. Reassess-ish," Stacy said. "I don't want to step on any toes here, but Jonny's second album hasn't done nearly as well as the first even though we poured in marketing resources for it and he had the shoulders of a major platform to stand on."

I pictured a huge platform with a pair of shoulders and no head that I was standing on.

Jane said, "Debuts traditionally outperform sophomore albums, if you've had the kind of market penetration Jonny had."

Stacy looked to Ronald for the thousandth time, and he was like, "Jane, we know that, but please hear us out."

"Jonny, you turn twelve in two months, right?" Stacy asked. "So the deliverables for your last album under contract would, best-case, be ready later this year, and when it hit shelves, you'd be around thirteen."

I wondered if anyone else noticed she'd said *last* album under contract, not *next* album. Stacy talked quickly, though, and turned back to Jane. "That's the perfect time to make him a tad more . . . adult. Nothing drastic—we're just talking clothes, hair, and songs and videos that connect more with the teen audience and not so much the tween demo."

"Once you do that, you're competing with everyone else," Jane said. "No other singers own the tweens like Jonny does. We've still got a few years."

"We have to think about the future and evolve," Stacy said. "They're not going to stay little kids forever. And neither is Jonny, you know?"

Jane stirred her gimlet with her straw and picked a mint leaf out and chewed on it. "What are you suggesting?" she asked.

"For starters, how do you feel about Jonny dating someone? Someone famous, obviously."

For a second the only famous person I could think of was Madonna, and how weird we'd look as a couple but that I could always say I once dated Madonna, and then I realized she meant someone my age. Jane's eyebrows moved together and wrinkled up her skin in this one spot over her nose. She calls it her thinking wrinkle. Botox can't get rid of it.

"Dating?" she asked, like she'd never heard the word before.

"Not real *dating*-dating," Stacy said. "We've got a girl in our stable named Lisa Pinto, about Jonny's age, done some TV acting, whose first album drops in February. She's a total sweetheart, and she's immensely popular with Latinos. It'd be great publicity for both of them if they were seen out together in L.A. a few times. If you're comfortable with that."

Jane said, "Well—"

"And who knows, maybe a real romance will blossom!" Stacy laughed. "What do you think about that, Jonny? Here's Lisa's album cover."

She pulled up the picture on her phone. Lisa had black hair in a ponytail and wore pink gym shorts and a white tank top over her tan skin and stood in front of a school bus, and the album's title, *School's Out!*, was spelled on the side of the bus. I felt the tingling that tells me a boner's coming, but I had a napkin on my lap so no one could tell.

"She looks nice," I said.

Whenever the media or fans ask me if I'm dating anyone, I have to say that I'm not seeing anyone in particular right now but I'm always looking out for that special someone and I love all girls. Jane says this makes all my female fans think they have a chance, especially the fat ones, who are the most rabid and loyal. And if I ever did date someone, it would crush them and they'd turn their attention to someone else.

Jane didn't bring that up. Instead, she said, "It's something we'll have to mull. I don't like the idea of Jonny . . . sexualizing himself at this age to sell a few more units."

"Totally understood," Stacy said.

She turned her lips into her mouth and raised her eyebrows, which was Ronald's cue to say, "We've also considered upgrading Jonny's dance routines and voice work. Stacy's got a great relationship with the woman who worked with Tyler, and she completely transformed him during his midteen years. I know you're loyal to Rog, but what do you think about Jonny meeting with this woman, to see if they hit it off?"

"Jonny really trusts Rog."

I don't know why she didn't tell them she'd already asked Rog to sit out Salt Lake City. Maybe because she wants it to sound like it's her idea alone.

"Sure, but Rog is"—Stacy laughed to herself again—"how shall I put this delicately? Rog's vocal techniques are antiquated, and his choreography is antiquated, and if we want to keep Jonny's message current, we've got to surround him with current support."

Jane chewed on another mint leaf. I swallowed a fry and said, "I really trust Rog."

Stacy said, "I know, Jonny, but maybe you could just meet Holly—I bet you'd like her—and pick up a tip or two and see how it goes?"

Jane was watching me. "No, I think I'd prefer Rog's techniques," I said. Jane hid her smile behind her gimlet, and it always makes me smile when I see her doing it, but I stuffed a few fries in my mouth so I wouldn't give myself away. A glob of ketchup dripped on the sleeve of my white track sweater. It looked like I'd punched someone in the nose and gotten his blood all over my sleeve.

"Okeydoke, gang, let's drop the shop talk for now and enjoy our lunch," Ronald said. "Jane, take a look at the rest of the folder when you get a chance. We'll meet again when the tour's over to review everything. Unless sales for the Garden show pick up, we'll have to make some changes going forward."

That was a pretty bad note to end the shop talk on, and I could tell Jane was covering up an angry mood the rest of the lunch. Her and Stacy ate half their salads and Ronald finished his steak as they picked up their gossip about real estate and restaurants and Ronald's new ski château in Germany. He joked, "I know, what's a five-foot-five Jew doing skiing in Germany?" When we signed with the label, Jane told me, "You always want a Jew to be in charge of your business," and she laughed and said, "But an *honest* Jew." Ronald's an honest Jew and an industry legend.

I finished my lamb burger, but when the waitress came to clear our plates, Jane handed her mine with half my fries left. Stacy said it was awesome meeting me and she couldn't wait to touch base again after the tour. Walter came in to escort us out of the restaurant, where a car was waiting for us with all the paparazzi. Jane let me do one trademark spin move before I got into the backseat, but when they asked me to sing the chorus from "Guys vs. Girls," she said, "Come to his concert tomorrow night!" She could work as my publicist if she wasn't my manager.

In the car with me and Walter she talked on her phone. I was drifting in and out of sleep, like Walter was, so I heard parts, like when Jane said, "Some bimbo he probably fucked once and had to promote so she doesn't file a harassment suit . . . No, no progress on the other thing." *The other thing* could've been a million things, but if I asked, she'd make something up about a sponsorship deal or whatever.

Jane lost the call as we drove up Laurel Canyon. She said to herself, *"Peruse."* Then she told me we were invited to the twelfth-birthday party that night of this TV exec's son.

"I'm tired."

"I know, baby. But we should go to this. We only have one free night in L.A."

"I just want to go to sleep tonight."

"You can sleep for a whole week straight after the tour," she said. "There are going to be a lot of film and TV people there."

"We can take a meeting whenever we want."

"Yes, but you know it's always better when you meet them socially. An exec comes up with an idea while he's drunk, he thinks it's the most brilliant thing ever. We have to, baby."

I thought Walter had been sleeping, but his mouth moved a little, like he'd heard it and wasn't saying anything. Or maybe I didn't see it right, because I was so tired and my eyes couldn't stay sharp. The outside was just a blur of green trees and brown roofs.

"Can't you just go without me?"

"It's not as fun without you," she said. "And they invited us both."

Which meant they really invited me, and she'd be letting them down if she showed up without me. My head was hurting like just after a 120-decibel concert and my eyelids were too heavy to keep arguing.

"Fine," I said. I fell asleep for real and woke up when we reached the security gate to our community. When you come home there should be a smell or sight or something you recognize, but coming back to our house hasn't felt like that yet after upgrading from the three-bedroom the label rented for us the first year in L.A. and buying our six-bedroom in the Hills. I asked why we needed six bedrooms when it's just me and Jane plus a couple staff and Walter in his bungalow, and she said that half of showbiz is about perception and you need to create buzz to sustain buzz, and real estate's an evergreen source of buzz.

But it felt more like coming home getting off the school bus in St. Louis or when Michael Carns's mother would drop me off when I was old enough to have my own keys, even if our apartment wasn't a source of buzz, because it only had one bedroom that Jane let me sleep in after my father left and she took the couch that folded out in the living room, and we didn't have fancy kitchen appliances the manufacturers give us for free now hoping we'll mention them in an interview, and it was always dirty since Jane hates cleaning and couldn't afford to pay anyone. We have a few pictures left, but that's it.

Walter went off to his bungalow since he had the night off, and me and Jane walked through the front door and past the paintings the decorator picked out in our foyer and some framed photos of me and Jane with other celebs in the entry room, and I cut through the awards room that I walk into every day for motivation, with all my plaques and trophies in a case, except there aren't any Grammys yet and it's mostly crap like the People's Choice Awards.

I said hi to Sharon in the kitchen while she was spraying the countertop. "How is the tour, Mr. Jonny?" she asked when she hugged me. Her smell was a combination of cleaning products and this cream that black women moisturize their hair with that she keeps like four bottles of in her bathroom. Sharon is from Barbados and one time she let me weigh her. She's 223 pounds and I bet her breasts and butt are at least forty pounds of that. They're the biggest of anyone I know, including singers and dancers with implants.

"It's good," I said. "We're working super-hard."

"You look skinny," she said. "We have to get some meat on those bones."

"I just ate," I said, even though I was still a little hungry since I didn't finish the fries. I was only skinny compared to Sharon.

"Okay." She went back to spraying. "But don't work too hard, Mr. Jonny."

Jane came in and told Sharon that the gardeners were coming tomorrow and the painters were coming two days after, and Sharon said, "Yes, ma'am," real quiet the way she always does when she answers her.

Jane said, "And you really need to do a more careful job in the foyer. I found a sheet of dust behind the white table."

"I'm sorry, Mrs. Valentine," Sharon said.

Jane told me we were eating at six before she went to her office. When she was gone, I told Sharon not to take it personal and that Jane was pissed at me because I didn't want to go to this dumb party and she was taking it out on her. Sharon said, "I know, Mrs. Valentine has a lot of pressure on her, too," which *isn't* what I meant, but I guess the important thing is Sharon didn't feel so bad. Jane's good at making people think they screwed up even when they didn't really. It does motivate you to do better, though, except I don't think Sharon needs much motivation to clean the foyer.

The staircase was being renovated with marble, which I didn't know about, but Jane's always working on improvements to the house, some for her, some for me. When I wanted a basketball court, she said it would cost too much, and I was like, Please, Jane, I'll add another concert to the next tour to pay for it, and she said what she usually says when I ask for something big, which is, All right, but just because I'm the only mother you have and you're the only son I have. I asked her a few months ago if we could clear out the land behind us and build a baseball diamond like the one me and Michael Carns used to talk about building in St. Louis so I can play with Walter on it, and with a springy backboard so I can play catch when he isn't around. She says depending on what tour and merch profits are, we can think about it.

That's partly why it's not familiar when I come home, because of the renovations and it never smells like much besides Sharon's cleaning products. I asked Nadine once if you replaced one thing at a time in our house until everything was new, would it still be the same house? She said that was a very smart question, and that the human body replaces all its cells every seven to ten years, so you could say that I was a completely renovated person from when I was born. We spent an entire session discussing it. I decided it was a totally new house. Nadine wasn't so sure.

I took the elevator upstairs and went to my room. A Jonny Valentine doll had fallen on the floor. It was one that sang the chorus from "Guys vs. Girls" when you pulled the string.

"If Jonny is reading this, he can contact me," I said to it. Then I smiled huge at it. "How's the tour? Any fun stories?"

I pulled the string. It played the "Guys vs. Girls" chorus up to *gotta* so slow you couldn't hardly make out the words and stopped. It must've broken when it fell.

In slow motion, making my voice baritone so it sounded like a broken recording, I said, "Kid's . . . got . . . a . . . work . . . eth . . . ic . . . like . . . a . . . Ko . . . re . . . an . . . im . . . mi . . . grant." I stuffed the doll back on the shelf with all the other Jonny Valentine dolls and action figures and angel figurines, under the shelf with the Jonny Valentine backpacks and messenger bags and lunch boxes, and above the shelf with the Jonny Valentine necklaces and bracelets and nail polish and purses and other garbage for girls that would be gay for me to have in my room if it didn't have my face on it, and next to the bookshelf that had about a hundred copies of my ghostwritten autobiography, by this skinny bald guy with thick glasses in his fifties named Alan Fontana who interviewed me for a couple hours, then just used Wikipedia to write a bunch of made-up stuff about girls and sports and music pretending to be in my voice, like one page has a picture of me looking in a jewelry-store window and it says, "Sometimes all I think about is getting jewelry for girls." They'd never write the real truth, like, "Sometimes all I think about is getting boners for girls."

The ketchup stain on my sleeve probably wouldn't come out, so I threw it in the garbage and walked into my closet and found the bin labeled TRACK SWEATERS and took out a new white one. I'd worn that sweater the last four days on the tour when I wasn't performing, so I felt a little bad throwing it out, since I don't get to wear old clothes much to keep up with the trends, and also because it was like, Sorry, sweater, even though it was my fault I got ketchup on you, fuck you, you have to depart the realm now.

Sharon had brought my five suitcases up to my room. I freaked out that she'd thrown all my clothes in the laundry, including the jeans with Albert Derrick Valentino's email address in them, but the suitcases were still filled. I took the piece of paper out and stuck it in the jeans I was wearing.

I started to play Zenon, but it wasn't as fun without other people in the next room, even if they're not paying attention. It's nice to know other people are near you at least while you're playing games. It's best when Walter's in the room with you, but he had the rest of the day off in his bungalow and said he was going to grab a shit-ton of shut-eye, brother, we were all getting worked to the goddamn bone on this tour. Walter finished high school though he talks like he didn't, but besides nonstrategy decisions, he's probably one of our smartest staff.

A new stack of tabloids and glossies Jane wanted me to study was next to my bed, right near this photo on my bedside table of me and Jane when I was about seven or eight that a friend of hers took. It's a nice photo, with her sitting on one end of the seesaw in the park near our apartment in St. Louis and me all the way up on the other end, but Jane doesn't want it out in a hallway because she has an ugly perm and about ten pounds more chub.

You have to give the glossies enough access so they're grateful but not too much or they think they can walk all over you with a character assassination. Jane's savvy at adjusting the level. My picture was only in one of them. It was an onstage shot during the Houston show, and the headline was JONNY HEATS UP HOUSTON! with a capsule description of my tour. That show was one of my worst so far, actually, but the glossies never review your performance unless you bombed so bad it becomes a media story.

I took that issue and one of the tabloids into my bathroom and locked the door and turned on the fan for sound. There wasn't any regular moisturizer, since my dermatologist doesn't want me messing with lotions and maybe causing acne, but on the sink was a bottle of the SPF 50 sunscreen Jane makes me slather on. I sat on the toilet and turned in the tabloid to a photo spread headlined FIT AND OVER 40!—THESE OLDER STARS STILL LOOK LIKE STARLETS! It was candids of a bunch of actresses in bathing suits and workout clothes. I got hard and rubbed with the lotion and touched myself to a photo of an actress with red hair doing yoga outside and bending over, and in one hand held the glossy picture of me onstage next to her. After about five minutes both arms got tired, so I packed the glossy in one of my suitcases. It wasn't going to happen yet, but I could feel myself getting closer, sort of like what I think the inside of our teakettle is like just before it boils the water for Jane's laxative tea. I bet within a year I'll be able to do it, way before I've had ten thousand hours of practice.

I got in bed to take a nap, but I couldn't fall asleep. First, I was looking at my stomach. A little chub folded up at the bottom even when I was lying on my back, and way more if I sat up. And when I bent my legs, right above my knees the skin pooched out. Maybe it was muscle, but even if it was, no one else would be able to tell.

The only way to find out if the fan-forum messages were really from my father or if someone just knew his full name would be to email him and see how he answered, which would mean setting up an email account different from the one I use for Nadine since Jane had access to it. I couldn't do it from Jane's computer, and there wasn't any other way to get on the Internet in the house. If she found out, she'd make sure I never got another chance.

I closed my eyes, but I kept seeing his name in my head like it was on the screen:

Albert Derrick Valentino

And I imagined what he might look like, sort of like when the police try to figure out what a missing kid looks like years later. All I could come up with was a combination of me and Jane, like if me and her had a baby and he was born already in his forties.

Even though I was so tired, I knew I couldn't fall asleep, so I took one over-the-counter sleeping pill from the bathroom and got drowsy, and I woke up a couple hours later. Sometimes you wake up, especially in a hotel or something, and for a second you're not sure where you are, or which direction you're facing in your bed. With me, sometimes it's like I forget I live in L.A. and I think I'm still back at our apartment in St. Louis and that I'm in the small bed there and I expect the walls to be closer and my bed against the one window with my Cardinals team-picture poster over my head, and instead I open my eyes and the other wall is like twenty feet away and my huge bed is in the middle of the room and there are all these photos on the walls of me with other celebs.

I took the elevator downstairs and asked Sharon to make me a cup of coffee. She always makes the same joke: "Black, like your women, Mr. Jonny," and I don't take it with milk but I say, "Ebony *and* ivory, Sharon," because everyone makes fun of that song, but Rog told me it was Paul McCartney's longest number-one Billboard hit after "Hey Jude," so the joke's on them.

I asked how Gerald was doing. She hasn't seen him in four years. They got engaged over Skype. She smiled super-wide and whispered, "I've saved enough that I think I can go back this summer."

"For a vacation?"

"No, for good."

"Like, to live there?"

"Yes. But don't tell your mother yet, okay?"

"What about your job here?" I asked.

"I know." She made this clucking sound. "I'll miss you a lot."

"Are you gonna work in someone else's house there?"

"Maybe," she said. "They have a lot of hotels I can work in, too. Right on the beach."

I remembered a line from a crap romantic comedy I'd seen on pay-per-view in New Orleans, and said, "So, you're gonna leave me for him? Just like that, after two years together?" except I did it with a smile to show I was joking, and then I fake-cried and improvised some new lines like, "You're gonna leave me, I always knew it, you never loved me, I can't believe you're gonna leave me all alone."

She knew I was messing around, but she got kind of serious with a gentle smile now and said, "You can always visit me, Mr. Jonny. Gerald's got a couch you can stay on."

I stopped fake-crying and said, "That's okay, I can just stay at one of the hotels you'll work at."

Her smile went away a little and she said I could and my coffee was ready and she had to finish up some cleaning upstairs.

Jane was ending her exercise in our gym. She probably did a light routine on the elliptical, because our trainer wasn't there today, and when she's on her own she wimps out and does like fifteen minutes at low intensity, not enough for cardio benefits and way below what you need for serious fat burning.

She came in with a water bottle and in her sweaty workout clothes and told me our food was waiting for us in the living room. Our chef, Peter, was also off today, so Jane had ordered in salads. When we sat on the couch, she said, "There'll be a lot of tempting junk food at the party tonight. What do we say to temptation?"

I said, "Temptation is for the weak," and she gave me a high five and turned on the TV and we watched celeb news on E! and the networks while we ate. Jane flipped through the folder Stacy gave her. In the middle she said, "These idiots in creative are all the same. They're only looking out for their own careers, not yours. Never forget that. No one else cares as much about your career as I do. If your sales tank, they can move on and get another client. I won't get another son."

She kept reading until one of the shows said that Tyler Beats was announcing his Asian tour for next fall. Her head popped up from the folder when the woman said the words *Tyler Beats*. "That's what we have to do next," Jane said. "The real money is in Asia."

"I thought that's why we're doing the Internet live-stream concert, to grab Asian viewers," I said.

"Yes, so we can get enough of a critical mass there to justify a tour. Once you do that, you're set. They have stronger brand loyalty."

A car commercial came on, and Jane's eyes stayed on the screen, but I could tell her mind was somewhere else. She said, "You have more natural talent than Tyler Beats. But he works harder than any-one else."

"I work hard, too." Jane doesn't watch most of my sessions with Rog, when I sing myself hoarse or dance till I get blisters or analyze songs for hours.

"Not like Tyler," she said. "The top person is never simply the most talented, or the smartest, or the best looking. They sacrifice anything in their lives that might hold them back."

I wasn't sure if she meant anything in particular, and if I brought up Zenon as an example, she might say, Yeah, you have to cut that out. So I shut up while we finished the show and our salads. Jane said she was showering and the car service was picking us up in an hour to take us to the party. I asked why we had to take the car service, since they always make us wait when we want to leave, and she said, "You know I hate driving at night." It's true that Jane's a safe driver and she doesn't like driving at night and I wasn't even allowed in the front seat until this year, but I knew it was so she could drink, and she never drives with me in the car when she's had any alcohol.

"Can Walter come and drive us?"

"It sends the wrong message." She sighed like she was tired of talk-ing about it and tired in general. I moved behind the couch and gave her a neck rub. She closed her eyes and made a few *mmm* sounds, and after a minute said, "You're the best at that, baby," and stood and kissed the top of my head and ran her hands through my hair. "I'm so happy when we get to hang out like this, just you and me. I miss this on tour, when we're running around in a million directions with a million people around us."

"Maybe we could find time to do it more on tour," I said as she walked away. We hung out together a lot more on our first national tour. Jane's been busier this one.

She paused, but her pauses are like pausing the game in Zenon, where the music keeps playing. Jane's never not thinking. "Sure, that'd be nice," she said and smiled at me. She left to shower and I watched TV on the couch but I really thought about Tyler. Like, did he work twice as hard as me, and is that what it took to get where he was, and would I want to do that? What if it meant sleeping two less hours a night and not playing Zenon but only practicing and extending my tours and reducing gaps between shows and never eating anything bad for me?

And though I wouldn't say it to Jane, in my mind I was like, No, don't make me. I don't even know how I could do that. I'm already working the hardest I can without departing the realm.

Jane always takes a year getting ready. I knocked on her door and told her the car service was waiting outside, and she opened it and said, "They get paid for their time." She was in her lingerie and had two dresses on her bed, a red one and a blue one, and asked me which I liked more, and I said the blue one, so she put it on and asked me to zip her up. "Do you think my stomach's getting fat?" she asked.

It *was* a little fatter than pretour, with some wobbly jelly chub over her gut. We went through a women's glossy a few months ago that ID'd problem zones. I didn't say anything, but Jane's were Belly Bulge, Bat Wings, and Muffin Top. She didn't have Turkey Neck, Armpit Fat, Thighscrapers, Cankles, or Back Fat. She thought she had Mom Butt, but she doesn't.

I went, "No, not at all."

In the ride over she told me who she thought was going to be at the party. I didn't know their names, but I knew who they worked for, and most of them were at top-shelf movie and TV companies and agencies. For a second I wondered if maybe my father had been waiting for me to return to L.A. and he might show up, but that was stupid for a million reasons.

Jane hadn't stopped talking. "We still have to find the right vehicle for you," she said.

"How about a Ferrari?" I said.

She smiled and pinched my cheek and said, "Maybe you *could* do comedy." That kind of joke was like my Victor joke to Nadine, though. You smile, but you don't laugh. Like a song you hum along with but don't tap your feet to.

The party was in Calabasas, and we got lucky with traffic, so it took about forty-five minutes. The house was behind a security gate like ours, and when Jane had trouble with the guard and her name on the guest list, she pressed down the window all the way, and he let us in.

We drove around the half-circle driveway past all the parked cars of the guests and up to a typical Calabasas mansion, with stone columns in the front and a huge set of double doors like a castle, and the house was white and light pink the way Jane likes her salmon cooked. There were torches along the walkway to the door and balloons and banners saying HAPPY 12TH BIRTHDAY MATTHEW! Jane checked her makeup once more in her compact mirror and knocked.

A woman with the kind of long skinny arms Jane is always trying to get—she calls them *flamingo arms* even though they're really like flamingo legs—and who didn't spray-tan and had straightened black hair that was a definite dye job answered it with a glass of wine in her hand. She smiled at Jane and said, "Hello!" and then saw me and her smile became real. "Hi, welcome! I'm Matthew's mother, Linda."

People who know better never say my name when they first meet me, but they try not to act like they *don't* know me, either. It's the fans who slobber all over you, and sometimes other celebs pretend they don't recognize you. It's always the male movie stars or rock stars who act like they're too cool, but I can tell when they're faking it and are secretly excited to meet me, since they're pretending not to be impressed. When someone actually doesn't care, like politicians who meet me for photo ops and don't hardly know who I am, they have to pretend to *be* impressed. That's how you know who's more famous, whichever one of you is more excited to meet the other. It helps that I don't really know a lot of older actors, but they all know me, besides the ones who are *seriously* old and culturally irrelevant. Jane says most male movie stars have career peaks from about twenty-five to forty-five, but a male pop star can start earlier and also probably ends quicker unless he's really savvy. Women's careers in both are over by the time they're thirty, which is why they all suddenly get interested in having kids then. Once you have a kid, you're basically saying, Fuck you, career, except if you're the type of parent who doesn't really care about his kid anyway.

Jane introduced us and handed Linda a wrapped gift, which I'm sure was my debut album and a concert DVD. Our basement has a room that's filled with like a thousand of each.

About eighty adults and kids were standing around eating hors d'oeuvres from waiters in the main living room after the entrance. I recognized a few of the adults from the glossies, but no one was nearly as famous as me, which sometimes is a rush and sometimes you want someone else to take the attention off you, since everyone either looked at me or pretended not to when me and Jane walked to the bar. Except when there *is* a bigger celeb, after you relax, you get pissed, like, Why is *this* guy more famous than me?

Jane whispered that Linda got small roles on a few TV shows but her career would be in the toilet without her husband. After she got her prosecco, Matthew's father came over and kissed Jane on the cheek and thanked us for coming and shook my hand and said, "Big fan," and I said, "Love your work." You're not supposed to say anything else except "Big fan" or "Love your work." He wanted me to meet his son, so he called Matthew over.

Matthew was wearing a button-down and nice pants. His father said, "Matthew, thank Jonny for coming to your party. I'm sure he's very busy."

He stared down at his loafers and mumbled, "Thanks for coming." For having such good-looking parents, Matthew was pretty funny-looking. He had buck teeth and he already had acne and his stomach was a little chubby. I felt bad for him. I wondered if my father was good-looking, and if he was, why him and Jane made a good-looking kid, but Matthew's parents didn't.

His father said, "Make eye contact when you're speaking to some-one, Matthew."

Matthew made eye contact, and this time, when he said, "Thanks for coming," his eyes turned into tiny hard stones and I could tell he hated me. I didn't know if it was because I was famous or cuter or more talented, which are the usual reasons, or because his father was embarrassing him, but I can always tell when someone hates me right away. A lot of times it's easier to tell than when someone loves you.

I said, "Jane, can we get Matthew and his parents VIP seats to the concert tomorrow night? If they're available and want to come, I mean."

Jane seemed surprised but said we could probably do that, and asked Matthew's father if that was okay. He said they had plans but they could easily cancel them, and I looked at Matthew sort of like, Fuck you, Matthew, now you'll have to make eye contact with me for a whole night *and* sit through an entire concert *and* your parents are gonna love me even more, and I don't even care that when you open Jane's gift you'll probably try to break the discs with your friends from school.

Jane saw someone else she knew and introduced me, and we spent the next hour schmoozing different adults in the movie and TV entertainment industry. A few mentioned they had a project in mind that I was perfect for and we should call their offices to take a meeting, and Jane said we'd be making the rounds when the tour was over. I was still tired and wanted to go home, so instead of talking shop, I ate every spinach-and-cheese-pie triangle and mac-and-cheese cupcake and all the other weird hors d'oeuvres from the waiters, most of which had dairy. Each time I did, Jane shot me a look like, Enjoy it, kid, because that's your last one, but I knew she wouldn't say anything in front of the others, so I kept pigging out. She owed me for making me take basically two different meetings in one day.

The kids were hanging out together on the other side of the room, playing with their iPhones and eating from the table that had Doritos and soda and gourmet caramel popcorn and sometimes glancing over at me. Most were around me and Matthew's age, but some were younger or older. They all dressed about the same, in expensive jeans and T-shirts that were the in-store versions of what designers send me. When you squinted your eyes, it almost looked like a team uniform. But if I stood next to them, you could tell there was something just a little bit different, like the stitching and buttons on mine are higher quality and tailored with new measurements every two months even though I haven't hit my growth spurt yet.

I was a few feet behind Jane and this woman who was a network exec, but they didn't know I was there. After Jane listed the highlights on the tour, the exec said, "It must be tough on Jonny."

Jane asked what was tough, and the woman was like, "You know. Not having a normal childhood."

Jane said, "What's abnormal about it?"

The woman said, "Sorry, poor choice of words. I just mean I . . . I wouldn't put my son through it, that's all."

Jane was like, "Not everyone could handle it."

"You're right, he probably couldn't," she said. "I apologize if I misspoke."

Jane's voice iced over and she said, "Well, it was really nice meeting you." She excused herself to the bathroom and wobbled off in her high heels, and the woman noticed me and fake-smiled and said she had to say hi to a friend, and I grabbed four more pigs in a blanket and stuffed them down while Jane was away. I didn't know who the woman's son was, but I looked around for the most normal-looking, average kid in the room. I found a boy with short brown hair, in a group of kids near the popcorn bowl. I tried to picture him growing up and staying normal-looking and average, going off to college, getting a job in an office, marrying a normal-looking woman, having a bunch of normal-looking kids who later went off to college and got office jobs, working another forty years, then departing the realm and having a funeral with just his family crying there because the public didn't know who he was and everyone else forgot about him since he was so normal.

I went to the bathroom near the kitchen, but Jane was still inside. There was another room with the door open, a study, to one side, and Matthew's father was inside at a desk with his back to me, on his laptop and making a phone call. I pushed the kitchen door a crack, and no one was there, so I walked inside to hide out.

All the extra food and drinks were on the tables, but I wasn't even hungry anymore, I was eating out of boredom, and Jane always says that's who the real chubs are, people who fill up their guts with food because they're missing something else. I sat on a chair and listened to the voices muffled by the door. You could separate different voices out if you strained hard enough, like isolating music tracks. Everyone was trying to be the one who was heard, making their voices louder or saying the funniest or smartest line they could think of. The stupid thing is that people always listen to me, even though I'm just a kid and I wasn't even that good in school when I went and the only people I make jokes to are Jane and our staff, and my jokes suck.

Then I heard some voices outside, in the back of the house. There was a door in the kitchen to the backyard. It was unlocked and I opened it to a big fenced backyard with patio chairs and tables and trimmed grass and a small pool without water. The noises were coming from right around the side of the house. It was numbskull of me to be out there in the first place, and even more numbskull to go see what the sounds were with Walter grabbing shut-eye forty-five minutes away in his bungalow. But Jane was getting drunk, so it's not like she was doing an A-plus job of watching me.

I walked to the side of the house and knocked into a recycling can filled with glass. Nothing broke, but it made a rattling sound, and I could hear whoever was around the corner going, "Shit, shit."

It was the older kids who'd snuck out. The two boys' hands were behind their backs, and the two girls had guilty looks. They were around fifteen or sixteen. That was about the oldest my fan base got, and they were always harder to talk to. Tweens were easy, since they only squealed and didn't have any real opinions, and adults try to be polite, but it's hard to know what to say to the teen demo, who do have opinions but don't feel like they have to act nice. "Hey," I said.

"Hey," said one of the boys, who had a haircut that was influenced by The Jonny, even if he didn't know it, with an asymmetrical sweep down almost covering the eyes. Everyone wants to think their look is their own, but it's always coming from someone way higher up on the style food chain. The boy brought his arm out. He was holding an open bottle of wine. "Want some?"

All the kids were staring at me like, Is he gonna drink with us or rat us out? "That's okay," I said. "But you guys can do it."

He smiled, mostly to himself, and said, "Cool, thanks for giving us permission." The others laughed, and he took a swig and passed it to one of the girls.

"I'm seeing your concert tomorrow with three friends," one of the girls said.

"Thanks," I said. "I'll give you a shout-out."

"Except it'll be like a joke," she said. "Like, pretending we're the kind of girls who are excited about a Jonny Valentine concert. No offense. It's just, we would never go to it, for real."

"Oh." There's nothing else you can really say to that, unless I said something like, "It's just, you're an idiot, spending your parents' money and putting it in my bank account for a joke. No offense."

"Don't be such a bitch, you're hurting his feelings," said the first boy. He grabbed the bottle back and held it up to me. "Sure you don't want some?"

"I better not tonight," I said.

"Right," he said. "Save it for tomorrow, before your concert. Like a fucking rock star."

"Yeah, maybe," I said. The boy smiled to himself again like he'd won. The air was a little chilly, but looking at that kid's smile, this heat rose up in my body, and I felt like if I didn't say something, I'd set myself on fire.

"Or like a fucking no-talent nobody whose father pays for him to go to private school," I said.

I didn't wait for him to answer, but when I got back around the corner I heard him call me a douche bag midget and they all laughed. I nearly yelled another insult back, but you can't control other people, Walter says. You can only control yourself, so it's not how they act that matters, it's how *you re*act. The most successful celebs never lose control.

I found Jane inside the party talking to a handsome guy in his early thirties. He had on a standard young-but-not-too-young-actor's outfit, dark jeans with a slim gray blazer and a collared pink gingham shirt under. Jane introduced me and said he was a detective on some network crime show. He said, "But don't hold it against me," and Jane laughed and grabbed his arm at the elbow and said I should totally do a cameo on the show, and the actor was like, "That's such a bad idea it might actually be good. Imagine the ratings: Jonny Valentine, murder victim."

Jane stopped laughing and said, "I was picturing more like a witness or something."

Matthew's father came by, and Jane grabbed *him* by the elbow, too. She's always grabbing people by the elbows at parties, like if she doesn't, they'll all float away. "When are you bringing out the birthday cake?" she asked, and he said in a few minutes, and Jane said, "I thought— never mind," and he said, "No, what?" and she said, "Well, I was thinking Jonny could sing 'Happy Birthday' a cappella, but if it doesn't make sense . . ."

Matthew's father was like, "Seriously? That'd be amazing. Jonny, would you be up for that?" I couldn't tell if his father had no idea Matthew hated my guts, or if he picked up on it but knew that if I sang at his son's birthday party, all the kids at school would be talking about it and Matthew would seem cooler to them.

Jane was telling me with her eyes to do it. It was supposedly a birthday gift for Matthew, but it was really a gift to Jane, for business opportunities down the road.

"If you think he'd like it, then sure."

He smiled and said he'd tell his wife, and I should come in the kitchen soon so I could walk out with the cake. When he left and the actor went to get a refill, Jane leaned down and whispered, "This will make a huge impression on all the brain-dead execs here." Jane says an exec is a businessman who's convinced he has the soul of an artist.

"Fine," I said. "But I want to leave right after."

"Deal."

"Like, call the car service now."

"Okay," she said. "One more prosecco first before they run out."

Her face looked dried out and red from the alcohol, but she joined the actor at the bar and I went into the kitchen, where Matthew's dad supervised one of the waiters lighting the candles on the cake. Before we walked out, he said, "Thank you so much for doing this for Matthew, Jonny. He may not . . . he may not be able to express it, but I know this means a lot to him."

Sometimes parents know their kids better than anyone, and sometimes they don't have a clue, even if they're the kind of parents who throw their kids fancy birthday parties. Maybe my father *would* understand me because he *hasn't* been around.

Matthew's father turned off the lights in the living room and asked everyone to stay quiet for a special guest performance. He opened the door and the waiter carried out the cake, with me right behind, singing. Matthew stood by himself in the middle of the room, and the other kids were all taking my picture, because once I was performing the regular protocol didn't apply.

When I got to "Happy birthday, dear Matthew," I stared right at him again. He seemed like he was sort of pissed I was hogging the attention but also happy for the reason his father might have wanted, that it made his party the juicy gossip item at school. And even though he hated me for no good reason, I still felt sorry for him. He'd probably get even funnier-looking as he got older, and these kids might not really be his friends, maybe they only liked coming to his house for his pool and all the other cool amenities he had and because his father controls the purse strings, and not because they like him.

He blew out the candles and the adults applauded, but it was like they were mostly clapping for me, and I found Jane standing next to the actor and told her I wanted to leave, now, and she said, "I'll call the car service."

"You said you'd call it before," I said.

"They were busy."

The actor asked where we lived and Jane told him off Laurel Canyon, and he said, "Awesome, I'm in Los Feliz, I'll give you a lift."

I could see where this was going. Jane would invite him in for a nightcap and send me to bed. In the morning, I might see him on his way out, and he'd nod at me or act like he'd come back to take a business meeting at our house, which I'm not that stupid. And that'd almost definitely be the last time he came over.

We could *all* see where it was going, but no one could say anything, just like you can't say anything besides "Big fan" when you meet a celeb.

Jane said, "Let me finish this drink and we'll go. And that was nice of you to sing for Matthew."

She still had most of her prosecco to go, but it was better not to argue now. Jane and the actor were flirting and he was teasing her about how high her heels were to make up for her being so short, so I slipped away to get some more of the mac-and-cheese cupcakes from the kitchen. But on the way over, Matthew's father's study was still open with his laptop on. No one was around. I closed the door behind me.

I was going to use a totally made-up name for a new email address, but then it might look like I was someone else. So I came up with valentinojonny@gmail.com, since a lot of times celebs use an email that's just a little different from their real name. It took a couple minutes, and I had to keep glancing up to make sure no one was coming. Once I heard a loud creak on the floor right outside and got on my hands and knees and hid under the desk. When it didn't sound like anyone was there, I got up again, but I was still nervous. In the movies, when the star hides and the enemy leaves, they come out of hiding and don't worry about them ever coming back, like that was the *only* chance to get caught, but in real life, people can surprise you and come back again.

I took the paper with his email address out of my jeans and wrote

Can you prove you are really Jonny's father? If you can,
I can find a way to get you in touch with him.

I sent it and sat there for a minute in case he answered right away, but then I remembered where I was and closed the browser and snuck out. I made it seem like I was waiting for the bathroom, and went in and flushed Albert's email address down the toilet.

I found Jane with the actor. She said she had to say good-bye to Matthew's parents and go to the bathroom before we left.

When she was gone, the actor turned to me. "I've got an eight-year-old daughter," he said. "She loves your music."

I figured doing my "If it wasn't for my fans I wouldn't be here" line wouldn't work on this guy, so I just said, "That's cool. Is she here?"

"Yeah, I'm just gonna leave her here by herself, she can find her own ride home," he said, and I thought he was serious, but then he went, "No, she's with her mother this week."

He kept going. "Actually, my band has this one song, 'Xanax is a Deified Palindrome,' that some people say sounds a little like you. We're called the Band-Its, but with a hyphen between 'Band' and 'Its.'" Before I could say something pretending to know the song, he said, "You wouldn't have heard of us. Our first album was on a no-name label, but it was before I was cast. We're gonna shop our next one around soon to the majors, now that I'm better known. And the show plays a new song every week over the credits, so I'm working to get us some airplay."

Airplay means radio rotation, not TV. Every celeb thinks he has a cross-promotional platform just because he's famous. Being an all right actor playing a detective on some crap TV show *might* mean you can launch a career in crap movies. It doesn't mean you can launch a music career. Acting is a talent that you're born with or not. You can improve a little with practice, but there are some eight-year-olds who are better than sixty-year-olds who've been doing it their whole lives. Music is a talent that requires cultivation. This guy didn't look like someone who'd put ten thousand hours into it.

"I'll be sure to give it a listen when it comes out," I said.

"Here, I'll give you our demo, if you want to give your label a sneak peek," he said, and he pulled a CD out from his inner jacket pocket. "Or do people do that constantly to you, so it's really annoying?"

People hardly ever did it to *me,* since Walter or Jane was always providing buffer, but they pushed demos on Jane all the time.

"It's not annoying," I said. "I'll show it to them."

"Seriously? That's really cool of you."

I stuffed the CD in my track sweater's pocket before Jane came back. "Ready, boys?" she asked, a little slurry.

"I'm so sorry to do this," the actor said, "but I just found out I have to take care of my daughter tonight, and she's up in Encino." He looked at me real quick.

"Oh," Jane said.

"I mean, I could drop you off after I get her, if you want." So he'd gone after Jane at first, but once he realized he had me, he didn't need her anymore. Or maybe he thought this was part of the deal, that he didn't go home with her if I told the label about him.

"No, that's fine," Jane said, with a strong voice like everything was all right and she was totally sober, but I knew better. "We'll be in touch, and have a good night."

They kissed on the cheek, he left, and she called the car service and guzzled one more prosecco while we waited, but I didn't say anything this time. She conked out pretty quick in the backseat on the ride home, so I played the actor's CD on low volume. He was the lead singer, and had limited range and a reedy texture that he compensated for with some yells and a put-on scratchy growl. The only way that's real is if you've been singing and smoking cigarettes for like thirty years, which this guy definitely hadn't done. The musicianship was medium-caliber, nothing special. Bland arrangement. Sloppy production. No real hook. Zero nuance to the vocal/lyrical relationship. My lyrics may be simple, but Rog says I'm the most subtle pop vocalist around. You need to exert control over the lyrics, not the other way around.

Plus he'd have to be the next MJ for me to help him now.

Sharon goes to sleep at like nine o'clock unless I'm coming home from a show, so no one was up. Jane headed to the stairs, because she forgot they were being renovated. I steered her to the elevator. She leaned against the wall inside and didn't budge when the door opened. I put her arm around my shoulder and escorted her to her bedroom.

She collapsed on the bed and I took off her heels. Then I got a plastic cup from my bathroom so she wouldn't chip her teeth and filled it with water and dumped out two Tylenol PMs. I brought them back to her and made her sit up to swallow them, and while she was up I pushed her under the sheets. Before I left the room, she said, "You wanna sleep here tonight?"

I really needed a good night's sleep, and Jane tosses and turns even when she's on zolpidem or an over-the-counter pill. But I said, "Okay," and stripped down to my underwear and sponsored energy-drink T-shirt. I closed the shades all the way so the sun wouldn't wake her early and climbed in next to her, and she sort of murmured to herself, "You're really a good kid."

She started snoring soon and moved around a lot and took up more than half the bed, but I put up with it and eventually fell asleep.

CHAPTER 3

Los Angeles (Second Day)

I let Jane sleep it off in the morning. In the kitchen, Walter sat at the table and nodded at me over his copy of the *L.A. Times*.

Peter put down his own copy of the *Times* and poured me a cup of coffee and separated three eggs for my omelet and got out the spinach. He's got muscular forearms with blue veins popping out like worms under his skin, but he's delicate when he cooks, and even though he used to work at a restaurant with buzz in L.A. until Jane poached him and now he makes food that's beneath his talent level, he cares about every meal. That's what professionals do.

"Morning, little sensei," he said. I told him I liked karate movies one time.

"Morning, Peter."

"How's the cuisine been on the road?"

"Not like yours."

He flipped the omelet and said, "Nothing like a home-cooked meal, eh, little sensei?"

"Nope." I looked at the front page of *Variety* and took the sports section of the *Times*.

"Your Cardinals doing all right?" he asked.

Peter doesn't follow sports and didn't know the baseball season ended almost three months ago, which anyone who put a second of thought into it would realize they don't play baseball in the middle of January. He thinks he has to make conversation with me as part of his job, but I'm happy just to eat and read the paper. Walter gets it. "They'll be better next year."

He served my omelet and went back to reading the living section. There wasn't any sports news I cared about, so I looked at "Today's Top Albums" in *Variety*. Tyler Beats still had his last *two* albums, *Tylernol* and *Beats Me,* in the top five for Amazon, and *Tylernol* was number two on iTunes. I *knew* I'd see them there, but I couldn't help looking. It's like picking a scab when you know it might leave a scar.

Jane came downstairs looking much better than last night. She rebounds quickly.

"Sound check time," she said, all business, except it wasn't because first we had to get my highlights touched up for the rest of the tour and maybe even a full dye job since my roots were showing and a touch-up trim now that my hair was dangling in my eyes, which my fans like, especially when I have to flip it away, but it screws with me when I'm dancing. Jane's always like, The hierarchy is your voice, your eyes, and your hair. And when it gets long, it grows all curly at the ends, and that looks too ethnic. Jane also needed a trim, and she doesn't trust anyone besides Christian.

Walter fist-bumped me and said, "Ready to kick some tail and take names tonight, brother?" and I never really know if he wants me to answer or if the question is what Nadine calls *rhetorical* and also what taking names actually means, like if you'd kick someone's tail and ask them their name after to put on a list to help you remember whose tail you don't have to kick anymore, plus I don't think kicking tail and taking names includes getting a ride from your mother over to a gay guy's hair salon on Beverly Drive to have your hair dyed blond, so I just said, "Yep." Maybe it's Southern-demo slang.

After the appointment, Jane drove the three of us to Staples Center, which is always exciting to play, even if L.A. isn't my hometown. The main thing we had to make sure was fully operational was the metal swing in the shape of a heart that carried me around for the finale of

"U R Kewt" and "Roses for Rosie" and the encore of "Guys vs. Girls." We'd done rehearsals on it but we were waiting until L.A. to debut it in the show. It lifted me about fifty feet high over the crowd and projected a million stars on the roof, including a heart-shaped constellation. Jane didn't want me to do it, and told Rog it was an unnecessary risk for a young boy to assume, but he convinced her it would make a huge impression on the crowd and I could throw rose petals on them during "Roses for Rosie" and it would really provide a midtour bump in Web chatter about the stagecraft. You have to come up with reasons why someone should pay to see you live instead of watching you on You-Tube, even if that's how I got discovered in the first place. Everything went right in rehearsals, but I was still nervous about it.

Musicians are supposed to be bored during sound checks, except I like rehearsing with the band and the dancers and the tech guys checking sound levels and Rog making sure the choreography fits the stage and Jane organizing everyone. Sometimes it's better than the actual show, because you're not doing it for the audience, you're only doing it for yourselves. It's like you're practicing on a team during sound check. When you perform, though, you're the star and you're on your own.

This was our last show with Mi$ter $mith as our opener before we got that rock band the rest of the tour. He was a nice enough guy backstage, and did his own thing when we were on tour, but he has middling talent. His repertoire is standard slow jams mixed with a little rap that he cleaned up for my audience. I overheard him one time in his dressing room complaining to his entourage how he couldn't believe he was opening for an eleven-year-old white boy. I'm like, Go triple platinum with *your* debut, and I'll open for you. His real name is Marvin Hilliard. Pop stars don't like people knowing who they were before they were famous, since part of their appeal is that they *are* famous. Rock and rap stars can get away with it more, because if you came from the streets, it gives you more cred, but only rock stars usually go by their real names. All we had to do was change my name from Jonathan to Jonny, and me and Jane both changed Valentino to Valentine. He calls me Jonny-Jon, but I don't know if I should call him Mi$ter $mith or Marvin or M.S., the way his entourage calls him. It's like with Michael Carns's parents. I just said hi and never used their names.

After sound check, I hung out in the star/talent room and drank warm Throat Coat and ate some of the filet mignon and other low-carb food because I was starving and had my hair and makeup done by this Asian woman who's new for this tour. She was coiffing and gelling my hair, but it takes a light touch, since you need to gel it enough so it mostly stays in The Jonny, but not too much that it loses its floppiness. Girls historically love singers with sort of floppy hair. Besides the Beatles, there's Elvis, Jim Morrison, Kurt Cobain, even MJ once he got whiter. When she was doing my foundation, though, she went, "Your mom's gonna hate this," and I asked what, and she said, "I think you may have your first zit."

"Really?" I asked, more excited than anything else. I definitely didn't want zits, but it would mean I was hitting puberty soon.

She looked closer and said, "You're lucky, it's a whitehead. They're easier to cover up. This might hurt a little."

She pinched my skin and said, "*Never* do this to yourself, you might get a scar and then we're fucked." She showed me some white liquidy junk on her finger before she wiped it off on a tissue. It was gross, but cool to know my body was making something I'd never seen before. Maybe it was making sperm, too.

It's funny how half my songs are about liking girls who don't wear makeup, and I'm a *boy* who wears makeup. I once told Jane I should do a song about only liking girls who wear tons of makeup and expensive clothes, and she was like, That's basically what most songs *are* about.

Later on, while I played Zenon, I could hear the vibrations of Mi$ter $mith taking the stage and kicking into his first song, which was supposed to be "I Loves Me Dat Ho, Don't You Know" but he had to change for our tour to "I Loves Dat Girl-O, Don't You Know," and I took some liquid Pepto for my preshow butterflies, which were worse than normal because it was L.A. I couldn't get past Level 64's minion, and when he damaged me to zero percent the third time in a row from my saved game, I yelled at the screen, "You fucking motherfucker!" and Walter ran in quickly from outside and asked what was wrong, and I said, "Sorry, I was just screaming at the minion," and he said, "Whatever the hell you're talking about, let's save the screaming for the show, brother, or Rog is gonna get pissed about you wasting your voice."

I invited Walter to sit inside with me and I showed him what I meant about the minion. Walter still didn't know what the hell I meant, since the last time he played video games was when he was a teenager and he spends his free time either watching sports or reading mystery books, but when I was describing the way the minion kept deflecting my side attacks and how I couldn't figure out his Major Vulnerability, I accidentally attacked him straight at the middle of his body with a sword-punch-kick combo. Usually a Major Vulnerability is an attack from an angle that's hard to reach, but with this guy, he was vulnerable to an attack right in front of him, where you'd think he'd be most protected. I damaged him and advanced to Level 65 and explained to Walter how it was like when soccer goalies jump to one side on penalty shots, so sometimes the smart move is to kick it straight ahead. He understood it, and I said, "Make sure Nadine gives me credit for doing my first Teachable Moment this month," and he said, "I don't think video games count." She gives credit for stuff that's not always about school subjects, though.

I got paged right before intermission, as Mi$ter $mith was closing out with his one hit, "Call Me $ir," and I got into what Walter calls the Jonny Zone, when I tune everything out and deep-focus. He escorted me backstage to meet Jane. "How you feeling, baby?" she asked.

I said I was fine. My crew moved everything into position and Bill handed me my mike while he adjusted sound levels on this little machine, so I did the usual line, "Microphone check one-two-one-two," over and over. They still want me to hold a wireless mike instead of wearing a headset so I look more like an old-school crooner.

"We're all cool here, Jane?" he asked.

"We're all cool, Bill," she said.

He left, and the butterflies flapped their wings harder. It's always the same backstage. You get worried you'll forget the words even though they're like the alphabet song by now. You're afraid your voice will crack when it strains for the high notes. You'll slip in a spin move. Your jeans will split and everyone will see your underwear. You'll say something in a banter interlude that offends people and viralizes. Or something you haven't even *thought of* will go wrong, and not only is your career hurt, but so are the careers of the 136 people who work on your tour, plus Jane's. And no matter what, for the first few seconds you get onstage, you'll look around and realize twenty thousand people are all watching every move you make, and you'll be like, Why am *I* up here and not one of those people? Rog says that's natural for musical artists to ask, and you've got to block it out right away and remind yourself that very few people in the world are born with the consummate performer's gene, and that's why everyone else is paying premium prices to see you, because they need entertainment and escape almost as much as they need food and water.

On top of all that, I was getting more worried about the heart-shaped swing. If you were the kind of person who had a fear of heights *and* of being trapped, it would be your nightmare.

I said to Jane, "I think I might throw up," and she was prepared for it and had a big bucket nearby like usual and got it in front of me just in time, and she rubbed my back and pushed my hair out of my eyes and said, "Get it all out, baby, all the crap you ate in the star room."

Once it was out I felt better, and Jane handed me a special Japanese-green-tea-and-honey drink she always requests for my rider, and I took a swig to flush out the phlegm. Jane did my psych-up routine, where she's like, You're the most talented singer and dancer in the world, everyone loves you, but not as much as me because you're my beautiful baby boy, and the page tapped her and I nodded and she kissed me on both cheeks and my lips, and I felt less nervous, and the house lights went down and the countdown timer on the big screen and on the small backstage monitor ticked down from one hundred to zero as the audience chanted "Jon-*ny!* Jon-*ny!* Jon-*ny!*" and the opening piano riff of "Guys vs. Girls" played and the crowd went crazy, and Jane patted me on the butt to send me through the talent passage and out onstage into the bright red smoke, and I could tell I was close to the Jonny Zone again. When I'm in there, I can do whatever I want and the crowd will follow me. But if you snap out of the Zone onstage, it's scary. It's like when you're in an airplane or a car and you think, If the guy driving this wanted to, he could kill us all in a second.

Normally people say you should focus on one person in the crowd, but all that works for is small-scale performances. With arena shows, there are too many people, and if you *think* about focusing on one audience member, there's a chance you'll think about the entire audience watching you. The trick, I learned from the house guitarist on my first tour, is to focus on a vendor, since the vendors never care about you, they're the only ones who *don't* want anything from you, they just want something from the crowd, so in that way you're on the same team, both moving product.

And once I sang, "Girls and guys, burgers and fries, all gets ruined with a coupla lies," I forgot about the nervousness, it was just singing and dancing in the Zone. The crowd got even louder and the stage shook a little. It was probably ninety percent girls and their mothers and just ten percent their boyfriends. Jane wants a better balance, like seventy/thirty female/male, what Tyler has, for career longevity, but girls are way more loyal so it's a good problem to have. I counted eight signs in the front rows that said something like JONNY, I WILL BE YOUR GIRL TODAY while I sang the first verse:

> *In junior high, we're going at it*
> *Boys throwing spitballs, pulling on twirls*
> *Fussing and fighting, tearing apart*
> *This is how it starts with guys versus girls*

When I hit the first chorus, they all sang with me and did the backup singers' echoes on *guys!* and *girls!*:

> *Guys (GUYS!) versus girls (GIRLS!)*
> *Why's it gotta be that way?*
> *Guys (GUYS!) versus girls (GIRLS!)*
> *Will you be my girl today?*

I was on the second verse, which is probably my favorite of the four verses, because of the lyrical repetition of *broke* and the way it goes from *gal* to *boy* to *guys versus girls,* singing

I once got my heart broke, broke so bad
By the kinda gal who wore diamonds and pearls
She said, See you later, said, Don't you know, boy?
Everything in life is guys versus girls

when I did a trademark spin move and one of the backup dancers, Roberto, was off his mark by at least a foot, and I got distracted so it made *me* go off-rhythm and I launched the next verse a beat late. I sped up my tempo to catch up and stumbled over the words. It sounded sloppy. I did a half-spin later in the song and gave Roberto a scowl, but I don't think he saw. It's annoying when you're pissed at someone and they don't even know.

When I finished, it was one of the three designated spots for crowd banter. Jane had someone at the label write me up new banter interludes for each show so no one would put it on YouTube or whatever and catch me making the same jokes and riffs each time, but what they wrote was always so stupid, especially that day's sheet I'd glanced at in the star/talent room, so I was allowed to improvise a little.

I shouted, "What up, L.A.! I love you!" and they all said that they loved me, and I turned down the volume and said, "You guys ready to . . . party?" They were like, "Yeah!" and I said, "You know what you need to do for a party to be polite," and they said, "RSVP!" and I gave Ronnie the signal and he strummed the first G chord of "RSVP (To My Heart)."

I picked one girl in the front row to make eye contact with, about a year older than me, sort of pretty but the kind of round face where she might get chubby when she was older. At the edge of the stage, behind one of the security guys, I kneeled down and sang to her. Jane tells me to pick a girl older than me so it can never come off as creepy and it makes them want to still be my fan when they're older so they have a shot with me. Everyone around the girl was trying to touch me and the security guys were probably thinking, Thanks a ton for making us tackle a bunch of rabid ten-year-old girls, it makes *us* look like child predators.

I waved for her to come onstage, so a security guy picked her up and put her next to me. She kept saying to herself, "OMG OMG OMG." She was actually *saying* "OMG," not "Oh, my God." I circled around her as I sang, and half the time she wasn't even looking at me but was checking out the crowd. So I took her hand and sang right up in her face, like, You're gonna have to pay attention to me, and tears dribbled out of her eyes and down her cheeks in two curved lines.

It's always weird when girls cry at shows. It's not like it is when Jane cries, because you're sad, or once in a while because you're happy. It's that they think they love me. But you can only love someone for real who loves you back. They're *in* love with me. You can do that for someone who doesn't even know your name.

At the end of the song I gave her a kiss on her cheek, and the tears dumped out faster and the crowd went wilder, and I covered the mike with my hand and whispered into her ear, "I love you, do you love me?" and she nodded and wiped away her tears and one of the roadies gave her a bouquet and walked her backstage. And the messed-up part is, when I said it, I believed it, too, even if she was only okay-looking since you don't want to pick someone who makes the fat girls feel bad about themselves.

The rest of the show was what Nadine calls *B-plus work,* good enough to get by though not great, and we should never be satisfied with a B-plus, except I am with tutoring but not with music. My texture was muddier than I'd like, and my lungs didn't have much behind them on "Breathtaking," when I have to suck in my breath over and over after I sing the word *breathtaking.* Maybe being nervous about the heart-shaped swing affected me. Just a little stress can really hurt a singer. And Roberto made one other screwup by lifting his left leg when it should've been his right that I bet no one noticed but me. Probably no one noticed I was B-plus, either, because when a pro is below average, he's still performing at a caliber no one in the crowd can come close to. Sometimes I think it's not that I'm so talented, it's that everyone else in the world is so *un*talented.

It was time for "U R Kewt" and the closing medley. The swing coasted down to the stage and I climbed in and a tech guy secured the latch. It hummed and lifted me up-up-up and flew over the audience as

I sang. You're already higher than the audience onstage, but the swing makes you feel like you're above them and better than them, like you're God watching over everyone from the sky with all the projected stars swirling around. The swing's vibrations trick you into thinking you've had an accident in your pants, and the first few times at rehearsals I even checked my underwear after to make sure, but it's safe, with metal bars all around you, and the only way I could fall out is if I climbed over the side and jumped out. When you make the mistake of looking straight down through the grate, though, you're like, Whoa, now I *really* might have an accident in my pants. If I jumped, my fans would probably let themselves depart the realm by breaking my fall anyway.

For "Roses for Rosie" it lifted me straight up, and I tossed the rose petals down to them. They all scrambled to catch them like I was throwing money. It was sort of pathetic watching them do it, and I started throwing the petals super-hard, like I was trying to hit them, even though they just fluttered down. On the moon me and the petals would fall at the same speed because there'd be no air resistance, Nadine told me. I told her I'd jump out with them when I play the moon in the year 2060 on my oldies tour with Tyler Beats, if I don't have early onset dementia yet.

At the song's bridge, as I was a few words into the line that lifts the melody from "Amazing Grace"—"You called me the angel to your eyes, yet your heart was full of lies"—I heard a clanking sound from somewhere in the swing, and all of a sudden, *whoosh,* it dropped.

People say your life flashes before your eyes when you think you're going to die, but that's stupid, because you can't think about your whole life in just a few seconds. So when the swing dropped, all I thought of was Walter jumping on the crowd, spreading his body out to provide buffer, like a soldier taking a bullet for his commander. He was backstage, so it wasn't possible, but I bet he would've.

It didn't matter, though, because after about five feet the swing stopped again like a car braking hard.

Once everyone in the arena figured out what had happened, they gasped like they were the ones singing "Breathtaking," and half the band stopped playing, and my chest felt like it was thirty feet above me.

I could stop and ask to be let down. But I got my balance and said, "It's all part of the show, folks," which is what you say for any major technical malfunction, and continued singing and the band started up after me. The guy operating the swing did slowly move me down to the stage right away, though.

At the end I gave one of my "This was the best show ever!" lines, but with Roberto's mistakes and no one being on point and the swing especially, it was one of my worst ever.

Backstage, Jane hugged me. "I'm going to sue someone," she said. "So help me God, I'm going to sue the shit out of someone."

She was stroking and kissing my head and squeezing me tight against her implants, which are kind of hard, so it hurt a little, and I also couldn't breathe too good, so I said, "Jane, I'm fine, okay? I'm not hurt or anything."

She let go and breathed out and crouched in front of me. "We're not using that swing again. You hear me?"

"No, I went deaf from the swing, I can't hear anything."

"Stop messing around. Are you upset?"

"I'm more upset at Roberto."

"Roberto?" She pushed some hair out of my eyes that had gotten sweaty and lost its stiffness from the gel. "Why?"

"He fucked up his moves twice. It distracted me."

"Don't curse, baby. Do you want me to fire him?"

He never even noticed when I gave him that scowl, and either didn't think he'd done anything wrong or figured I didn't catch him and he'd gotten away with it or that I just didn't care much. I didn't know which was worse.

"Yeah," I said. "Fire him."

She kissed my forehead and wiped the sweat away and said, "You do your encores and then play games in the star room. I'll deal with all this and meet you there later."

I did my encores with the instrumentalists, not the dancers. We always do two separate encores, with a minute in between each. When you come back the first time, the crowd gets so amped up, and it sounds like they can't possibly get crazier, but you do it the second time and they're even happier because they really thought you'd left. Jane and Rog say three encores would be too much, since they'd never believe you're going away and it doesn't mean as much when you come back.

I went to the room and filled up on desserts to make up for what I'd vomited, and also because Jane wouldn't get pissed this time since she was upset about the swing. I took a slice of Eureka lemon cheesecake and an espresso crème brûlée from Spago that the salad bar had kept cold and warm, and took bites while playing Level 65 of Zenon. No one came in after shows, not even Walter, who stayed outside and said, "Good show, brother," like he always did. I think he thinks I want to be by myself postshow, which I mostly do, but around him, I don't have to be on, the way I do with other people.

As my character was coming up on a farmhouse in the middle of nowhere, I heard Walter and another voice outside my door, and Walter did his two knocks and a pause and a knock. He stepped in and said, "Roberto wants to talk to you."

I said okay. Roberto slumped in and closed the door and sat down on one of the beanbag chairs. I kept playing Zenon.

"Hey, Jonny," he said. "I'm real sorry about tonight. I was off, and I know it fucked with your rhythm. That's on me."

I went inside the farmhouse, and there was a mother and father and daughter eating stew at a table lit with one large candle. The father said, "Greetings, noble warrior, we are honored by your presence and invite you to share in our supper, meager though it be." I sat down with them.

"So," Roberto said, "I wanted to man up in person."

I nodded and ate the stew and took a bite of the Spago cheesecake.

"Your mom." He ran a hand over the back of his buzz cut. My male dancers aren't allowed to have longer hair than me. "Jonny, your mom wants to fire me. Just for what happened tonight."

I stood up from the table and took the candle. "Yeah, she told me." I brought the candle over to a curtain and put it against the material. It caught fire slowly before ripping into an orange rectangle. The father leaped up to fight me, but I drew my sword, and he ran out of the farmhouse with his wife and daughter behind him.

"It was a little mistake, Jonny. We all make mistakes."

"I don't," I said. "That's why I'm in the star/talent room and you're in the band/vocalist room."

The flames caught on the wooden walls and floor of the farmhouse and spread out on both sides. Out of the corner of my eye, Roberto was looking down and shaking.

"I know," he said, like he was crying even though there weren't any tears. "I'm real distracted lately. It's my pops, man. He's real sick."

The fire blazed on the entire wall and the screen was turning reddish from the heat, like when you close your eyes after staring at a bright light. "What does he have?"

"I don't know." He was shaking more now but he still wasn't crying. "Something's fucked-up with his heart and he's got all these doctor appointments and his insurance doesn't cover shit. And I'm the only one in my family who makes any money."

The fire was everywhere, and the screen got so red I couldn't hardly see anything, way thicker than the red smoke onstage. The farmer probably thought I was crazy for staying inside so long, but I'd never seen it get so hot like that in the game before. I ran out of the farmhouse in the direction I remembered the door was, and knocked against something solid with a sound effect, but I found the door and the screen lost all the redness and I could see again in the cool blue night air with the white moon hanging like a fingernail clipping, and my body was all blackened but not burned or damaged, and I dropped to the ground and sucked in air like a fish in a boat.

I'd gained twenty-seven experience points.

I finally turned to Roberto. "I'll talk to her."

He took a long time getting up, breathing slow in and out of his nose. "Thank you," he said. "I won't fuck up again."

He left and closed the door like he was trying not to wake up a baby, and I ran away from the farmhouse once I could breathe again, past the family who was beating their fists on the dirt and moaning at the smoky sky, and the level's gem appeared on the ground before me.

Walter came in and told me we were ready to go, so he gave me an Angels hat I squashed down almost to my eyes because I forgot my sunglasses, and he escorted me through the personnel exit. Jane's car

was waiting right near the entrance. I jumped in the back and slid down
into my usual postshow slouch even though the windows were tinted
almost black.

We had a smooth venue exit since only a couple paparazzi were
camped outside the personnel lot, and Jane just got the car pretour so
they didn't recognize it or the plates. Once we were on the freeway I told
her I'd changed my mind about Roberto. She only nodded and said,
"So I talked with Bill about the swing."

I'd forgotten about the swing because I was so happy about getting
the gem on Level 65. "What'd he say?"

Usually Jane looked at me in the rearview mirror when she talked to
me about something serious, but she just faced straight ahead and her
hands tightened around the wheel. "He said they figured out what the
issue was and resolved it, but there are apparently three separate safety
devices on it, so even if it happens next time, you're protected by three
levels of defense."

Walter's eyes shifted over to Jane before he turned his head out the
window.

"It didn't feel that safe," I said.

"I know, baby. That's what I told him. But he swears it is. And it
really is the technical highlight of the show, and the fans are going to
expect it now."

I thought about climbing back into the swing. When something
bad happens once, you always think about it after. It was like how I'd
choked onstage one time on my bottle of water, in New Orleans, and
now every time I took a sip I worried I'd do it again, mostly because
choking on water would be such a crap way to depart the realm. At least
crashing in the swing would be cool.

"If you say so."

"Great," she said. "We're going to use it for a lot of visual promo
content. And Bill knows what he's talking about."

Walter laughed quietly to himself. "Something funny, Walter?" Jane
said.

"If he knew what he was talking about, it wouldn't have gotten broke
in the first place."

Jane kept driving without talking, but it was the kind of not talking that said a lot. It wasn't the smartest thing for Walter to say that to her, but I thought again of him jumping in front of me to catch a bullet. General Jonny and Private Walter.

"Don't mind me," Walter said. "It's not my place. You going out tonight, or are we driving straight home?"

"Home," Jane said. "And I'd appreciate it if you kept your mind on security issues, Walter."

He kept looking out the window. "Sorry, Miss Valentine."

Jane turned on the radio to a classic rock station. We didn't talk the rest of the way. When we got home, Walter mumbled good night to us and went off to his bungalow, and Sharon was still up and asked us if we wanted anything. Jane said she was going to sleep and reminded me we had a six a.m. wakeup.

My body was tired but my mind was racing from the concert, so I asked Sharon to make me some decaf green tea with honey from the kettle, not the microwave or the hot-water faucet. It would take longer that way.

It was just me and Sharon awake in the house. She leaned over the island counter. "How was the concert, Mr. Jonny?"

"One of the dancers kept messing up and it threw me off, and then the swing that carries me over the crowd, it broke when I was inside."

She put her hand over her mouth. "It broke?"

"But there are three safety devices. So I didn't get hurt."

"Oh, good." She swept my hair to the side. "They're not going to make you do it anymore?"

"No," I said. "Jane said she wouldn't let them put me in it again for a million dollars."

Sharon said that she worried so much about me when I did tricks in my concerts, but now she could relax. I finished my tea while she read the front page of the *L.A. Times* on the counter. She's taking an adult-education writing class and they have to read the front page every day. When I was done, she looked up from the paper and said, "I love watching you drink your tea. You're so serious about it."

She took my mug and opened the dishwasher and bent over to put the mug in the back of the bottom row. Her butt was like two huge boulders guarding the entrance to a cave in Zenon. And I felt like I wanted to disappear inside that cave and close out the world around me and hide in there. I imagined running around the island and grabbing the chub around her hips and under her purple sweatpants and humping her. Thinking about it got me hard, and in my mind I was holding on to her so tight, she was captured like an animal and could never escape. Sharon wasn't just chubby, she was fat, but there was something about a fat body that was better than a chubby body. Like, either be skinny or be fat, but don't be somewhere in the middle. It's sort of like how it's okay to be super-famous or not famous at all, but don't be a D-list celeb.

She went to bed. I was still hard, so I tried in my bathroom, but couldn't make it happen. At least a groupie could never accuse me of getting her pregnant, except I'd have to issue a public statement like, "It's impossible, I can't even do it on my own," and a policeman would have to watch me in private to see if it was true, and they'd give me an adult glossy to help, and we'd also have to bring in Walter to make sure the policeman wasn't a child predator. I was wired, and I figured Jane was asleep from her zolpidem by now. She probably hadn't locked her door since she hadn't been drinking, and I didn't know when my next chance to go on the Internet was. At her door, I heard her breathing heavy, almost snoring, so I crept inside. Her computer was on top of a suitcase so she wouldn't forget it. I took it into her bathroom and booted it up. If she caught me, I'd tell her I couldn't sleep and was researching slave autobiographies for Nadine.

There were eight new emails, and my stomach jumped up like it did when the swing fell. But they were all spam. He hadn't posted anything new that I could find in my fan forums, either. I looked at my Facebook page to see how many new likes and comments I had. Jane had posted a photo of my Phoenix show, and there were 31,158 likes and 5,385 comments.

I didn't want Jane to catch me, even though browsing my Facebook page wasn't that bad and showed I was interested in growing my social media platform, and I closed out. An over-the-counter pill wouldn't cut it tonight, so I popped one and a half zolpidems from her medicine cabinet. It's like the sleep command in Zenon, when you can select how many hours you want to sleep for, and you do it right away and wake up refreshed. Only it's not as deep as regular sleep, and plus you have to be careful not to take it too much or it doesn't work as good. That's Jane's problem.

CHAPTER 4

Los Angeles (Third Day)

I woke up to Jane tapping my head. It didn't make sense, but I was still so sleepy that for a second, with my eyes closed, I thought it was my father waking me up, except I imagined him as the soldier in that war movie we saw.

"C'mon, make hay while the sun shines, you sleepy numbskull," she said. "You have an estimated twenty-three thousand, three hundred and sixty days left on earth. Make this one worth it."

That was Jane's Jonny Valentine Departing the Realm Countdown. I mumbled okay, but when she left the room I fell asleep again. She came in again. "Jonathan, seriously, we have to be out the door in forty-nine minutes."

I looked at my Cardinals alarm clock. I'd taken the zolpidem six and a half hours before. In Zenon, the only time you get woken up early is because of nearby enemies.

She watched to make sure I got out of bed. I was really out of it, though. My legs were spaghetti, and I felt like if I inhaled too much my chest would pop open.

I leaned against the wall of the elevator going down. When I sat at the island counter I put my head down by the newspapers as Peter prepped my breakfast. He refilled my coffee mug. "Looks like you need a double today, little sensei."

"Thanks." I tilted my head up. "Maybe some food will wake me up."

The entertainment section was buried at the bottom of the newspapers pile, and I saw why: A photo of me was on its front page. I pulled it away just enough so I could read the article. Peter was too busy cooking to notice.

THE CULT OF JONNY

Exactly how does a 46-year-old male music critic open a review of a Jonny Valentine concert he is forced to attend? And to maintain proper journalistic house style, must he *really* refer to an 11-year-old boy hereafter as "Mr. Valentine"?

Well, *forced* is an unfair verb. Mr. Valentine (indeed, my sadistic editor grinningly assures me, I must) has world-class pipes and dancing talent and stage charisma to spare. A few songs are downright catchy, even to ears from which poke a few stray hairs. Besides the annoyingly can't-get-it-out-of-your-head chorus of "Guys vs. Girls," several other numbers in the Angel of Pop's repertoire last night at Staples Center showcase the singer's live-performance attributes, notably "Breathtaking" and "Crushed."

Yet no one, not even Mr. Valentine's most enthralled fans, goes to a Jonny Valentine concert expecting a fully developed auditory experience. Rather, they go for the spectacle, to surrender and sublimate and take part in the cult of personality swirling around a human being who, I suspect, may not yet be in possession of, you know, *an actual personality*. (Perhaps that's the point: Onto this blank canvas his audience can paint whatever image they desire of him, or, even better, through gender metamorphosis, of themselves-as-Jonny.)

If Jonny Valentine is ever to grow as a pop artist, he will have to ditch everything about his act, from the infantile lyrics to the cheesy choreography to the overproduced packaging, and deliver something that speaks to who he is, if and when he eventually figures that out—not to his management's carefully crafted presentation of an innocuous crooner of the bubbliest bubblegum. I, for one, wouldn't mind seeing his vocal cords matched up with something a little more authentic. With his chops, he might even be—gasp!—great. Until then, we'll have to make do with limp offerings like "RSVP (To My Heart)" and "Roses for Rosie," which—

Peter pushed my plate over, so I stopped reading and hid the entertainment section under the pile. I felt dizzy again and took one bite of my omelet, thinking it would give me some strength. But as soon as it went down my throat, my vision went all fuzzy like a TV when the cable isn't plugged in and all these walls crashed around my head at once like the trash compactor in *Star Wars,* and I fell forward on the counter and heard Peter say, "Jonny! Fuck!"

I must have woken up soon, because Peter was shaking me awake and Jane was just getting there. I hadn't fallen off the chair, but I'd spilled my coffee and food all over the countertop.

"I don't know what happened," he said. "He keeled over—"

"He's waking up!" Jane said. "Give him some air!"

Peter backed off but Jane leaned in real close to my eyes. "Jonathan, can you hear me?" she breathed in my face.

I blinked my eyes a few times. "Yeah."

"Are you okay, baby? Do you feel faint?"

I was moving and speaking in slo-mo. "I feel . . ." Her eyeballs popped out huge and scared right up against mine. She couldn't find out I'd taken zolpidem without her permission. "I feel fine."

She put her hand on my forehead and kissed the skin to test my temperature. It always felt nice when she did that, cool and soft. Like she wasn't afraid of catching whatever I had. "I'm taking you to the doctor."

"But the bus."

"They'll wait."

She drove us to Dr. Henson's office fast. He had a lot of celeb patients, and there was a special waiting room for us so the normal people wouldn't Tweet that they were in a doctor's office with us. Even his super-rich patients might do that.

I got sent to the examination room right away while Jane filled out paperwork. The nurse told me to strip to my underwear and measured and weighed me. I was down to eighty-six, so at least there was that. While I waited I thought about the *L.A. Times* article. Normally I don't pay attention to the critics, because they either decide from the start that they hate me, or they come up with a lot of big words to explain why they actually like me, because they can't just come out and admit they're into my music. Smart people always have to give reasons. But this guy was saying he *could* like me, if my image was completely different. I couldn't bring it up with Jane, though, especially now that the label was reassessing me. She'd say music critics are guys with ponytails and potbellies who never got good enough at an instrument to be in a band, so they take it out on the real musicians. Even when they *love* something in a review, they have to mention a few things they don't like in the second-to-last paragraph, to prove they're smart, and then the next sentence is always, "But these are minor quibbles in a near-masterpiece of an album."

Dr. Henson came in in a few minutes. He was fake-cheerful like usual, with his kind of chub face but slim body. Some people can't lose weight in their face no matter what. Jane doesn't have that problem.

He always put out his hand when he came into the room and said, "Jonny, high five! Now down low!" and pulled it away before you could hit him and he said, "Too slow!" and giggled like he was the first guy to invent that trick. I guess it's like me doing interlude banter, acting all upbeat and saying pretty much the same lines even when I don't feel it. Jane gives him tickets to L.A. shows for his daughters so we always get excellent service. He was probably there last night, but we don't discuss it. It's not professional.

"I hear you've had a little fainting spell?" he said as he perused some papers. Doctors never talk right to you. They're always reading something else at the same time like you're not interesting enough.

"This morning," I said, and in case he *wasn't* there, I added, "I had a show last night."

He put his stethoscope on my chest in a few different spots. It felt like an ice cube. "Give me some deep breaths with those powerhouse lungs of yours," he said. "Did you eat normally?"

I made a tiny tear with my fingernail in the thin paper covering the table. "Yeah. But I vomited preshow, like I usually do."

"We've discussed that. Your singing teacher doesn't want you to take the antinausea medication because it causes dry mouth?"

Rog is a voice coach, not a singing teacher. "Right. I can't sing with it. And if I don't eat before at all and I vomit, I feel even weaker."

"Did you take anything to help you go to sleep last night?"

I pulled the tear in the paper further, so it looked like one of Jane's dresses being unzipped in the back. *Fussing and fighting, tearing apart.*

"Only when I'm on the road, like we said."

"You getting enough rest out there?"

"Mostly. If I don't get a good night's sleep I can always sleep on the bus."

Jane did her usual knock on the door, three sharp raps, and Dr. Henson let her in and told me I could get dressed. She said hello and sat down on one of the blue folding chairs. "Did he tell you about the swing?" she asked.

"What swing?"

"Oh, just that there's this machine, like a metal box, that carries him around in the air over the crowd," she explained. "And something malfunctioned and it dropped him a few feet before the safety devices kicked in. But there are three safety devices and they figured out the malfunction, so it's not something to be concerned about. Anyway, I wondered if that could've frightened him and caused the fainting."

He smiled like she was a total moron. Doctors must think about regular people the way I think about people who are tone-deaf. "No, it couldn't. What could is dehydration, vomiting, strenuous exercise, and both physical and mental exhaustion. This is not what a typical eleven-year-old can handle. Even child actors have far less punishing schedules."

"He turns twelve in under two months," Jane said.

Dr. Henson wrote something in his papers. "How long has this tour been going for, when does it end, and when's the next concert?"

"About two weeks, it ends on Valentine's Day, and we're driving to Utah today but the concert isn't till tomorrow night."

"He should be fine for that, if you give him plenty of fluids and food today with little exertion," he said. "But you're going to have to find a way to get Jonny more rest. I'm serious about this."

If I admitted I took a zolpidem last night, he'd make sure Jane hid them from me. I don't think he even knew she gave me some of hers.

"We'll come up with something," she said. It was her this-conversation-is-over voice.

"Jonny, would you let your mother and me speak alone for a minute?" Dr. Henson asked. I said sure, and he high-fived me again but didn't do the down-low part this time. Jane came into the celeb waiting room a few minutes later. On the ride home I asked what he talked to her about.

"I had some questions about my period. He's my doctor, too, you know," she said. "Stop talking for a while, okay? You need to rest." I definitely wasn't interested in hearing what her questions about her period were, and didn't even make the joke I thought of, which is that if you wrote out a question about your period, you'd end the sentence with a *period mark*. It was more Nadine's kind of joke anyway.

At home she had me lie down on the living room couch and eat a new omelet as her and Walter got ready. She even asked Walter to carry me to the car. I was like, Jane, I'm good now, but she insisted. Walter was cool about it. He threw me over his shoulder and said, "You can carry me next time I'm on a bender, brother." I didn't mind him carrying me, once he did it. It was kind of fun, actually, and felt familiar, but I couldn't remember him doing it before.

The car service took us to the studio parking lot, where the buses and eighteen-wheelers were still waiting. We weren't that late, and all of them except the star/talent bus could've left, but I guess they needed to make sure I was really going before they took off, because without the star, the apparatus is irrelevant. The EVP of creative Stacy was standing by my bus, typing on her phone. She looked up when we arrived and inhaled and exhaled like I did with Dr. Henson. I told Walter I could walk fine and he shouldn't carry me.

"Are you feeling okay, Jonny?" she asked when I came by.

"I was just tired," I said. "When we find a way to get me more rest, I'll be fine."

Her eyebrows were worried. "As long as the doctor cleared you," she said, looking at Jane. "You up for meeting the Latchkeys?"

"The who?" I was watching Nadine, who'd come out of my bus and was talking with Walter while they both looked over at me.

"The Latchkeys. Your new opener. They've boarded their bus, but I can ask them to come out."

I said sure, and she went into the band/vocalist bus and came out with four guys in their twenties. Three of them were unshaven or had beards and wore regular clothes and looked like normal guys, but the one in back was thin and tall and had midnight black hair that almost covered his eyes and a maroon leather jacket that was all scuffed up. It was the kind of look a stylist would never be able to come up with. Or if she did, it would feel like a stylist did it, instead of it being the look this guy had his whole life.

"Hal, Steve, Tim, Zack, meet Jonny," Stacy said. "Jonny, meet the Latchkeys."

They all shook my hand and wore these goofy smiles that older guys always have when they meet me, because they don't know if they should be impressed or think it's silly. People say that girls are hard to figure out, but they're much easier to handle, even the older ones. Guys are the ones who have to think they're always in control, so they act the way they want to act.

Zack was the tall and thin one, and he was the only one that said something more than hi. "Pleased to meet you, Jonny. I'm Zack. We're excited to open for you."

"Me, too," I said. "I mean, for you guys to open for me."

He laughed in a way that made me feel like I'd made a funny joke even though I'd messed up. "Just last night a friend who's a kindergarten teacher said to me, 'Have a good tour,' and without thinking, I said, 'You, too.'" Zack looked at one of his bandmates. "But the thing is, she *is* going on a huge kindergarten-teacher East Coast tour, so it made sense."

They laughed, but it was still early in the morning, so not that hard, and said bye and returned to the bus. After he left his cologne hung in the air. It smelled like the woods mixed with cigarettes.

Stacy said, "Jane, if anything comes up, don't hesitate to call my personal phone."

"This isn't creative's responsibility, right?" Jane asked. "Olivia's our usual tour liaison."

Stacy smiled at me. "Well, I sometimes make an exception and prioritize talent like Jonny."

Jane pinched her lips and said bye and walked onto our bus. When I got on, she told me I should sleep on my bed for as long as I wanted, since it was like a twelve-hour drive, and Nadine and I could tutor later. So I took a long nap and didn't need any pills to fall asleep. When I woke up I felt super-strong. I bet if I was alone I could've gotten close to coming.

I went out to the seating area and told Nadine I was ready for tutoring. But Jane said she wanted to talk to me about something quickly first, and she came into my room and sat down on the bed with me. "Do you feel better?" she asked.

"A lot."

"What do you think it was? We got home from the concert too late?"

"No," I said. "I think it was getting home from the party late the night before."

She looked down when I said that. "Anyway, I've been mulling our options for the next six months or so," she said. "Even if album sales have lagged, the gate receipts have been respectable. If the live-stream sells well, I think the label would be open to a bigger tour to expand your fan base."

"To where?"

"I'm thinking Asia and Europe both. If there's ever a time, it's now, because if we don't make a splash at the Garden—" She cut herself off and smiled big, like it'd make me forget what she just said. "But it would mean a lot of work right after this ends. We'd start recording new songs and have to orchestrate a whole new show. The album would drop and the tour would begin next fall, and it'd continue through the winter."

"Uh-huh."

"The other option is this." She fiddled with her silver ring. "We can do a smaller repeat tour on the West Coast next fall, and we record the next album in the summer."

"What would I do the next six months?"

"There's this school in L.A. that a lot of celebrities and children of celebrities attend. You could just go to school for the spring semester. It starts right after the tour ends, and I'm sure we could pull some strings to get you in."

"So I'd be going to school and that's it?"

"Basically. We could see how you like it. But remember that going to school full-time can be hard, too."

"I know. It's hard just with Nadine. She's making me read three whole autobiographies by slaves this unit."

"Slaves, huh? Well, you don't have to decide now. But we need to figure it out after the tour ends."

I said okay. Before she left she said, "I bet we could schedule free time in Japan to look at samurai stuff, so when Peter calls you 'little sensei,' you'd actually know what he's talking about, right?"

"That'd be cool," I said. But I looked out the window at the side of the highway and thought about what it might be like to not be on tour anymore. I hadn't been around regular kids in a long time, not including times like at Matthew's birthday party. All I was around were fans. Me and Michael Carns from St. Louis hadn't talked since I moved to L.A. I couldn't hardly even remember what school was like by now. When you live one way for a while you sort of forget how you lived before. Except Jane remembers working at Schnucks. She never goes into supermarkets anymore, not even the fancy organic ones.

And then I thought about my father maybe getting in touch again with Jane, and how he wouldn't like the celeb lifestyle, but now that we were having a normal life, he wanted to come back. We'd have enough money to keep Walter on staff and in the bungalow, and him and my father would become friends and lift together and come to my Little League games, so he'd be more like Uncle Walter than my bodyguard, but if anyone messed with me or my father, he'd still be there to provide buffer.

I'd also be able to sleep in again and not have to spend months recording and rehearsing and traveling and performing. I hadn't had a real hiatus for two years.

Nadine came in to tutor, and a million times she was like, "How are you feeling?" and "Do you feel like you need to take a break?" and "Are you sure you're feeling okay?" Finally I said, "I *feel* like you can stop asking me how I *feel*," and she laughed and said sorry, she lets her caretaking tendencies get the best of her sometimes. After we played word games at the end, I almost told her about Jane's offer, but I realized that would mean she'd be out of a job. I didn't feel *so* bad about that. She could find other celebs or rich kids to tutor or work at a school, and I bet Jane would keep her on to tutor me part-time if she had openings. But I hated the idea of telling someone they had to leave. Even when someone fucks up like Roberto did.

During the word games, I told her the period mark joke instead. She gave me credit for a Creative Stroke, but warned me not to repeat it in any interviews.

CHAPTER 5

Salt Lake City

Jane said that me and Lisa Pinto were going to do an exclusive photo op of a staged date for a glossy on our next stop in Denver. I didn't ask her why she changed her mind. There were always two reasons: Ronald told her she should do it, or there was a lot of money. I didn't care, though, since I'd get to see how cute Lisa Pinto was in person. You can't always tell from photos. Sometimes girls are disappointed when they meet me. I've read a few blog posts.

Before I left in the morning, Rog knocked on my door. He seemed twitchy. "Good luck tonight," he said. "You know the warm-up routine?"

"Rog, I've done it like a million times."

"Just let me know how it goes later, okay?"

"Roger that, Rog," I said, which he never finds funny.

"And try to remember the name of whoever works with you. Can you do that?"

"No, I'm a numbskull who can't remember anyone's name. Who are you, again? And who am I?"

"No kidding, Jonny, as a favor to me. Please."

I promised him I would. "Thanks," he said. "This is a really tough time in the industry. So . . . I appreciate it." He beat it down the hall, because he must've been afraid Jane would catch him. It looked like he had a little limp when he walked fast. It wasn't hard to see why he was worried about someone younger teaching me.

When we got to sound check at EnergySolutions Arena, Jane introduced me to this English woman named Patricia and said she'd be helping with my warm-ups. I couldn't figure out a way to ask her last name for Rog without being obvious. She looked young enough to be one of my backup dancers. Her arms were like toned snakes in her tank top and she had a pretty smile like white piano keys even though she's from England. The English musicians I've met have the worst teeth, except for the young ones who are pop singers. They've got American teeth. Jane stayed and worked on her computer while we did vocal exercises in the star/talent room but glanced up a bunch of times.

The Latchkeys sound checked next, and though I'm supposed to rest up in the star/talent room and drink Throat Coat and I wanted to play some Zenon, I watched them. It wasn't a full performance, but they had a tight sound, with lots of ambient noise. Zack was what made them different. He was the lead singer and rhythm guitarist, and his musicianship was fine, but his voice was sonorous and had real range. Most male baritones can't reach the high notes easily or give them any feeling. And he wore a dark green velvet suit. I couldn't make out the lyrics, but each song had a different girl's name in it and other words that began with that letter, like "Erica's Elfin Ears." I found a copy of their set list to read the names of the others, and one called "Vera's Vulva" was crossed out and next to it someone had written, "R-rated! Oh, my!"

When I was back in my room playing, I found myself humming along to their song called "Jealous Julia." I wanted to hear it again, but Jane was always busy before shows and wouldn't be able to download it for me. So I asked Walter to escort me to the band/vocalist room. Outside their door I said, "Walter, you can wait out here if you want."

He smiled and said, "No problem. Like dropping you off a block from school." You didn't have to explain anything to Walter, and his feelings never got hurt.

I knocked on the door and the bassist opened it, I forget his name, either Steve or Tim. He said hi and invited me in. It was the four of them, and they were sitting around eating food and reading books and magazines that weren't glossies. Some up-tempo rock was playing with a male singer. Zack put down his book whose name I couldn't see except for a huge letter *U*.

"Stately, plump Jonny Valentine," he said.

I looked down at my stomach. The hotel scale that morning said I was maintaining at eighty-six. "It's a joke, you're not plump," he said. "Your sound check rocked, by the way. I listened in."

I smiled wide and said I'd heard theirs and wanted to download their songs but I didn't have the Internet. "There's no Wi-Fi in your room?" he asked.

"My mother doesn't let me go on." Two of the Latchkeys looked at each other like this was the funniest thing they ever heard.

Zack took my iPod and plugged it into his laptop. "Not letting children go on the Internet anymore." He made a *tsk-tsk* sound. "What *is* the world coming to? I'll give you not only our first album for free, but the rough cut of our next one. But don't leak it to anyone, right?"

I said, "Right," and he gave me a handshake and said, "All right, I trust you because you're the man, and because I don't have trust issues despite what my therapist says." I stared at the laptop while it was transferring to my iPod. "If you want to hang out and surf the Net, like the kids say these days, feel free. I won't tell your mom if you don't."

I said thanks and he went back to his book. There were like fifty emails, but it was all spam. That's what my regular email account usually looked like, too. If you were an alien and looked at someone's email, you'd think the only merch they sold domestically was prescription sex pills.

An email in the middle was from "Albert Valentino." There was an attachment of a photo of a driver's license with the name Albert Derrick Valentino. I almost said something out loud, and looked up. No one was paying attention.

The guy's hair was almost the same chestnut color as mine is naturally, except it was thinner and he didn't have it in The Jonny, obviously, but more slicked back. His skin was much paler than mine but that's also from living in L.A. and spray-tanning once a week with Jane at this salon where they serve you sugarless pink lemonade, and his eyes were also blue like mine. He was a pretty good-looking guy, better bone structure than Jane. I got my pug nose from him, and Jane's right, it's cuter on a kid than it will be when I'm an adult, but it still worked for him. He was six feet tall. Jane is only five-two, so if it was really my father, I might not be so short, but shorter pop stars are more successful because they're better dancers and your head is oversized for your body, which plays better on TV, and plus it helps since people love seeing a huge voice coming out of someone tiny. If I was bigger it wouldn't be so impressive to them.

He'd turned forty-four years old in November, so he'd had me when he was thirty-two. The license showed an address in Pittsburgh, and it expired over a year ago.

When you've seen a million pictures of yourself, you start to see yourself in other people's features sometimes. I guess part of it's because you almost forget it's you in pictures. Instead it's the glossy magazine version of you, so you compare that person with other people. And depending on what the picture's in, like a glossy or tabloid or newspaper or website or teen glossy or whatever, it feels like a different version of you, even if it's the same exact picture. Most people don't see themselves so much besides in the mirror, which is the opposite of how you look in real life to others, so when they see pictures of themselves something always feels off. But I see so many photos of myself that I can picture myself in them better than I can picture my own reflection. Except everyone takes a ton of photos of themselves, so they probably react a little more like celebs.

Anyway, I could see myself not in his eyes themselves but more *around* the eyes, since he had deep purple bags there, and when I didn't sleep enough I got them, too, only not as purple. It really was my father. All those times I'd imagined what he looked like, and now I knew. Or knew from a driver's license. If he'd sent a thousand pictures, I would've studied each one in close-up.

He might have a whole new family in Pittsburgh. I played it on my last tour. Maybe he came, or even took them. The oldest any of his kids could be was around five, which was just outside my base's age range, but some were that young. Or he could have a boy, one he played catch and watched Pirates games on TV with or took to games, and taught him how to swing and the proper fielding position and how managers do a double switch, which is the hardest thing to understand, and I had to watch a million games before I figured out how it worked. I don't know why, but that last part about the double switch made my stomach feel like it does preshow, all knotted up and swirly at the same time and like I had to throw up. Except preshow you *do* throw up and you feel better. This sat there like a huge bag of Doritos you wished you hadn't eaten but you couldn't stop yourself.

My face must have moved a lot because I heard Zack say, "Everything working okay?" and I said, "Yeah," without moving my eyes. I read the email:

> Please send this to Jonathan. Jane still calls him that right?
> Here's my license but I don't live in Pittsburgh anymore. I
> live in New York, just moved here last year after a few years
> in Australia mostly working in construction. Now you have to
> hold up your end of the bargain. Send me a regular picture of
> Jonathan to prove you know him and tell me something about
> Jane only he would know.

So he wasn't taking some other kid to Pirates games, unless he'd had one there before he went to Australia. I could easily see the guy in the driver's license bouncing around Australia, living with different women who took him in, seeming all exotic to them since he had an American accent and knew how to operate forklifts and cement mixers. Jane thought about adding an Australia/New Zealand segment on the first tour, and to work in an appearance at a big Sydney music festival, but the label didn't think we had enough of a foothold there yet. I wonder if he would've come to the concert.

I'd passed by a million guys doing construction on the street in my life, but I never thought that that's what my father did. Jane just said he didn't do hardly any work.

Jane was always worried about child predators getting ahold of candids of me, even though I didn't see any difference between those and published shots. And I couldn't tell him anything too personal about Jane in case he was still just pretending to be my father or was going to go to the media. The more we limit awareness of Jane, the more freedom she has to operate behind the scenes.

I checked again to make sure the Latchkeys weren't watching me. They weren't. One of them was on his iPhone, and Zack said, "Please tell me you're not on Twitter again."

He said, "We've already gotten a thousand more followers since our profile in *Vice*."

Zack was like, "Because our fans definitely aren't sheepish hipsters. I mean, sheeplike hipsters. Sheepish hipsters would be, what, bashful practitioners of countercultural lifestyles."

One of the guys said, "And neither are we."

A second one said, "So we're all in agreement that we're not sheeplike, right? Guys? Yes?"

The third one said, "And neither is the guy at our Austin show who wore the ringer T-shirt that said I HATE IRONIC T-SHIRTS."

The first guy said, "Doing anything meta is a hipster thing. So is saying that anything meta is a hipster thing."

The second one said, "And disavowing your hipsterness is the surest sign that you are a hipster."

Zack said, "Some of my best friends are black hipsters."

They hadn't laughed until that last one, and then they returned to doing what they were doing. The Latchkeys were like the Harlem Globetrotters with words. I'd pay $19.95 to watch them talk on Internet live-stream. They must've known each other for a long time, the way they talked so fast and all sounded like each other. I didn't sound anything like Jane or even Walter.

I asked the guy with the iPhone if he could take my photo and email it to me. "So I can make sure I'm able to download photos," I said, since it was a strange thing to ask.

"Sure," he said. "With all of us?"

"That's okay, it can be just me."

"As long as we're not being narcissistic," he said. Fuck him for making fun of me for asking for a photo with myself, when I was just trying to protect them in case I was emailing with an impostor.

Zack got up. "Can I get in there? I'll be the envy of everyone back home who said I'd never amount to anything." He winked at me. "Or I'll sell it on eBay and we'll split the profits."

Maybe it was okay if only Zack got in there, and even if the guy was an impostor and was going to email the photo to a gossip site, it'd look cool that I was hanging out with Zack backstage in his green velvet suit. I told him yeah, and he said, "Copacetic," and put his arm around my shoulders. He smelled like the woods and cigarettes again.

I gave the other guy my email and Zack said to send it to him, too. It showed up in my inbox. I had to figure out what to tell him about Jane. And I didn't want to let him know it was me who was emailing him. I wrote

Jane is very allergic to peanuts.

That wasn't too private, but I don't think many other people know about it. Jane's savvy about containing info in our circle.

I Googled "Albert Valentino Pittsburgh." I didn't find anything till a few pages in, a short article in a no-name Pittsburgh newspaper from four years ago.

CRIME BLOTTER

TWO MEN ARRESTED IN BARROOM BRAWL

Two men were arrested early Sunday in connection with a dispute in the parking lot of Schmidt's Tavern in Southside Flats.

According to a police statement, Jefferson Smithfield, 35, and Albert Valentino, 40, turned to fisticuffs after a verbal dispute. The owner of Schmidt's, John Schmidt, is suing the two men for damages to the exterior of the bar sustained during the altercation.

Smithfield has a prior conviction for unlawful possession and delivery of a controlled substance. Valentino has no prior record.

Both men were processed and released Sunday evening.

They didn't have a picture of his mug shot or anything. But I thought of the guy in the driver's license posing in the police station, which wasn't hard because ID photos already look like mug shots without the height marker behind you. If you see a celeb who still looks good in a mug shot, then you know that person's *really* good-looking and doesn't need to rely on makeup and lighting and Photoshop.

Then I imagined him getting in a fight outside a bar. The other guy, Jefferson Smithfield, was drunk and insulting my father and telling him he sucked. He was like, "And I don't believe Jonny Valentine is your son, like you always say." Finally my father was like, "I *am* Jonny's dad, and if you say one more thing to me, I'm gonna kick your ass," and the other guy smiled like in the movies and said, "You're a loser and a liar." My father didn't say anything. He just threw an uppercut and knocked him out cold through one of the bar windows, which is why he got sued for damages to the exterior of the bar sustained during the altercation. He waited there for the cops because he hadn't done anything wrong. That wasn't how it could've actually been, since I wasn't famous four years ago, but maybe he'd gotten in fights like that outside bars in Australia and they didn't have muscular enough media there to report it.

The newspaper didn't have any more stories about him, and I couldn't find anything else by Googling his name with Pittsburgh or Australia or New York. I told the Latchkeys I'd see them later and asked if they wanted anything from my food spread, but Zack said, "Thanks, we're solid."

Walter was waiting outside like he was picking me up from school. I don't think he's ever made me wait once. Back in the star/talent room, I didn't listen to the Latchkeys yet. Jane made sure I rested before I went on, and she watched what I ate before, too, to try to prevent me from vomiting. She made me stick to cold soup and promised I could eat whatever I wanted after.

I didn't vomit, but that could have been luck. The performance went fine, an A-minus, and Roberto didn't make any mistakes. A couple times I thought about Albert, like when I saw some fathers with their daughters in the crowd, but mostly I didn't. That's the good thing about doing a show, you really block out everything else in your life when you're onstage, because you're not only selling the emotion of the songs to the audience, you're selling them to yourself, and you can't imagine feeling anything other than the way the songs are supposed to make you feel. If you're going through the motions, the audience can tell. I've done it before, and those are my C-minus shows.

I was nervous when I first got in the heart-shaped swing, but then I was like, Well, if I die, everyone else will feel like shit for telling me it was safe, and the crowd will feel like shit for wanting me to do it just so I could be closer to them. So by going on it was sort of a fuck-you to them, and at one point when I was over the crowd and the keyboards were blaring on "Roses for Rosie," I hummed and whispered, "Fuck you all, if the EVP of creative didn't prioritize me and get me coverage in all your glossies, none of you would give a shit about me," quiet enough so the mike couldn't pick it up. When you're acting angry it's hard to also be scared.

CHAPTER 6

Denver

We had two shows in a row in Denver, and the heart-shaped swing worked good, Rog acted like he hadn't been replaced in Salt Lake City, and the Latchkeys' base broadened our audience like the label hoped. I really should have been focused on the shows, but all I could think about was how on the second day I was going to meet Lisa Pinto. She was doing advance publicity across the country for her album, and the label thought it was a perfect chance to prove our relationship was serious if we were going on dates outside of L.A. Normal people went on vacation together, but celebs met up when one of them was performing or on set in a different city.

It was going to be a panel of fake candids of us getting ice cream together and then ducking inside a car with tinted windows. The whole thing would take less than an hour, and it was all staged, but I kept picturing Lisa Pinto on her *School's Out!* album, and how maybe when we met she'd turn out to be cool and would want to date for real in L.A. Or even just watch TV or play Zenon together or something.

In the morning, Jane and Walter came with me in the car service to the ice cream place. We were about ten minutes late, because of Jane. "Ice cream in Denver with snow on the ground," she said on the ride over. "It's official: Stacy's as brilliant as she looks." Stacy actually *did* look pretty smart with her glasses, but when Jane's in a mood, it's better not to argue.

At least no one was going into the ice cream place and the parking lot was mostly empty, so we could shoot without much crowd interference. Crowd interference is the worst. A Range Rover with tinted windows was in a corner of the minimall parking lot. We parked near it and stepped out onto the crunchy ice. Walter stood nearby and a woman with short black hair got out and came over to us. "Hi. Denise, Lisa's manager," she said.

"I'm Jane, Jonny's manager, and mother," Jane said.

"We weren't sure when you'd show up, so Lisa's putting on some more makeup."

"Sorry we're late."

"It happens," Denise said. "Good to meet you, Jonny. I'll introduce you to the photographer. He only has an hour before he has to fly back to L.A."

She waved to a guy smoking a cigarette at the other end of the parking lot. He stubbed it out in the snow and came over. I'd guess he was thirty-three and he wore a plaid Western shirt under his jacket and glasses with thick black frames.

"Hey, Jonny." He didn't shake my hand or anything. "I've already gone over this with Lisa, but what we want is a set of photos where it looks like you don't know I'm taking them, then a set where you're on to me, so to speak, and you're trying to get away."

I nodded as he explained the different setups and angles he'd use. He was professional about it and knew what he was doing, but what a weird job for a guy in his thirties. There was *no* way when he was a kid he was like, When I grow up, I want part of my job to be flying into Denver for a few hours in January, directing a couple tween celebs in a staged photo shoot to pretend they're dating and giving me a paparazzi freeze-out, and flying back. Though I guess most people don't end up doing what they really want. I'm lucky.

"Jonny, why don't you stay warm in the car and meet Lisa before we do this?" Denise suggested.

"I can go with him," Jane said.

Denise gave her a look. "I think it's best if they had a chance to get to know each other a little on their own first," she said. "It might make the shoot look more authentic."

Jane said, "I'll be in our car." The only person she's used to taking orders from is Ronald. And now maybe Stacy.

Denise led me to the Range Rover. My whole body was shaking, so I said, "Brrr," and wrapped my arms around myself like it was cold, which it was, but not that cold.

Denise opened the back door for me and I climbed in. Putting on lipstick with a small mirror was one of the cutest girls I ever saw in my life. I knew a lot of girls thought *I* was the cutest boy *they* ever saw, but I didn't really think about it except for when I saw a girl like that in person, and then it made sense why they acted so crazy around me, besides me being a celeb. Most celebs are what Jane calls celeb-genic. They look good on video and in photos, but in person, nothing about them stands out, and if they weren't famous and all made up, you'd pass them on the street without giving them a second glance.

Lisa looked good in her photos, but even better in person. Her skin color was like she had a naturally dark spray-tan, with straight, soft black hair, and when she smiled at me with her perfect rows of tiny teeth, her brown eyes crinkled underneath and made two dimples on the sides of her button nose. She smelled like flowers, too, but you wouldn't expect a girl who looked like that to smell bad. Even her clothing was cute, a blue coat that seemed like something a British actress would wear. I felt so dorky and clumsy in my puffy winter jacket and winter boots, like a beefy middle-aged white guy with no rhythm on the dance floor.

"So nice to meet you *at last,* Jonny." She snapped her mirror shut and shook my hand, and her voice sounded like she was ten years older than me, too. Her hand felt like luxury-hotel sheets. " 'Guys vs. Girls' was a huge influence on me." She probably meant the song, not the album. Everyone always means just the song.

"Thanks," I said. "I haven't had a chance to give your album a listen yet." That was stupid. I should've said I was looking forward to hearing it.

"Please *don't,* ever!" she said. "I'd be mortified."

"Okay." I didn't even know what *mortified* meant, but that was also a dumb answer. This was worse than my first live radio interview, when I mumbled through the whole thing and Jane had to keep answering for me.

I hadn't stopped shivering from nervousness, so Lisa asked, "Are you all right?"

"I'm just cold," I said. The temperature readout on the dashboard said seventy-five degrees.

"I can ask Denise to turn up the heat some more. I'm *such* a wimp about winter."

"No," I said quickly, because I didn't want Denise interrupting us. "I'll be fine in a second."

She smiled, and when neither of us said anything, she asked, "So, I imagine the label is running you ragged on this tour?"

"It's not too bad," I said. She said things like *mortified* and *running you ragged,* and I said things like *okay* and *It's not too bad.*

"I've only had to do a few press junkets for shows. I feel completely out of my element with touring."

I couldn't imagine how this girl could ever be out of her element. I could do media-training classes for a solid year, like I did for a few weeks when I moved to L.A., and I still wouldn't barely be able to talk like her. "I wasn't good at first," I said. "It takes some practice."

"Listen to Mr. Humility over here." She hit my shoulder, and it probably would've given me a boner except it actually stung a little, even through my puffy coat. "You absolutely *own* the stage, Jonny Valentine."

I had no idea what to say next. I wish I always had something funny or smart to say like Zack did. I don't know how people like him come up with a line whenever they want. Maybe that's why he's a songwriter and I just sing other people's words.

Denise bailed me out by opening the door for a second to say they'd cleared the ice cream place and we were going in in two minutes.

"Are your parents here?" I asked.

"Why would my parents be here?"

"They don't work with you?"

She laughed. It sounded sort of like when an actress laughs in a movie. "My parents can hardly speak English," she said. "I wouldn't exactly trust them to negotiate royalties."

"They didn't get you into show business?"

"I don't think they knew the *phrase* 'show business.'" She laughed again. "A casting director came by my school one day for some parts in a TV movie, I signed up, that led to a few more spots, and now here we are. A parking lot in Denver in winter. *Finally* made it." She blotted her red lips on a tissue. "This is a bit silly, don't you think?"

"Yeah," I said. "Do you know what they want us to do?"

"I think walk next to each other with ice cream and get into the car."

"And, like, kiss or something?"

"No, definitely not. That was clearly specified in the contract."

All my excitement drained out of me like blood leaking out of my body in Zenon. "Right," I said. "I forgot. That's good."

Denise knocked on the window, which meant I might not get another chance to ask if she wanted to hang out again. "Maybe we should do another date in L.A.," I said.

"Smart idea. I'll have Denise look at my schedule for another photo shoot."

"No, like getting ice cream for a real date. On our own."

"Huh," she said. "Maybe in the spring? Things are totally crazy for me right now with the album dropping and my shooting schedule. Like I'm telling *you* something you don't know, Mr. Double Platinum."

It was triple platinum, but I didn't say anything. "So, should my mother call your manager then?"

She grabbed the door handle and said, "Um, I prefer to keep my professional and social lives separate, you know?" It felt a lot colder in the car all of a sudden, and it got even colder when she opened it and a hard wind blew in. "We better move before Denise throws one of her famous tantrums."

I felt like an idiot during the shoot, acting like this girl was into me when she'd just dissed me. I should've spun it like I meant we'd get ice cream on our own so the paparazzi would get real candids of us, but it was too late. The photographer stayed outside the ice cream place and shot us through the window. We pretended to order, but they already had a chocolate cone with rainbow sprinkles for me and vanilla with a cherry on top for Lisa. It *was* dumb to be getting ice cream when it was freezing out, but no one reading the glossy would figure it out, even with us in our winter coats. Your brain pretty much turns off when you read those things.

The photographer shot us from a short distance as we walked back to the parking lot, like he was trying not to get caught. As we approached the car, he said, "Now pretend you've spotted me and look back."

We turned our heads, and when we were getting into the backseat, he said, "Lisa, I want you to shield your face, and Jonny, stick your tongue out at the camera, like, 'Screw you, man, I just want to hang out with my girl.'"

I did it, and we got inside and shut the door, and Lisa opened the other side and dumped her ice cream on the ground when Denise called out that we were done. Since it was vanilla, it was like the ice cream disappeared into the snow, and the cherry was on top of the whole parking lot. She stuck out her hand for me to shake and said, "It was an honor meeting you, sir, and, of course, playing the illustrious role of your lady friend." From her seat she did a fake curtsy and bow before tapping on her iPhone. I didn't know if I should wait for Jane or what, but without looking up she said, "Door's unlocked."

I went back to our car, with Walter escorting me. Jane kept typing on her phone and said, "Well, *that* was a really good use of our time."

Even if I was way more famous, Lisa acted like she was twice my age, and I should've known from the beginning she'd say no to going out. It'd be like me dating a six-year-old. She'd make it as an actress and as a singer, because she wasn't a normal kid. She was an adult in a kid's body. If you were just a kid in a kid's body, you *might* make it, too, as long as you had good management. If you weren't either, it was harder to tell.

CHAPTER 7

St. Louis (First Day)

At the end of the grueling first leg of the Midwest stretch of eight shows in eight nights, the glossy came out but without anything about me and Lisa in it. The label told us it was bumped till next week. The glossy would never bump a Tyler paparazzi spread, if they were lucky enough to get him in the first place.

Even though we were all traveling together, I didn't have any downtime to hang out with the Latchkeys again, and I was so tired each night that I didn't need anything, I just fell asleep after doing my homework and writing my first slavery-unit essay, on Harriet Tubman and the Underground Railroad. She didn't write her own autobiography, though. A white woman who knew her did the actual writing. Her own Alan Fontana.

There was no chance to check email, and I got worried that maybe the guy was an impostor and I'd given him a candid and some info on Jane, not that the photo or info were so private. But the guy could think that *I* was an impostor, too, pretending to be a celeb by acting like I didn't want him to know who I was. The idiot impostors on the Internet announced right away they were me, like it was no big deal to confab with possible child predators.

I hadn't played a show in St. Louis since we moved to L.A., to distance my image, so I'd never been back. Jane had gone three times, to visit Grandma Pat on her way to meetings in New York. Now that the heartland was a major plank of our new marketing strategy, Jane wanted to ramp up my Midwest connection a little more, at least here. So she'd set up a feature profile with a national morning show that was traveling to St. Louis and filming me here, and then we'd do a live interview the next morning with an abbreviated outdoor concert.

I didn't recognize the city much when we got in. I probably never really knew it except for our neighborhood in Dogtown and my school. The Four Seasons where we were staying, for instance, could've been any city and I wouldn't have known the difference. But most places in America are like that, so it's not St. Louis's fault. And I was young when we left so it didn't have the time to get into my memory.

We had a few hours to kill before we filmed the feature in the afternoon. Jane told me she was going to visit Grandma Pat in her old-age home. "You can rest up," she said in my hotel room.

I hadn't gone there the last year we were in St. Louis. It was hard to remember what Grandma Pat even looked like. She wouldn't remember what I looked like, either, unless she followed me through the media. And maybe there'd be a chance to ask her about my father.

Before Jane left, I said, "Wait, I think I'll go."

"You sure, baby?" She almost seemed like she was going to cry for a second, like she didn't really want to go by herself and couldn't believe I was offering to do it with her. "You don't have to."

"I know. I want to."

"She may not know who you are. Her mind isn't all there." She calls her once a week, and the calls have been getting shorter and shorter.

"I don't mind," I said.

Jane thought about it and said okay. The car service drove us to a place that was more like a hotel than an old-age home. I forgot we'd switched her to a luxury one after I signed with the label. Everywhere we went were old people with wheelchairs and walkers and canes. A lot of old dancers have to use canes because of arthritis and injuries. The one cool thing was I didn't have to wear my hat or sunglasses, since no one knew who I was. Old people don't know anyone famous unless they're their own age. The best would be an old guy who used to be a businessman and didn't have any grandchildren. I wonder if the tweens today will remember me when they're old. They'd remember someone like MJ, but that's a deeper level of cultural penetration I haven't achieved yet.

Grandma Pat's room was what you might get in a two-star hotel, with a small bed and an armchair and a TV and bathroom but not much else. I've asked Jane before if we could send her memorabilia, but she said it's a hazard to have small objects around because she might try to swallow them, like a baby. At least when you're a baby you don't realize everyone is running your life for you. I guess some old people don't realize it, either.

She was sitting in the armchair. She has Jane's nose and forehead, except Grandma Pat's has all these age spots and wrinkles and red splotches like zits for old people. Jane had to tell her her name a few times, and Grandma Pat said, "Jane is my daughter," and Jane was like, "Yes, Mom, *I'm* Jane, *I'm* your daughter."

Grandma Pat saw me for the first time and said, "Hiya, boy."

It was strange how she didn't know what the hell was going on but she could speak fine. Jane asked, loud, "Do you remember Jonathan? Your grandson?"

Grandma Pat looked longer this time. She finally said, "Michael?" I guess she'd met Michael Carns a lot of times when she used to babysit for me. I didn't know if it was more sad or weird that she'd remember his name and not mine.

"No, Mom, not Michael, *Jonathan*," Jane said. She seemed really upset by the mistake, like she was watching her mother's brain depart the realm in front of her. "He's *Jonathan*."

Grandma Pat didn't say anything. I probably should've been upset or scared by her because she had early onset dementia, and it would've been nice to have a grandmother who gave you gifts and played with you, but in a way it was relaxing. She didn't know about "Guys vs. Girls," she didn't know about Tyler Beats, she didn't even remember what my name was. I was just a boy to her. And not even *a boy*, only *boy*. But I definitely wouldn't be able to ask her about my father, even if Jane left the room.

"So we made a lot of additions to our house in L.A.," Jane said.

"That's nice," Grandma Pat said.

"It's going to be featured in a big magazine in a few months."

"That's nice," she said again.

Jane said, "Actually, we're living in a halfway house." There was silence for a few seconds, and you could see Jane feeling bad that she'd messed around with her. She asked in a cheerful voice, "What did you do last night?" Grandma Pat didn't answer, so Jane repeated, "Mom, what did you do last night? Can you remember?"

Jane pointed to a DVD case of a movie next to the TV. "Did you watch that movie?" Grandma Pat nodded, but she had no clue. "We met him, Mom." Jane grabbed the DVD case and showed her the cover. It was one of those comedies where the lead actor and actress are back-to-back with their arms folded, like they can't stand each other, even though you know they'll get together. It didn't make any sense for Grandma Pat to watch something like that. Bad content-demo pairing. "We met the star of it a few months ago at a party. Isn't that exciting? That your daughter is meeting movie stars?"

Grandma Pat shrugged. She *really* didn't care about celebs. The nurse who gave her her meds each day was more famous to her than the movie star everyone in America knew. A celeb is only a celeb if you remember them. It's like we disappear if no one is paying any attention. We think we have all the power, but it's actually the public who decides, just like with politicians. Except it's really the record and movie execs and probably a few guys in a room in Washington, D.C., who control the purse strings and give the public the next number-one Billboard singer and movie star and president, but they make it seem like the public chose it so no one gets too upset.

Out of nowhere, Grandma Pat said, "My daughter put me here. She works at the supermarket."

"Mom," Jane said. "I've been telling you, I don't work at the supermarket anymore. We have a lot of money now. Jonathan's a famous singer and I manage him."

"My daughter failed a class in high school. But she didn't want to go to summer school. So she never finished."

I couldn't imagine Jane being in high school, taking math tests and writing essays and talking with boys. It would've been over twenty years ago. Jane probably couldn't imagine herself at that age anymore, either.

"I got my GED," Jane said. "And it wasn't that I didn't *want* to go. You and Dad were pressuring me to—"

"Have you met Robert?" Grandma Pat asked.

"Yes, of course. He was my father."

Grandma Pat turned to me. "Have *you* met him?"

"He died before I was born," I said.

"That's too bad. Robert was a very nice man."

I wondered what she would say about Albert, if she remembered him at all. Jane snorted and said, "Pretty selective memory over here." She asked a few more questions about how the staff was treating her, but Grandma Pat either didn't give a straight answer or she nodded a bunch of times to herself. She wasn't mean or anything now, but I got the feeling she hadn't been the funnest person to be around when her brain was working right. If it was hard to imagine Jane in high school, it was harder to imagine Grandma Pat with a normal brain and Jane hanging out with her. I'll visit Jane at least once a week when I put her in an old-age home.

Grandma Pat said she needed to use the bathroom, which meant we had to call a nurse. I got really sad watching the nurse hold her with her walker, that every time she went to the bathroom she needed help. Then I was like, Wait, if *I* ever use a public bathroom, I need Walter's help for protection, too. Except with me, it's because a million people would try to get in there with me, to make out with me or molest me or take a picture of my penis. No one wants to be in the bathroom with Grandma Pat.

Jane whispered that we should go. She kissed Grandma Pat on top of her head and told me I didn't have to say good-bye and could wait in the hall. But I squeezed Grandma Pat's arm anyway when she stood up in her walker since I was afraid a hug might knock her over.

Jane was quiet on the ride back to the hotel and didn't multitask. She scoped out the Scottrade Center and took care of other business while the film crew drove me to Carson Elementary. The school looked really small when we drove up to it, a couple short redbrick buildings with a soccer field behind them. I remembered it being humongous, but that's what happens when you get older, the things that used to impress you now seem stupid, like how even though I still get nervous before performing I don't think it's a huge deal, but if you'd told me two years ago that I'd be playing Madison Square Garden on Valentine's Day, I'd have had an accident in my pants.

They'd set it up so we had access to the grounds and field without anyone watching. I walked around and talked to the camera and the interviewer, a blond lady named Robin, and said things like, "Here's where we used to have recess and gym and where I got into baseball," and when we came by a rock near a tree, I lied and was like, "I had my first kiss here," and when the interviewer asked who the girl was, I said, "I don't want to say her name, but she's in every song of mine in some way."

I'm usually good at tuning out what a taped video appearance will look like when it airs, because if you think about it in the middle of filming you screw yourself up, just like you can't think about how you're singing onstage, but I realized my father might see it. He'd be on his couch watching me in my old school, except he might have left before I started there.

"When I was a student here, I used to have a fantasy about traveling around the world, singing my music," I said. "I most wanted to go to two places: Pittsburgh and Australia."

Robin laughed for the camera. "Pittsburgh and Australia? Why those two?"

"I did geography reports on them both," I said, and I looked straight into the camera, which is a no-no. "I've played Pittsburgh, but I still haven't made it to Australia." If it really was my father emailing me, there's no way he could think I was an impostor now. And if Jane asked why I chose those cities, I'd say I thought it would help with my domestic-brand extension and foreign-market outreach.

They made some calls and said it was time to go inside. I spend half my life waiting for someone to tell me it's time to do something. They'd arranged it so we went in while everyone was in class, but to make it look like school was still going on, a few kids who'd won a lottery could be in the halls at the same time as me. A couple years ago, I used to walk down those same halls afraid that an older kid might push me into a locker or something.

When I got onto the main hall I was supposed to walk through, there were like forty kids hanging around, and they started screaming, which meant all the kids stuck in the classrooms pressed their faces up to the windows in the doors. I wished Walter didn't have the day off. The security guard the TV crew had hired didn't look big enough to prevent a stampede.

The producer Kevin was like, "If you guys want to be on TV, you have to act normal and like it's no big deal Jonny's here, all right?" Which was idiotic, because why would I be walking through a school hallway with the students acting normal? But it was Jane's idea, and maybe she was right that it branded me as a regular kid.

The school only went up to fifth grade, so there was no one I would've known from before. The kids tried to pretend to be normal, but almost everyone who walked by looked at me. Only really they looked at the camera. They weren't too obvious about it, since they probably knew they'd get edited out if they did, and the smarter ones just walked by with their faces and eyes visible but without staring directly in. Everyone wants to *be* famous more than they want to *see* someone famous.

I walked down the hallway and another one. The walls all had artwork by the students and stupid posters like one that said BEE-LIEVE IN YOURSELF! with a picture of a bee reading a book, though I had a track called "This Bird Will Always Bee There for You" so I couldn't call it too dumb.

I kept looking over at the kids behind the glass windows of the doors, which was unprofessional camera protocol, but I couldn't help myself. If I went back to school, and a celeb came to visit, I'd be one of those kids behind the glass. Except I wouldn't cram my face up against it like they were doing. That's one of the ways I could never really be like them again.

I made up more stuff, like "I had this locker" or "That was my third-grade classroom." The truth was I didn't remember much, except for the smell, which was chalk and hissing radiators. I knew I'd been there before, but I couldn't place any details, and when we got to the end of the hall, Robin said I should take them to the cafeteria. I didn't even know where it was anymore. So I said I thought they moved it after I left, and they escorted me. After we finished in the cafeteria, Robin stood next to me on camera and said they had a big surprise. "We know what you miss most about St. Louis is all your friends," she said.

Into the cafeteria, about thirty feet away, walked a boy.

"So we found your best friend, Michael Carns," Robin said.

He looked how he used to, same pale skin like he'd been scared and lived underground, but a few inches taller and his hair was shorter now. He'd become sort of funny-looking, with his ears sticking out, and was wearing dark blue Champion sweatpants and a sweatshirt, same as before, at least the way I remembered it. People always wear the same thing in your mind, like Jane in St. Louis is the Schnucks black polo shirt and khaki pants, but in L.A. it's a black skirt and top and stockings because black is slimming.

The last time I saw Michael was the night before we left. Jane let me do one final sleepover. With Nadine I once figured out that I probably slept over at his house about two hundred times. We tried to stay up all night together, watching TV and eating junk food in his room like we always did, but we couldn't do it, and we both fell asleep around five a.m. When Jane picked me up in the morning, I didn't want to wake him up on so little sleep, so I just left without saying good-bye. I guess I thought I'd be seeing him again soon. I felt like running over to him now and telling him I wished I'd woken him up, but maybe he didn't remember it anyway.

They must not have told Jane about this, because she would have definitely leaked it to me, and the surprise would be ruined. Most of the time that stuff is faked on TV, which I know from doing it a few times, and when I see it on reality shows I can always tell who's pretending to be surprised. You have to be a high-caliber enough actor to pull it off. I'm just good enough to do it, but I guess they didn't know that.

Michael glanced at Kevin like he didn't know if he was supposed to stay at the door or come to me. He was pretty uncomfortable with all the cameras on him. Those lights are hot, and it's hard when you're not used to it. Kevin motioned to him to come over, so Michael walked up to me and said, "Hi," all quiet, and I said, "Hey, Michael."

It was weird. I knew it would read bad on TV if I didn't do something, so I slapped him five like Dr. Henson and said, "It's awesome to see you!" and he said, quietly again, "You, too." Then we stood around waiting for something to happen and he looked at his feet with his face angled away from the crew. I couldn't tell if he was so quiet because of the cameras or because of me or because that's what he was like now. Robin looked at Kevin, who said they'd clean it up in editing and told me they were taking us someplace special.

Kevin said me and Michael would go in a car with each other so we could catch up off-camera. It was a town car, not a limo, so the crew guy who drove us could hear us in the backseat.

"What's new?" I asked Michael as we pulled away from the school.

"My parents adopted a baby boy last year," he said. "From Ethiopia, in Africa. His name is Justin. He's pretty fun, actually."

I couldn't imagine Michael with a younger brother. We always said we were like brothers and it was better than having a real brother since we got to choose each other.

"From Africa," I said. I didn't really want to look straight at him, and I tilted my head down. Under my unzipped winter coat and jacket, my black graphic T-shirt had a picture of Brangelina as farmers standing in front of a house with a pitchfork, but they've got white makeup and jet-black hair and lipstick and mascara, and it says AMERICAN GOTH. "Cool. Like Brangelina."

He looked at my shirt and the rest of my outfit. "They give you those clothes?" My jeans were distressed and my jacket under my winter coat was shiny black leather with metal studs and my sneakers were custom-made red Nikes with heart shapes on the tongue.

"Who?"

"The TV people."

"No. This is from home." He didn't say anything, so I added, "Well, the designers give them to me. They send me stuff and pay me to wear it. There's a lot of contracts involved. I have to wear certain pieces a certain amount while out and at photo ops." As I was saying it I was wishing I wasn't, but I couldn't stop myself. It got quiet again, so I asked him, "Is Jessica Stanton still the hottest girl in our class?"

"No, she got fat. Luann Phelps is now."

"Luann?"

"Yeah. She got contacts this year and became hot," he said. "She has a crush on you."

"For real?" I got a little tingle. I don't know why I was so into the idea of Luann Phelps having a crush on me. She used to be this dumpy girl with thick glasses and a lisp. For a second it was like she was the celeb and I was the fan.

"All the girls do. Whenever you say your songs are about this one girl, they all say that they're your ex."

I had to stop using that line so much. Or maybe I should use it more. "They didn't used to," I said. "Have a crush on me." I knew I could date any girl at one of my shows, but somehow it seemed cooler to be able to go to a school and date any student I wanted to. If there was ever a dance, I could ask whoever, and I wouldn't call attention to myself with a dance-off or anything, but everyone would know I was the best dancer there.

"You left in the middle of fourth grade. They didn't get crushes till the fifth grade. The boys didn't get crushes till this year."

I wondered if he'd hit puberty yet, or if any of the other boys did. If I asked him in the back of a town car if he had any pubes, though, then *I'd* be like a child predator.

"Who do you have a crush on?"

He played with the string on his sweatpants. "No one, really."

"Does anyone have a crush on you?"

"I don't know," he said. "Girls don't talk to me much. Except when they want to know about you."

"Oh." Neither of us said anything. The more I tried to come up with things to say, the less I did. All I could think of was, "My record label wants me to date this actress and singer Lisa Pinto. You know her?"

"She's on that show," he said. "So what do you do? Like, go to a movie or something?"

"No. Not real dates. Fake ones, for publicity. That's how most people do it in L.A. Celebs, I mean."

He didn't respond but he sort of smiled to himself, so I closed my eyes and pretended to fall asleep. Soon the crew guy told me we were there. I looked out and we were at our old apartment. And I got that feeling I don't get when I come home in L.A., times a million, but right after, for some reason, and it's not like I would really do it, I felt like I wanted to throw a rock or something at the windows.

I wondered for a second if maybe the third surprise would be that they'd found my father and brought him to meet me where we all used to live together, but then I saw Jane standing outside, stamping her boots in the cold while talking to Kevin, and there was no way she would have signed off on that. She said, "Hi, Michael, what a nice surprise," and made a little face to me that meant she'd just found out I was hanging out with him, but she didn't say anything because he was still there. She probably wished my old best friend was more telegenic. Me and her were going to do a quick tour of the apartment before I'd throw a football with Michael in the park like we used to.

Our apartment was in a row of buildings that all looked the same, two floors each with pinkish concrete on the outside and a short walkway leading up to a red door. We were on the upper floor. Kevin said we had to be careful not to mess anything up inside or the family that lived there now would charge the show even more. I would've thought they'd be happy enough that their apartment was on TV and they could say they lived in Jonny Valentine's old apartment, but people are always trying to find ways to monetize you.

Robin took me and Jane inside with a few crew guys. I was glad Michael stayed outside. The place looked different with the new furniture, but it felt familiar, with the pipes clanking and the way the floor creaked under your feet when you took your first step inside and how it always smelled like something had burned a little.

Jane showed them around, fast, since there was only the bathroom, the living room, the kitchen, and the bedroom. Nothing in it was that nice. They'd put in an ugly tan wall-to-wall carpet that wasn't there before. Jane said to the camera, "So, obviously, the new tenants have decorated it their own way."

It felt like I was a burglar in our old home, and I was scoping it out to steal from the younger Jonathan and Jane from two years ago. I could almost see myself sleeping in my bed, with me from now creeping around the room and taking sports equipment and schoolbooks and clothes from Jonathan Valentino and replacing it with Jonny Valentine merch.

The whole strategy with footage like this was stupid. It was like, Let's see how you're like a normal person behind the scenes, but the more we want to see you acting regular in private, the more you have to hide there and throw up a bunch of public buffers, so if we *really* saw you behind the scenes, it wouldn't look normal at all, that's why we have to show you pretending to be normal in your old apartment.

There was one picture up on the wall near the kitchen. It was a man and woman in their thirties, and they were holding a baby between them in the hospital bed after she'd given birth and was all sweaty and tired. There was a crib in the corner. The baby was cute, but for a second I thought, Fuck you, baby.

Robin asked me if it brought back any memories. I knew I should come up with something, but nothing from the past hit me when I was in the main rooms. Nearly the first ten years of my life had happened there, so it's not like it was easy to pick out one thing. When we went into the bathroom, though, I thought about the time I'd gotten sick from eating crab cakes at Ben Marton's birthday party at Captain D's, and I spent all night vomiting, and Jane stayed up with me rubbing my back and giving me water even though she had the six a.m. shift at Schnucks. Probably I remembered it because of my preshow routine with her.

"I used to come home from school every day and have a snack before starting my homework," I said.

"What did you eat?" Robin asked.

"Peanut butter and jelly with the crusts cut off. Jane would make it." That was another clue for my father, since she's afraid to go *near* peanut butter because of her allergy. She actually made tuna sandwiches with a ton of mayo and the crusts on and left them in the fridge for me, but she doesn't even let Peter buy mayo anymore since it's so fatty.

Robin looked over at Jane, who was staring at the stove like she was watching something boiling. "Were you as involved in Jonny's life back then as you are now?"

Jane turned back to her quickly. "Well, obviously. I'm his mother."

"But now you're his mother *and* his manager. Before, you were just his mother."

"I consider it a blessing that we get to spend so much time together."

"Does it ever feel like it might be too *much* time?" Robin asked.

Jane looked ready to kill her, but she adjusted and smiled huge. Never lose control.

"Of course, you have to give your child room to breathe," she said, totally composed in a cheery talk-show voice. "But I do fear that parents aren't spending enough time with their children these days and are just scheduling them for activities without them or letting them entertain themselves."

"And was it a hard decision to bring Jonny into show business?"

"The hardest decision I've ever made." She shook her head and made a small frown like it still tore her apart. *Jane* could star in a dramatic vehicle. "But it was really Jonny's decision. He wanted it so badly."

"It was always my dream," I said, to help her out.

"Since he was old enough to sing," Jane said. We were like a veteran shortstop and second baseman on joint interviews, me flipping the ball to her to turn the inning-ending double play. "So we prayed on it, and we felt it was the right time to share Jonny with the world."

That was really smart brand strategy, because it was just enough religious stuff to make her look good after she'd snapped at Robin, and also coastal media never probes when you bring up religion, because the risk of controversy is too high.

Sure enough, Kevin said the family was gouging them on each ten-minute block and we had to leave. I was kind of surprised they hadn't set up a museum, like "Jonny Valentine's Childhood Home."

When we left, we passed by the TV, which used to be on the other side of the living room, because they'd switched where the TV and couch were, since it was better to sleep in the other position but better for people to sit in now, but *before* even that, when my father lived there with us, I had a bed in the living room and Jane and my father slept in the bedroom. And it brought back another memory.

It must have been right before my father left or I couldn't have remembered it. It was rainy and gray and cold out, and Jane had been staying with Grandma Pat for like a week. She must have been sick or something. The Cardinals were on TV, on the road because they couldn't have played in the rain, and I guess my father decided I was old enough for him to explain the game to me. I bet I didn't get much of it since I was so young, but he talked nearly the whole game, in this really fast way, and he was sweating even though he was only lying on my bed and getting worked up every time the Cardinals got a hit or something. But one reason it stands out is that the Cardinals got into a brawl with the other team, both benches clearing out, and my father called someone on the phone and asked if they were watching this shit. That must be nice, to have a friend you could just call up like that and know they were watching the same thing as you. Me and Walter don't follow the same teams, so I don't call him in his bungalow when I'm watching a game.

The Cardinals scored a few runs off the other team's errors, and I kept asking what an error was because the announcers kept bringing it up. My father tried to explain. He was like, "It's when you make a mistake, and it screws everything up for your team." Then the Cardinals gave up a few runs after *they* made a bunch of errors, and the announcer said, "The Lord giveth and the Lord taketh away," and his color man said that was always true in baseball, and it was the first time I'd heard that saying so I asked my father what it meant, even though he was pissed the Cardinals had let the game get tied.

He said something like, "It means right when you get something good, you lose it."

"Like the toy car?" I asked. They'd gotten me a remote-control car for my birthday, and I'd been all excited to use it, but it broke right away.

"No," he said. "We returned that to the store when it broke, and we got a new one that worked." He didn't say anything for a minute as we watched the Cardinals lose, then he spoke real slowly so I can still mostly remember it. He was like, "What it means is what our neighbor Mrs. Warfield said to me the other day, which is that God has a plan for everyone and it's not our place to question him."

He turned the TV off. "So if anyone ever tells you that in the future, you'll know they're as big a moron as Mrs. Warfield." Up till then Mrs. Warfield had just been this nice older lady who gave me candy, but after that I knew she was a moron.

Just as we went out the door to the apartment, I got this empty feeling in my chest, like this would be the last time I'd ever see it. I turned back to look inside, but the final crew guy had already closed the door. Maybe if I reconnected with my father we could visit it again together, without a TV show.

Outside, the camera crew walked with me and Michael to the park down the block. "Should we be talking?" I asked Kevin.

"If you want," he said. "Or we can cut footage with music over."

But I didn't know what to say. I wanted to ask Michael if he ever thought about our sleepovers, how we'd stay up late and sneak out of his room to watch the TV on low and raid the kitchen for cookies and chips and soda when his parents were asleep. His house always had a million snacks. I didn't feel like it, though.

I used to lie in bed at night sometimes before sleep and I'd think about what if Michael died, and I'd imagine me being at his funeral and staring into his coffin like they do in the movies and seeing him in a suit even though he should've been in his Champion sweats, and knowing no one else knew the jokes we had together, like when we'd crack each other up by saying, "There was a weasel in here?" after Elinor Burt once asked that in the middle of science class when Mrs. Potts said the word *weasel,* and I'd make myself cry even. I wondered if I could even do that anymore. I could make myself tear up onstage when I sang "Heart Torn

Apart," but I didn't have to think of anything to do it, I only had to tell myself to cry and the tears were waiting for me, like the song brought it on, not anything from real life.

It would sound pretty gay if I told Michael about that, or asked if he ever thought about anything like that for me.

No one else was at the park. It looked empty, just a swing set and a small field I also remembered being bigger that was all dirt now from the winter. Michael was always the QB and I was the receiver, so I tossed him the ball.

"Do you still play a lot?" I asked.

"I'm on the intramural flag-football team," Michael said.

"I just play with Walter."

"Who's Walter?"

"My bodyguard." I shouldn't have brought him up. "He's not here today, because it wouldn't play good on camera." Michael just picked at the grip on the ball, so I asked, "What was the name of that play we made up?"

"'Oh Baby,'" he said.

"Right. Why'd we call it that again?"

He shrugged. "I don't know." But it looked like he did. I couldn't ask him on camera, though. I couldn't even really ask him off-camera.

I ran deep. Like I'd practiced it every day the last two years, I thought, "Oh baby oh baby oh baby *cut*." You cut left after the third "Oh baby." I still couldn't remember why we called it that. Michael's pass sailed behind me.

"You're supposed to cut right," he said.

It was true. There used to be a seesaw to the left, the one with me and Jane in the photo in my bedroom, and I had to cut right. It wasn't there anymore, so I forgot.

I said, "Sorry."

We ran it a few more times until we completed a pass for the camera crew. I spiked the ball and did my trademark spin move when Kevin asked me. He said they had enough tape, and told me and Michael to say our good-byes before they drove him home. "Bye, Michael," I said.

"Bye."

"Stay in touch."

He smiled. He needed braces soon. "Yeah," he said. "Like when you left the first time." He didn't sound sad when he said it. It was like his eyes were seeing through me and through the seesaw that wasn't there anymore.

I thought he was done, but he kept going. "My parents wanted to fly me out to visit. We couldn't get through to you."

"I never knew that." I really didn't. "The label doesn't tell me a lot. They probably thought you were a fan. There are a lot of impostors who pretend to know me."

He would've loved going into the locker rooms of any team and backstage at any concert we wanted. Maybe I could still invite him out to L.A. He could sleep in one of the extra rooms and we could finally try staying up all night, now that I knew how to make coffee.

"I know." He shuffled into a car without looking back at me. "You're busy with your label. And getting free clothes. And going on fake dates. Like all the other celebs."

He shut the door. I stared at the tinted window he was behind. I wanted to knock on it, open it up and tell him I was sorry, I didn't mean to talk to him like that, this is how people talk in L.A., I'm still the same kid who played football with you for hours after school and ate Doritos till three a.m. while we watched infomercials and used to cry imagining your funeral, and there was a weasel in here?

Except I wasn't the same kid, and neither was he, and if he visited we wouldn't have a fun time together and I wouldn't be able to stay up all night because it would throw off my schedule for the next day and I wasn't allowed junk food and he probably didn't even remember the weasel joke.

Jane came over and asked how it all went as his car took off. "I think they'll edit it good," I said.

"Was it nice seeing your school?"

"I guess."

"And Michael?"

I traced the pass route for "Oh Baby" on the ground with my red Nikes. "He was fine."

"Just fine?"

"I don't know. It was sort of weird. He said he tried to visit but couldn't get through to me. I told him the label doesn't pass on personal messages."

She nodded. "I've explained to you before how it's hard for people from your past to adjust to you. They can get jealous, or resentful, or try to use you. You know that's why I cut everyone from St. Louis off."

"Michael wasn't like that, though."

She stroked my hair out of my eyes and gave me a kiss on my forehead as if I'd fainted again. "I know, baby. I'm so sorry."

"It wasn't you who was acting weird, it was Michael."

"Yeah, but—" She straightened up and got into her business mode and said, "They're taking us somewhere else. It's a surprise, so we have to be blindfolded. We'll ride together."

They had a limo for us, and Robin and a camera guy sat inside with us and made us put on blindfolds. In the dark, I imagined it was like a hostage situation. Me and Jane were being kidnapped, and the kidnappers told Jane they would only let one of us live, so she told them, "Fuck you, let my baby go," and they let me out of the car, but then I found my way back to them because the car left a trail of gasoline, and I killed them all even though it was too late to rescue Jane, since they'd slashed her neck and blood was oozing everywhere.

They took our blindfolds off, Jane's first, and I heard her say, "No way. Absolutely not." I wriggled out of mine. We were in the parking lot of Schnucks. "Turn the camera off. *Now.*"

Robin said, "Phil, turn it off."

"First, how did you know I worked here?" Jane asked.

"It's not exactly classified information."

"Well, I'm not going in, if that's your plan."

Robin sighed and said she'd talk to Kevin. The camera guy left with her. "This is ridiculous," Jane said to me. "They're deliberately trying to belittle me."

"Won't this help the heartland ID with us?" I asked.

"I don't care."

Kevin came inside. "Jane? You have a problem with this?"

"I'm not doing it."

"Listen," he said. "We made a lot of concessions already, namely not interviewing any family members or friends. We need more footage. So I'm afraid this is a deal breaker."

"Me not agreeing to humiliate myself is a deal breaker?"

"What's humiliating about this? It's a job you used to have. I used to work at a hardware store. This is what people do. If you don't want to do it, we won't run the profile."

I almost said out loud what I knew Jane was thinking, that this guy didn't know what it was like to be a celebrity, even a backstage celebrity like Jane, that he might run a TV show but no one cared what dumb job he had before, but Jane had image maintenance to worry about.

She looked out at the Schnucks again, the big red letters over the brown front. "B-roll footage only. Robin doesn't come in. If anyone I know works there, we're not talking to them. Deal?"

He agreed. Jane's good at bargaining. She always reminds me how the label tried to screw us on our first deal and her business advisers were pressuring her to sign but she knew she had leverage and used it when less sophisticated people would've just buckled. You extend a fair offer to the other party but make it clear you're not giving them anything beyond that. People respect that you're not conning them and you're also not a pushover.

She put on her sunglasses as she got out of the car. "No sunglasses, please," Kevin said. She took a sharp breath in through her nose and placed them on top of her head and walked fast to the entrance. The camera guy raced to catch up.

I asked Kevin if I could go in. I hadn't even been inside a supermarket in forever, and I'd been in this one hundreds of times. He said, "You can put on your hat and sunglasses and go in, but stay away from your mom, okay?"

Kevin walked inside with me and the hired security guard. The doors dinged open. Everyone knows how music can make you remember something, but even a sound like that double-ding brought me

back to how I imagined the double-ding sound was saying, Jon-*ny*,
when Michael's mother used to drop me off after school before she took
Michael to his violin lessons or his tutor or his speech therapist, and I'd
do my homework in the staff room, and when her shift was over Jane
would let me choose a candy bar to use her employee discount on. For
a long time I always picked Butterfinger, but when I was old enough to
know Jane was allergic to peanuts, I switched to 3 Musketeers in case
the crumbs fell in her car and made her depart the realm, and then we'd
drive home together.

I hung around the front fruit displays as Jane went down the main
aisle, not saying anything while she walked ahead of the camera guy
and Kevin and the security guard. A few people turned around because
of the camera, but not all that many, since it was a small handheld and
it's not so strange to see a camera out in public, even in a St. Louis
Schnucks.

I followed a little farther in, ducking behind the other displays like
in Zenon when projectile weapons or spells are coming for your head.
She made it about three-quarters to the end of the aisle when a woman
from an empty checkout register in one of the Schnucks polo shirts
intercepted her. *"Jane?"* she asked. "Jane Valentino, is that you?"

Jane stopped. The woman was around her age, with a lumpy body
like a potato and her hair in a bun. "Yes?" Jane said.

"It's Mary Ann. Mary Ann Hilford?" She pointed at her name tag.
"Remember?"

Jane looked blank. "Of course. Hello, Mary Ann."

I barely remembered her, or any of them, except for this one black
guy named Vaughn who snuck me M&M's when Jane wasn't looking.
Mary Ann reached out to hug her, and Jane kept her arms mostly by
her side and didn't hug her back. "Vanessa and Lillian and Phil and me,
we all follow Jonathan's career. Or Jonny's career."

"That's nice of you," Jane said. "I hope you're all doing well."

Mary Ann said, "Look!" and she went back to her checkout line and
came back with something. "He's on the cover."

I couldn't see it, except that it was a tabloid and definitely not the
glossy we'd contracted with. She handed it to Jane, who looked at the

cover for a few seconds, and turned to the camera guy and said something. He took the camera down off his shoulder and pointed it at the ground. "Is he here?" Mary Ann asked.

I crouched lower behind the cantaloupes and watched through a small space in the pile. They smelled rotten. Bottom-shelf supermarkets are always kind of sad, with all the D-list merch they're trying to get rid of that no one wants. "No," Jane said. "But we have to get running. It was great seeing you."

She walked away. Mary Ann said, loud enough for Jane to hear, "I'm sure."

Jane turned. "Excuse me?"

"I see how it is," Mary Ann said. "Thought you were better than everyone back then, still do."

Jane's face twisted around. She seemed a little hurt, even. I didn't know how this woman from Schnucks with a bun could say anything to hurt her feelings. "I'm sorry you feel that way," she said quietly.

Mary Ann looked like she hadn't expected this. "Wait." She shook her head and sighed. "Jane. That was bitchy of me."

Jane smiled at her. I couldn't read if it was a fuck-you smile or an I-forgive-you smile. "That's okay. All this stuff"—Jane pointed to the camera guy and waved the tabloid—"makes people say and do things they don't actually mean."

"Yeah." Mary Ann didn't say anything else because you could tell she *did* mean it but just felt bad about it.

"And it makes it hard when you meet people who knew you before," Jane said, even though it wasn't like Mary Ann asked her to keep talking about it. The camera guy was still there, and he was itching to turn the camera back on and catch this, but he couldn't do it. "So I understand why you'd feel the need to say something hurtful like that."

Now Mary Ann *really* didn't know what to say. She nodded, and Jane said, "Anyway, it was so nice seeing you again, Mary Ann."

Mary Ann mumbled something that sounded like she was apologizing. Jane's a natural at spinning.

I rushed out through a different aisle and an empty checkout line so Jane wouldn't see me running out ahead of her.

I climbed into the limo before she could see that I'd been inside the supermarket. When she got to the car I heard her say to Kevin, "We're not using the end of it or else we're canceling the interview tomorrow, and that's final." She got inside and slammed the door and said TV people were paparazzi with fancier job titles.

She was holding the tabloid Mary Ann gave her against her chest. My photo was splashed on the cover. Central real estate. "What are they saying?" I asked as the driver pulled out of the parking lot.

She turned it away from me before handing it to me. "You may as well see it."

The cover was me getting into the car with Lisa as I stuck my tongue out at the camera. But it was a tabloid, which is much less valuable to your image than a glossy for gossip. The headline said GUY *AND* GIRL: JONNY VALENTINE AND LISA PINTO.

A few pages inside, there was a short article with a few more photos:

> According to raven-haired songstress **Lisa Pinto**, 12, when **Jonny Valentine**, 11, asked her out last month, he did so by quoting a line from his hit single "Guys vs. Girls": "Will you be my girl today?"
>
> The two young lovebirds have become a serious item and were recently photographed canoodling outside an ice cream parlor in Denver, where JV passed through on his *Valentine Days* tour and Lisa was promoting her upcoming debut album, *School's Out!,* before its Feb. 14 release.
>
> "What I love most is hanging out with him away from the spotlight, when 'The Jonny' comes off and he's simply Jonathan—that's what I call him when it's just the two of us," says Lisa, referring not to her new boyfriend's angelic halo of golden locks, but his public image. "He's a normal kid who doesn't take himself too seriously."
>
> Which means what, exactly?

"Jonathan's a huge dork," she says with a trilling laugh.
"A total nerd. Yet so am I. And I love that about him."

The feeling is mutual, according to a person close to
the young "Breathtaking" songster. "Jonny's completely
obsessed with Lisa," says the source. "I've never seen him
like this with another girl."

"I can't believe they sold it to a tabloid without my consent," Jane said.
" 'I've never seen him like this with another girl'—Jesus. Not to mention this *Jonathan* garbage."

I didn't know why she was acting like it was a character assassination
when it was all positive press. I closed my eyes to pretend I was trying to
nap, but what I really was doing was imagining that Lisa replaced Jane
in the limo, and there were paparazzi outside but the windows were too
tinted for them to see into, and Lisa looked at me and said, "Door's
locked," and we humped each other and I stuck my tongue inside her
mouth. I turned on my side so Jane couldn't see I was getting a boner.
As I was picturing this, I kept wondering why she called me a dork
and a nerd. She called herself one, too, I know, and female celebrities
always do that so ugly girls don't hate them, except they never admit to
being what a dork actually is, which would be like saying to an interviewer, "Yeah, I'm a huge dork, I have bad social skills and no one likes
me." But you don't need to call male celebrities one. I *really* shouldn't
have asked her on a date. The way she kept calling me Mr. Something
would've annoyed me after a while. I bet if she ever met Mi$ter $mith,
she'd call him Mr. Mi$ter $mith.

Jane tapped one heel hard on the floor a few times like she does
when she's pissed and took out her phone and made a call. "This is Jane
Valentine calling for Olivia. Yes, I'll leave her a voice mail," she said.
"Olivia, this is Jane. I saw the story about Jonny and Lisa, and I'm not
happy that it was sold to a tabloid without my knowledge. If this is
Stacy's doing, please tell Ronald that I never signed on for it and this is
not the way I want to run things in the future."

I opened my eyes. She hung up and turned to me and shook her
head. "You're eleven years old," she said, wiping some snot from my

nose that had turned crusty from the cold air. "They forget that you're eleven."

"I'm almost twelve," I said.

She pulled me close to her and hugged tight. She had on more of her Chanel No. 5 than usual that this movie actress told her she should wear after we moved to L.A. My boner was going down but it was still there, and I had to adjust my hips so it wasn't uncomfortable.

"Not just yet," she said.

CHAPTER 8

St. Louis (Second Day)

The morning after my concert, which was a straight A, me, Jane, and Walter hustled down to the Arch. I was worried the show had invited Michael to watch, but even if they'd been thinking about it at first, they'd have to be blind not to see how bad he played on camera.

They'd set up a circular outdoor stage underneath it, and the crowd was already surrounding it and hollering when the show's security guys escorted me onstage. It was my usual audience, girls with their mothers or sometimes fathers, plus a few stragglers. When people see a crowd, they always feel like they're missing out if they're not part of it. Kevin reminded me they'd air the video from yesterday, Robin would do the ten-minute interview, and then I'd sing three songs over a musical track. They estimated a 3.2 and twenty-two share, with a 1.1 in the twelve-to-seventeen demo, solid numbers for morning TV.

They showed the video on a small screen near us. It was all the regular stuff, video and photo clips of me with voiceovers talking about my career, spliced with shots of St. Louis and me walking around the school. I could be a TV director. It's pure formula.

They cut to me and Michael meeting, and they edited it as B-roll so it didn't seem awkward. We walked to the park like a weirdo pair, with him in his Champion sweats and me in my sponsored wardrobe. But they cut it so it seemed like we were having fun, and with "Kali Kool" in the background instead of a love song, it didn't look too gay, even though it didn't make any sense to play a song about partying on a beach in California over shots of an empty park in St. Louis in the middle of winter. If you didn't know, you'd think we were still best friends. I let my eyes get blurry like when I've been playing video games for a long time, so I had a sense of what was happening on the screen but didn't have to watch.

After I could tell they were done with me and Michael, they ran a few shots of our old apartment before the segment wound down. They'd cut the whole Schnucks thing.

I wasn't nervous for something like this, because I've done plenty of live TV, but when they were counting down, it was the last thing I wanted to be doing. I wasn't tired, so I didn't want to be sleeping, and I didn't want to be playing Zenon, either, or hanging out with anyone in particular. What I suddenly wanted was, I wanted to be back at our old apartment, and I wanted to tell Jane to buy it back. We could afford it easily, and we could decorate it the same exact way it looked back then. We wouldn't stay there or anything, because it was still a crap apartment, but when we came back to St. Louis for shows we could just pop in and remember that it was still around.

But she'd say it was a wasteful expenditure and these kinds of purchases were what bankrupted musicians with stupid business instincts.

Being a consummate professional means doing your job when you don't want to, so I sucked it up and pasted on a huge smile when the camera light blinked and Robin introduced me as America's Angel of Pop and the girls screamed like they were getting attacked and I got ready to give answers in Auto-Tune mode, where they sound right but have nothing behind them.

She asked me how I got my start, and I'd gone over this story so much I could recite it in my sleep. I talked about my music teacher in second grade and how I won second place in a local talent competition that year, and like every other interviewer in the history of the world, Robin asked what the kid who won first place was doing now, and I said what Jane coached me on, "I hope she's still singing, because she was hella good." You can say *hella* on TV, even at seven in the morning, Jane told me, but not *hell*. Networks are idiots.

I talked about how me and Jane decided I was old enough to busk on weekends in the Central West End, and a couple videos of me singing exploded on YouTube one week and my record label called, and a couple years later, with God's help, here we are. I'm supposed to mention God once in a while, but after Jane's lie the day before about us praying, it might have been too much Bible thumping.

"Everything happens for a reason," Robin said.

Something about the TV-host smile on her face made me want to be like, No, it doesn't, that's the coastal way of believing in God without actually believing in him, and it's a stupid thing morons like Mrs. Warfield tell themselves when bad things happen so they feel better about it, that's why The Secret Land of Zenon is so good, things happen and no one's keeping track of if it's for a reason or not, experience points either come or they don't and you can never totally predict why and sometimes it's the opposite of what makes sense, like Jane can't sing and my father probably can't but I was born with a perfect voice from good luck, and if Jane had gotten an abortion then everyone here would be watching someone else get interviewed right now, or if YouTube hadn't been invented I might never have been discovered and would be a normal kid in St. Louis who was the star of his school choir but nothing else and Luann Phelps wouldn't have a crush on me, and there's a girl in the audience in a wheelchair and if you think *that* happened for a reason, you have a fucked-up idea of why things happen.

"Totally," I said.

"Did you ever think you'd become this famous?" Robin asked.

"I don't think of myself as famous. I'm just a normal kid who likes normal things, sports, video games, hanging out, and who's getting the chance to live out his dream and share the music and the love. And that's why I love coming back to St. Louis"—the crowd cheered—"because I never want to forget where I came from."

Right when I finished, I heard a guy in the crowd shout, *"Faggot!"* There was some whispering and Robin pretended like she didn't hear it, but I could tell from her eyes she did and hoped like hell the mikes hadn't picked anything up, which they probably wouldn't. I glanced around for Walter, but I didn't see him and didn't know where he was. This was the problem with letting someone else run your show. You don't have full control over performance protocol.

She segued quickly to the next question. "We hear you've been dating the actress Lisa Pinto, who has a debut album out on February 14—which is, of course, Valentine's Day. Can you confirm if you two are going to be celebrating her release together?"

The way she said it, slipping in the reference to the drop date, I knew Stacy in creative had planted it, even though Jane had told the label to lower the volume on it after the tabloid. But Stacy could always claim that the show people just saw the story and ran with it. So I repeated what Jane had told me to say if anyone brought it up.

"Me and Lisa are just good friends," I said, which was almost less true than saying we were dating, since you could get ice cream once with someone and say you were dating, but to be good friends you'd have to spend a long time with each other, like I did with Michael. "I'm still looking for that special girl to share myself with in my personal life, but until then the best connection I get is when I'm onstage, with my fans."

"And you have a lot of them," she said. "Here are some Tweets from two of our viewers." They showed the Tweets on-screen, and while she read it and the camera was off her, her eyes were scanning around, I think to see if they found the guy who'd shouted before.

i love 2 listen 2 Jonnys voice when everything is Bad it makes me feel like theres something Good in the world thank u Jonny

That NOT awkward moment last night when @TheRealJonny sings "Crushed" and makes eye contact with you in the front row #willyoubemyBOYtoday

"It must make you feel great to hear that," Robin said.

"If it wasn't for my fans I wouldn't be here," I said. "Everything I do belongs to them."

She lobbed a couple softballs, like, "What's your best feature?" and even though I really think it's my arms because they've got zero chub, I always pretend to be a little embarrassed and say, "Well, I don't know, but people tell me they like my eyes," and she said, "Can we get a close-up on Jonny's baby blues?" and the camera zoomed in on them and I batted them like I was shy and the girls went nuts like they always do, it's like they know they're supposed to from other times they've seen audiences react.

She asked how I'm so natural onstage, and I said I always felt at home performing, which is bullshit and it took me a long time to fake being comfortable and if I told her I usually vomit before shows she'd cut to commercial. She used it as a segue to the music, and I sang "Crushed" and "Chica" and ended with "Guys vs. Girls."

When I got on "Guys vs. Girls," though, I heard the same guy again. The music was too loud for the audio to pick him up, but he kept saying things like, "Fag! Sing your faggy love song, faggot!"

My first thought was, Wait, what if *this* is my father? Like, what if he's out to get me, or is crazy, and the emails were just a decoy?

And my second thought was, Or one of the Latchkeys? Which didn't make sense, because the label would drop them in a second for a prank like this, plus Zack wouldn't let them.

I scanned the crowd, which I shouldn't have, but I had to see who it was. It wasn't my father, unless he'd gotten really fat since his driver's license and had grown stringy hair like sound equipment cables all twisted up backstage. And now he was right next to the stage, and the only people around him were all these little girls and their mothers who were clearing away from him so they were actually making it easier for him, and security wasn't nearby since the stage was high enough to prevent any girls from rushing it, like five feet tall, but if an adult really wanted, he could find a way to jump it.

We locked eyes for a second behind his thick glasses and sweaty face even though it was February. He smiled this gross smile, like he knew he'd gotten my attention, and he shouted, "You want me to fuck you in your little faggot ass?"

I knew the mikes wouldn't pick it up because the music was so loud, but security was taking a decade to break through the crowd. If there ever was a time to stampede a bunch of tween girls, this was it, when the talent's safety is compromised, which is the result of amateur event planning and operations.

He put both hands on top of the stage, like he was maybe going to climb it, and I'd been worried before, but now I was seriously scared, even if he was fat enough that he might not be able to get up. I turned away from the guy and danced quickly to the other side of the stage, to move away from him but also to make sure the camera didn't catch him at all, and *finally* I heard some commotion, and when I had the guts to turn around, Walter was a few feet away from the stage, on top of the guy and wailing at him like it was a bare-fisted battle in Zenon, punching his face with a right-left-right combo. It would've been fun to jump in as Walter held him down and be like, "You think I like performing in front of child predators who want to fuck me in my ass? How about I kick you in the teeth first?" and bash away until he didn't have any left. I wish I'd seen how Walter tackled the guy. He played defensive end in high school.

Then security peeled Walter off and led the guy away, but he kept trying to yell the whole time they dragged him away. It wasn't the first time some asshole had yelled at me during a show or on the street, but usually it was a young guy who was doing it to impress his friends, not some scary-looking child predator. And plus this time it threw me off and I accidentally switched the second and third verses, which I hadn't done since my first tour and probably no one noticed, but it got me pissed.

When we wrapped up I was supposed to do autographs, but Jane grabbed and hugged me and said, "Are you okay, baby?" I said yes, and she said, "You're not doing autographs. They're supposed to screen the crowd. You don't let in a fifty-year-old man who looks like a crazy. And you always have security at the perimeter of the stage."

I let her bitch Kevin out and went with Walter and additional security into the car service in a restricted area behind a building. I guess I was playing around with the buttons inside more than normal, because Walter asked, "Everything cool?"

"Yeah," I said. "And thanks, for before."

"It's my job, brother," he said. "Just wish you hadn't been in that situation in the first place."

"Unprofessional performance protocol," I said. "But what do you expect, with a morning show plus a public event in a third-tier city?"

"I guess." He scoped out the windows, in case any more crazies were thinking about breaking into the car. "Hey, when we get to Nashville, I saw we've got the night blocked off. You feel like visiting my daughters with me? If Jane clears it?"

"Like, at your house?"

"My ex-wife's house."

Some bodyguards might have been like, I just saved you from getting attacked or molested by a child predator, the least you could do is give my kids a story to tell their friends, but that wasn't what Walter was about. Plus I was curious to see what his old house was like and to meet his daughters. "That'd be fun. I'll ask Jane."

"They'd like that," Walter said. "Thank you."

We were quiet for a minute or two while we heard Jane still yelling at Kevin outside. It was pretty loud and she was cursing a ton. Walter said, "Your mom doesn't take shit from no one, huh?"

"She's good at business."

"There are always gonna be people who don't like you just because, you know?" he said.

"The haters, who are insecure so they have to tear someone down to feel better themselves."

"And there are gonna be people who love you."

I'd gotten this speech from the label and Jane about fifty times before. "And those are the ones who count."

But he shook his head. "They do, but that doesn't matter."

"I know. You have to love yourself and everything."

"Nah," he said. "That's the kind of bullshit they say on TV shows like this. There's a saying, 'What doesn't kill me only makes me stronger.'"

In Zenon, you can sometimes drink an invincibility potion that makes it so the world can't hurt you, but it lasts just a minute, and after that you can get damaged like normal. It's a little different from Walter's saying, which would be like if your damage percentage got lowered, you somehow became healthier. The only way that was kind of true in Zenon is that when you're at a hundred percent health, you're always worried someone's going to damage you and make it so you're not perfect. When you're already pretty damaged, you stop caring as much.

"Except when child predators are at my show," I said.

He smiled. "That's why you've got me around."

Maybe having Walter nearby didn't make me feel like I had an invincibility potion, but it was at least like being inside the fort me and Michael Carns used to make from his couch cushions, and he was the cushions providing buffer.

Jane finished up outside and got in the car and snapped at the driver to go and not let any fans stop the car if they spotted us. She typed angrily on her phone, and me and Walter were both afraid to make any sounds. When we arrived at the buses, though, she seemed calmer.

"Jane," I said, "I don't think I want to come back to St. Louis on my next tour." Even if it meant never seeing our old apartment again. Or Michael.

She gave a tired smile, where you could see all the cracks and wrinkles around her mouth and eyes that the makeup couldn't cover, and pulled her sunglasses off the top of her head and over her eyes. "Me neither, baby," she said.

CHAPTER 9

Memphis (First Day)

We had to wait for some bus maintenance before we could take off for Memphis, so I stretched in the cold air. The Latchkeys were outside their bus, smoking and talking with each other. Zack waved at me to come over. "Sir," he said, and he shook my hand. He always did when he saw me.

Zack looked good in photos, but he was more handsome in person, even at nine in the morning. His hair was a little spiky but soft and long, like black ferns, and he hadn't shaved yet so he had stubble on his face like the rough top of a mike. "How was the prodigal son's return?" he asked. I took a few seconds trying to figure out what *prodigal* meant from the context, like Nadine tells me, so he said, "How was it playing your hometown?"

If he hadn't heard about the crazy guy, which it sounded like he hadn't, I didn't really feel like telling him there was a child predator who nearly got onstage and kept shouting that he was going to fuck me in my ass. "It was okay. I'm glad we're leaving."

"Tell me about it. Thank God Memphis is next. Before this we were touring the sticks." He turned to his bandmates and said, "We've got to do Europe next time. I'm through with this Walmart bullshit. No offense to your fans, Jonny."

"I might tour Europe next time," I said.

"That right?"

"And Asia. Maybe you guys could come along." I was going to add, "To tap their markets," but that wasn't how Zack and the Latchkeys spoke.

He put the cigarette in his mouth and held it there while he clapped my shoulders with both hands and said out of the corner of his mouth, "That's why I like this man right here. Spreads the wealth through globalization. Like a young Bill Clinton." I wasn't sure what any of that meant except for "That's why I like this man right here," but I tried to play it cool and not smile too big. Zack added, "We're partying tonight in Memphis. You in?"

I looked behind me. Jane was still on the bus. "I'm kind of supposed to stay in the hotel at night."

"We can party in the hotel, too. I'll come get you late, okay?"

I didn't exactly know what Zack meant by partying in the hotel, or what late was to him, but it would be lame to ask. "Okay," I said.

The driver of his bus said they were ready. "Looks like this bus is bound for glory. See you tonight, Jonny," Zack said. He ground his cigarette beneath his boot and shook my hand again, and him and the other guys piled into the bus and I went back to mine and sat behind Jane near the back.

She was on the phone. I could hear the voice a little on the other end, because Jane's hearing isn't great and she has to turn the volume way up. It sounded like Stacy. "I simply want your assurance that this won't happen again," Jane said. I thought she was talking about the security breach, but she continued. "I didn't want to do this in the first place— he's just a kid. And we certainly didn't sign on for tabloid coverage."

I knew what Jane meant, we always want to have as much control as possible over my image, but the Lisa Pinto exposure made sense from a packaging-strategy perspective, since even if it was driving off some of the fat girls, it would bring in more of the pretty girls, and if they liked me then the fat girls would like me more to try to be like the pretty girls, plus the pretty girls would bring their boyfriends to my concerts, which effectively doubled gate receipts and they also had to buy them crap merch to make them happy, but the fat girls didn't have boyfriends. They had to buy the crap merch for themselves to feel happier. But Jane says we're in the business of making fat girls feel like they're pretty for a few hours and that most pretty girls are afraid other people think they're fat anyway, so maybe it's all the same.

If the media kept covering me and Lisa, I wondered if we'd get a combo name like Jonnisa, and I imagined the tour bus was the school bus on her album cover, and put an issue of *Rolling Stone* from the back of Jane's seat over my lap to hide my boner, and since no one was behind me and Jane was in front of me, I rubbed myself under the magazine but over my jeans.

Stacy talked but I couldn't hear, and in my mind me and Lisa were wrestling in the back of the school bus, with me pinning her down so she couldn't get up, and then Jane said loudly, "With *Tyler*?"

I popped open my eyes and stopped rubbing and leaned forward to listen. "A joint appearance on the show, February 13," I heard Stacy say. "Terrific exposure for Jonny's concert."

"And his people suggested this?" Jane asked.

"No, I did, but they were on board from the start."

I couldn't see Jane's face, but I could tell from the way she paused that she was pissed she hadn't come up with the idea. "All right," she said. "That's a scheduled free day, so we can do it, as long as our crew doesn't have to work."

Stacy said something about the house band backing us and they hung up. I pretended to be trying to sleep when Jane turned around and told me what I already knew, that I'd be meeting Tyler Beats for the first time and performing with him the night before my Valentine's Day concert on one of the big late-night shows.

A week ago I would've been super-excited and nervous to be bundled with Tyler Beats. But I didn't think he was all that cool anymore. The Latchkeys were cooler.

"Copacetic," I said, and I faked going back to sleep.

I did fall asleep soon. When you fake something, a lot of times you end up doing it for real. When I woke up, Jane was in the seat next to me and petting my hair lightly. "Did I oversleep?" I asked.

"No," she said. "I've just been sitting here, watching you."

"Why? Did I do something wrong?"

She smiled, but with her Botox it almost looked like she was close to crying sometimes. "Not at all, baby. It's time for tutoring now."

I went into my room where Nadine was waiting for me. Walter was in there, too. It looked like they'd just stopped talking once they'd heard me come in. He said he'd get out of our hair.

My corrected essay on Harriet Tubman was on Nadine's lap. She cleans it up enough for me to learn from without changing it to her style. I like that about her, it's like she wants to help you but is really doing it for you and not so she can feel better about herself, even though I know she gets paid well by Jane.

She said she read about my morning show performance on the Internet. "What about it?" I asked.

"I heard about the . . . incident."

I was sure it hadn't been picked up by the mikes or the cameras. "It was a hater. Whatever."

"Yeah, but . . . a knife. It's scary to think what might have happened."

"What knife?"

"You don't know?"

"Know what?"

"Jane didn't say anything?"

"No."

"Oh, Christ," Nadine whispered to herself.

"What happened?" I asked.

"I don't know much else about it."

"Yes, you do."

"All he said—" I could tell she didn't know if she should keep going or stop. "It's just that when they took him in they found a knife on him, and the police said he'd written all these . . ." She flattened out my essay. "You should talk to Jane. I'm being paid to tutor you."

Nadine probably thought she was scaring me by talking about a crazy guy with a knife who was also a child predator. It'd be easier when I was an adult, because they aren't interested in you anymore. It must have been strange for MJ to go from worrying about child predators to people saying *he* was a child predator. I don't know if he did it or not, but if he went through half the stuff as a kid that I deal with, I can't believe he'd ever do anything like it to someone else. Unless it's done to you so then you feel like you're allowed to do it to someone else, like how rookies have to carry the veterans' bags, then when they're veterans they make the rookies carry *their* bags.

I was getting pissed more than scared at the crazy guy, and at security for not doing their job, and at the TV show for not caring about my safety, just about ratings. I pictured the guy working his way up to the stage during "Guys vs. Girls," all calm, then in the chorus jumping up and stabbing me through the heart a bunch of times with a huge knife. I'd die singing the song that made me famous, and I'd splatter the girls in the front rows with blood instead of rose petals, and this time they'd be screaming because they really were scared, and all of America would be watching it on live TV and it'd viralize. *That* was something people would spend $19.95 on for Internet live-stream.

We did our work, and she gave my essay an A-minus and said my vocab was improving. I said, "You mean it's *ameliorating*," and she laughed since it was the one word I'd gotten wrong on the vocab test two weeks ago, and she said that's not quite the correct usage but close enough.

When she was packing up she said, "Jane told me you might tour again next fall."

"Yeah." I didn't know if Jane had told her the other option.

"Or that you might enroll in school."

I nodded. Doing that was also being like, Uh, sorry, Nadine, you're fired.

"I just want to tell you, if you want to go to school, you should do it."

"I don't want you to lose your job."

"That's really nice, Jonny, and you know I love doing this with you, but don't worry about me. Besides, I can't do this forever. I'm not building a real teaching career."

"You're teaching me."

"I know, but it's not the same as being in a classroom. And I turn twenty-seven in a few months, and I sometimes go weeks without seeing my boyfriend. Someday I'd like to start a family, and you'll need a tutor for another four years at least, and I can't do both."

My chest felt like someone had pulled the lungs out of it. "So are you saying you want to quit?"

"No! I mean, not now, at least. But at some point I'd like to go back to teaching in a regular school. The point is, don't factor me into your decision. In fact, don't factor anyone else in. Even your mom."

"Why shouldn't I factor in Jane?"

"Because it's about you. What *you* want to do with your life. You don't have to do something just because other people say you should."

When the conversation started, I was scared Nadine would think we were firing her. Now it sounded like *she* was firing *us*.

"When you're a celebrity, it's *not* just about you," I said. "When I give a concert, the jobs of a hundred and thirty-six people on this tour are standing on my shoulders, plus hundreds of people in that city."

"You don't have to be defensive," Nadine said. "I'm just trying to let you know that I'll respect whatever decision you make."

I didn't say anything, and two of her books fell out of her bag when she stood up so it took her longer to get out. It felt quiet in there. That was the first time we'd had a real fight, because the other fights were about stuff like me forgetting to do an assignment.

I avoided Nadine the rest of the drive to Memphis, which wasn't hard since she was usually reading a book with her iPod on but the music off, which only I knew about, so no one would bother her. She didn't bring her laptop on the bus because she says we're becoming increasingly dependent on the sensory stimuli of technology to fill our interior lives. Jane's the opposite, she usually has her computer and her iPhone and if we're at home the TV on. She doesn't listen to music besides for work, though.

A few hours in, I was in my room and heard her and Jane talking. They don't discuss much except about scheduling and other business, but I could tell from their voices that it wasn't about that. I wasn't playing Zenon, but I turned it on for the background music and opened my door a crack to listen.

I heard Nadine go, "I believe he has a right to know," and Jane went, "Frankly, I don't think *any* eleven-year-old needs to know about something like this, let alone the one it's happening to," and Nadine said, "If you're putting him in that position, and everyone else in the world knows, then he *does* have a right," and Jane said, "Nadine, you're an excellent tutor and Jonny likes you, so I'm not going to say any more except that you haven't raised a child." Nadine said, "Well, I've said my piece, and I hope you're putting Jonny first here," and went back to her seat.

"Rog, Walter, I suppose you have something to add, too, or are you just watching the show?" Jane asked, and Rog said, "I'm just the voice coach," and Walter said, "Bodyguard." I closed the door quietly.

I wondered what the guy wrote. It couldn't be much worse than some of the things I'd seen on the Internet. People write whatever on the Internet and don't even remember anything, but if you write it on paper, you really mean it.

When we got to Memphis, Jane made me rest at the hotel until dinner because she's been on my case about that ever since I fainted. I had Zenon to keep me company, so I didn't mind. When Jane came to my room, I asked if we were ordering room service or going out. "Actually, it turns out I have to go to dinner with a regional promoter," she said.

I got that weird feeling in my stomach that came when Jane said she had to go after she'd made it sound like we'd be hanging out. It wasn't like preshow nervousness. I never vomited, but it was almost like I was losing part of my guts.

"I could come along."

"You'd be bored. All shop talk. So you should order room service."

At least I'd get to play Zenon all night long without her around, plus I didn't know when Zack was getting me so this made it easier. "Can I order whatever I want?" I asked as she was leaving.

I could see she wanted to say no, but I also knew what she'd answer now that she'd blown me off. "Go easy on the barbecue," she said. "That's why everyone here's a tub of chub."

She stopped again before leaving, and looked at me, and scampered back in, even in her heels, and I knew what was coming. She tickled me on the couch and squeezed my stomach, and I squealed, and she sang our song and I joined in on the second verse through my squealing:

> *Oh, we don't like our chub*
> *We put it in a little jar*
> *We hide it very, very far*
> *No, we don't like our chub*

She kissed my forehead and said, "Don't play games all night long, baby." After she closed the door I heard her check it was locked a couple times.

I was more interested in the corn bread Walter had been talking about anyway since my stomach prioritizes carbs over meat even though they're the enemy, so after she left I ordered three pieces of it and some fried chicken and mashed potatoes. If I lived here full-time I'd gain twenty pounds of chub.

I played Zenon the rest of the night as I got more excited to hang out with Zack, plus this would be my one chance to check my email, since there hadn't been any computer terminals around at any of our venues and the ones in our hotels you either had to pay for with a credit card or get someone over eighteen to authorize you. I could email asking if he saw me mention Pittsburgh and Australia and peanut butter on the morning show for him and if he heard about the child predator, and maybe he'd be like, Yeah, I wanted to fly to St. Louis right away and kill that guy when I heard about it.

By nine o'clock he hadn't come, and I was supposed to go to bed by 9:30 the night before a concert if I didn't have a show that night, and maybe he didn't know which room I was in or he'd forgotten or he'd changed his mind or the other guys vetoed me.

I didn't want to get in my pajamas in case he did come, and I definitely didn't want to take a zolpidem, but I was getting tired, so what I did was, at 9:30 I stayed in my regular clothes and got in bed and left the bedroom door open so if he came I could pretend I was still up.

For a little while I stayed up since I thought every sound outside was

Zack knocking on my door, but I must have fallen asleep because then I heard this loud banging from out of nowhere. I scrambled out of bed dizzily and turned on the light in the living room and opened the door, and there was Zack.

"Oh, fuck," he said. "Were you asleep? It's only, like, ten-fifteen. I figured you'd still be awake."

Maybe he thought I was older than eleven. "No, I was up." I could feel my hair going all directions like I'd been electrocuted. That's the main problem with The Jonny, it looks messed up when you wake up. Plus after rides in convertibles. Ronald has one.

"Can I see your room?" he asked, and he came inside before I could say anything. He smelled like alcohol and cigarettes more than his cologne. "Goddamn. So this is the real rock star room. We should be partying in here instead of our hovel."

I got nervous that he was going to move the party here and Jane would catch us, so I said, "It's all right. Usually they're nicer than this."

He smiled. "Tough crowd, little man. You want to come over?"

"Yeah. Except I'm not really supposed to be out now." That was lame, so I added, "On a night before a concert. The doctor said I had too many late nights."

"Then we'll have to evade the authorities," he said. "Come on."

I got my sneakers on and took my key-card, and he turned off the lights and cracked the door a few inches and poked his head out in the hall both directions and whispered, *"Let's go!"* and walked-ran out and I did the same behind him down the hall, and my body felt tingly and light all over, because I was afraid Jane might catch me or a fan would see me but also because it was the most fun I'd had not in Zenon since probably Phoenix, when they'd opened an amusement park at night just for me and Walter and we go-karted and played laser tag. Zack probably weighed about half what Walter did, but I felt safe with him, too, in a different way, like he could talk us out of any trouble we got into.

At the end of the hall Zack opened the door to a stairwell, and he raced and jumped down three flights of stairs before stopping at another stairwell door. Two escaped slaves in the Underground Railroad, hiding at safe houses until we reached freedom.

Zack crouched down, breathing all heavy like he'd finished a marathon, and put his arm around my shoulders and said, "We got one more sprint and we're safe. Ready?"

I said ready, and wasn't hardly breathing, because I was in better shape from being a dancer and all-around entertainer, and rock stars smoke cigarettes and stand in one place all night besides the ones like Mick Jagger who add a few dance moves to their stage repertoire, but my heart was still beating like the drum and bass in a techno song, and we dashed through the door and down another hallway and he put his key-card in a door and it made that click sound and he pushed it open and got us inside to the free states. It's funny how in real life, though, we were still in Tennessee.

His bandmates were on the sectional couch in the living room, which was smaller than mine but not at all a crap room, with an iPod stereo on the coffee table playing a gritty-textured punk-rock song with a British singer, and they were all drinking either bottles of beer or whiskey in the bathroom cups. There were four girls with them. The girls weren't that hot, really. They were wearing tights and two of them had bangs and one even had glasses and was a little chubby. Maybe it's because the guys in the band except for Zack weren't that good-looking, but whenever Mi$ter $mith was with a girl, she always looked like a model or an actress, and they definitely never wore glasses. In a way I respected the Latchkeys more for not having model groupies. These girls probably had better personalities. Unless they wanted the model groupies but they couldn't get them, since that was the whole point of becoming a rock star for a lot of guys. I didn't know that when I started out, but once you see seriously ugly bassists backstage with models, you figure it out. For a normal guy, becoming a rock star is like Luann Phelps getting contacts and losing her lisp.

Mi$ter $mith had an entourage, too, like most black pop and rap stars, and they probably helped him get models. The Latchkeys didn't have any friends with them on tour, but that was smart financial strategy. It's hard to have career longevity when you're controlling the purse strings for twenty people everywhere you go.

One of the girls looked better than the others, though. She was sitting by herself in the center, and was tall and thin, and her nose was long but it still fit her face good. But it was the way she sat, with the posture Jane wants me to have, that you knew she was their leader. Zack sat next to her and put his arm around her, and told me to sit next to him. He said, "Jonny, this is Vanessa, and these are Clara and Samantha and Jane."

I almost said that that was my mother's name but I stopped myself in time, and I also knew that if I asked to check email one of the Latchkeys might tell them that Jane doesn't let me go on the Internet. Zack wouldn't do it, but I didn't trust the other guys not to.

The singer on the stereo kept singing "1977" at the start of each verse, and the bassist of the Latchkeys was like, "If we wrote a song named after this year, and someone was listening to it in three or four decades, what would it be about?" and the drummer said, "Like, fucking Facebook," and the lead guitarist said, "No, articles *about* Facebook," and Zack picked up an acoustic guitar from the floor and paused the music and played a pretty riff that was like the textural opposite of the song we'd been listening to, and one of the Latchkeys cupped his hands over his mouth and said, "He's playing acoustic! *Judas!*" and Zack said, "Except for acoustic it would be, *'Jesus!'* and he'd whisper to his band of disciples, 'Play fuckin' quiet!'" Then he cleared his throat and said the name of the year all serious in a way that made everyone laugh, and made up these lyrics on the spot and sang them soprano:

> *Status updates and Internet dates*
> *I'd rather eat out a Middle East date*
> *Get your filthy minds outta the gutter*
> *I'm referring to consuming the biblical delicacy*
> *Not cunnilingus on a woman*
> *From a historically war-torn and oil-rich region*
> *Whom I've been set up with by our mutual friend, John*
> *Who thinks we have a lot in common*

Everyone laughed throughout the song and especially at the end, and so did I to play along but I didn't get most of the jokes. Zack turned the music back on to a new song and said, "You like the Clash, Jonny?"

I didn't want to admit I'd heard of them but didn't know their music. Punk was a genre Rog and Jane didn't allow on my iPod since the singers were almost all low-caliber, but I'd seen on the iPod that they were the band playing, so I said I liked that song before, and he said, "This song is criminally underrated."

"Oh, God, not 'Complete Control,'" said the bassist. "You worship that song. It's so banal."

"It's the greatest meta-critique of the music industry in a rock song," Zack said.

I tried to listen to the lyrics, which were hard to make out, but I liked how it was part singing, part shouting. Normally this music, it's all shouting because the singer's got zero vocal chops. I could tell it was about how bad their label was, which is a major no-no. When singers play antimedia songs, they think they're getting the fans on their side, but the fans don't actually care and all you're doing is alienating your ally and mouthpiece. But the fans *really* don't care about a song slamming your label, even if most people hate their boss. They don't even understand what the label does. They just know what's put out in front of them, like a roast beef sandwich on an airplane, and have no idea anyone else had to feed and kill and cook and package the cow before serving it on their tray. And the funny thing is, they all wish they could *be* the packaged cow.

It wasn't MJ, which pumps straight into my veins, and I don't know how you could listen to him and *not* dance, but when Zack saw I was tapping my foot to it and turned the volume up, it didn't make me want to dance. It made me want to throw or break something. When it was over he said, "I'll put it on your iPod next time. Because fuck the major labels, right?"

"Right."

The Latchkeys weren't guys who'd leak something you said to the media.

He ruffled my hair and said, "We're gonna convert you to a punk before this tour is over, right here in one of our three-star suites." He looked at the bassist. "Also, you pronounce it *buh-nahl*?"

"Yeah," the bassist said. "What do you say, *bay-nul*?"

"*Buh-nahl* sounds so pretentious. What do you guys say?"

He asked the room, but it was obvious he was only asking the guys in the band. They both pronounced it the way the bassist did, and the lead guitarist, Steve, said, "Zack, you lose the pronunciation battle once again, you working-class Jersey boy."

It was the first time I'd seen them make fun of him at all. Zack smiled but his eyes dropped when he did, not a real smile, and he said, "You're so banal-retentive, Steve." They laughed, and he said to Vanessa, "So you know, I'm only doing this if you're into banal sex." She thought it was funny, and he said, "I'm into doing it hard-core banal. Banal sex, all night long, while watching interracial banal porn. Double-banal penetration, where it's twice as banal as normal." He did a fake bite of her neck, and said, "Jonny, you want a drink? Beer, whiskey?"

Everyone was waiting to see if I'd drink with them. If I said no the wrong way, like I did with the kids at Matthew's birthday party, they'd know I'd never had alcohol before. Before I could answer, Steve said, "Milk?" like it was the funniest line anyone had ever come up with, the asshole, and the girls all giggled.

"I'm good," I said to Zack. Then I looked straight at Steve. "But I'll take some of your mom's milk."

There was silence for a few seconds. Everyone looked around at each other trying to figure out if what I said was funny or not, until Zack said, "Oh, snap, Jonny *schooled* you, Steve-o, lactation-style."

Everyone laughed again at what Zack said, but it was like they were really laughing at my line, and he put his arm around my shoulders again and pulled me into him, and while the others were talking he said to me, "You coming out tonight?"

I'd been planning on lying about a media interview early in the morning and how I couldn't stay up late. "For sure," I said.

We hung out in the room awhile longer. I didn't talk much, but I picked up that they had all met at college at Harvard and formed there under the name the Archdukes of Hazzard, which Zack said was the most preposterous band name of all time, and graduated a few years ago, and they released *The Latchkeys Open Up* last year. It sounded like college was a lot of fun for them there, that they were celebrities at school but not real celebrities. Maybe that's why they didn't seem to let it get to their heads now, since they'd had it build up slowly, from nobodies in high school to sort of famous in college to not famous again after college to pretty famous now, not like some musicians I've met who go straight from nobodies to super-famous and act like they were never nobodies. Last year I asked Jane if she thought I should go to college. She'd said, "I didn't go, and I was as smart as anyone at that marketing firm and would've been promoted soon if I hadn't had you and lost my job." That was all she said. I wouldn't want to study for an extra four years anyway, or five, when you count the year I don't have to get tutored for if I get my California GED when I'm seventeen. But Jane was smart in a different way from the Latchkeys.

The other Latchkeys, even Steve, were nicer to me than before. They almost seemed like they were relatives more than friends, the way they teased each other. All my dancers and vocalists and musicians are at least seven or eight years older than me, and Jane makes sure I don't hang out with them too much because they might be bad influences or cannibalize my focus. Watching the Latchkeys mess around with each other was like when the Cardinals win a big game and they have a pile-on at home plate. It made you happy to see them do it, but part of you was jealous since you wanted to be in the pile-on, too. The only time I get close to that is when all my backup singers and the band sing a line with me, like in "Love Is Evol," where they yell the last line of the chorus, "Love bleeds you dry, never leaves you full, love eats you up, *love is evol!*"

I went to the bathroom. Someone's iPhone was charging on the sink. This was really dumb to do, but I went into the Web browser the way Jane does and checked my email. Still nothing from Albert, and it'd been over half a week. I Googled "Jonny Valentine St. Louis concert." A million articles came up about the concert with headlines saying things like "Stalker Threatens Jonny Valentine at Concert." I clicked on the first one, from a media blog:

Jonny Valentine Receives Violently
Sexual Threats During Televised
Performance from Old Man;
NAMBLA to Produce Next Album?

So! As if we needed further confirmation that Jonny Valentine
concerts are attended exclusively by lovelorn prepubescent
girls and rapey old men, the ***St. Louis Post-Dispatch* is
reporting** that a 57-year-old St. Louis man was arrested after
hurling a slew of violently sexual epithets at the Angel of ~~Poop
Pap Smears~~ Pop during his **live televised performance**
(many of which the mikes picked up; listen to **some genius's
sound edit** in which *only* the slurs are audible and remixed
over the insipid instrumentals of "Guys vs. Girls"). The would-be
ass-ailant was found with both a knife and a journal on his person,
which allegedly further detailed the actions he would perform
upon Jonny's nubile body (is it just us, or is he looking a little
tubby in this clip?). As the sexual and musical deviant awaits
legal judgment, let's all listen to the **Jonny Valentine sexual-
epithet remix** a few more times, shall we?

I didn't feel like listening to the remix, plus they'd hear it out in the
main room, but I did read the comments below:

Sick. And yet profoundly gratifying. I'm a horrible person.

Proposed title of remix: "(rapey old) Guys vs. (lovelorn
prepubescent) Girls"?

Yes. Just . . . yes.

OK, don't take this the wrong way, but give Jonny seven years and I'LL be writing the same things in my diary. Just sayin'.

Best. Heckler. Ever.

Once you start reading them it's hard to stop when it's about you, even though you know pretty much exactly what you're going to find and they just get worse and worse the farther you go down. It's like people are afraid to be the first one to be an asshole, but once some others clear the way, they get super-excited about it. Except with most blogs, the blogger himself is the biggest asshole, so all the commenters think it's okay to write whatever they want from the start. They think they're being clever, making fun of me, but it's just a bunch of losers who're angry they're stuck in boring jobs at offices all day and this is their only way to be creative. If they were actually creative, they wouldn't be *reading* the media blogs, they'd be the ones the media blogs are *covering*. Which is what they wish happened, and that's why they were reading a media blog in the first place, just like how Jane used to read all the glossies when she worked at Schnucks. But even the guy who wrote the post wasn't creating anything. He was only linking to other publications and writing a little filler, like a crap DJ who remixes other people's songs so it seems like he's done something new, but he's really just spliced them together like anyone with half a brain could do.

Zack's toiletry kit was on the counter. For a second I thought about opening it but I didn't. Next to it was a bottle of cologne, except it wasn't like a regular cologne you buy in a store or see an ad for, it was a specialty cologne with no name, just a handwritten label listing ingredients. I unscrewed the top and sniffed it. It was definitely his woods smell.

It was probably worse to do this than to peek inside his toiletry kit, but I dabbed a little on my finger and smeared it on my neck. Now I smelled like Zack. I sucked my gut in and joined the others.

After an hour or so the drummer called a cab company and requested three cars for nine people. Zack said, "Jonny, Vanessa, and I will take one, you all split the other two."

One of the girls said, "How should we divide it up? Guys versus girls, Jonny?"

She said it sweetly, you could tell, so I quickly half sang, "Why's it gotta be that way?" and this time everyone laughed and didn't need Zack to make a follow-up joke. I was going to hang out with the Latch-keys every night on this tour, and I didn't care if I was tired all day.

We took two elevators down to the lobby, and I went in Zack's. It wasn't that cold out, but Zack gave me his leather jacket so I didn't have to go back to my room. It was big on me, like an overcoat, and it smelled like him mixed with cigarettes. He took a red wool hat out from the pocket. "Wear this," he said, and he pulled it over my head and ears. "For warmth and cunning disguise."

Two cars came first, and Zack told the others to take them, and him and Vanessa smoked cigarettes while we waited. "Don't ever quit smoking these," he said to me.

Vanessa hit his shoulder and said, "Don't listen to him, Jonny. Don't *start* smoking them. Seriously."

"I won't," I said. "I don't want to fuck up my voice."

"You do have a pretty goddamn golden voice," Zack said. "Not like me. I've got the bronze. But I can write a verse-chorus-verse to opiate the masses. Other than that, I'm basically useless as a member of society." I don't think he really thought that way about himself, but if he did even a tiny bit, he was wrong. His friends loved him and people wanted to be around him and he made people feel smarter and funnier. If I told him, though, it would sound gay.

Zack told the cab driver the Velvet Lounge and gave him the address. The guy looked in the rearview mirror once at me, but I didn't know if it was because he recognized me or he was wondering why a kid was with two adults.

Would the nightclub let me in? Or did it not matter if you were with adults? But maybe they had to be your parent? Zack looked too young to pretend to be my father. Except he could've had me when he was very young, and we were more like friends who partied than a father and son. You see some father-son actors like that in L.A.

Vanessa sat in the middle, and Zack made out with her. She allowed it for a minute but kept whispering, "Not now," and finally she said, "Heel, boy," and straightened out her skirt and turned to me and asked, in a teacher-type voice, what I usually did at night on tour.

"I usually have dinner with my mother and do homework and play video games and watch TV," I said.

That definitely sounded like I was a little kid, but Vanessa wouldn't make fun of me. She said, "You must miss your friends at home."

"I don't really ha—I don't really miss them. I only tour a few times a year, and I have a lot of fun."

"Jonny falls into the proud tradition of the rogue wandering troubadour," Zack said. "All's he needs is his harmonica and guitar"—Zack pronounced it *gee*-tar—"and a warm place to rest his head and nothing else, no, sir."

I knew he was joking around, but I kind of liked that idea, me as the traveler who only needed his instruments. Except I wasn't that type of musician. I needed instrumentalists and vocalists and dancers and buses and eighteen-wheelers and a bodyguard and a manager and a PR liaison. Sometimes I look around at the people and equipment and promo materials put together and am like, No one would notice if I disappeared, even though it's all there because of me. If I was never famous, the people whose lives would be attached to mine would be Jane plus Michael Carns.

Also Zack said *sir* in a much less annoying way than Lisa Pinto did.

Zack paid with a twenty-dollar bill when the cab stopped. There were lots of adults in their twenties in a red-velvet-rope line before a black bouncer who made Walter's body look like mine. The other Latchkeys came over while Vanessa found her friends near the door. "We tried to skip the line," Steve told Zack, "but no dice."

"Sounds like we're huge in Memphis," Zack said. "Jonny, come with us?"

He put his hand on my back and walked us up to the bouncer with the other guys behind us. Halfway there, Zack took his hat off my head.

"Hello," he said all polite to the bouncer, who was letting in a couple women in short skirts and wasn't looking at him. He stood between me and the other people in line so they couldn't see, which made me less nervous, since I didn't want people taking photos. This was getting more and more dangerous, but if I had to be doing this with anyone, I was glad it was Zack. "My name is Zack Ford, and I'm the lead singer of the rock group the Latchkeys. We're opening for Jonny Valentine here tomorrow night, and we were hoping to enter your establishment."

"Got to get to the end of the line, sir," the bouncer said.

"Jonny has a curfew, unfortunately, so waiting in line isn't a great option."

The bouncer turned to us, and the way he sized me up, I could tell he'd heard of my name but didn't know what I looked like, and for all he knew I could've just been some kid pretending to be Jonny Valentine, the way the guy emailing me could be some perverted pedophile pretending to be my father. I don't have much penetration into the urban-male demo.

Zack pulled out his iPod and shuffled through some albums before holding it up. "Look," he said. "Jonny's debut album. Triple-platinum smash. You still want to send us to the back of the line?"

The bouncer compared the iconic close-up of my face with *The Jonny* just brushing my eyebrows on the album cover and me in real life. I didn't want to smile, or it might look like we were fooling him, but it was hard not to when I'd seen that Zack owned my album *and* he knew it'd gone triple platinum. "Hold on," the bouncer said.

He went inside, and came out soon with a redheaded woman in her twenties, who looked at us and asked, "How many in your party, Mr. Valentine?"

I pointed to the other Latchkeys and the girls and told her nine. The bouncer unhooked the rope and let us in, and Zack let me go first but I could tell he was right behind me. The woman said her name was Irena and if we had any problems or wanted anything to ask her. She led us inside and through a door on the right, not the main entrance to the nightclub, and down two long hallways that must have been a special access for celebrities, and I could hear the girls behind me getting excited since they never did anything like this. I tried to pretend I'd done this before, but really I'd only been to industry events that were like nightclubs with Jane, not a real nightclub, and definitely not without Jane.

Finally we came out into the main room. It wasn't decorated like a regular nightclub, it was more like a huge living room with wooden furniture and old couches and chairs like the kind Jane said she wants to decorate our living room with after she saw a spread of an Oscar-winning actress's house in a glossy, and part of me thought about asking Zack to invite her over, but it would be super-lame to call my mother and also I'd be in serious trouble.

We were in a roped-off section that had another bouncer guarding it, with thirty or forty people in our area and a lot more in the rest of the room, either talking or dancing to the DJ, who was playing some bad hip-hop song, I forget the rapper's name, but it was one of those where the guy tries to sing and he doesn't have the range. I want to be like, Stay in your element. You don't see me trying to rap. I've tried it on my own, and I know it's out of my talent reach.

Irena brought us to a free area with two couches and two chairs around a chipped and beat-up coffee table. It was sort of like what they had in the hotel room, only we were paying to be here and have other people around us that we weren't talking to. Zack grabbed one of the chairs and I sat on a couch right near him. Irena took everyone's order, which was still whiskey or beer, and when she got to me, she looked at Zack to see what she should do. "Jonny, what soda do you like?" he asked.

"Ginger ale," I told him. All soda is crap for the vocal cords, but ginger ale has a little less sugar and doesn't cause as much mucus production. I couldn't ask for diet in front of everyone, though.

"Ginger ale on the rocks," Zack ordered, which is what I was going to say from now on. He whispered something else to Irena before she went off. When she came back with our drinks and was handing out the last one to Zack, the DJ kicked into the Latchkeys song "Frog-Legs Franny." I caught Irena smiling at Zack, and I figured he'd requested it, to impress the girls, but they were already impressed, so maybe he just wanted it anyway. "Well, that's embarrassing," Zack said after Irena left. By now a bunch of people in our section were looking over at us, mostly at me and Zack.

The Latchkeys talked about books and movies and musicians I hadn't heard of. They all had opinions on everything and used words like *aesthetic* and *ideology* and *polemic*. Maybe I knew more about slave autobiographies than them, but that was it. I thought about asking if they'd read *The Confessions of Nat Turner*, which was the best one I'd read so far, because it was short but also it has the most action and Nat Turner kills a bunch of white people just with a small sword, like he's in Zenon, except he says he wants to slay his enemies with their own weapons, which in Zenon would mean stealing someone's weapon and using it against them, and I don't think the game actually lets you do that since you can't inspect an enemy's inventory until he's dead.

They wouldn't know about Zenon, though, so I stayed quiet. The girls didn't say as much except for Vanessa, who used those kinds of words and argued with them all, especially Zack. Making smart music got you smart groupies who understood what you were doing with your sound, even if it meant a smaller overall base. I had fans who'd never even heard of MJ.

They were discussing the one movie I *had* seen, *Back to the Future*, and Zack was like, "It represents not merely a nostalgic desire to regress to the safety of adolescence, but to the conservative fifties, the notion that we only have to roll back the biological and temporal clocks and we'll be happier. It's a total by-product of the anxieties of the cold war . . ."

The song that was playing switched into something familiar, and after a few bars I picked up that it was "Summa Fling," but a remixed club version I'd never heard before. It sounded decent, but it cut down my lyrics to the words "Summa fling, two-month thing, I wanna sing to my summa fling," and overlaid a lot of other beats not in the original song. My producer for that album, Charles, had the philosophy that the music had to hook the listener but the vocals were what kept them there, and when you had someone with my vocal strength, you didn't mess around with overproduced songs. We probably got a good royalty rate for the sampling. Jane watches that stuff like a hawk.

"This one of yours?" Zack asked me, and he gave me a little wink no one else could see so I knew he'd requested it from Irena. I said it was, and he said it was cool and told the other Latchkeys they should do their own remix about briefly dating the valedictorian of summer school called "Summa Cum Laude Fling," and took Vanessa's hand and danced with her. A ton of people in the crowd were dancing, too, and even if it was only like a quarter of my original, it somehow felt cooler to watch people here dancing to it while I drank ginger ale than it did when they danced at my concerts. Part of it was because the crowd was older and where we were, but the biggest reason was that Zack had requested the song, which meant he knew about the club remix already, and he was dancing to it.

The one thing I didn't like about the remix was the original has a long fadeout, where I'm singing the chorus over and over for about thirty seconds, and what I like about fadeouts is how, after the song is over, it feels like it's still playing somewhere, only you can't hear it. It's a nice idea, that just because you're not listening to a song in front of you doesn't mean it doesn't exist somewhere else. It works even better for "Summa Fling," since it's like, Even this two-month relationship is going on in some way, that's why I'm singing about it forever. The remix had a hard stop. You *know* a song is over then.

They ordered a second round of drinks from a new waitress, and Zack asked for a double rye. When it came, he said, "Jonny, let me get some of your ginger ale?" I handed it to him, and he brought it down below the coffee table with his rye and poured half his drink into mine. He passed it back to me without looking.

The drink smelled mostly like ginger ale, but also like Jane's breath when she drank. I took a sip. It was sweet, but it stung my tongue like an arrow piercing your armor in Zenon and slid down my throat like a mage's fireball that caused some damage. But it got easier with each sip, until when I was halfway through Zack reached for my glass again and dumped in the rest of his drink. The fireball fell inside my stomach, but it was a relaxing fireball, and it spread out like a smoke cloak in Zenon for hiding yourself, and then it was like the damage was healing. What doesn't kill me only makes me stronger. Now I got why Jane does this.

You don't worry about anything anymore. I could say something dumb that everyone knew about *Back to the Future* and not care how the Latchkeys reacted, like that I thought the coolest part was how different everyone's lives became in the future after one little thing changed in the past.

By the time I was almost done with my drink, Vanessa was sitting on Zack's lap on his chair and making out with him like in a music video. My vision was getting blurry, and I didn't have the energy to keep it straight, so I only saw their outline, and then I had this picture in my head of Zack sitting in an armchair like the one he was in, but it was in a home, in a real living room, and there was a fireplace behind him and he was reading the newspaper, and I went up to him as he patted his lap and I crawled onto it and sat there while he read the paper.

And the weirdest part was, I was getting hard. Probably it was because my eyes were sort of on Vanessa's legs where her skirt was riding up on her thighs and I could almost see her underwear, so I focused my eyes on her there and got harder and shut my eyes totally and put my drink on the table and thought about what Vanessa looked like naked and humping her.

Next thing I knew, someone was shaking me awake. It was Vanessa. "Wake up, sleepy boy," she said, almost like Jane singing, "Go to sleepy, little baby."

I don't know how long I was out for, but it was way worse than waking up early from zolpidem. The Latchkeys and the girls were all getting their stuff together and leaving. The nightclub was still pretty packed, though not as much as before. I swung my feet onto the ground and wobbled back to a sitting position on the couch before Vanessa broke my fall backward with her arms. "Easy there, fella," she said. "Zack, help?"

Zack bent down right in front of me. His eyebrows looked concerned. A long lock of his hair touched my forehead. "You okay, little man?"

I made sure I wasn't going to fall again before I stood up. "I'm solid."

Zack gave me a fake punch on my cheek, lightly touching it with his knuckles, and said, "Cool. Walk out with me." He put his jacket and hat on me and his hand on my back again, but this time I think it was to make sure I didn't collapse or depart the realm.

We left through the secret passage from before and there was a long line for cabs, but Irena let us cut in front and told us to come back anytime. I went with Zack and Vanessa again. The cab ride seemed longer than the way there, since we were quieter and time always goes slower after you've left something than before you've arrived. Zack sat in the middle, and after a few minutes Vanessa leaned on his shoulder and fell asleep, and I got tired, too, and my head found its way onto his other shoulder, but I wasn't falling asleep and I didn't really want to be asleep, I just wanted to stay like that forever, smelling the cigarettes in his jacket I was wearing and his cologne me and him were both wearing and resting on his shoulder as we drove silently in the dark of a strange city.

We arrived at the hotel after the two other cabs. Zack and Vanessa took me up to my floor in the elevator. I was hoping we'd pretend to sneak around again, but I think they were too tired. They escorted me inside my room and took Zack's jacket and hat off me. "Change into pajamas," Zack said. "You don't want your mom asking why you're still in your clothes."

While I changed in the bathroom, I was hoping Zack and Vanessa would say they were so tired, could they just crash on my couch? And I'd be like, "Yeah, I don't really like my bed and I kind of want to sleep on the couch, too," so I'd go on one of the couches and they'd take the other two, and we'd have a sleepover like I used to have with Michael and maybe even make a cushion fort. I changed my clothes super-fast so I could tell them they could crash there if they wanted, in case they were afraid to ask.

But when I came out, they weren't in the living room. "Zack?" I called.

They weren't in the bedroom, either. I guess they wanted a real bed. I got under the covers. It had that feeling of being too big, like it was an ocean and I was a stone someone skipped in it, where you watch it carefully at first to count how many times it skips, and then it sinks, and you pick up the next stone and forget about the last one.

CHAPTER 10

Memphis (Second Day)

I had a hangover. I should've put out a glass of water for myself like I do for Jane, and I woke up like three times in the middle of the night but was too tired to get up for the bathroom, even though I knew it would make me feel better. Usually I'm good about doing hard things now that will help me in the future. Deferring gratification, Jane says. An extra hour of vocal practice targeting your weaknesses in the present means an extra thousand in sales a year from now. It's what separates one-hit wonders from musicians with career longevity.

I took a couple baby aspirin from my toiletry kit when my wake-up call rang at eight a.m., which helped a little, but I still felt like I'd just done thirty minutes of high-intensity cardio on a zolpidem. I got down about half my omelet, but had to run to the bathroom and barely made it in time before it came back up.

I don't know how Jane does this.

By the time Nadine met me for my morning tutoring, I'd recovered enough so that she didn't notice anything, except for once when I forgot what eleven times twelve was and she said, "Come on, slowpoke, what's with the lethargy?"

I tried napping in the afternoon before sound check, but I only turned around in my bed a bunch. Zack probably had good hangover advice, but I couldn't remember his room number. I called the front desk and asked for the room of Zack Ford.

"One moment, sir," the woman said, and I was so surprised, I didn't have anything planned to say when Zack picked up and said hello. I guess they weren't famous enough to have to use fake names. Or maybe they did it so groupies could find them. That was Mi$ter $mith's trick. He'd mention how cool his hotel was during his interlude banter, and you'd see all these girls in the lobby waiting for him postshow. He sings about hotel groupies in his song "$ext $candal," which he couldn't play on our tour. It wouldn't work for me, because I couldn't exactly be like, Hey, your Marriott is really cool, I've got an awesome room with a view right down the hall from my mother.

"Hi," I said.

"Hi. You have a name?"

"It's me. Jonny."

"Jonny." He laughed. "I thought you were some girl."

My speaking voice was high, but I didn't think it was *that* high. I made it a little lower, enough so it wasn't obvious what I was doing. It's easy for me to control, which is one thing Rog says is a huge weapon in a singer's arsenal, impersonation, since it means you can be a different singer to suit the subject. I've been working on an impression of Walter, to spring it on him one day when it's good. It kind of hurts my throat, since his voice is so gravelly, so I can't practice too much. "No, it's me."

"So, as my Uncle Morris from Nebraska says, what can I do you for?"

I realized if I told him I got sick off two drinks I would sound like a kid. "That was fun last night," I said.

"Yeah, we'll have to do it again."

I waited for him to say something else, but he didn't, so I said, "That was all I wanted to say."

"The soul of wit. I like it," he said. "I've got to get ready for sound check, but I'll catch you later." He hung up before I could say good-bye. My stomach jabbed me when I heard the dial tone, but I think it was because I needed to go to the bathroom again.

I didn't know where the Latchkeys' room was at sound check and didn't see them, but it didn't matter since I was feeling more and more like junk the rest of the day. For my sound check I took it easy, almost spoke the words, which I was allowed to do if I felt like it, so no one paid attention. In the star/talent room there was a super-big spread with barbecue and buffalo wings and ribs and sweet potato fries in addition to my rider requests, and I knew Jane hadn't approved it and she hadn't scoped out the room, but I couldn't imagine putting anything in my stomach anyway, so I told Walter to go nuts. When the Latchkeys went on to open, I realized I hadn't eaten anything after my morning omelet, and I was starving, so I ate a few sweet potato fries to test it out, and my stomach seemed fine. I moved on to the wings and ribs and some meat loaf, and before I knew it I'd eaten probably two dinners. I added up all the calories from the nutritional listings, and it was around seventeen hundred. I'd have to offset it with high-intensity cardio for ten thousand hours.

I hadn't vomited before a concert since I saw Dr. Henson, from getting rest and being back in the performance groove, so I thought it would be okay. While I was waiting backstage, though, I had lethargy again, and Jane asked if everything was all right, and when I said yeah, she wiped all this sweat off my forehead that I hadn't even noticed and had the makeup woman give me another coat of foundation.

The second I went onstage, I knew I'd made a mistake with the barbecue. I opened with "Love Is Evol," which requires a lot of dancing around from me, and when I did my first split, my stomach gurgled and was like, Fuck you for poisoning me, Jonny. I adjusted and made it more of a crooner-style walk-around onstage, which Rog lets me do if I don't feel up to the choreography, and I had my dancers do the heavy lifting. It settled my stomach a little. I just wouldn't do any serious dancing the rest of the show.

But my singing was off, too. I'd drunk all the Throat Coat in the world in the afternoon, but it was like I kept running out of saliva, and when I reached for high notes, which are usually a meaty fastball down the middle of the plate for me, I could feel my voice cracking, so I had to rein *that* in also, which screwed me for "Breathtaking," where I'm supposed to hit a high C that sounds like my breath is being taken away.

I wasn't even sharp on "Kali Kool," which is my easiest song, but at least it's a sing-along so I could hold the mike out and let the crowd carry it.

I was sweating over my face and down my back, and when I brought this chubby girl with glasses onstage to sing to, she almost looked scared for me, because the sweat was dripping down my nose and I had to keep wiping it off with my sleeve.

The feeling passed for a few songs, and I got greedy and danced a little before the heart-shaped swing finale, and right when the swing came down my stomach bubbled again, and it turned a lot worse as the swing locked down and lifted me up. This was my nightmare, having an accident in front of all these people where they could tell I'd had one. I couldn't crouch down and puke, since it would fall through the holes in the bottom, and vomiting wasn't even going to help anything. I was trapped. And the more I worried about it, the gurglier my stomach became, which made me think about it more. The vicious cycle of performance anxiety, Rog calls it, but usually it's about singing worse because you're afraid you will, not about having diarrhea in your pants.

The audience was pretending to text and singing along with "U R Kewt" so loudly that I couldn't hardly hear the band or my own vocals, which made me pissed. If they actually cared about hearing me sing they'd let me sing, but it's really all for them, which is why like eighty percent of pop lyrics are about *you,* not *her* or an actual name, so the listeners can pretend it's them. Or so they can pretend to be me for a few hours, even though they're almost all girls, like the *L.A. Times* writer said, except at that moment if they knew what my stomach was going through, none of them would want to be me, and I couldn't stop the show or anything, so for their sake I had to clench my muscles and fight through it and hold everything in while it was bursting to get out.

And then I had the thought of what would happen if I said fuck it, and pulled down my pants and sprayed diarrhea all over their heads and their iPhones shooting unauthorized video and their Be Jonny's Valentine heart-design T-shirts with the picture of me next to a Photoshopped picture of them, just me coating the entire stadium with Jacuzzi jets of endless diarrhea. It was like, you all caused this in me, even though this one time it was the alcohol, but if I didn't have to perform it wouldn't be so bad, so now you get to feel what I'm feeling.

Thinking about that made me laugh, which I never do in concert, and the laugh helped the terrible feeling pass again. I made it through to the end without any problems. I was going to tell Zack about it. He'd find it funny. Except I'd have to make it seem like the diarrhea was from food poisoning and not from the alcohol.

After the concert I ran to the bathroom just in case, and I'm glad I did, since whatever I'd been keeping in was super-excited to get out. When Jane came to pick me up, I must have looked drained, because she asked if I felt okay and I told her I'd had some diarrhea but I was fine now.

But as we pulled up at the hotel, I grabbed my stomach and Jane quickly took me to her room to use the bathroom. I was taking awhile, so she opened the door, and I squeezed my legs together a little to hide my penis, but not all the way or it would look like I had a vagina. "How do you feel?" she asked.

"Not so good."

"What did you eat?"

"A lot."

"Did you sleep okay? Or take any pills?"

She'd turned into Dr. Henson all of a sudden. "No."

She ran cold water over a washcloth and wiped off my face and gave me a glass of water and told me to drink all of it, but it squirted out a few minutes later. *Diarrhea* would be my new word for a song that you listen to and forget right away.

Jane sat on the garbage can near the toilet. It was an expensive-looking garbage can, gold-plated with a sturdy lid, so it supported her. It was kind of stupid to have such a nice garbage can in a place where people go to have diarrhea. She kept sponging up the sweat on my face and feeding me glasses of water and gave me a couple anti-diarrhea pills, but it didn't do much to stop it. "I should call a doctor," she said.

Maybe the doctor would take a blood test or something and find alcohol in there. "Don't," I said. "It's embarrassing. And I'm already feeling better."

She got a call on her phone, told me she'd be back in a minute, and closed the door behind her. I tried to listen, but it was hard because of the door and she was talking quietly and every fifteen seconds or so I'd shoot out another stream of water. All I heard was two sentences: "I'm staying in tonight . . . Not here."

She came back a minute later. "I think you should sleep here with me tonight," she said.

I was trying to figure out who could have called her and what it was about. But she'd lie if I asked. "Okay," I said.

I stayed on the toilet another hour, and Jane got my pajamas from my room. And this is the most embarrassing part, but she ordered the smallest size of adult diapers from the lobby. Somehow they had them, and she made me wear a pair to be safe, because she said she didn't want me shitting on her in bed. I had just enough strength to smile but not enough to laugh.

Jane wore her white satin nightgown to bed, and I climbed in and turned onto my side so my stomach hurt less. She spooned me and rubbed my stomach lightly, which might irritate it, but it was soothing. For a second I pretended it was Lisa Pinto doing it, but I was too sick to get a boner anyway.

She stroked my stomach some more and put her arm under my neck and cradled me inside it. "Can you sing the lullaby?" I asked.

She didn't answer, but she sang it. I liked this part the most this time:

> *Way down yonder*
> *In the meadow*
> *Lies a poor little lamby*
> *Bees and butterflies*
> *Flitting round his eyes*
> *Poor little thing is crying Mammy*

I said, "It's like the bees and butterflies are the diarrhea now flitting round my stomach."

She laughed and said to make sure I told that to Nadine for extra credit. Then she said, "We haven't done a sick night in bed in a while, huh?"

"I think the last time was that Christmas you gave me season tickets to the Dodgers and I ate some bad sushi."

"Right. Two Christmases ago."

On my father's last Christmas with us he gave me my first baseball glove. I didn't start playing Little League till after he left, and I don't remember ever playing with it with him, so he probably left when it was winter. I used it the rest of the time in St. Louis, but we lost it when we moved. It was fake leather and a child's model, and my new glove is premium leather and bigger and was autographed by Albert Pujols when we visited the locker rooms at Angel Stadium last year. It'd be nice to have my first glove still, though.

"Did my father play baseball?" I asked.

Jane's breathing stopped its regular flow for a second. "What do you mean?"

"In high school or something, did he ever play?"

"I don't think so."

"Were the Cardinals his favorite team?"

"Jonathan, I know you're curious," she said. "But it's really best not to think about him. Some people get good luck, and they get two good parents. Some people have bad luck, and they don't get any. And most people end up somewhere in the middle, and that's what you got."

"I only want to know if the Cardinals were his favorite team. Because he lived in St. Louis, but he grew up in Kansas you said, so maybe he liked the Royals."

"I don't know, baby," she said, and kissed the back of my neck. "But it doesn't matter. The Cardinals are *my* favorite team, because of you, and I'm the one who stuck around."

"Why didn't he?" I asked, but I knew what she'd say.

"It's been a long night."

"I just want—"

"We're not discussing this any further. Go to sleep."

She waited a few seconds. "Remember this?" she asked, and gave me a wet zerbert on the back of my neck. I squirmed and giggled, and she pretended to chew my neck with a *myum-myum* noise.

Neither of us took a zolpidem, since it would be dangerous for me to have one and she wanted to be able to wake up in case she had to help me.

CHAPTER 11

Birmingham (First Day)

I felt way better in the morning, and when we got to the parking lot, I couldn't wait to tell Zack my idea about crapping on the audience.

But the Latchkeys were already on their bus, I guess because Jane let me sleep late, so I didn't get the chance. I didn't want to tell the story to Nadine in the middle of tutoring. I wasn't sure she'd get why it was funny and she'd probably ask me to *articulate* why I had that idea. Halfway through our session, Jane came into my room without knocking. Usually she knocks.

"Nadine, I need to speak with Jonathan alone," she said in her business voice. Nadine got out without even gathering her stuff. Jane kept standing over me. "Did you go out to a nightclub with the Latchkeys in Memphis?"

"What do you mean?" I said, but my heart was drumrolling at 120 beats per minute.

"Never mind," she said. "I know the answer already. What I really need to know is if you drank alcohol or not. Don't lie to me."

I wanted to say, But you lie to me all the time, you never tell me where you're going at night, you don't tell me when my father is trying to reach out to me, for all I know he's a nice guy and not a bastard like you say. But I said, "Why are you asking this?"

She showed me her phone. There was an article on a news site head-lined BREATH*A*LYZER-TAKING? 11-YEAR-OLD JONNY VALENTINE ACT-ING DRUNK AT NIGHTCLUB (EXCLUSIVE VIDEO). It had all the standard search-engine terms below, like "Jonny Valentine" and "Celebrity" and the name of the nightclub, plus things like "Scandal" and "Underage Drinking" and "Busted!" and "Citizen Journalism."

There was a low-def phone video of me that Jane played. It was so dark you couldn't see it too good, but they'd edited it to when Zack handed me my glass of ginger ale both times, and paused it and put a circle around the handoff, then it showed me drinking from it and sleeping on the couch and almost falling down when I stood up. I wish Walter had been with us after all and could've beaten up the person who took the video like he did with the child predator in St. Louis. Or at least provided visual buffer with his body. But if he'd allowed me to go, Jane would've fired him on the spot.

"Only a little," I said. "It was an accident, though." She looked at me hard. "I mean it was my fault. I asked for some. I wanted to try it."

"How were you there in the first place?"

"I asked the Latchkeys if they'd take me. I think they were afraid if they didn't, they'd get fired or something."

"Exactly how much did you drink, and does anyone have proof that you did? The entire truth, this time."

I told her the entire truth, mostly. "Two drinks. No one has any proof. I made Zack do it under the table. The other Latchkeys didn't know."

"If that's the truth, we can work with it," she said. "That *is* the whole truth?"

"Yes. I swear."

She told me to finish up with Nadine while she consulted with the label on how to spin this. Then she said, "This is the stupidest thing you've ever done. When we get to Birmingham, you are not to talk to any of the Latchkeys. You hear me?"

I told her yes. Before she left, I said, "I'm sorry, Jane."

She just told Nadine to come in. I didn't tell Nadine what we'd talked about. She must have known something big had happened, especially since I couldn't concentrate on my reading comprehension passages. Jane was going to get even angrier at me later and also at Zack, this was only crisis-control mode when she's actually calmer, and I wanted to warn him but I had no way to do it. But Nadine didn't ask about what happened or lecture me for not paying attention. She was always cool about things like that.

I stayed in my room the rest of the ride to Birmingham, and when we got there, Jane escorted me to my room and told me to stay there all night and that she'd be checking in every hour. I could've called Zack's room, but by now she'd definitely have talked to him already, and I was worried I'd get him in even more trouble. I turned on the TV to see if it was on the news, except Jane had parentally blocked all the channels, so I played Zenon and did my homework but was crap at both.

Jane came in at 9:30. "Here's the story," she said. "No one's come forward saying they saw you ingest alcohol. We're going to say you were drinking soda, and you were tired from being on tour and fell asleep, but that you regret going to an over-twenty-one establishment. If we're lucky, this will be a blip on the radar and pass."

I didn't want to say anything where she'd get upset. This was a worse feeling than when she told me *Valentine Days* had debuted at twenty-eight on Billboard.

"The label's set up a photo op tomorrow at a children's hospital before sound check," she added.

"Is Zack coming, too?"

"No. The Latchkeys have just left."

"Left where?"

"L.A., I suppose. The label is sending a new band on a red-eye. Some Christian rock group. But not *that* Christian. Ticket holders are permitted refunds if they want. We figure we'll get as many additions as refunds."

"They're not on tour anymore?"

"Of course not. We couldn't keep them after this."

I felt like a tough minion had just delivered a sword-punch-kick combo straight to my gut. My dumb, beefy gut.

"It's not their fault! They shouldn't have to leave just because I was stupid!" I said. "You can't do this."

"It's already happened, and they *do* have to leave. I've told you repeatedly, an entourage is the downfall of any celebrity," she said. "What do you care anyway? They probably brought you along just so they could get into the club."

My eyes got all hot, and I could feel I was going to cry, but I fought it back. When you can fake-cry onstage like I do for "Heart Torn Apart," it's easier to stop real tears, too. "That's not true."

"You don't understand how these things work." She stood up from the couch to show the discussion was over. She looked about ten years older to me, with all her wrinkles popping out under the bad lighting.

"It doesn't matter. I don't want the Latchkeys to leave."

"This is to save your fucking career," Jane hissed, like she was trying to hold in her anger the way I was holding in my diarrhea the other night. "The label has a morality clause in your contract they can try to claim you're in breach of, and they'd love any excuse to back out of your next album. You want that to happen? You want to sell the house, go to a shittier label, get no promotion next time, put your career in the toilet?"

"They don't want to back out of my next album," I said. "They just want to do brand extension."

"Everyone knows that's a nicer way of saying rebranding," she said. "And you don't rebrand something unless it's not selling."

Sales for *Valentine Days* weren't great compared to *Guys vs. Girls,* but I wouldn't have thought they were *so* low that they'd drop me after just two albums. A lower-tier label would pick me up in a second, but Jane was right, it wouldn't be the same. I'd be one of those artists who was lucky to crack the charts for a week or two. Everything I'd killed myself for the last two years would be erased. I'd never get fans like the kind the Latchkeys had, and definitely not like what MJ had. We wouldn't be able to afford Walter, either. We might not even *need* Walter. And it wouldn't be worth Jane's time to personally manage me, so she'd get some cut-rate hack to do the job instead. My career would be in the toilet. No one would care about me anymore or remember me. I'd be diarrhea.

"No, I don't want that to happen," I said.

"Then don't argue anymore. *You* screwed up, and this is what happens when you screw up. Internet presales are flat as it is, we don't need some uptight parents' group banning us." She let out a long breath. "At least this is partly on Stacy, for picking them as your opener."

I didn't know presales were flat, too, which meant less money for promoting the MSG concert, which meant even flatter Internet sales. The vicious cycle of marketing budgets. There was nothing I could say. It was my fault.

I listened to the rough cut of the Latchkeys' new album on my iPod in bed. One of the tracks began with a few seconds of Zack talking in the studio. They would cut it out of the real version, but you can hear him say, "For real this time, no more fucking around, especially you, *Timothy*," and everyone laughs when he says *Timothy* before the drummer counts it off. The song itself was B-side material for sure, but I put it on repeat, and every time it looped back, it was like Zack was in my room, coming back to the same moment in a time machine, saying, Good night, little man.

CHAPTER 12

Birmingham (Second Day)

Jane woke me up early in my room with my iPod repeating the Latchkeys song. "We've got an hour booked at the children's hospital," she said. "There'll be photographers from a few glossies on hand."

"Where will you be?" I asked.

She looked at her phone. "I'm coming along."

It made me want to ask why we couldn't have brought along the Latchkeys to help with their PR problem, too. But they probably wanted that image. You can get away with a lot more as a rock band.

The car took me and Jane because it wouldn't look good if we brought Walter, though I was surprised she wasn't taking Rog along for support. The glossies with photographers there had to embargo the information, so there wasn't any other media. It was easy to get in, and the PR rep for the hospital met us and brought us to a waiting room that had been cleared out.

Jane was silent the whole ride in, I guess since she was still pissed and thinking about how to fix the problem, and when the PR woman was telling us about the different wings we could visit, Jane nodded along but it looked like she wasn't even listening.

I stayed in a waiting room they'd cleared out for me while Jane and the PR woman filled out some forms with the three photographers in another room. There were only travel and fashion and home-decoration and golf glossies on the table, but then I saw the front page of the *New York Times,* and at the bottom it said "Jonny Got His . . . Gin? Op-Ed, Page A30."

The article had a drawing of a mother in a hooded robe holding her baby, with this light glowing around both their heads, except the mother's face was a drawing of *my* face, and the baby's face was Jane's face.

> The latest granular amateur video to swallow up Internet bandwidth and tabloid headlines depicts 11-year-old Jonny Valentine, the tweeny-bopper known for such saccharine pop confections as "Guys vs. Girls" and "RSVP (To My Heart)," dizzily imbibing drinks that may or may not have contained alcohol in a Memphis nightclub. That such an exposé registers as merely mild surprise to the jaded public makes it all the more dismaying.
>
> Still, that jaded public gulped down the gossip like it was one of Jonny's possibly non-virgin drinks and pointed fingers everywhere. While any number of parties should bear at least some responsibility—the venue, for starters—there is one person justly deserving the criticism heaped upon her the last 24 hours of the voracious news cycle: Jonny's 39-year-old mother-manager, Jane Valentine, renowned for her own hard-partying lifestyle, who was spotted at another exclusive Memphis club the night her son was reveling with 20-something rock stars whose most-quoted lyric is the deathless couplet "I drink and I drug / No, I don't wanna hug."
>
> Paraphrasing the old public service announcement: It's 10 p.m.: do you know where your parents are?
>
> To be sure, we live in an age of over-parenting, where babies are trained from the womb for the Ivy League and every precious exhalation from junior is deemed worthy

of a picture and status update. Ms. Valentine, who has a reputation in the music industry for meddling too heavily in her son's affairs, might be accused of a Hollywood strain of this practice. Yet a far more egregious fault is the blithe under-parenting she practiced the other night when indulging in behavior befitting someone half her age, desperately seeking attention and stimuli while neglecting the stewardship of her child.

Although we may have not yet fully regressed into an infantile nation of Jane Valentines, disseminating photos of our vacations so that we can feel famous and glamorous for 15 seconds to 15 online acquaintances—but not paying any real attention with our own eyes to our surroundings—we are not far from the tipping point. As a mother of three toddlers juggling a career in law, I feel traitorous in passing judgment on the hardworking and single Ms. Valentine, although I—

I heard the door opening and Jane's voice with the PR rep, so I turned the paper over. The rest of it, I could tell, was slamming Jane for not paying enough attention to me. I wished I could tell them how she stayed in bed with me two nights ago when I was sick. Newspapers always get only half the story. They're even sloppier than glossies, because their deadlines are tighter. Internet media doesn't even try to fact-check.

And this writer made it sound like she was above it all, better than Jane and better than celebrity news, but she was using us for content the same as a gossip blogger to advance her career, and gulping it down just like the public. The people reading it weren't above celebrity news, either.

But now I knew why Jane had to be in the photos and why she was acting so strange today.

The PR rep told me she'd lead me on a tour of a few wings with the photographers trailing behind. The first hallway was all slick and shiny and fluorescent, with nurses and doctors and regular-looking people who were probably parents of the sick kids. The rep opened a door and said this was a playroom for children with leukemia, and several of them were fans of mine, and would I mind singing a song to them?

Jane never likes for me to sing for free, but she jerked her head up and down a few inches, so I said sure. Some of the kids wore masks, and a bunch didn't have hair. There was a TV and some toys and games, with a few parents and staff hanging out, but not much else. It was a pretty depressing place to have to play in.

They clapped a little when they saw me. The PR rep said, "This is Jonny Valentine, and he's a very special guest. He's going to say a few words and sing you a song."

I didn't know anything about saying a few words. Jane was staring at the kids, and one kid in particular. He had no hair, like all the others, and was even skinnier than the rest, almost a skeleton with skin pasted on top, and his cheeks were sunk into his mouth so deep it was like a skull.

"Hi," I said. I was quiet for like five seconds. All I could think of saying was something like, "The one reason I'm here is because we're doing a PR scramble to save my career and you guys have such crap lives it'll make people forget I drank alcohol with the Latchkeys, even though if I saw a photo spread of a pop star doing this I'd see through it in a second, but people only remember the last thing about you."

"It's awesome to be here with you guys," I said.

I sang "You Hurt Me," which sounds good a cappella. It was going fine until I got to the chorus:

> *Oh, yeah, girl, you hurt me*
> *You always make me cry*
> *Oh, yeah, girl, you hurt me*
> *You make me wanna die*

As I was singing the last line I was like, This is a bad choice for kids who might *actually* die. The PR rep stiffened, and I wondered if she knew I was supposed to sing the chorus like six times in a row at the end. And this fucked-up part of me *wanted* to sing it, and get super-falsetto on the word *die,* and sing it in the PR rep's face.

Jane was still staring at the kid with the skull. Every other part of him was all shriveled up but his eyes seemed huge. When I got to the chorus again I replaced *die* with *cry,* even if rhyming with the same word is a hack move. I bet the kids didn't notice, though.

I signed some autographs and posed for photos with them and Jane, and we moved to another wing. This time, I thought I heard the PR rep say, "Now, Jonny, this is the playroom for the bird unit. Do you feel comfortable going in?"

I didn't see why she'd think I'd be uncomfortable around birds, as long as they were in cages, or why there'd even *be* birds at a children's hospital, so I said, "Totally."

I realized my mistake the second we walked in and saw a few kids who had parts of skin like the leftover cheese mixed with tomato sauce that gets stuck to the top of a pizza box. The PR rep explained that they were kids who had recovered enough from their burns to play, but a bunch of them still had to wear gloves and masks. I stared at my red Nikes, but I couldn't help turning my head to look, like I was checking where Tyler Beats was on the charts. She whispered, "Sure you're okay?" and I knew I couldn't back out of it, so I mumbled yes and went on with her.

A nurse brought us over to one blond girl around my age who wasn't burned that much, at least her face wasn't at all, but you could see a big bandage like a tank top on her chest before it got covered by her blue hospital shirt.

She got excited and said she owned everything of mine and listened to it all the time. I thanked her and told her I needed the love of my true fans like her and sang "U R Kewt," but as I was singing I had another fucked-up thought, which was that when she grew up she might have a beautiful face but if a guy ever got her shirt off he'd lose his boner, so she'd dream of meeting a guy who loved her even though her breasts were all burned, but she'd always try to hide it until she found that person, and the more she hid it the more she'd be embarrassed by it, until her being embarrassed by it would be *worse* than the actual burns, so after a while if she finally found someone who *did* love her still, she'd think something was wrong with them for loving her and wouldn't want them anymore, and everyone in this unit and in the whole hospital was like a character whose body was damaged bad in Zenon and couldn't hardly walk anymore and what didn't kill them did *not* make them stronger.

When I finished the song I told her to always follow her dreams, and that if you're following your dreams no one can ever take anything away from you, which is even more of a crap idea for someone like her. I whispered to the PR rep that I had to use the bathroom, and she got the hint because she said we could move on somewhere else. Before I could go, though, the girl said, "You know why I love your songs?"

I said no. She said, "Your songs are always nice to listen to." That was the most broad-spectrum compliment I ever heard, but I said thanks and walked away. "Most of the time they're pretty," the girl added, and I stopped. "But once in a while they're not. That's my favorite thing."

"You mean the lyrics?" I asked.

"No, the words are," she said. "But the way you sing them isn't always. Even when the song is about having fun, sometimes it sounds like you aren't having any at all. It's like the song is happy, but you're not. Like when someone's smiling in a picture, but their eyes are sad. It's really beautiful."

I couldn't believe a tween girl had this response to my song. This was the sort of thing a critic would write about a Latchkeys song, or even Vanessa would say to Zack about one of their songs. Or how someone might feel about an MJ song. It was way better than the usual stuff I heard from fans, about how they listened to me nonstop and followed all the news about me and I was their favorite singer. They only listened to me nonstop because we courted the radio stations, and they followed the news about me because our publicists fed material to the media each week, and I was their favorite because the label had marketed me to them. If none of that happened, they wouldn't actually care about the music. This girl did. I wanted to ask her if she meant I sounded punk, but she wouldn't know what punk was and Jane would wonder why I was asking that and she was signaling with her eyebrows for me to hurry up, so I said, "Thank you."

I found the bathroom down the hall and locked myself in a stall and tried to pee, but nothing came out. While I was pushing like crazy but nothing was happening, I wondered if I could get hard now if I tried, after everything I'd seen, like if it would still work properly. At first I couldn't, even when I pictured Lisa Pinto and Vanessa's legs and the time I walked in on one of my dancers changing in Houston.

I opened my eyes and looked down. A tiny black hair poked out of the skin around all the peach fuzz. I pulled on it and it didn't come out. *Then* I got hard, and I even had to wait a little for it to go down before I left, since I didn't want to be walking around dying kids with a super-hard boner and a grin on my face after finding my first pube.

I was going to turn left to join up with everyone outside the burn unit, but to my right there was a glass window with golden light coming from inside. All these rows of babies were inside, hooked up with wires inside clear rectangles. "What's here?" I called to the PR rep, who was talking with the photographers and Jane.

"I see you've found our premature infants," she said.

"Jonny, don't wander off," Jane called.

"What are they inside?" I asked the PR rep.

"Those are called incubators. They simulate the mother's tummy for babies that are born too early, to help protect them."

"Cool," I said, which was stupid, but I was really thinking about how they were like the force-field spell in Zenon. "Can I see them?"

"Yes, but we have to be very quiet, and it's best not to touch them," she said. "They need some attention, but too much isn't good for them."

Jane was like, "You know, I think we're running behind schedule."

"I want to go in," I said.

"We're very late," she said.

The PR rep said, "It'll only take a minute."

"Thank you, but we're late to Jonny's sound check," she said, which was a lie. Sound check wasn't until after I tutored with Nadine and we could always cut that short and make up the time later.

"I'm going in." Jane wouldn't stop me now.

"I'll wait out here," she said. Her face was icy, the most since she'd been at the hospital, even more than in the burn unit. Her body was turned sideways, and she hadn't looked inside the window once the whole time.

It was weird. When we walked into the room, I felt like I'd already been here, right in the room with all the premature babies, like at the start of the tour or something. That drawing of Jane as a baby in the *New York Times* had mixed me up. But I stopped thinking about it once I saw them. They were like half the size of regular babies and were sleeping in their little boxes, with bluish skin and pinched eyes and tiny arms and legs and scraps of hair. One of the nurses asked us not to go closer than a few feet and told the photographers not to snap any photos, so we stood and watched.

I wished I could hold one of them, since I'd never held a baby before and they were still pretty cute. It's kind of hard not to find a cute baby. And it's just as hard *to* find a cute adult. Jane says that's a reason I'll maintain my appeal, my naturally boyish looks. The second I develop facial hair I've got to learn how to shave.

The nurse talked about the challenges premature babies face, and it sounded bad, like a lot of them develop brain and vision problems, and unlike most of the other kids in the hospital who'd gotten bad luck later in life but at least they probably had some normal years first, these babies were damaged from the start all because they were born too soon. It could happen to anyone, but it happened to these babies. I could've been one of these babies, or the girl in the burn unit, or the kid with leukemia, or the girl in the wheelchair in St. Louis, or that fat woman Mary Ann in Schnucks, or Walter or Nadine or Rog, or the PR rep, or even Tyler Beats, which is the best of all those, but it wouldn't be anything I chose, just something that happened to me, and maybe you choose a few things after that, but it's mostly not up to you.

Right away I wanted to get out of the premature infants room and to leave the hospital completely, so I whispered to the PR rep that I was ready to go to my sound check, and she led us all out. Jane was typing on her phone a few feet away from the window with her back to us.

We went to the PR rep's office, and she told me I could wait in there while her and Jane and everyone dealt with photo release forms in another room. Her computer was on, and the screen showed the hospital's website. I didn't wait, I just went around to her side of the desk and opened a new window and got into my email account. As I waited to sign in, I noticed a framed candid photo next to the printer of the PR rep and this bald guy with a big smile and a bulky polo shirt and dorky jean shorts and their son, hiking somewhere.

My email had tons of spam again. One message said "How to become rich and famous in 30 days!" which sounds like something only idiots would fall for, but I *did* do it almost that fast, if you time it from when Jane uploaded my first YouTube videos to when we signed with the label. Most successful musicians take much longer to make it, Rog always tells me, and I'm the lucky exception, and he thinks that when stories like mine get so much press, it gives young musicians the wrong idea that they can hit it big overnight, so they don't work as hard at their craft, they just hope someone will come along and discover them on the Internet.

I searched for Albert's name, and my stomach jumped up to my chest because there was one new email from him, written a few days after I'd sent him the photo. I opened it but it was longer than his others and I was afraid of Jane coming back and catching me reading it.

I've had to print Nadine's homework instructions from hotel printers before, so I figured out how to print it. Except the printer got jammed, and I had to yank out the smeared page and reprint.

I heard different voices down the hall. The page started printing, and I signed out of email and closed the window and hoped the printer would work this time or else I was screwed.

The voices were coming closer. The page came out halfway and stopped for a second and I nearly punched the printer, because it was like it kept delivering a premature infant. But it restarted and got the rest out. I grabbed it and folded it into my pocket and sat in the guest chair and pretended to look bored while my blood drummed a hip-hop beat inside my head as Jane came in with the PR rep to get me. I couldn't get out of that hospital soon enough, and neither could Jane. In the car service, she said, "I hope those vultures are satisfied."

I didn't get a chance to read the email since she took me straight to my room at the hotel and waited with me until Nadine showed up for our session. The letter was like a heat source in Zenon burning up my pocket as Nadine chattered on about word problems and why water freezes and other stuff I couldn't focus on. Finally we took a break and I went to the bathroom and read the email.

> So it looks like you might really know Jonathan or maybe I am writing to Jonathan himself. Please forgive me for being suspicious. When I tried to reach out in the past I only heard from people who are pulling my leg. If you aren't him, please pass this on to him:
>
> You must be turning 12 pretty soon. I don't remember much about being 12 except that was when I started thinking about girls. I'm sure you have a lot more options than I did! If I'm able to send you a birthday present, I'll do it.
>
> Did you know I played drums in high school? I was even in a band for a year. We called ourselves the Wrecking Balls. It was heavy metal. We were pretty bad, so I know you didn't get your musical talent from me!
>
> I couldn't get in touch the last few years on account of being in Australia and I feel awful about it. Jane doesn't want anything to do with me. It's hard to make amends when you're not allowed to make them. There are many things I would like to say to you but I don't feel comfortable saying them over an email. But I do want to say one thing, better late than never. I'm sorry to you for not being there because there are some things in life you can't replace, and one of them is a father's love.
>
> Al
>
> P.S. When you have your concert in Cincinnati I might be there too.

I had a million questions. Did he mean he'd be *at* my concert, or he was only going to be *in* Cincinnati? And if I even wanted to meet him, was it against the law because of the letter in Jane's room? And when he tried to contact me before, did he go through the label and no one believed him or Jane stopped him like he made it sound and like I bet she did with Michael Carns because his image wasn't cool enough, or did he just put it out on the Internet and I never saw it?

I pictured me and my father taking a plane to Sydney for the music festival there I almost played in and him inviting all the friends he'd made there to come hear me. He'd introduce me to the crowd, and he'd be as famous in Sydney as me, and he'd manage my Australia/New Zealand tour because he had so many connections there. He'd be like the Australian Jane. Except he'd also play drums to back me up, and for the drum solo in "RSVP (To My Heart)," when it's supposed to sound like my heart beating faster and faster because the girl just sent her RSVP to be my girlfriend, I'd do my trademark spin move right next to my father while he played, and you wouldn't be able to tell who the crowd was cheering for, him or me, because they all knew him and they didn't really know me since I didn't have a foothold in the Australian market yet. And at night we'd hang out with his Australian friends, who were normal guys who had no idea who I was. They just liked my father.

Then I figured out where I'd heard the words *better late than never* before. I'd been at this boy Richard Nester's birthday party. It was a fancy white house, with a huge lawn we played Red Rover on. All the other parents picked up their kids at the end, and after a while it was just me and Richard and Richard's parents. They kept calling Jane at Schnucks, but she wasn't picking up or available, and when they asked me where my father worked, I said he didn't work at a place, my mother did, and even at that age I could tell they were a little embarrassed for me. Finally he showed up in our crap Dodge, and he didn't even come out to get me or apologize to them, he only honked a few times from the big circular driveway they had. When I got in the car, he said, "Well, better late than never, kid." He must say that a lot. In the car he talked on his phone to Jane and got angry, and instead of going home he drove for a long time on the highway without talking. I didn't know where we were going and knew *he* didn't have a plan, either, but there was something cool about that. We ended up at a diner on the highway and he said I could order whatever I wanted, he didn't care, so I ate French toast for dinner, and by the time we got home it was dark. They got in one of their big fights, I remember. They must've broken up soon after, because that's the last time I can remember him driving me anywhere.

Nadine called out that break was over. I folded the letter again. It would have been smarter to tear it up and flush it down the toilet, but I didn't want to do it. I kind of liked having it inside my pocket, even though it would've done bad on one of Nadine's composition tests since it didn't use evocative language, which was actually what we did next.

I was writing the composition, on Nadine's logic question:

> The police are separately questioning you and your friend about a crime, and offer you both the same deal. You can either testify against your friend (say he is guilty) or claim he is innocent. (1) If only one of you testifies against the other, then the person who testified is freed, and his partner is put in jail for 12 months. (2) If you both claim the other is innocent, you are both put in jail for 1 month. (3) If you both testify against each other, you are both put in jail for 3 months. What should you do?

I couldn't think straight, because the last few words from my father's email kept playing on repeat in my head, and it was like I saw them written all over the walls in a jail cell: a father's love a father's love a father's love a father's love a father's love

I finally said, "You should say the other guy's innocent and hope he says it, too, because then you both have just a month in jail."

Nadine explained that you should actually say the other guy is guilty, because you can't guarantee he'll cooperate and say you're innocent. So if he *does* say you're innocent, you get freed, and if he says you're guilty, it's not as bad as if you said he was innocent, and the other guy is probably using the same strategy, so you have to plan for that. I bet Jane would've figured it out even if she hasn't studied logic, because of her street smarts.

"That's not very nice to do, if it's your friend," I said.

"Well, it's the right answer for a logic problem, but I agree. In real life I'd rather hang out with someone who says his friend is innocent," she said. "Hey, you doing okay today?"

"I'm fine."

"I forgive you for being somewhat distracted. You've had a lot of stressors recently."

"I'm good at handling stressors."

She smiled and said, "I apologize for the pop-psychology jargon."

"I forgive you, too," I said.

This time she laughed. She has a pretty laugh. I should tell my next producer to sample it and see if we could use it somehow. I bet she wouldn't charge us, either.

"Maybe you'll be okay after all," she said, like she was watching me from very far away.

"I'll be fine. This is a blip on the radar. The vultures will move onto the next thing in a minute."

"That's not what I meant," she said. "But, yes, that's true."

I didn't ask what she meant. The last line of my father's email was still bouncing around in my head as we drove to the venue and during sound check and in the star/talent room before the concert and while the Christian opener, which was called 3 Days Dead, played their fake alt-rock. They'd been drinking beer preshow, which if it wasn't against Christian protocol, it still probably wasn't the most religious thing to do and definitely not professional, and it got me pissed that the Latchkeys had to go home when these guys were way worse people and musicians. The concert finally snapped me out of it. You really do have to focus when you're singing and dancing, and it ended up being a strong show, since the crowd was into it and I fed off their energy. There were all these signs up about the nightclub incident like LET THE HATERS HATE, WE ♥ U JONNY and *THIS* BIRD WILL ALWAYS BEE THERE FOR YOU and NO MATTER WHAT, YOU ARE THE ANGEL TO MY EYES. I told my instrumentalists not to come out for the second encore, and did an a cappella version of "You Hurt Me" instead because I liked how it sounded with the kids with leukemia even though it was an idiotic choice for them. At the end of the concert I stayed out extra-long when they were cheering and invited up *two* cute girls onstage, which I never do, since it looks like I'm not a one-girl guy, which is the image we want to promote, and looped my arms around them and let them kiss me on each cheek at once.

But the minute I got back into the star/talent room, I reread my father's email and still couldn't figure out if he meant he was coming to my Cincinnati concert. I was hoping for more clues to his life, like what sports he liked, or what he thought of my music. I'd want him to like it, but the idea of some guy in his forties listening to my music was weird, too. Except he wasn't just some guy, he was my father, so maybe it was okay.

Jane came in but I'd put the letter away and was unwinding with Zenon, and she told me she was going out for a late dinner with a promoter, and Walter would take me home and she'd see me in the morning before our ride to Nashville. "You sure that's a good idea?" I asked.

"I'm having dinner with another adult in a restaurant, Jonathan," she said. "I think that's allowed."

I was going to tell her about the *New York Times* article, but I kept quiet because this meant she'd be gone from her room and I had a chance to get inside it and write back.

Me and Walter took the car service back to the hotel, and because it was our first real face time since the scandal broke, he told me not to give a shit about it, it was just tight-asses who had nothing else to do and they'd quickly move on to the next thing because they love getting worked up over bullshit so they don't have to think about things like wars and people starving and bankers stealing from everyone, and anyway part of being a rock star is acting wild, and I reminded him, "I'm not a rock star, I'm a pop star," since the difference is that rock stars might seem bigger to people like him but they also drive off a lot of listeners with either their sound or their image, so most only secure a niche audience, but pop stars have a chance at dominating the entire market because there's fewer offensive elements. To be a rock star, you basically *have* to push your freakiness, but pop stars in my mold have to be more relatable and push their normalness, which is not the regular normal, it's like a super-normal, so all I'm supposed to talk about in interviews is sports and girls and spending time with my family and friends even though the only family I see is Jane and now I'll probably never talk to Michael Carns again, but if fans don't love you as a person, they won't love your music.

He took me to my room and made sure everything was secure before going to his room. I waited until I heard his door click shut to make sure he hadn't gone down to the hotel bar, and waited another twenty minutes to be safe. Then I pulled my Florida Marlins cap down and wore sunglasses and went down to the lobby. If I got busted by Jane, I'd say it was her job to be watching me, not going out at night. Anyway, I wasn't nearly as scared this time, now that I'd done it by myself in Vegas and with Zack in Memphis. Jonny Tubman.

I found a woman with a helmet of dyed blond hair at a desk who looked young enough to recognize me, and went up when no one else was around and took my hat and sunglasses off and said, "Hi, I'm Jonny Valentine, and I'm a guest in your hotel."

"Oh, hi!" she said in this super-friendly Southern accent. "I heard you were—how may I help you, Mr. Valentine?"

"I need to get into my mother's room, but she's out. It's under Jane Valentino, room 1722. I'm 1723."

She typed on her computer. It always sounds the same when workers like her type on a computer, like a million little clicks in a row. It's got to be depressing spending ten thousand hours to be that good at a job like that.

"I see something was messengered here for you today," she said.

I wasn't expecting anything, and when we got sent print clips, they usually went to Jane. I gave her my label's name and asked if it was from them.

"Bergman Ellis Jacobson and Walsh," she read off the screen. "It sounds like a law firm."

"And it's for me?" I asked, which was stupid, because then she read more closely and said, "Oh, my mistake. It's for Jane Valentino. They mixed up the room numbers."

That was really dumb of me. I could've read it without Jane knowing, then returned it. It wasn't worth trying to get it from the woman now, when I was already hoping to get access to Jane's room. She typed some more.

"I'm terribly sorry, Mr. Valentine, but I'm not authorized to let anyone but Ms. Valentino into the room," she said.

"But I'm her son. That's the name she uses for hotels. We've both been all over the news."

"I know, but we'd need her to list you, and she hasn't done that. I could call her on the number listed here, if you want?"

"No," I said, probably too quickly. I slowed down. "She's at a big business meeting with a promoter and she told me not to interrupt her. This is important. My leukemia medication is in her room and I need to take it."

"You take medication for leukemia?" the woman asked.

"To prevent it," I said. "It's to prevent me from getting leukemia, and it's really dangerous if I miss a day. It runs in my family. My father had it."

I couldn't tell if she believed it or not. People get freaked out by anything to do with health. "I can't call her?" she asked again.

"No, she'll get worried and it'll ruin her meeting. Please, miss, I have to get in there."

She peered around like Angela did in Vegas, but she was slicker and did it just with her eyes. She made a key-card and said she was only doing this because it was an emergency. I asked if she wanted an autograph, but she said, "Um, thanks, that's all right."

I sped back to Jane's room and listened outside the door and went in. Her computer was in the bedroom, which was lucky, since sometimes she brought it to concerts. If she caught me using it, I'd say I was reading about the nightclub incident and my own key-card worked on her door.

While it booted up I looked around, but I didn't see any more legal letters, only her usual junk and clothes on the floor and even more dumped on the bed, though I kept the light off so I didn't get a great look. Except she had a copy of *The New Yorker* magazine open and facedown on the desk, which didn't make sense because she never reads it except once when they ran a profile of Ronald and it mentioned me a few times. When I turned it over, though, I saw why:

SHOUTS & MURMURS
RACIAL HARMONIES

BY ANDY TWEEDY

Jonny Valentine's concert last night was anemic even by today's nadir of pop-music standards. One would be hard-pressed to imagine a hypothetical performance an audience might find more alienating.
—The Kansas City *Star*.

When my manager's manager told me I'd been invited to perform at the historic Apollo Theater in Harlem, I was so excited that one of my handlers screamed for me with excitement.

The day before my performance, an old movie called "The Jazz Singer" was on TV. The star, Al Jolson, had really great makeup, with black paint all over his face. Not only did he look badass, but it seemed like the perfect way to cover a pimple—and, boy, I had a honker right on my button nose! It also made his lips look a lot fuller, and I've always been insecure about my thin lips. So I sent my handler's manager's handler to buy me some industrial-strength Midnight Black Hole paint and bright red gloss to make my lips really pop.

I wanted to surprise everyone, so I didn't put on the paint until just before I went onstage. There was another movie I'd seen a couple weeks before that I also thought was cool, because it starred a guy with a kick-ass mustache. I don't have much facial hair, but I let it grow in the week leading up to the awards, then just before I put on the black paint I shaved everything but the mustache so I could look like him. I also had the movie playing behind me on a big screen with a close-up of the guy I was trying to look like, so everyone would know the mustache was on purpose. Check it out sometime, even if foreign movies normally suck— "Triumph of the Will."

It was time to sing my song called "I Like Girls with Curves." But I wanted to do something special for this performance and tweak my lyrics a little. Fortunately, there was a book lying around backstage that had a similar title. I just plucked out a few lines and mixed them into the verses, and changed the chorus to "I Like, and Whole-heartedly Endorse, the Bell Curve."

Yet the star is only as good as

his backup dancers. It was almost Halloween, so I thought my dancers should dress up—and my all-time favorite costume is ghosts. My second favorite? You guessed it: dunces. I got all my dancers ghost outfits with dunce caps, and told them to cover their faces, too. Hey, *I'm* the star, you know? But I felt bad that they weren't getting as much attention, so I researched which shape is most visible from a distance, got them some wood in that shape, and had them light the wood on fire for better visibility. I also wanted to single out the three dancers who'd been with me longest—Krista, Carl, and Kiersten—by putting up a banner with the first letters of their three names. Except the guy who made the banner thought Carl was spelled with a "K"! Maybe we'll get a discount next time. They were doing this new dance I'd choreographed in which they go around in a circle totally in sync on horses. Aww, yeah: Ghosts in dunce caps on horseback with flaming crosses!

In the middle of all this perfection, something went wrong—suddenly the big-screen video stopped, the background music cut, and the house lights went down. What a low-budget production! The TV crew was still filming, though, so to show everyone I was against "The Man" and wasn't afraid to stand up to corporate America, I started yelling about how cheap they were. I've been studying vocabulary lists—stay in school, kids!—so instead of saying "cheap," I decided to whip out one of my bigger words.

"Y'all are niggardly!" I shouted. "Goddamn niggardly! Get 'em for being niggardly!"

I then repeated the word *niggardly* seventeen times.

Everyone started talking, probably to ask what *niggardly* meant. "Oh, I'm sorry," I said. I figured I had to speak down to the level of people who don't understand big words, so I should have shortened it and referred to it just by its first letter. "I guess I should've called it 'the N-word.' Is that better?"

I kept getting calls after the show from a group named the NAACP, which I assume stands for the National Association for Awesome Costume Parties. They probably want to know where I got my ghost costumes and dunce caps.

I'm going to ask the NAACP if they want to sponsor my next tour through the South! ♦

I recognized the writer's name, because he flew in from New York to hang out with me for a day for a softball profile in a music glossy last year. I must have made him a few months' rent on his crap apartment by now. Not only did he not sound like me at all in this article, but we only released "I Like Girls with Curves" as a digital single because we knew it was weak. I understood the jokes about the KKK and a bunch of the rest, but I didn't think it was that funny. People in the cultural-elite demo usually aren't. They just like making fun of my music so they feel special about liking their own boring classical music that no one listens to anymore, the same way that *New York Times* writer bashed Jane to feel better about how good a mother she is. They're probably even happy that no one else listens to classical music now, so they can feel *really* special. If you listened to Mozart when he was alive, it was like saying you listened to MJ. And they're just as into reading and talking about celebrities, only their celebrities are politicians and serious musicians and writers and movie directors. Jane's big into publicity that reaches people high up on the cultural food chain, though, even if they're way out of my fan base, because there's always a trickle-down effect. I'm sure she was happy about this.

I almost forgot what I'd come in for, so I signed into my email and read my father's letter again, and it was different here, since it was like he'd written these words himself, not ones I'd printed out later.

I'd had all these questions before for him, but now I didn't know what to write. Or I knew some things, but I couldn't click on the reply button and type them in. I just stared at it.

I heard the elevator ding down the hall and two people laughing, and one of them sounded a lot like Jane, so I signed out of the email fast, which I was getting a lot of practice at, and closed the computer, which made the room completely dark, and the voices were louder and one of them was *definitely* Jane's, I can ID her laugh a mile away, and I remembered there were closets in the living room, so I ran out of the bedroom and almost tripped over a suitcase, but I heard Jane sliding her key-card and it kept beeping from her not doing it right, and I didn't have time to hide in the closet so I crouched in the small space between the back of the big white U-shaped couch and the wall. I was doing that a lot lately, like I was in the movies. General Jonny, hiding from the enemy.

"Abracadabra," Jane said, slowly. She was drunk.

There weren't any sounds for a few seconds as the door shut, and I didn't want to lift my head. But then there were footsteps, and something bumped hard against one of the sides of the couch. A man's voice, low and steady, said, "Don't fucking move." I couldn't tell whose it was, but it sounded familiar.

"Yes, sir," said Jane in this little-girl voice that was a million miles from what she used when she was bitching out the TV producer. I could tell she was putting it on, that she wasn't actually in danger, but the guy sounded like he wasn't pretending at all.

Then shoes hitting the ground one after another, high heels falling to the floor, a zipper unzipping, jeans being shaken off, keys and a belt and change jingling and clanging when they hit the ground, and the man saying, "Take off your clothes and stand there." I still couldn't place his voice.

I held my breath, since I was sure they could hear me breathing. Once you pay attention to the sound of your breathing or your heartbeat, it's like the loudest sound in the world and you have a hard time doing it regularly. It's the reason why you're supposed to be *aware* of your breathing while you sing but you should never *think* about it, because you'll screw it up.

The man said, "You like being my little slut, don't you?" and Jane again said, "Yes, sir," and I heard a loud slap and Jane moaned and the guy said, "Shut up," and Jane said, "I'm sorry, sir," and heat rose up in my body like it wanted me to jump over the couch and tackle him, even though I knew from her voice that Jane was playing along. But I'd get in *major* trouble.

My eyes had adjusted to the darkness, and I peeked up a tiny bit to see if I could watch them without them catching me, since their eyes probably hadn't adjusted yet and they were off to the side. Jane's back was to me, and the guy was standing in front of her totally naked except for dark socks and his boner sticking straight up out of his pubes. A man looks weird with just long socks and a boner. I couldn't see him too good, only that his arms were covered with tattoos.

Oh, man. The head crew guy. Bill.

Bill had joined us when we began assembling the crew for this tour and getting the stagecraft down, so the longest this could've been going on was a few months, but he'd never been at our place in L.A. He didn't talk to me much.

"God, you're so beneath me," Bill said.

"I'm sorry," Jane said in her little-girl voice.

"You don't even deserve my cock tonight," he said. "I'm just gonna jerk off on you."

"Yes, sir," she said again, and I heard him jerking off. After a minute he said, "I need moisturizer or something," and she ran in and out of the bathroom and handed him something, and he took a few more minutes, and I closed my eyes and thought of me telling Lisa Pinto she was my little slut and her calling me *sir*, but the way Jane said it, and then Bill took a step toward her and made this sound like an animal growling.

He went to the bathroom and peed and used the sink while Jane pulled a bunch of tissues from a box and wiped herself off. Bill came back and Jane went to the bathroom, and he sat down on the couch. I peeked over again. His hands were behind his head like a pillow, and it looked like his eyes were closed. He was still naked. His penis was small now and hanging to one side. That looked even stranger than a boner, a grown man with a soft penis that wasn't all that much bigger than mine.

When Jane came back, she sat down next to him and asked, "Want some?" Bill took a long gulp of water before giving it back.

"It's my birthday on the sixth," Jane said. Bill grunted, though it wasn't like one of the grunts from before. "Maybe we could do something special that night."

"Maybe," Bill said. "Where are we gonna be?"

"Cleveland."

"Beautiful," he said. "You can really paint Cleveland red in early February."

She was quiet until she said, "I had to go to the children's hospital today. For photo ops."

"Yeah?" he asked, but it was more just saying it than a question. "How was it?"

"I'm never going to a children's hospital again."

"It's no worse than a regular hospital, when you get down to it."

"It is, to me."

"Right," Bill said. "My sister lost a baby, too, you know."

Too? I almost asked.

"You told me," Jane said. "You said hers was stillborn. Mine lived two weeks."

I thought it was hard not to jump out before when he slapped her, but it took everything in me to stay still now. I couldn't remember Jane being pregnant. Maybe it was before I was born. It wasn't something I could ask her about normally, but now I really couldn't be like, Oh, I know about it because I heard you talking about it with Bill after he jerked off on you in your hotel room I'd broken into so I could email a guy who says he's my father but he still may be a child predator.

And she didn't lose *me*. I was right next to her. Closer than she would've wanted.

There was a long silence. Jane said, "I missed you. I don't like going this long without seeing you."

"It's only been three days."

"I know." I could hear her tracing her fingers over his chest. "Still."

For some reason this made me even more upset. I tried to remember all the other times Jane had said she was meeting with a promoter or something so she wasn't coming back to the hotel. Sometimes I bet it was real, and the rest it was Bill.

"You want to go to the bedroom?" she asked.

"Mmm." He stretched and stood up. "I gotta go."

"Can't you just stay a little?"

"You know I have to check in with Elsa before she goes to sleep, and I won't do it from here."

"You can come back after."

"I never sleep well with you, and we're loading up early tomorrow."

"Okay," she said, even more quietly, like she'd really been slapped this time.

He put his clothes on there, and when he was dressed he gave her a quick kiss on the mouth and said, "We'll do something nice for your birthday, okay?" and she said, "Uh-huh," and he walked out quickly and let the door shut on its own behind him.

Jane didn't move, but I knew she was awake, probably with her eyes open. I could almost hear her thinking in the dead quiet of the room. I didn't know what was going through her head, but I was sure it wasn't about my digital apps or the Asian market or anything like that. Finally she went to the bathroom, and I thought about making a run for it, but it was risky. A pill bottle opened with a popping sound. It was smarter to wait it out.

From now on, when I looked at Bill, I'd know he was cheating on his wife. I kind of hoped I'd run into him in the hall, even if it meant getting in trouble. I'd ask him if Elsa was a fan, because I could make a courtesy call to her to say hi. Just to make him sweat.

And when Jane told me she had to go to an unexpected dinner with a regional promoter, I'd know she was lying. It's also probably why she defended Bill for the heart-shaped swing. Plus it made me pissed that of all the guys on the tour, she chose him. He was muscular and good-looking and the best at his job, but he was an asshole. If she had to pick someone, it should've been Zack. He's not much younger than some of the other guys she's been with.

She started snoring like a quivering bird from the bedroom, and I climbed out carefully from behind the couch and left. When I got to my room, I called the label. It was late, but someone would be there. A girl picked up, and I identified myself as Client 463, password *Breathtaking*, and asked if I could get Zack Ford's cell phone number. She said he was no longer a client of the label but they still had it on file.

I called his number. It rang a few times, and I thought it was going to go to voice mail, but then Zack said hello.

"It's Jonny," I said, so he didn't think I was a girl again.

"Jonny," he said in a flat voice. That was it.

"Where are you?" I asked.

"In my kitchen. Making couscous. It's a glamorous life."

I'd meant what city, in case Jane was lying about that, too, but she'd told the truth. "So you're not with the label anymore?"

"Nope," he said. "Their lawyers found a variety of clever ways to cleave us. Cleave in the sense of *separate,* not *join.* That's called a *contronym,* by the way, when a word means its own opposite."

If he'd stayed on the tour I could've learned all this stuff, plus new bands I'd never heard of and ideas about movies and smart jokes. Now I couldn't.

"I'm sorry I made it so you had to leave," I said. "If I'd known, I wouldn't have even come to the nightclub with you."

"It's okay. We'll find another label."

"And I wouldn't have had any of the alcohol."

Right when I said it, I could hear him tense up in his kitchen in L.A. "Anyway, it was nice talking to you, Jonny," he said. "And watch out for yourself out there. It's a cutthroat industry." He hung up before I could even say good-bye.

Maybe he thought I was taping him for a tabloid or something, except that would make me look worse than him. That was probably the last chance I'd get to talk to him. I didn't blame him. I'd left Michael Carns behind in St. Louis and I'd left Zack behind in Memphis, even if officially we made him leave. I was like the criminal who told the police my friend was guilty.

CHAPTER 13

Nashville (First Day)

The next morning I watched out the bus window as Bill directed the final loading of the eighteen-wheelers near us. He just did it like normal, like nothing had happened the night before. A silver wedding ring was on his finger. Elsa.

I told Walter I was getting air for a second and stepped outside and went up to Bill. "Hey, is Els—" It wasn't worth him asking Jane how I knew his wife's name. "Is there anything else to know about the Nashville setup? Is it standard or special prep?"

He said, "Standard." He never said more to me than he needed to.

Jane looked hungover but not too bad on the bus. I waited until we were a few hours on the road and she'd had a chance to hydrate before I reminded her that she promised I could go with Walter tonight to visit his daughters and I was giving them a game system and a copy of The Secret Land of Zenon that was supposed to be waiting at the hotel for me.

"Sure," she said. Her eyes were closed and she was reclining in her seat. I was going to ask her to call the hotel to confirm the game system was there, but I didn't want to push it. She asked Rog to sit next to her, which was my cue to leave her alone and let them talk.

At the hotel, before I left with Walter in the car service, Jane called to say she was staying in that night. I wasn't sure if it was because she was seeing Bill or she was actually staying in. "Do you want to come with us?" I asked.

"No, thanks," she said, and she was so tired-sounding, I was pretty sure she was hanging at the hotel. "You sure you don't want to stay in tonight, too? You don't have many days off coming up."

"I promised Walter."

"Just because you promised doesn't mean you *have* to do it. We could order room service, watch pay-per-view."

"I love hanging out with Walter," I said. "He's the best."

"All right. Do what you want," she said, and hung up.

"Yeah, and do what you want with Bill every other night," I said to the dial tone. "Maybe I'll die tonight like your other baby you never told me about."

We brought the game system and Zenon along in the car, and Walter was jittery in the backseat. He hadn't seen his daughters since last summer, or his ex-wife, Callie. He's all calm when he has to push away a hundred fans who might stampede me and him, but seeing his own family got him nervous.

Callie's house was in an okay part of town, with streets that had some trees and grass, but her house was kind of depressing. It looked thinner than my bedroom and connected to the houses on both sides of it, with flimsy wood that was painted yellow and peeling. Walter was *really* jittery when we walked up to the house and he rang the bell. Callie opened the door in her winter coat. She wasn't fat, which I was expecting, but she also wasn't cute. Walter wasn't that handsome, either, so I guess they were a good match. "Hi, Walter," she said.

"Hey, Callie," he said.

He waited a second before leaning forward to hug her. I'd never seen him hug anyone before. Standing there for five seconds with them was so awkward, it felt as painful as sitting on the tour bus for eight hours. He returned to his spot, and like he'd just remembered I was there, too, he said, "This is Jonny."

"I know," she said. "It's great to finally meet you, Jonny."

I said hi and handed her the game system in a box and told her it was for her daughters. She thanked me and set it down inside and said she'd head out and would be back at eight. She called out, "Girls, your father's here!" and walked out before they could get there.

They were six and seven and ten years old, and the youngest two, Danny and Pris, squealed a lot when they saw Walter and jumped on him and called him Daddy, which was weird for me to see. They didn't know who I was. But the oldest, Sally, was quieter, and she only let Walter hug her the way Callie did, with her arms mostly by her sides. She knew who I was, so maybe that was part of why she was shy. It's okay to be shy if you're a girl, but it's really bad if you're a boy, like Michael is, except a lot of it was from being on camera. I'm less shy on camera than I am off it. Someone's going to watch it later, so you have to step it up.

"What do you girls want to eat for dinner?" Walter asked.

"Pancakes," Pris said.

"The pancake place," Danny said.

"They're into pancakes now," Sally said.

"Okay," Walter said. "How about we make them here?"

"The pancake place," Danny said again.

"You sure?" Walter asked.

I could tell Walter didn't want to go out to dinner. It wasn't because he was cheap, though, since he was always sneaking me little presents in L.A. And I liked the idea of him making pancakes for dinner for his kids. Plus I didn't want to deal with crowd interference, especially after Memphis. I pointed to the box and said, "I've got a video game system for you guys if we can eat here."

Danny ran over and ripped open the box's packaging and it was like she'd forgotten all about the pancake place. Little kids are easy to distract. That's why it's annoying to have girls younger than eight or so at concerts, because they lose interest in the whole concert if they don't like one song. Older kids, it takes a few songs in a row they don't like before they're gone. That's why you have to keep producing and pump out an album every eighteen months max, or your fan base will forget about you and move on to the next artist.

I helped them set up the system in the living room and explained how to play Zenon as Walter poked around the kitchen right next to us. I'd never seen Walter cook before, since Peter always made him food at home or he ordered in, and here he was getting out pancake batter and butter and pans and everything. But he actually knew what he was doing, and once I got the girls set up with Zenon, I watched him cook. His face was super-serious, like making these pancakes was the most important job in the world not to fuck up.

Me and the girls played Zenon and ate the pancakes Walter made fresh batches of every few minutes. One time, when he thought no one was looking, he stuck a couple twenty-dollar bills in one of the girls' pink backpacks on the floor. I ate and tried not to think about how much cardio I'd owe and let the girls switch off playing and stepped in to show them how to do certain actions, though later I stopped touching the controller, because sometimes with games it's best just to let kids figure out for themselves what to do and what not to do, even if their characters keep getting damaged. Also they didn't get the idea of experience points, even Sally, who asked, "How do you know what to do if you don't know how many points it gets you?" and I was like, "That's why it's different from other games, you have to play it a long time to get a sense of what helps you, but sometimes it still surprises you."

Pris laughed at the voice of this archer Shamino who sounded like a baritone demon, so I turned off the character sounds and did the voices for all the characters in his voice. She laughed every time I did it, and Danny did, too, even though it wasn't really funny. Then I whipped out my impression of Walter, whose voice wasn't far from Shamino's, and made up dialogue in his voice, like, "Pris, you must bestow upon me the last pancake in your inventory or I will eat you, brother."

Walter never laughs, but he smiled and said, "You got me, brother." It hurt a little to do the impression, since I had to make my voice all gravelly and scratchy like Lennon on "Twist and Shout," but it was worth it, and after a few minutes even Sally started laughing, so I said everything in his voice the rest of the night, like, "Where's the bathroom, brother?" It was a fun night, like hanging out with the Latchkeys, even if it was cooler to say you were with a rock group at a club instead of eating pancakes with three little girls and your bodyguard at their mother's house.

When I went to the bathroom, I saw an old desktop computer in a small room next to it. I thought they might not have the Internet, because they were so poor, but they did. Everyone has the Internet except me. So I closed the door behind me, even though Walter wouldn't actually care and I could just tell him I was doing an assignment for Nadine. A spreadsheet was open called "budget.xls." Callie only budgeted $150 a week for groceries for her and her daughters, and I could tell from the ingredients Walter used that she shopped at supermarkets way below Schnucks. I sometimes saw Peter's receipts for food at the organic stores, which was for me, Jane, Walter, Sharon, and him, and they were over a thousand dollars each time, but some of that was wine and liquor.

I went into my email. I wondered if my father had heard about Memphis and everything or if he was the kind of person who didn't hear about things like that. There was one more email from him, written a few hours ago. It was strange to picture him going on a computer somewhere in New York today and writing to me. It was strange to think of him at all in a way that wasn't just like, I wonder who the hell my father is.

> I thought I would have heard back from you if you really were Jonathan or knew him. Now I guess it was a joke. Please don't screw around with people like that in the future. It's not nice. I just wanted to connect with my son and tell him a little about my life.

I wanted to write that it was me, I wasn't making it up, I wanted to hear more about his life, but I didn't have a chance to do it because I could never get on the Internet, and he was the one who didn't make it clear if he was coming to my concert in Cincinnati or not. I almost even said to the computer, Fuck you. But I wrote

I don't get to go on email alot but it is really me. Did you see my TV morning show appearance where I mentioned Pittsburgh and Australia and peanut butter? Where did you live in Australia? Why did you move there? Do you have any pictures you can send? Or from when you were in the Wrecking Balls? And are you coming to my concert in Cincinnati?

I didn't have anything else to say, so after I sent the email I looked up a bunch of Australia facts that I could ask him about until they called me to come back in and help them fight one of the Emperor's minions. We played another hour before Callie came home and the car service picked us up. Callie and Walter were weird again when they spoke, since he had to tell her he'd cooked pancakes for them and she was maybe pissed that he'd made them breakfast for dinner, and she looked doubly pissed in a more serious way when Walter said good-bye to his daughters, and Pris and Danny grabbed his legs and said they didn't want him to go. He put both their heads in his palms and pretended to pick them up by their heads. Sally stayed on the couch and kept playing Zenon.

Walter sat with his eyes closed and was quieter than usual on the drive back. I didn't want to break the silence, but eventually I asked, "How did you and Callie meet?"

"High school," he said. "I thought she was way out of my league, but I asked her to the senior prom, she said yes, and there you go."

I was surprised he thought she was out of his league, but I just said, "I guess I'll never go to the prom. I'll just sing about it in 'The Big Dance.'" I don't even sing it much. It's a crap track from before the label figured out my voice.

"Never know, maybe you will." I hadn't told him Jane's idea about school. I bet she hadn't, either. Nadine could've. I didn't want to discuss it with him.

He was quiet for another minute. "I fucked that one up, didn't I?" he said.

"That was a fun night. You didn't fuck anything up."

"No, not tonight," he said, and I understood what he meant.

"Then why'd you leave?" I'd never really asked Walter before about why he left his family. Jane told me not to once when I asked her.

"I didn't," he said. "She kicked me out. But I had it coming."

"Why?"

He did this half-smile/half-frown thing he does sometimes. "We had creative differences." He added, "Sometimes I forget you're ten years old," but instead of reminding him I was almost twelve, I said, "Do you wish you could go back?"

"Nah. I like working for you guys, and getting to hang out with you, and I've got my friends in L.A. and everything."

He didn't have that many friends in L.A. besides the guys he knew at his gym, though. He mostly hung out in his bungalow when he had time off, and if the label hadn't recommended him as a bodyguard from a connection he had, he'd be a trainer in some bottom-shelf Hollywood gym.

"I read a fortune cookie just after I moved to L.A.," he went on. "It said, 'To live in the future you must break with the past.' And I know these cookies tell you whatever you want to hear, but still."

"So that's why you came to L.A.? To break with the past?"

His eyes were still closed. "Yeah. But it's more like a break in your head. Like that song of yours, 'I Loved a Girl'? Where you realize it's over, so you have to let it go?"

I'd always thought that song, which was actually called "Once Loved a Girl," was just about an ex-girlfriend who didn't love you as much in return. The chorus goes, "Once loved a girl, in the past tense, she never committed, stayed on the fence." Maybe Walter was right.

"I had to keep telling myself, 'I don't love Callie anymore,'" he said. "Because when you really love someone, it means they can hurt you. I even had this picture of us kissing, from a photo booth, and I tore it apart in the middle. Like that other song of yours."

He meant the chorus from "Heart Torn Apart": "Before I felt whole, now there's a hole in the part, where my heart used to be, 'cause you've torn it apart." It's not a hack rhyme because it's *the part* and *apart*.

"So you did it enough that you really don't love her anymore?" I asked.

He opened his eyes for the first time. "I'm tired, brother."

He closed them again, and I left him alone and listened to MJ on my iPod until we got home. Walter told himself Callie couldn't hurt him anymore, but anyone could see she was still his Major Vulnerability, right in front of him, even if she was halfway across the country most of the time. Maybe that's what it was with most people, the person closest to them. I always figured Jane and my father both wanted to end things because of creative differences, but maybe he had it coming, too, and they were each other's Major Vulnerability, and so she kicked him out. My songs are always about a girl dumping me and I still love her and want her back, but dating is different from people who have a kid. Except it could be that he wants to come back now, like Walter does, even if he won't admit it.

CHAPTER 14

Nashville (Second Day)

When the wake-up call rang at seven in the morning and I said, "Thank you," it felt like forks scratching away at the bottom of my throat. I hoped the coffee might soothe it, but it made it worse. I couldn't find any Throat Coat in my suitcases, so I knocked on Jane's door. She opened it in her towel.

"Jane," I croaked, and she gave me a look like, What the hell is wrong with you? "My throat is really sore."

"Do you feel sick?"

"No, only my throat."

She ordered up a pot of hot water and some honey and steeped Throat Coat in a mug for me, but I still sounded like junk. "I bet it was that stupid impression," she said. I'd shown it to her when I got in last night and she told me it was bad for my voice and to knock it off. "How long did you do it for?"

"Maybe two hours."

"For Christ's sake," she said. "I can't believe he let you do it for that long."

"Who?"

"Walter. He knows you're not supposed to strain your voice."

"He didn't know it hurt my throat."

"It hurt, and you *still* did it?"

"A little. I didn't think it would do this."

"Jesus, how old are you? Okay, stop talking, just stop," she said. "Don't talk again, and keep drinking the tea. Can you sing tonight?"

I didn't know if I was allowed to talk, so I shrugged. I could tell from a few minutes of this that it would be a pretty frustrating life if you were totally mute. I wasn't sure what would be worse, being mute or deaf. For one, you couldn't sing music, and for the other, you couldn't hear it.

"Let me figure this out. In the meantime, get ready for your session with Nadine, and I'll tell her you're not supposed to talk."

I just did writing and math exercises and a new vocab test with Nadine, but my performance was *subpar,* which means the opposite of *superb.* I wondered if that was like the word Zack used when it sounds the same but means the opposite. I broke the rule of not talking by asking Nadine if there was a name for words that sound like they're mixed up and also mean the opposite, but she said she didn't think so. It's like those guys who can sing two different tones at once with their throats. I've tried a million times and can't do it. The only way is like we did on an alternate take of "Breathtaking," when they overlaid me singing the chorus in a lower octave, but my producer didn't like it. You have to keep the emotional message in pop songs pure, or you confuse the audience.

When Jane picked me up in a few hours for sound check with a thermos of Throat Coat and honey, she asked me to speak, and I still sounded like a frog. "If you can't sing by tonight, we'll lip-synch it," she said. "I had to fight tooth and nail with the venue to let us do it. They wanted to back out of various clauses in the contract."

I suck at lip-synching. It always looks fake. I've never had to do it for a full concert before. "Where's Walter?" I whispered as we got in the elevator.

"He's got some appointments in town this afternoon. Stop talking and keep drinking."

My voice was softening and I knew I could handle the banter interludes, but at the start of sound check, when I tested out the lines "Please don't send a text, please don't you depart, please send an RSVP to my heart," it sounded terrible and made my throat worse, and Rog told me not to sing anymore. I had to stand there like a numbskull and pretend to sing while they piped in my vocal tracks and I got worried that everyone would catch me faking it later. People get more upset over someone pretending to be good and lying to them than someone who's horrible but open about it. Jane told me they wouldn't, that concertgoers don't hardly even listen to the singers, they only want to see you and feel like they're connecting with the star by singing along, and I would've asked how they could connect with me if they're not even listening to me, but I didn't want to strain my voice.

Except for one time where I came in late to the line "I picked you flowers, you picked apart my life" in "Roses for Rosie," which no one noticed because I was in the heart-shaped swing, I pulled it off during the concert. It kind of made me think there wasn't much point in *actually* singing. Rog said I gave a powerhouse performance, and he always tells the truth after shows. Jane walked me to the star/talent room and joked that we should do it for our next concert in Cincinnati, even though my voice would be better by then.

I'd forgotten Cincinnati was next. I wondered if he was coming to the show.

"Get your stuff ready quickly, baby, so we can get out of here," Jane said outside my room.

"Okay," I said as I opened the door. "Where's Walter?"

She whipped out her phone and said, "Hmm?"

"Where's Walter? He wasn't here all night."

She typed into her phone on my Twitter account, "Thanx 4 the love and support, Nashville! Next stop: Cincinnati! #ValentineDays," and linked to a candid stage shot of me.

"I told you," she said. "He had appointments."

"What appointments?"

"I don't *know*. He used to live here."

"Call him."

"I'm not going to call him now. The venue security can escort us to the car," she said. "Come to my room when you're ready."

She walked away. "Did you fire him?" I asked.

She stopped and waited there. Then she came back and pushed me into my room and shut the door. "He was irresponsible in letting you do that impression of him, when he should have known it would hurt your voice, and it almost caused us to lose a lot of money."

"You *fired* him?"

"He'll be paid for the rest of the tour."

My legs turned to noodles. "You did this with the Latchkeys. You can't do this with Walter."

"Walter understands he made a fireable mistake. He'll find someone else to work for."

That almost made me more upset than her firing him, the idea of Walter being the bodyguard for someone else like it was no big deal. "He's my best friend." Saying those words made me feel like I was about to cry.

"You can't be best friends with a man thirty years older than you."

"Yes, I can." I could feel tears filling up in my eyes. I tried holding them back.

She took a step closer to me and said, "Stop crying."

"Hire Walter back," I said.

"I said *stop* it, Jonathan." She tried to put her hands to my face, I guess to wipe my tears away, but I pushed her arms away and she accidentally sort of rapped her knuckles on top of my head, which wouldn't have hurt if it was only the knuckles, but the huge silver ring on her right hand caught me hard and it stung. I pulled back from her quickly and touched my head. It pounded like an echo.

Jane's mouth was in an *O* and her eyes were stuck in place. I could tell she was *really* upset now, so I just let myself bawl, more than I do for "Heart Torn Apart," a bunch of ugly heaving sobs.

"I'm sorry," she said, still stuck.

I shook my head no and forced the tears out faster.

"I'm sorry," she said again, and she moved her arms out a little to see if it was okay to hug me, so I pretended to flinch, and then I waited until she saw that before I hurled myself into her arms and cried the hardest yet into her chest. I didn't even hardly have to force it, smothering my tears and snot into her dress over her implants, and she was half crying, too, and said, "I'm so sorry, baby, I'm sorry, I'm a terrible mother."

I waited a minute without letting up the tears. Then I squeaked out, "Bring him back," and she said, "Okay, Jonathan, okay, I'll get him back."

I took a little while to calm down, since I really did get myself worked up even if part of it was acting at the end. Maybe Jane's right. I *should* be in the movies.

CHAPTER 15

Cincinnati

Walter joined us on the bus in the morning. He was quiet around Jane and kept to himself near the front of the bus, but later, when she went to the bathroom for like the fourth time in two hours, he came up to my seat and said, "Thanks, brother," and fist-bumped me.

Jane kept talking to Rog about her fortieth birthday in two days, and he was telling her age is mental more than physical and the more she thought about it, the bigger a deal she was making it. The vicious cycle of aging.

"Look at me," he said. "I don't think about it or talk about my age, so no one else does."

Jane looked at him like, Um, other people *do* think you're old. But she said, "It's different for women."

I looked back at Nadine reading in the bucket seats. Jane was only about thirteen or fourteen years older, but from their faces, she looked like she could've been *her* mother.

Rog gave her a back rub like he does a lot when she's upset. It's also usually a way to get her to stop talking. She went on for another hour, though. He's a pretty patient listener. Jane thanked him for being her human Xanax, and it reminded me of that detective-show actor's song about Xanax. She said, "You'll make a good manager someday, after you retire from dancing," and Rog said, "Well, that's a ways off, but I've had the best teacher."

On our driver break at a rest stop, I went outside to get some air and Walter came with me. He said, "Mind if I smoke?"

This was the first time I'd seen him smoke on this tour. He's always trying to quit but never lasts more than a few weeks. I said I didn't mind. We didn't talk, he just smoked facing away from me. Rog came walking back to the bus with a cardboard tray from Starbucks with two chais for him and Jane. He got her hooked last tour. "Walter, would you please smoke away from Jonny?" he asked.

"I am," Walter said.

"The wind is carrying it back," Rog said. "Do what you want to your own lungs, but let's not ruin his, okay?"

Walter flicked away his cigarette. Those two didn't talk too much.

We didn't have anything scheduled for that night in Cincinnati, so me and Jane watched TV in her room and ordered in. When I asked for lasagna with sweet potato fries on the side, she didn't say anything, even though it's a double-carber. She was being super-nice to me because of Walter, but I didn't push it with dessert. Besides, I'd eaten a ton of salads the last week. "Can we do this tomorrow night?" I asked when she walked me back to my room.

"You've got a show."

"I mean after. Can we watch some TV together?"

"Sure," she said.

The second we got into Cincinnati, I looked out the bus, in the hotel lobby, through the hotel window, everywhere I could, for my father. Maybe he was going to come to my hotel, since sometimes if a fan spots me they leak where I am on the Internet, or the media knows about it. If you really want to find out where I'm staying, it's not so hard, which is why we have to take so many precautions and throw up so many buffers. Or he might be coming to my show, except I didn't know how he'd meet me.

I didn't see him. So I did my best to tune it out and got into the Jonny Zone way earlier than I normally do. I felt rested the next day, zero damage, my voice was back in condition, and I had an A-plus workout in the hotel gym in the morning with Jane, where we competed to see who could do more crunches and had less stomach chub. I won both, but it's not fair because Jane's a woman and she was turning middle-aged the next day.

I kept scanning the crowd for my father at U.S. Bank Arena, which is impossible because you can't pick out one guy from thousands of people mostly in the dark, even if it's the one grown man there by himself, except for a couple child predators.

Still, it was going good, maybe because I was trying harder in case he was there. On "Breathtaking," I really went for the high C and nailed it, and I could tell even my backup singers were like, Shit, Jonny's *on* tonight. When you can do whatever you want vocally and everyone in the stadium knows it, it's like gulping down the invincibility potion in Zenon.

Then, when the spotlight whirred around the crowd right after "Breathtaking," starting out all slow at first with my drummer playing a solo, so I could pick out a girl to bring onstage in the new set list Jane reordered to avoid performance fatigue, it went over a guy in one of the front rows. I only saw him for a second, but he looked like the picture of my father in his driver's license, just with a beard. In "Breathtaking," I'm pretending to lose my breath, but now I really did.

All of a sudden, I came up with an idea that would make it so Jane wouldn't figure out what I was doing. I walked toward the edge of the stage and said into the mike, "Al."

I was close enough now that I could make out the front rows a little, and when the spotlights flew over I could see them better. The guy was looking straight at me, but so was everyone else in the capacity crowd of 17,090. Except they were all standing in their seats, and since he was the only guy in a row filled with tween girls and a few mothers, he was way taller than everyone else.

The first concert I remember going to was a free outdoor show in St. Louis along the riverfront, so it must have been the summer. I don't know what the music was, but I was with Jane and my father, and we were standing far back in a packed crowd and I couldn't see anything onstage. So I walked through the bodies to get a better look, but it was even worse, just a lot of tall adult bodies over me, and after I walked for a little, I couldn't see Jane or my father anymore.

I'm not sure how long I was gone, because I didn't know I should've been scared to be off on my own like that, but later my father grabbed my arm and told me to never leave them again like that, and he carried me back to Jane, who hugged me. They both looked really worried, and I remember liking how much me being gone like that scared them.

My father put me on his shoulders the rest of the show so I could see, even though a guy behind us kept complaining, but my father finally turned, with me still on top of him, and said to him in a baritone, "This is the only way my son can see. You have a problem with that?"

The guy didn't say anything, and I was just old enough to tell he was backing down. We watched the rest of the show like that, with my father holding me on his shoulders above everyone else like he could do it forever.

I was at the perimeter of the stage, right in front of the security line, and the spotlights were whirring faster now and I had to pick someone soon. I said, "Al," one more time, and watched the guy closely. But he wasn't responding in any special way, like how I would if my father was onstage and I was in the crowd and he said, "Jonny," twice in a row while staring at me.

He just put his arm around the girl next to him, who was my age. It wasn't him. And if it had been him, I didn't even have a plan for what I'd do next. All the momentum I was feeling during "Breathtaking" departed the realm.

So I quickly sang, "*Al* always be there for you, too," a line in "This Bird Will Always Bee There for You," and used the same trick of switching a name to a regular word like I did for Elsa's name with Bill, which must've made my band be like, Huh? because it wasn't in tonight's set list.

I still had to pick someone. In the front row, there was a group of older-than-normal girls, like sixteen years old, when my fan base usually topped out around fourteen or fifteen. One with black bangs was wearing a tight T-shirt with my picture on it. She was short but had a big chest. I almost got a boner onstage seeing my own face stretched out across her breasts like that.

Normally I don't pick such a hot girl, but if my father *was* somehow here I didn't want him to think I could only get ugly girls, so I called her onstage, and all her friends looked jealous. She came up and I sang "Chica" to her, and when I got to the part with the half-rhyme where it goes, "Oh, chica, you make me loco, can't figure you out, you're like Sudoku," I sang it right in her ear, and with her head blocking the view of the crowd, I stuck my tongue in her ear for a second but made it seem like it could've been an accident from singing.

After the song, I hugged her so I could feel her breasts and moved the mike away and whispered, "Stay backstage and meet me after," and she nodded. I didn't know what I'd do with her. It's not like I had any privacy. I walked her to the backstage entrance instead of returning her to the crowd, and finished my set thinking about her more and more and how I hoped someone posted photos of us on the Internet that Lisa Pinto would see, and her PR people would issue some statement in a glossy through her like, "I understand other girls will be interested in Jonathan, but we have a relationship built on mutual trust," and I forgot about my father.

When I came backstage I couldn't find her. She wasn't waiting around my room, either. She probably figured I wasn't serious about inviting her or someone told her she had to leave the backstage area. Or maybe she got bored and went back to her seat to be with her friends. Now it was like the opposite of a boner. A *no-ber*. A subpar no-ber.

I did find Jane and asked her if we could order some food in at the hotel while we watched TV since I didn't like what they gave me in my room. "Something came up and I have to go out," she said. "But you can order whatever you like. Even dessert. And we'll have a birthday lunch tomorrow."

She gave me a kiss on the head and left. She didn't even try to make up an excuse like a promoter this time. Just because you promised doesn't mean you *have* to do it. At least this meant she didn't ask me why I'd said "Al" twice in a row before singing a line from out of nowhere.

So Jane left, the girl left, and my father never showed. Walter came up to me and said, "Ready whenever you are, brother."

I said, "Walter, I want you to find me a girl here."

"What?"

"Find an older girl who's here without her parents and invite her to my room."

He made his smile/frown. "That's not gonna happen."

"I'm allowed to meet my fans backstage. It's like my senior prom." I added what I knew would get him: "I won't tell Jane."

You could see him weighing it in his mind, like I'd said he was innocent and bailed him out before but here was something that could get him thrown right back in jail with the death penalty.

He played with the all-access pass hanging around his neck. "Just this once."

I went into my room and waited, but I was getting nervous and pacing around the room, so I turned on Zenon. I was on Level 96 and close to the end, though the final levels were the toughest and taking longer to complete, and I couldn't get past the minion on this one. It might look lame if a girl came in while I was playing video games, but I didn't have anything cool in my room the way the Latchkeys did, like guitars or big books, so I rested on a beanbag chair and kept trying different positions that looked like the most relaxed.

A groupie would probably expect me to have some music on, so I plugged my iPod into my portable speakers and chose a playlist with "Billie Jean" on it to pump myself up. It's an iconic opening few bars, and even though it sounds like a million other drumbeats with a kick, snare, and hi-hat, you know what it is right away. Then that bass line starts up, and if you didn't know what it was before, *now* you definitely do. That's the best, something unique so you instantly recognize it but also similar enough to what you've heard before. You can't challenge the listener that much, but if you only give them what they already know, you might have quick commercial success but no rotation stamina. And if it's too complex, you don't like it till you've heard it a few times, and it's more important than ever to hook listeners within the first seven seconds or they switch to the next video on

YouTube or the next song on the radio. Rog tells me MTV cut down the audience's attention span, but MJ had it *way* easier with television than the Internet, even if MTV didn't play him at first because he was black.

It's a perfect pop song. The tempo is 117 beats per minute, which I think is the best for a dance song, right about where your heart rate should be for low-intensity fat-burning cardio, and the spare instrumentation highlights the vocals while still driving the song, which is a tough combo. It would be nice if I ever had a song like that, which a broad-spectrum audience will remember forever and which anyone with a pulse loves, instead of singing for tween girls and having them forget about it six months later.

It took ten thousand hours, and I checked outside my door a couple times. After twenty minutes Walter knocked. "Mr. Valentine, a fan of yours would like to meet you," he said in a serious voice after I unlocked it, but he didn't do it in a winking way.

Behind him was a girl who was fifteen or sixteen. She had a cute face, but she was also kind of chubby. Like, *really* chubby. Even under her winter coat, I could tell. I didn't know if because Walter was such a big guy she seemed thin to him, but I bet there were skinnier girls in the crowd who would've come to my room. Except maybe he'd picked someone who, if she blabbed on the Internet about this, no one would believe them since she wasn't hot enough. That was probably it. "Hello," I said.

"Hey," she said, and she walked past Walter and into my room before I could invite her in. She looked around. "So this is it? I thought it'd be fancier."

Walter made eye contact with me, and I nodded, and he closed the door from the hallway. "Most of the time they are," I said. "This venue sucks."

"This *city* sucks," she said. "Where do you live?"

"L.A."

"I heard L.A. sucks, too. The second I turn eighteen, I'm moving to New York or San Francisco."

"For college?"

She snorted. "I'll work in a coffee shop or something. I'm friends with this older girl? Amanda? She moved to San Francisco and makes enough at this yuppie teahouse to pay rent and go to shows. That's all I want." She took off her coat and threw it on a chair. She wore a skirt with black fishnet stockings, and her chub muffin-topped out under her T-shirt. "What do you have to drink here?" I listed all the diet sodas and chilled teas. "I meant like alcohol."

"There isn't any," I said. "Tonight. 'Cause the venue sucks. Usually there's whiskey and beer."

"Whatever." She went over to the food spread but didn't touch it, and was like, "So, we gonna turn the lights off?"

"Okay," I said, and I went over to flip the switch, and when I turned around she was right next to me in the dark and leaning down to cleave her mouth to mine. My lips were closed at first, but they opened up when her tongue pushed between them. It was like a wet worm darting around inside.

She cleaved our mouths again, the other meaning. "I used to think your music was shit," she whispered, "until I heard this band here, the 99 Percent Dilution, do a punk cover of 'Guys vs. Girls.'"

"Thanks," I said, before I realized she'd also insulted me.

The beanbag chair was near us, so she pushed and lowered me onto it, where it made a crunching sound. "Have you heard it?" she asked.

"No. What's it like?"

"It has this, like, angry energy?" she said. "And so then I listened to your song. I mean, I'd heard it before, at the mall or on the radio or whatever, but I wasn't really listening. And I still think it's a shitty pop song, but I heard all this pent-up anger from you, too. It's like you're punk and you have no idea."

I said thanks again, but it was another insult, like I was too stupid to know who I was. At least she sounded smarter than most of my fans. She reminded me of the girl in the hospital who said I sounded sad when I was singing about happy things. Everyone sees what they want in songs, the way Walter said they do with fortune cookies.

She climbed on top of me and kept kissing me and licking my neck. I wasn't hard yet. I got boners every two minutes except when a girl was actually humping me. I thought of the things Bill had said to Jane, and got a little bit of something. Maybe if I said something he'd said out loud, I'd get fully hard. "You like being my—"

I couldn't say the final words. She stopped and pulled her head back a few inches. "Yeah?"

"You like being my fan?"

"I told you, I only like that one cover of your song. I just want to give you the best blow job of your life."

That did get me sort of hard for a second, hearing the words *blow job*, or maybe it was *blowjob*, one word. My computer dictionary wouldn't have it, and I couldn't ask Nadine. Maybe Walter would know. It was right in time, because she unzipped my jeans and stuck her hand down my pants as my half-boner was going up. A half-erection would be an *Eric*. She grabbed it and wrenched her hand around it a few times like she was unscrewing a stuck jar. It didn't feel too good. Like, except for the fact that a girl was touching my penis, it would've been better to do it myself or not have anything happen at all. If I asked if she had moisturizer, or checked if they had butter or olive oil in the fridge, she might have thought it was weird.

It hurt so much, actually, that my Eric turned into a no-ber, and though my eyes were closed, I could tell it was shrinking a lot. The more I concentrated on getting it hard, the softer and tinier it got. Pretty soon it was going to become like negative size and turn into a vagina. She moved her hand faster, which only hurt worse and made me more nervous that she could tell how small and soft it was.

She stopped. "Are you even old enough to *get* a hard-on?"

"Yep," I said. "It's just that I already had a bunch today."

"Oh." She went back to trying to jerk me off.

I wished Zack could somehow see me doing this. Not like a video or being in the room, but knowing I was getting a hand job now, even if it wasn't working and was mostly painful.

Suddenly I got hard again, and she pulled my pants down to my ankles and tried to do the same to my boxers. But I didn't want her to see that I only had one pube, so I stopped her from doing that and instead poked my penis through the fly.

She put her mouth over it, which felt a ton better than the hand job, and if all hand jobs were the same as that one, then I was fine never getting another in my life. The blow job was the opposite. It was like melting inside the heat of her mouth, and I didn't feel anything else on my body, except when her teeth hit it a couple times. I'd be okay getting some more of these in my life. I bet real sex is like your body completely disappearing inside the girl's body.

After a minute she took a break. "I'm Dana, by the way."

"I'm Jonny."

"No duh," she said.

She went back to the blow job, but I could tell there was no way it was going to happen. I wasn't even getting as close as I got when I masturbated by myself. Finally she asked, "Are you gonna come soon?"

"Probably not," I said. "I already comed a couple times today."

She stopped and I stuck my erection back inside my boxers and pulled up my jeans and was careful not to zip up my penis. She sat down on the beanbag chair to my side, but there wasn't enough space for us both to lie down, so I sat up on it, too.

"Have you done that before?" She smiled like she had a little secret. "I feel like I totally corrupted you."

"No, I do it all the time."

Her smile went away. "You really know how to make a girl feel special."

I could have told her she was the first girl I'd even kissed except for Alyssa Hernandez in a game of Spin the Bottle in fourth grade. But I've heard that you never want to tell girls you like them too much. When you *sing* about how much you like them, it's okay, because you're not singing to one girl, you're singing to all of them, so they're all competing with the others. It's like Jane giving access to the glossies, just enough but not everything, and they all want to nab an exclusive.

Still, maybe the right thing to do now was to kiss her again or squeeze her breasts or something. It would've been good to have Zack around for advice on things like this. I wasn't sure what would be best, so I put my hand behind her head to give her a little neck rub. She flinched, but then she saw what I was doing and let me. Her muscles stayed pretty tight while I rubbed, though.

"How'd you get here tonight?" I asked. "Did your parents drop you off?"

I thought back to my father carrying me in his arms back to Jane at the riverfront concert. That was maybe my only real memory of them being in the same place together besides in our apartment.

"Yeah, right," Dana said. "They don't drive me *anywhere*. I can't wait till I get my license. I took the bus."

Every time one of us moved, the beanbag popped and snapped at a million decibels. I didn't know what to say to girls offstage or when I wasn't signing autographs or posing for pictures, and I *really* didn't know what to say after something like this. "What bands are you into?" she said.

I could tell if I said MJ, she'd think it was gay. She might not even know what MJ stood for. And I couldn't say Tyler Beats, who I bet she thought also sang shitty pop songs. There's no way all the members of the 99 Percent Dilution combined had the talent that either of them had in their toenails. If no one's heard of you, there's a reason for it.

"The Clash is a major influence for me," I said.

Right after I said that, the song "Stay" by Maurice Williams came on the playlist, which made what I said about the Clash sound like a lie. That was when Rog was teaching me how to sing falsetto. I don't like doing it other than for MJ songs, because I sound like a girl, so it's only on "You Hurt Me." "Stay" is very short, about a minute and a half. That's part of what makes it such a strong song, right as you're getting into it, it ends and leaves you wanting more. It makes you feel what Maurice Williams is singing about, which is what any good song does, but usually not with track length.

"They're cool," she said. "I'm more into the Pistols. But I mostly listen to Cincinnati bands. You know the Upper-Middle Classmen? I've seen like nine of their shows this winter."

"No. You know the Latchkeys?"

"Ugh. They suck. They're like corporate indie rock for the masses. The Urban Outfitters of bands."

I stopped rubbing her neck. "What do you mean?"

"They're the type of music you can tell was cooked up in some laboratory by a group of record executives to sound exactly like it *wasn't.*"

"No, they met in college. And they sound like the Stones meets the early Strokes."

"Whatever," she said. "They're still rich white boys pretending to be something they're not. Their front man, Nick something?"

"Zack. Zack Ford."

"More like Zack Fake. I saw an interview with him? He was trying so hard to be clever. Only rich white boys try to be clever. I was like, '*Really?*'"

"He *is* clever. He can make up funny songs on the spot. And he's not rich. He's working-class from New Jersey."

"He's rich now," she said. "All that matters is what you are now."

That wasn't true, because you always knew who you were before and you kept thinking of yourself like that even if no one else did, but once she said that, I knew Zack wouldn't even care if he knew about me getting a blow job. He probably wasn't thinking about me at all except for being pissed that he took me along to the nightclub even though I'm the one who got them in because no one in Memphis gives a fuck who the Latchkeys are, which was why they were lucky to be asked on my tour in the first place with my Walmart fans.

"You want any food?" I said. "You looked super-hungry before."

"No," she said. "If I'm not back by ten I'll be in deep shit." I'd wanted her to leave before that, but once she said *she* wanted to leave, I kind of hoped she'd stick around.

She opened the door. Walter was right outside on a chair. I asked him to get the car service for her. "You gonna remember me?" she said.

Dana probably gave blow jobs to everyone in the Upper-Middle Classmen, whoever they were, and to all the other Cincinnati bands, but she wasn't hot enough to get backstage for any bands with national profiles, so I was the most famous person she'd ever give a blow job to, which was the only reason she'd remember me, and down the road she'd probably change what happened in her memory so she could feel proud of that one time she made Jonny Valentine come.

"Totally," I said. "What's your last name?"

"Hollister."

"Like the clothing company. They send me stuff sometimes."

In my head so I wouldn't forget I repeated to myself, Dana Hollister, Dana Hollister, Dana Hollister.

"Diana Hollister," I said out loud.

"Dana," she said. *"Dana* Hollister."

"Right. Dana."

Walter escorted her out, and after I closed the door, "Stay" finished and the playlist ended and it was quiet. I played Zenon while I waited for Walter. I had my game saved right before the level's minion who kept killing me, but this time, instead of running into the room and attacking him, I realized I could run in, attack him once, and run out before he could counterattack. It took a lot longer, but eventually I wore him down and advanced to the next level. Sometimes in Zenon you just have to take your time and not be in a rush to attack.

Me and Walter didn't talk about it on the ride back except when he said, "Don't expect that to become a regular service, brother. When you're older you can do it all you want." I guess I couldn't ask him how to spell *blow job* now. And I didn't tell him I didn't want to do it again for a while anyway. Unless maybe I got a skinnier girl next time.

CHAPTER 16

Cleveland (First Day)

On the morning of Jane's birthday, Nadine gave me my first set of final exams on the bus and in the hotel before she went back to L.A. in two days for winter break. The next day was going to be history plus language/reading, which meant an essay on slavery. I think I did okay overall, because it was vocab (superb), math (middling), and science (subpar), but I wasted a few minutes at the start imagining taking them in a real classroom, with all the other students getting nervous before and comparing the answers after. It wasn't exactly like having teammates, because you were basically competing against them, but it sounded sort of fun.

When I finished, Jane said she'd reserved a nice lunch for us. She didn't look so hot. All these tiny blue veins I'd never noticed before popped out under her eyes like the roots of a plant, and she was really skinny, skinnier than when the tour started, but not in a good way. She still had chub in some areas, like her stomach and hips, but was too skinny in others, like her forearms and face. Rog is always stressing the importance of a balanced dancer's body to prevent injury. Jane's is *im*balanced.

Walter escorted me and Jane out the hotel through the lobby to the car service, since Cleveland doesn't have anything set up for celebrities.

Right after the revolving doors, this guy was standing there in a cheap suit, holding a big white envelope. "Jane Valentine?" he asked.

"No autographs or interviews, sorry," she said, and Walter started to move between them while keeping an eye on me.

He quickly pushed the envelope on her before Walter could provide buffer. "You've been served," he said, and walked away. She watched him for a few seconds and folded the envelope up and stuffed it in her bag.

"Why'd he say that?" I said.

"It's nothing," she said. "Walter, get the door, please."

I slid into the car. "What's in the envelope?"

"Just some papers I needed," she said.

"What kind of papers?"

"Boring business stuff."

"But why did he dis you?"

"What?"

"He said, 'You've been served,' like what people say when they dis someone or block their shot in basketball. Only they usually say, 'You got served.'"

"It's to let you know he's from the delivery service." Her body seemed smaller and her face was tighter than usual, like she'd shrunk into a Jane Valentine doll. Walter looked like he didn't know what just happened, either. "Can we have quiet time until we get to the restaurant? I need to email a few people back."

The restaurant was an Italian hot spot for Cleveland, the type of place where there'd be write-ups of us locally and they'd get syndicated out to the nationals. Maybe that was why Jane chose it, to show me and her went out to eat in restaurants like a normal mother and son. But when it's a third-tier city, their trendy places always feel desperate, like they're trying to be a cool place in L.A. or New York but not coming close. Jane always puts down pop acts that imitate someone else, because they'll never do it too good and it looks worse when they fail. She says you have to make your own brand, no one wants a knock-off. I'm like, But you're always trying to make me into the next Tyler Beats. She says we're imitating his *career trajectory*, not his *music*. She's always on the label about getting songwriters and producers who understand that distinction, except I'm not sure she can hear the difference herself in the music.

Jane ordered a mimosa when the waiter seated us and went to the restroom and had another waiter stand by me since Walter had stayed outside. When she came back, the white envelope was poking out of the unzipped part of her bag and was opened. Without making it obvious, I peeked at the writing in the corner. It said "Meacham Weiss & White," and it had a New York City address. So it was another legal letter, and not from her L.A. lawyers. I don't think she had lawyers in New York. It could have been something about business, or about me and her drinking, or about my father. No way she'd tell me, though.

She kept watching the room like there were paparazzi everywhere, and slurped down her mimosa by the time the waiter came back for our food order. When she asked for a third in the middle of her Caprese salad, I said maybe she should switch to water. "It's my birthday, Jonathan," she said. "I'm entitled to a couple drinks."

The waiter was this young guy, and he looked like he was about to piss his pants because he had a tough logic question of who should he listen to, the adult or the child celebrity, so Jane held up her glass and said, "Refill it."

She left for the bathroom before he came back, and when he did I said, "If she asks for another drink, can you make it very low on alcohol?" and he was cool about it and said, "Certainly, sir." He wasn't the kind of guy who'd talk to the tabloids. Plus he'd lose his job if he did. That was the best defense against employee leaks.

She didn't ask for a fourth drink, but she also didn't finish her salad. Her walk to the car service for the Wolstein Center was a little wobbly, but she held it together and didn't slur her speech or anything. That was the thing with Jane, you couldn't always tell if she'd had too much or not. *She* could be a decent actor.

The concert was tight, because we all knew it was one of our last tune-ups before New York. I pulled out the hottest girl from the front rows to sing to, and I didn't care if it made the others jealous. But

I didn't try telling her to wait for me backstage this time. Even if it worked and Jane wasn't around, Walter would shut it down.

When I did get backstage, Jane was pacing around the hallway near my room. She had a glass of white wine in her hand. White doesn't stain your teeth. "Are you going out?" I asked.

"Yes, I am." The words came out fast, like she was vomiting them.

"Why are you walking around here?"

"I'm not allowed to walk?" She spilled a little wine on the carpet.

"Tell Walter I'll be in my room," I said. Jane seemed not like she wasn't herself, but like she was *super*-herself, two or three times the regular amount. She had tiny drops of sweat covering her nose and her face looked white in parts and splotchy and red in others.

Before I turned the doorknob, Jane said, "Make sure you warm up your vocals more before New York. You were flat a few times tonight."

I *wasn't* flat at all. It was one of my best performances on the whole tour. I was going to say, "Maybe Bill can help me with my warm-ups," but when I turned, she was wavering and put one hand against the wall for support and dropped the wineglass in the other. It broke in a few big pieces, and then she crumpled in the opposite direction onto the carpet.

I screamed, "Jane! Fuck!" What Peter said, with my name, when *I* fainted in the kitchen.

Her eyes were closed and she was breathing, but when I shook her, she didn't wake up, and for a second I thought I was going to faint, too. "Help! Somebody help me!" I yelled, almost the lyrics to that Beatles song. It's like I was derivative of other people even in an emergency. A voice down the hall shouted for someone to call the medical team. Sometimes a few girls faint during my shows and the medical teams from the venues have to help them, but this wasn't normal fainting.

I stopped shaking her, because it could've been making it worse. I kept saying, all quiet, "Jane, wake up." And then this was stupid, but I whispered to myself, "Don't depart the realm." She was the one who was sick, but I was having trouble taking full breaths and my heart was squeezing up and releasing like some animal that hides in its shell and pops out once in a while to see if the coast is clear. All this commotion whirled up around me, walkie-talkies crackling and people running and barking directions at each other and a few adults I didn't know testing her pulse and breathing. In a minute a couple guys from the medical team ran over with a stretcher.

"Clear some space!" one of the guys said, and even though I was glad they were helping, in my mind I was like, Fuck you, she's *my* mother. But I moved over and he listened to her heartbeat and checked her breathing. They carefully put her on the stretcher and carried her off to an elevator down the hall.

Walter rushed up to me as the elevator doors closed, wheezing like an accordion. If he ever has to carry me away from a crowd racing after us, we're screwed. That's the downside of strength training over cardio.

He asked what happened. "She just collapsed," I said. "I think she's been drinking all day."

He looked at the broken glass on the ground near us. "That must be it. She'll be okay."

I wasn't sure she would, but when Walter said it, I mostly believed it, and my heartbeat started to go back to normal, the slow verse after the fast chorus. We found the medical offices on the basement level, where a woman was eating fast food. *Girls and guys, burgers and fries, all gets ruined with a coupla lies.*

"They've already taken your mother to the hospital," she told us.

"What happened to her?" I asked. My heart sped up *again*. The last five minutes were like an album with a bunch of different tempos for each track. You don't want too much variation if you're trying to craft an iconic sound. Only critics care about versatility. Fans want consistency.

"I don't know," she said. "You'll have to find out at the hospital."

In the car service to the hospital, Walter said, "I've been through shit like this before, brother. Don't start getting worried before we see what's what." Walter usually knew what to say, but this time he actually made it worse, because if he had to warn me not to worry, maybe there *was* something to be worried about.

Before this week I hadn't been to a hospital since I was born.

I had on a baseball hat so I wouldn't be ID'd, but Walter walked right next to me the whole time we went into the hospital, just in case.

He found a receptionist and told me to stay in his sight but to stand by a water fountain about fifteen feet away, I think so I wouldn't hear anything, since he'd never let me stand fifteen feet away in a public space. He must've told her who I was so we could get special treatment, because she got all excited before controlling it and shooting a quick glance at me.

While he was still talking to her, Rog came into the receptionist area. He spotted me first, then saw Walter and went over to him. It looked like he was taking over the job of talking to the receptionist. He doesn't like Walter, I don't think, and I bet Walter doesn't like Rog but he's better at hiding it. After a minute, Walter gave up and came back to me. "Rog is finding out what's going on," he said. Rog's voice got loud a few times, until he motioned for us to come over and told us we could wait in a special room.

A Latina nurse with chubby upper arms led us to a small room on another floor, a conference room with nothing in it but a round table with glossies and a few chairs. Rog left with her to find out more details about Jane. Me and Walter didn't say anything until he asked, "You want to play a game or something?"

"What game?"

"What games do kids play now?"

"I only play Zenon and other video games. I don't know any other games, really."

"Me neither."

I imagined playing games with my father, but maybe he'd be too old to be into them, so then I thought about playing with Jane's dead baby, and that he was a boy and my younger brother. I'd teach him how to throw a baseball, and Jane would definitely build us a field then. Maybe he'd have musical talent, too, but if he didn't it wouldn't matter, and even if he did, when he got old enough I'd say to him, You don't have to go into the industry, just stay in school, I'll do it alone and support our family, little man.

If something happened to Jane, would Walter move in full-time with me? He was fun to hang out with, and I asked Jane a million times if he could move into the house from his bungalow but she wanted to establish some boundaries. But he didn't know how to do half of what Jane did. Nadine was too young to take care of me. I still didn't really know my father, and he never even came to the concert in Cincinnati like he said he might, so there was no guarantee he'd do anything if Jane died. And I'd have to find a new manager, and they might steal my money or make career-killing business decisions.

I thought about Jane's funeral, the same way I used to picture Michael in his coffin. All her industry friends and acquaintances were there, like Ronald and Rog and the TV exec and his wife and everyone who worked for us at the house. They were all listening to whoever was onstage talking about Jane, but none of them actually knew her. Anyone she was friends with, she'd known for two years at the most. We wouldn't be inviting the people who knew her from Schnucks, and she definitely wouldn't want Albert there. And there'd be no point in flying Grandma Pat out there, if she even could fly anymore. I'd be the only one who knew her from before.

They'd probably play a song of mine at the funeral, or ask me to sing live. The only one that would make any sense for a funeral was "Heart Torn Apart," even though that's about breaking up with a girl.

In her coffin, Jane was wearing a black dress and had a lot of makeup on to make it seem like she was still alive. I finished singing "Heart Torn Apart," and I looked at the crowd and said, "Fuck you all, you did this to her but you want to pretend like she did it to herself," and climbed into the coffin with Jane and closed it on top of us and locked it from inside, and in a few hours I'd run out of air and depart the realm next to her.

"Can you find out what's going on?" I asked Walter. He said he'd find Rog and to only unlock the door for him or Rog. He left, and I distracted myself by singing "Heart Torn Apart" quietly. He didn't come back when I finished, so I picked up a men's glossy. The table of contents mentioned my name, and I didn't normally get any coverage in men's glossies. It was a half-page fashion spread, with a stock photo of me and some text:

Kickin' It Elementary School

The most stylish singer these days may just be
JONNY VALENTINE

Yes, yes, we know what you're thinking: fashion cues from some-one whose mother might still lay out his clothes for him? But before you recoil and go back to home-brewing your own beer (see page 87), take a gander at Jonny Valentine's ensemble. Little dude's got *game*. From his bespoke track sweaters and graphic tees to his snazzy (usually red) sneaks and perfectly fitting jeans that are just relaxed enough to bust a move in, the kid outdresses musicians twice his age. And we haven't even brought up The Jonny, that coif for the ages you should seriously consider requesting next time you're getting sheared instead of your lame-ass crew-cut. Your girl-friend will surely thank us—and so what if your d-bag bros laugh at you? (Why *does* it gotta be that way?)

There were a bunch of arrows pointing at my different clothes and nam-ing the designers and their off-the-rack prices, and then one at my head with how much a haircut costs at Christian's salon for normal custom-ers. I might've usually been excited at getting a positive fashion write-up in an adult glossy, even if the guys who wrote for this one really do love clothes and hair products, but they're afraid people will think they're gay, so they write like they're the least gay guys out there. But when you're waiting in a hospital to hear if your mother's dead, a fash-ion spread seems like a pretty stupid thing, especially when you think of how many adults are involved in something like this. When I've done staged fashion shoots, not like the fake candids we did in Denver, there's a photographer, his assistant, the glossy staff that needs to be on set, plus all the people who helped plan it. *Then* you've got all the staff it takes for production at the glossy, whatever number that is. Even if someone's quoting me, it takes a bunch of adults to make it happen. All that work, just because an eleven-year-old opened his mouth near a mike. If they'd spent as much time studying medicine, they could all be doctors.

At least they didn't figure out that I started wearing track sweaters in the last year to cover up my gut chub. There was a big discussion with the label about how to do that.

Finally Walter knocked. "You were right," he said. "She drank too much and wasn't eating enough. But she's gonna be okay."

"Can I see her?"

"She can't see anyone till tomorrow, no exceptions. I tried."

There are a few places where being a celebrity or rich doesn't get you everything you want, whenever you want it. Not many, but a few. I guess hospitals were one of them. "But she'll be okay? You sure?"

"I'm sure," he said. "I told you not to worry. This happens all the time. Happened to *me* once in Nashville. Got the shit pumped out of my stomach."

Walter weighed about three times what Jane weighed, so it wasn't exactly the same, but that made me feel a little better. I said, "And maybe the stomach pump will even make her a little skinnier, because she's been worried about her love handles lately."

He looked down at the men's glossy on the table, which was open to my spread, and at me for a couple seconds. "Hey, you know you can walk away from all this, right?"

"We're using the car service to get home, aren't we?"

"No," he said. "This whole thing. You don't have to sing if you don't want. You've made enough money to live on the rest of your life. You can walk away from it if you don't like it anymore."

This was like what Nadine had told me, except Walter never came close to saying anything like this before.

"Why are you telling me that?" I asked. "Do you want to quit or something, right after I got your job back for you?"

"That's not it," he said. "There's a lot of other things in life, and maybe love handles shouldn't be the most important to you."

"It's not *my* love handles. It's Jane's." Except I *did* worry about growing my own, sometimes.

He closed up the men's glossy and looked at me for a few seconds. "Sure. Forget what I said, okay?"

It wasn't so easy to forget something like that, but I told him I had to use the bathroom before we left. He walked me to one down the hall, cleared the area inside, and stood guard outside. As I went in, he said, "I'm gonna find some coffee. Don't come out till I'm back, okay?"

I went inside a stall and peed and waited inside for Walter while holding my breath because it smelled like crap and piss. The room's door swung open, and before I called out Walter's name I heard Rog's voice. He was talking on his phone at the urinal.

"I know," he was saying. "It's awful timing. Except the Super Bowl's tomorrow, right? So that'll take away some of the attention." He *uh-huh*ed a few times while he zipped up. "Yeah, I'm handling the press on this, I don't trust anyone at the label." He washed his hands and left. In another minute or so Walter came in and called for me.

"Let's find Rog," he said, and we saw him still on the phone in the conference room.

Rog covered his phone for a second. "I'm staying here tonight." He looked right at me. "Hey. You doing okay?" I was doing okay before he asked, but now with Rog being so concerned about how *I* was, too, I didn't feel so hot.

"I'm okay," I said. "Call me at the hotel if anything changes."

He told me he would. I was a little more relaxed knowing Rog was handling it. He knew how to do this stuff. Walter wasn't media-savvy.

CHAPTER 17

Cleveland (Second Day)

I watched TV as I ate breakfast and Walter waited in his room. Some morning show was running down entertainment news, and the host said, "We have word that Jane Valentine, the mother and manager of pop star Jonny Valentine, was hospitalized last night in Cleveland after suffering an anaphylactic reaction related to a severe peanut allergy. We'll let you know more when we do. In the meantime, our thoughts are with the Valentines."

Yeah, sure, I almost said out loud. Last week your thoughts were a character assassination slamming Jane for being a bad mother. Your thoughts are whatever boosts your ratings, you vultures.

Jane probably *would* get rushed to the emergency room if she ate peanuts, but she's super-careful about making sure anything she orders doesn't have it as an ingredient. It was a good story, whoever came up with it, because if we needed to, we could get a doctor in L.A. to confirm she's allergic, and if the venue staff leaked to the press, we now had a reason for why she collapsed. People believe anything once it's in the media as long as it's the first story.

Nadine came by a little later to give me my final. "You feeling okay?" she asked.

"Jane's the one who ate peanuts and got sick."

Nadine looked at me like she wasn't sure if she knew I knew that was a lie. I don't know if she knew, either. But neither of us could say anything about it. We were sort of like the criminals in the logic question, guessing what was going on in the other guy's head.

"Well," she said, "given the circumstances, I've decided we should delay your final exam. I'll give you the question, but you don't have to finish it until my vacation ends next week and you're back in L.A. You can just play video games now if you like." She handed me a piece of paper.

Final Exam: History and Language/Reading

Write an essay of approximately 1,000 words in response to this prompt: What does it mean to be the property of another person, and what does it mean to be free? What are the advantages and disadvantages of each position? Make sure you have a beginning, middle, and end, and cite at least three primary sources.

Nadine always asked strange questions like this. They were never simple, like, "Why did America start the Revolutionary War?" She'd be like, "How might a Loyalist in America feel during the Revolutionary War?" and since I never have any clue, I'm always saying, "He'd feel ambivalent." *Ambivalent* was Nadine's favorite word to describe anyone in history's feelings, like, "Abraham Lincoln felt *ambivalent* about freeing the slaves," or her other favorite word was *complex,* like, "The causes of any historical event are always *complex* and cannot be reduced to a single explanation." But by now it had become a joke between us, so I couldn't use either one anymore.

Unless the answer was the obvious one, that when you're a slave you don't get to do what you want but everything's taken care of for you, and when you're free you get to do what you want but that means finding your own food and shelter and clothes, I didn't know what Nadine wanted. It was a good thing she'd given me the extra week, or else I probably would have gotten a C or a D. I'm crap at history.

Someone knocked at the door, and it wasn't Jane's knock or Walter's. "That must be Jason," Nadine said as she got up. "He's meeting me here."

"Who's Jason?" I asked.

"My boyfriend," she said. "I've mentioned him, haven't I?"

She had, though I doubted she'd ever told me his name, because I always pay attention to *Jason* since it's one of my fake IDs for hotels, but she already had the door open. This young guy in a suit stood there with a goofy grin and his luggage. He pulled a bouquet of flowers out from behind his back.

"Happy anniversary," he said, and Nadine hugged him and kissed him on the lips. After they, like, rubbed each other's backs, she said, "Jason, you've never met Jonny before, have you?"

"Nope." He barged right into my room to shake my hand. "Jason McKnight."

His hand felt sweaty and cold at the same time. "Hi," I said.

We all stood there. I didn't know if this guy thought he was going to move his stuff into my room or something, but Nadine said, "I'll be done in five minutes. Here's my card, 1933."

He took the card and said, "Nineteen thirty-three, good year," and she said, "Except for the Depression," and he said, "And the rise of the Third Reich," and they laughed and kissed again and he left.

"Sorry for the interruption. Where were we?" Nadine said.

"Why is he here?" I asked.

"Jason? He had to go to Cleveland for business, so we planned to meet up while I was in town, then we're going to Paris."

"I thought you were going back to L.A. for our break."

"I was, but Jason surprised me with this trip, and we realized it was our one-year anniversary, so . . . Anyway, I wanted to talk—"

"What's he do? In business?"

"He's a consultant for an investment bank."

"What does that mean?"

"It means—I'll explain another time. I wanted to ask you a question before I left," she said. "I know you've got a lot going on, but I was wondering if you'd made a decision about what you're going to do in terms of school. Jane said she'd pay me either way this semester, and I'd be helping you out after school, but it'd be good to know so I could start my job search. If I need to find one, I mean." She seemed uncomfortable, like she didn't want to have to ask this.

Then leave, Nadine. That's what you want to do. Everyone wants to do what's good for them and they don't care how it affects anyone else. Just leave. Tell the police I'm guilty and watch out for yourself.

"I'm thinking about going back to school," I said, but I still didn't really know. Maybe she'd feel sorry she brought it up.

"You are?"

"Yeah. I should probably have a bunch of different teachers who each know a subject instead of just one."

"Right. Right." She nodded a few times. "Almost forgot," she said, and took a greeting card out of a folder. It was a get-well-soon card, and she'd gotten everyone in the crew to sign it for Jane and was saving me for last. I picked up a pen, but because I was imagining Nadine teaching in a real school, with all these other students who weren't me, I wasn't concentrating and wrote a big loopy "Songs, Smiles, and ♥ JV" on the card. Everyone else just wrote their name or "Feel better!" or something like that. If I crossed it out it'd look worse, so I left it like it was.

When I handed it back to Nadine, I turned my head like I was distracted and kept my hand going forward until it touched one of her breasts. She doesn't have big breasts, like one-tenth of Sharon's, and I didn't feel much, but they were still soft and like super-nice chub. She made this quick gasping sound, but I think she couldn't tell if it was an accident or not, so she didn't say anything. She gathered her stuff real fast and didn't hug me like she usually does when she leaves on vacation. When she walked out she let the door close on its own, and hotel doors always swing shut hard so that you don't accidentally leave them open, and it was like a hard bass beat that closes out a song.

The hotel shut down the gym for forty minutes so me and Walter could sneak in a workout. Walter has me spot him even though he doesn't need the help, and he lets me lift the five-pound dumbbells. He doesn't push me on the cardio the way Jane and Rog do, he just tells me to go for it, but it's funny, I usually end up working out harder with him.

Walter had a voice mail from Rog, who said Jane was ready for visitors but was staying in the hospital at least another night to play it safe, and we could see her tonight after dinner. It was supposed to be Walter's day off, so I told him I'd hole up in my room. I was on Level 98 now anyway, and I wanted to finish bad.

I had a hard time focusing on the game because I was wondering what I'd say to Jane. Like, should I tell her it was stupid to drink so much without eating? Or did she already know that and she didn't need to get yelled at? I hate it when Rog criticizes a vocal glitch in a concert that I knew about, or when Jane says I shouldn't have answered an interview question the way I did when I already realized I messed up. When you mess up, if you've got any brains, you know it and you don't need someone reminding you. It almost makes me *want* to mess up again. So I wouldn't say it to Jane, in case she was like me that way. But if I didn't say anything, she'd think I was okay with it. Maybe the best thing to do would be not to go. Then she'd be *wondering* what I thought, and she'd be so embarrassed and sorry she wouldn't do it again.

I screamed through Level 98 in a few hours and had no trouble at all with the minion at the end. I wish Nadine tested me in Zenon instead of history. It was like working out with Walter. No one made me do it, so I was good at it. I wish I did more stuff like that, where no one else cared but me.

I ordered room service for dinner, pad Thai with mashed potatoes on the side, and didn't care that it was a double-carber because of my good workout with Walter and also since Jane was in the hospital and Rog never checked up on me in person, except he was calling every hour now to make sure I was all right. I even found a jar of mayo in the minibar and smeared a glob on the mashed potatoes to make it like potato salad. I watched a TV channel playing songs while I ate, but they weren't any of mine, only derivative pop.

Walter knocked on my door at six o'clock and said, "You ready to go, brother?" I was about to tell him, "I'm really tired, I think I'll stay in tonight and see her when she gets out."

But the channel with songs was still on, and I heard the first few notes of the track Rog convinced Jane to leave off my first album because it didn't fit organically, "Baby, Please Don't Ever Leave Me," where the piano quietly tinkles up a little like raindrops on a roof and then my voice drops in like sunshine through the rain. I should sing it more in concert. It's an underrated song in my library.

All of a sudden I got worried that Jane might have to stay *two* more nights in the hospital and she'd miss my concert in Detroit. She'd never missed a concert once. I grabbed a Detroit Tigers hat. "Let's go," I said to Walter.

Rog had arranged it so a hospital rep met us and took us straight to Jane's room. She had a room on a floor with all private rooms. There were concierges in the halls, and it even looked like a hotel, and the food coming into a few rooms was room-service caliber. If I had to go to a hospital, I'd want it to be a place like this. Definitely not the children's hospital. That was like a bad school where you don't even get to stay at home if you're sick. Walter told me he'd wait outside and said, "Unless you want me to go in."

"No, you can wait," I said. I don't know why he thought I'd need crowd buffer inside a private hospital room.

I thought the private rooms would get prettier nurses, but Jane's was around fifty and shaped like a snowman. She reminded me I could only talk to her for a few minutes, and opened the door and softly called inside, "You have a visitor."

Jane was in bed, watching network entertainment news. She didn't look all that bad. Her face was like she'd been putting on not moisturizers, but *de*-moisturizers. I'd seen worse hangovers on her, though.

She tried to smile, but could barely lift up the sides of her mouth. She muted the TV and said, "Hi." Her voice was pretty weak.

"Hi." I walked up to her bed, and didn't know if I should sit on it or if I should let her hug me or if she even *could* hug me, so I stopped about a foot from the edge. It was as awkward as it was with Dana after she gave me the blow job. I bet even Zack wouldn't know how to handle this situation.

I nodded at the TV. "Anything about you on that?"

"No. Thank God."

Her voice was super-weak, like it was filtered and the decibel level was cut by seventy-five percent.

"You getting out tomorrow?" I asked.

"I hope so," she said. "The doctors haven't cleared me yet."

I didn't ask how she'd catch up to us when we drove to Detroit if she didn't get out in the morning. I hadn't really thought about telling her about my father emailing me before, but this could've been the time to do it. She owed me, and she didn't have the energy to fight, and there was a chance she'd say it was okay. I could tell her I wanted to see him on my own when we traveled to New York, and if it went good, I wanted the two of them to meet again, and maybe when she saw him she'd change her mind. I bet she never even talked to him on the phone.

But it would be stupid. She'd get upset and say no and have her lawyers make him stop. I couldn't risk it.

We watched the entertainment show on mute. I think Jane didn't want to unmute it, since we'd be admitting we didn't know what to say to each other. It didn't really matter. You could sort of guess at what they were saying without hearing them.

When it cut to commercial, she said, "Will you sing me a song, baby?"

I couldn't always talk, but I could always sing. But it was the same problem with the children's hospital. None of my songs would fit here.

"Please, Jonathan?" she asked again. "It's all I've wanted the whole day."

I *still* didn't do anything for a few seconds, but I'd figured out what I was going to do. After I'd made her wait long enough, I sang

> *Hush-a-bye, don't you cry*
> *Go to sleepy, little baby*
> *Go to sleepy, little baby*
> *When you wake, you shall have*
> *All the pretty little horses*
> *All the pretty little horses*

I ended after the first verse. "I have to go," I said. "You're supposed to be resting."

She looked more beat-up than she did at the start, with bags under her eyes and her skin pasty and uneven without any makeup. I got this image in my head of Jane in a hospital bed, like she was now, only she was holding a baby to her chest. And the baby's face was mine. Probably from that stupid drawing in the *New York Times,* or maybe I'd seen her in the hospital when she'd had the other baby, after all, and that was why I felt like I'd been in the room with the premature babies before. If she didn't look like such crap right then, maybe I even would've asked her about it.

Before I could open the door, she said, "I'm sorry," quieter than before.

I didn't ask what she was sorry about. I didn't answer or nod or turn or anything. I just stopped, to let her know I'd heard it, and said, "How are presales?"

"They're . . . good," she said. That pause meant they weren't. "Better than before."

I left. Walter dropped me off at my hotel room and made plans for when to wake me up the next day. He said me and him and Rog would get Jane at the hospital in the morning. I figured they wanted me there in case any paparazzi were around when she got out.

I turned on the second half of the Super Bowl. It was a blowout, and I didn't care about the teams, but I kept it on anyway. My hotel room felt huge, like a football stadium, with me the only fan inside it that no one could see.

Tyler Beats starred in a big soda commercial. It was a sixty-second spot, and it was funny, and he even got to promote his new single during it. My commercials so far have all had crap production values for crap products.

I double-locked the door and dug out the glossy I'd packed in L.A. from the bottom of a suitcase. That seemed like forever ago. I turned up the volume of the game and found the FIT AND OVER 40! spread. My hand rubbed over my jeans, and I unzipped them and reached inside my underwear, and once I was hard I slid out of my jeans completely.

I was still wearing my black track sweater, but I didn't want to take it off and lose my boner. It felt like a strong one. Except I didn't have any sunscreen on me to use.

I opened up the minibar. The mayo jar was still there. I unscrewed it and scooped out a big glob and spread it over me. It felt slick and like the inside of Dana's mouth, but cool instead of warm. I kept the jar open in case I needed more, but I stored it in the minibar, with the door open so I could get to it easily, since you're not supposed to ever leave mayo out.

I went back to get the glossy and put it next to the minibar and stood there, with the cold air washing over me and the pictures of all the actresses, and I kept pumping harder and slathering on more mayo, and it felt like I was disappearing *inside* the mayo, surrounding myself in all this greasy whiteness.

I shut my eyes and imagined Lisa Pinto coming to my hotel room, hanging a DO NOT DISTURB sign on the knob and closing the door behind herself and locking it with those swinging hotel-door locks, and I opened my eyes again at the actress doing yoga in the glossy and I said out loud, "You like being my little slut, don't you?" and there was this tingly click inside my penis, and I knew it was happening for real this time, and the middle of my body felt like the most super-intense massage ever, like someone had punched me except the punch made you feel amazing, and there was a huge buildup like the silence in the middle of the third verse of "Breathtaking" before I belt out the words, "Yeah, take away my breath," and I comed.

It shot up and all over my black track sweater in a splattery line, but I didn't care, and each spurt was like a small electric shock that felt almost as good as the last one. I breathed heavy and leaned on the minibar for a minute like I'd just done an hour of cardio.

If I could do this each time I tried, I don't know why I'd ever do anything else.

I screwed the mayo lid back on and closed up the minibar and ran my sweater under the faucet, in case a hotel employee saw it, before I tossed it in the garbage. I nearly forgot to clean myself off, which would've been dumb in case the mayo spoiled on me, too.

Some of the come was between my fingers. It was sticky but also slippery. I could make a baby now. I could find a groupie by myself and nine months later be someone's father.

You had to be careful with that, though. Mi$ter $mith had two different women who said he'd gotten them pregnant, and he said it wasn't true but they made him take medical tests, and it turned out they were his kids. All the glossy headlines were like MI$TER $MITH LO$E$ PATERNITY $UIT.

If I had a baby with Lisa Pinto, it'd be cute and talented, but I bet she wasn't on her period yet. The only other girl I could think of was Dana. We'd end up having a chubby baby, but not cute-chubby, and I'd have to visit it every few months, and each time Dana would have some new local band she was going on about with her gimlet eye for spotting Cincinnati talent. I could sort of see why Mi$ter $mith pretended he wasn't the father.

CHAPTER 18

Detroit (First Day)

A knock at my door woke me up, but it wasn't Walter's. Through the peephole I saw Rog pacing around. Before I could say anything to him when I opened up, Rog was like, "We have to go to the hospital immediately. Get changed." He looked serious. I was afraid to ask why we were in such a rush, but I did.

"She's fine," he said. "Just get moving."

He left so I could change, but I got my answer when I turned on E! A reporter said that an anonymous tipster had let the media know that Jane's hospitalization hadn't been from a peanut allergy, but allegedly from a cocaine overdose. I called Rog's cell and told him about it.

"I know," he said.

"It wasn't that, right? It was alcohol, wasn't it?"

He took a long time to answer, and the longer he took, the more sure I became that it wasn't actually alcohol. "I don't know. That's why we have to talk to her at the hospital."

He got Walter and we headed over there again. "This is the last time I'm going to a hospital for a long time unless I get sick myself," I told Walter.

"I'm with you, brother," he said. Rog wasn't talking, though. He was emailing like he'd had eight cups of coffee.

The hospital rep met us again but we knew the way. Walter waited outside and me and Rog went into Jane's room. She looked a little stronger and had her phone out and was typing on it when we came in.

"Jane—" Rog started, but she put up her finger and he shut up.

She finished and said, "So, we have another little problem on our hands from America's worst mother." I knew she was joking, but when she called herself that, it made me think for a second that the media was right. It's like when backup singers apologize for being flat that day. After that, they sound way worse to you, even if they're not.

"We need to tackle this head-on," Rog said. "A press conference."

"First of all, the doctors are making me stay here another night," she said. "So that's out for today."

"How are you going to be at my show tonight?" I asked.

"I'm not. I'll have to miss it."

I knew the whole point of being there was to talk about the cocaine overdose, but her missing the concert felt like the bigger crisis to me. If I brought it up now, though, they'd tell me it wasn't.

"Second of all, there is no *we* anymore, Rog," Jane said.

"What do you mean?" he asked.

"It was an anonymous tip from someone on tour."

He looked at her and at me and back at her. "I don't follow."

"Rog, don't make this any harder than it has to be."

"I honestly have no idea what you're talking about, Janie."

She took a deep breath in through her nostrils. I couldn't tell if it was because she was upset or she had a hard time breathing. "I'm going to let you go. You'll be paid the full amount of the tour."

His mouth was open, and then he smiled. "You're joking, right? You're setting me up? Is this like a hidden-camera show?" She shook her head. His face and voice turned desperate. "Janie, this is insane. I didn't say a word. Why would I do that?"

"You tell me. Maybe to make me more dependent on you."

"Dependent!" Rog said. "What does that even—look, I did everything I could to keep this under control. *Everyone* knows you sometimes do—"

She shot him a mean stare and he looked at me and realized he'd messed up. He got quieter. "I'm not the one who did this. And for you to throw two years out the window because of . . . I don't even *know* what, is—"

"I have it on good authority that you're behind the leak," Jane said. "I value your previous work with us. Save your receipts for getting to the airport and your flight home and the label will reimburse you."

He smiled again, but it wasn't the smile he had when he thought he was on a reality show. "This is an excuse to get rid of me."

"Please leave now before we both say things we'll regret."

"I didn't say anything," Rog said, "but there's a hell of a lot I *could* have said. And I never have."

"You say whatever you want. No one will believe you, and I'll make sure you never get work again. Or I can give you a nice recommendation and say we amicably parted ways. Which way do you want to go?"

Rog bit his lower lip and waited for what felt like an hour. "This is a fucked-up way to treat a friend." He turned to me. "Hope you get along with my replacement." He slammed the door. Jane stared at it for a few seconds.

"You and me, kid," she said. "Just the two of us."

"I don't think Rog did it," I said. "I heard him talking on the phone in the bathroom and it sounded like he was the one who came up with the peanut story."

"That doesn't mean anything. I have trusted sources."

"More trusted than Rog?"

"These things are more complicated than you think. Rog and I have had conflicts you don't know about. I'm sure you and Michael used to have fights that I didn't know about. Can you try to understand that?"

No, I can't understand it. This is worse than what you did with the Latchkeys, and even worse than what you tried to do with Walter. Rog was your best friend for two years, and even if he wasn't the most in-demand voice and dance coach anymore, he worked hard and groomed me. You don't fire your friends because someone told you they messed up, especially if they say they didn't. And I didn't fire Michael as my best friend. You moved me away from him. Plus you didn't tell me he wanted to visit.

And maybe it's what you did with Al. You fired him as your husband and as my father and didn't tell me he wanted to see me again.

"I understand," I said.

I didn't ask her how often she did cocaine, or what she was going to say to the public. The tabloids really go for your throat if you get caught doing cocaine, but she was good at spinning, and they'd shield me from the media until we got to New York, and by then it would blow over. She'd be fine. Rog would be fine, eventually. I'd get a new voice and dance coach when I went back to L.A. who'd be fine. My image would be fine. Jane knew what she was doing.

"I'm going to meet you in Detroit tomorrow, baby. Okay?"

"Fine."

"Don't worry about any of this. Just focus on tonight's show." I nodded, and she told me to go back to the hotel with Walter because she needed to rest and deal with the label.

In the car, Walter said, "So, she fired Rog?"

"Yeah."

He whistled. "Damn. I didn't like the queer much myself, but he doesn't deserve that."

The ride to Detroit was weird with no Jane, no Rog, no Nadine, only me and Walter on a huge bus by ourselves with Kenny the driver. Three fans in the football stadium. Walter should've had the day off yesterday, so I let him sleep and I tried to think about my history essay, but I kept coming back to how Jane wouldn't be at my concert tonight, and Rog wouldn't be there to warm me up even though I could do it on my own, and the only person I'd have was Walter, who was the best in some ways, but he couldn't make up for everyone else.

If my father was around it'd be different. Having someone related to you nearby when you were with strangers would be cool. He'd probably comanage me with Jane, or do something else behind the scenes. I wouldn't have to worry about Jane going out late at night or doing cocaine, and she definitely wouldn't be with Bill. He wouldn't let her fire people who'd worked hard for us.

If Walter had a smartphone I could've checked my email to see if he'd written again, but he's not into gadgets, sort of like Nadine, and he says having one would make him less alert to protect me.

Kenny dropped me and Walter off at the hotel, where I napped and ate lunch, and the car service took us to the venue for sound check. The audio was junk, and usually Jane or Rog takes care of it and yells at whoever to fix it, but I didn't know who was really in charge, and Walter definitely didn't know what to do. I could've asked Bill, but I didn't want to talk to him. And he could've been behind the leak. Maybe Bill wanted to get out of his relationship with Jane and this was a way. She should've fired him, not Rog. Rog wouldn't do something like that.

I played Zenon in my room preshow and ate three slices of pepperoni pizza, which was dumb and totally off-limits if Jane or Rog was around. It would make me too full and the dairy would destroy my voice, plus the pepperoni might make me burp. I vomited, partly from overeating and partly I made myself.

This was already going to be a subpar concert because of the audio system and the pizza and everything else going on with Jane and Rog. I got jittery about my performance, then I got angry that *I* was the only one who got nervous before concerts, and *I* was the only one who looked bad if the concert was subpar, and everyone else could relax backstage even if they were part of the reason it didn't go good, and no one was reviewing *them* in the *L.A. Times* or making fun of *them* in *The New Yorker*.

So screw them. If this is what they were giving me, I wasn't just going to do a bad job. I was going to make it my worst show ever.

I started feeling a little bad about my plan and was afraid to go through with it, but once I got ready, with no one except Bill prepping me backstage, I knew I wanted to go all out. I began with "Guys vs. Girls" like I always did on this tour, but I didn't want to mess up too bad at the beginning. I sang a little flat, enough so that what Rog calls the lay listener could pick up that something was off. Or what Rog *called* the lay listener. Not that he'd departed the realm or anything, but in a way, he did. When someone is out of your life and you'll never see or talk to them again, it's sort of like they're dead.

On "RSVP (To My Heart)," I flattened it out more, and I moved slower than my dancers so it looked all out of rhythm and it might make them go off pace. I basically spoke the words to "This Bird Will Always Bee There for You" and didn't even move. By then the crowd could probably tell I was tanking it, even the seven-year-olds. On "You Hurt Me," I made it seem like I forgot the words and stopped singing halfway through, and came in late on purpose to the third verse.

Eventually the boos began. I'd never been booed at a concert before, only a couple times at other events where there are haters, because if someone pays seventy-five dollars or whatever to see me, they probably love me, especially girls. And once there were a few boos, from the older girls and their parents, more came in. If I'd been giving a concert to ten people and one booed me, no one else would follow. When you get people in a big crowd, they're sheep, like Internet commenters.

I waved my hands like, Bring it on, and the boos got louder until it seemed like the whole audience was yelling, and even though it was what I'd wanted, once I actually heard it, it was the worst feeling in the world. I couldn't tell what was worse: no one paying attention to you, or everyone hating you. I felt *ambivalent* about it. I didn't even know if I could recover now or if I should just give up and end the show, and so what if it meant we had to issue refunds.

I looked at my dancers and singers and instrumentalists, who were all staring at me like, You're screwing us, too. When I turned back, I saw a person in a wheelchair on the wings of the stage, hidden from the crowd.

Jane.

Walter was standing behind her, and she was still looking pale and weak, but she was there. She looked confused, I guess because of the audience reaction, but gave me a little wave.

Something switched inside me. I didn't want to hear the boos. One more second of it and I might die. All the bodies in the darkness around me were people who only wanted me to sing good, and I'd make their night. Their *month*. I wanted to hear their applause again, more than anything.

I faced the crowd. "I'm sorry, everyone," I said. "My voice was off before, but it feels better. I'm gonna sing an a cappella number to make it up to you." The band wasn't expecting this, but I motioned for them to let me go, and I sang

> *I want you here, I need you here*
> *Baby, babe, you always grieve me*
> *I want you here, I need you here*
> *Baby, please don't ever leave me*

It blew out of the water all the a cappella renditions I'd ever done. Even better, I drew the crowd into a sing-along by the third verse. And I knew I'd won them back, and that now they loved me more than they ever had before because for a while I made it seem like I didn't care if they loved me or not, and that they could just as easily turn on me again but it didn't matter to me. They worshiped me. Fans are like babies that way. You don't give them their milk, and they cry their eyes out, then you give it to them and they suck it down and shut up and forget they were ever upset.

The rest of the concert was A-plus work, and I went out for a second encore and did an a cappella version of "Guys vs. Girls," which I rarely do, but I couldn't do anything wrong that night. Jane was waiting for me in her wheelchair when I came backstage.

"You were great," she said.

I didn't smile or anything. I just stayed in the Jonny Zone. "I know."

"Sorry I got here late."

"I thought you weren't coming at all."

"I bargained to get out early, and took a cab all the way here. I couldn't stand the idea of missing one of your shows."

I shrugged.

"You want to clean up and we'll go to the hotel?" she asked.

I nodded and walked past her, but when I was right behind her I smelled her perfume, and I know it's Chanel No. 5 but to me it smells like Jane, and I couldn't help it, so I hugged her from behind around her shoulders and neck for a second, and she seemed a little surprised but put her hand on my arm, and then I let go and went to my room.

CHAPTER 19

Detroit (Second Day)

Jane had basically made a full recovery by the morning and didn't need the wheelchair anymore. She was supposed to take it easy the next few days, which I think even she was going to stick to. The original plan was for me and her and Walter to fly to New York ahead of the others, who'd take the bus and would have a day off, so I could do press and prep for my miniconcert with Tyler Beats. But I didn't know how much publicity they'd want now with everything that had just happened.

Me and Jane took our own car to the airport, and Walter rode in a taxi ahead of us. He's too big for all three of us to fit into the backseat sometimes, and Jane's luggage fills up the trunk. A few minutes into the ride, I said, "I've been thinking more about school."

She put down her phone. "What about it?"

"Like, maybe going to it."

"Why's that?"

"I don't know. It seems like it's something a regular kid should be doing."

"Uh-huh," she said. "I can understand that."

Boxy warehouses passed by us along the highway. Most cities were ugly on the way to the airport. It's like they didn't give a shit anymore since they knew you were leaving anyway. "The thing is, you know, you're not exactly a regular kid."

"I know."

"Other people go to school because they have to. You don't have to."

"But what if I want to?"

"No one's stopping you, if it's something you want to do. It'll be a tough adjustment, but Nadine can tutor you after school. And we could refer Walter somewhere else."

"Refer Walter somewhere else?"

"He wouldn't be your bodyguard anymore. The school wouldn't let you bring a bodyguard. The point is that you're supposed to be a regular student. None of the other celebrity kids are allowed to have one."

I hadn't thought about that. I might not even be the most famous student there.

"What about after school?"

"That wouldn't work. He wouldn't be able to live on a part-time salary, and if we're not working, I can't justify spending a full salary on someone who works only a few hours a day. I'm sure we could find someone else willing to do it, though."

"But when I go back on tour, he'd work for us again?"

"I imagine he'd be someone else's bodyguard by then. And we'd have whoever we end up with."

The sky was the color of a mouse and matched the highway and all the buildings. The outside was like an animal that changed its color to blend in. "I'm still mulling it."

"Entirely up to you, baby." She returned to her phone.

We found Walter outside the airport and did our thing where we get special treatment and skip all the lines, even the business-class line, and killed time before the flight in the private lounge area. They were always filled with businessmen working on their laptops, so I didn't need to wear my baseball hat and sunglasses.

The TV above us was showing a morning talk show on closed-captioning, and I was watching because I had nothing else to do, and after a couple boring minutes, Rog appeared on it. I elbowed Jane. She perked up. "He didn't waste any time, did he?" she said.

The closed captioning was screwing up a lot, like a few times it called me "Jenny," but the interviewer was grilling Rog all about Jane, and he was saying things like, "She's paranoid and a control freak," and "She thinks she knows how to run Jonny's career, but she doesn't understand music—it's everyone else who makes the smart decisions," and "I only hope Jonny makes it out of this in one piece." Every time he said something mean about her, my gut twisted up like it was my fiftieth crunch in a row. Jane had screwed him over, but I didn't see what the point of bashing her in return was, unless he was trying to score a book deal or become a judge on a reality show. When people commit reputation suicide like this, it's about money.

Jane made little sounds like she couldn't believe him. She said to me, "If anyone interviews you about this, take the high road and say gracious things about Rog. Say he was a great coach and, unfortunately, sometimes people go their separate ways. Kill him with kindness."

When they put up a bad photo of her near the end, she said, "The coffee here's terrible. I'm finding a Starbucks." After she left, I noticed a complimentary computer terminal in the corner of the lounge. This could be my only chance.

"I need to send Nadine follow-up questions for my slavery essay," I told Walter, and I pointed to the computer. He nodded, and I ran over to the terminal and checked my email, though I really should've been asking her questions since I still had no idea what to write about. There was a message from him from a few days before:

I'm sorry I wasn't in Cincinnati. I thought I might have the chance but it didn't work out. Was it fun? Maybe I can see you perform in New York. I lived in Sydney, Australia. I moved there because it seemed like a place where you could really have an adventure and a friend of mine told me there was lots of construction work. Here's a picture I took of my friend Dave on a hiking trip we took in Australia.

The picture was of some guy wearing sunglasses in the desert. I didn't have time to think about what I wanted to say, so I quickly wrote

If you can get a ticket to my concert in NYC at Madison
Square Garden on Feb. 14 I will find some way for us to meet.
I can't buy the ticket myself or get you on the list.

I ran back to my seat and picked up a glossy Jane had out and pretended
to be reading it when she came back. It was published a few days ago,
so there wasn't anything on me or her. Anyone who says all publicity is
good publicity never had actual bad publicity.

Jane typed something into her iPhone and said, "Rog's career is
essentially over, as of this email." She said it loud enough so that Walter
would hear, too.

She was trying to project confidence like you have to do onstage, but
I knew *my* career might be essentially over if things didn't go right the
next two days. That was how quickly your star could fall. And I might
meet my father. I tried not to think about either thing, and took out
my slavery books and a piece of paper to outline my essay, but I couldn't
focus, and just stared at the blank page.

CHAPTER 20

New York (First Day)

Jane's face sort of lit up when we landed in New York. She loves L.A., but wherever she is, she always feels like she's missing out on the real business in New York. She says L.A. is for entertainment-industry people who dabble in business, and New York is for business-people who dabble in the entertainment industry, and business is what makes entertainment possible even though entertainment sucks up most of the media attention.

We had a few short-form interviews and one business meeting in the morning before my late-show performance with Tyler Beats. Jane cut out interviews with anyone that might be hostile press, and she'd had our publicist make sure that questions about Jane would be off-limits, so they were all softballs I've had a million times, like, "What's your favorite song to sing?" ("Guys vs. Girls" is what I'm supposed to say, but it's actually "Breathtaking") and "What do you look for in a girl?" (a nice smile, which is something any girl can have, and someone who's got a really fun and nice personality, because every girl thinks she's got a fun and nice personality). Once in my life I want to answer something like, "I want a super-chubby girl so I feel less beefy compared to her."

I asked Jane if I could skip the business meeting. She shook her head. "We make more off branding and ancillary deals than we do with the music. The music is the plane that flies you to the branding."

"But the music's still the most important thing, right?" I asked.

"Yes, of course," she said. "I didn't mean to put it that way."

Maybe Rog was right. Jane knew a lot about some things, but she didn't know much about music. So I went but didn't hardly speak, just shook the hands of all these men and women who told me their daughters were big fans and asked me to sign all kinds of crap merch for them, which was funny, since the meetings were mostly about producing more crap merch, like a cell phone decorated with pictures of me and with all my songs preloaded for ringtones. *I* don't even have a cell phone yet. I was worried about overexposure, but Jane says it only seems like overexposure because we're looking at it all, and the average consumer has to see something seven times before they decide to buy it. Maybe that's another reason so many songs sound the same, to trick people into thinking they've heard it six times before and now they're finally ready to buy it.

The whole time we bounced around the city in the car service, I looked out the window like I did in Cincinnati. I knew I wouldn't spot my father on the street, but I kept thinking about how he *was* out there somewhere, and on every street I thought something like, My father could have walked on this street before. By now he'd probably read my email, and maybe he was trying to get a ticket. I wish they weren't so expensive, though. They'd cost even more from a scalper.

We arrived at the late show in the afternoon for the 5:30 taping. The fans were already lined up, and a few held signs for me, but most were for Tyler, which wasn't a positive audience predictor if he was supposed to be there supporting me in a secondary role. He even had some guy fans, and they were all older than mine, some in their twenties and thirties. His manager had done a really savvy job broadening his base through his music and image maintenance. I bet if Tyler got busted for drinking, he'd find a way to spin it into a positive.

Walter and the show's security escorted me into the star/talent entrance. Tyler wasn't arriving till later, so the show coordinator had me rehearse on my own with the house band and do a mock-interview with her. Since it was a special performance of two singers, we'd get three songs, then our joint interview. First I'd sing "RSVP (To My Heart)," Tyler would sing "Beats Me," then he'd sing backup on "Guys vs. Girls." I was worried that we wouldn't get a chance to rehearse it together, but she said, "Don't worry, Tyler's a total pro, just do your usual thing."

After I'd finished my rehearsal, Tyler came into the dressing room by himself. I wondered where his bodyguard was. He was smaller than I expected him to be, and his tight leather jacket and jeans made him seem even smaller, but with his head so big, it almost looked like his body hadn't fully grown. He was good-looking, but nothing special, like someone had picked out enough decent features and zero ugly ones and mashed them together.

He spotted me in one of the star chairs. "Hey," he said, and did a military salute.

"Hi," I said.

Jane shook his hand. "Very nice to meet you, Tyler."

"Likewise," he said. "Uh . . . can I ask your name?"

"Of course," Jane said, like it was no big deal, but she hates when people think she's just my mother and not also my manager. "I'm Jane Valentine, Jonny's mother and manager."

"Right." We all knew he was thinking back on the headlines the last couple weeks. "I'm sorry about that. Jet lag."

Jane pasted on a huge smile. "Is your manager here?" He said he was outside, and Jane excused herself to talk to him.

Tyler sat down in the other star chair a few feet away from mine. He sized himself up in the mirror and stood and leaned in closer. He squeezed his left nostril between two fingers. A bunch of white lines popped out of his skin like flowers sprouting out of the ground in fast-forward. Then he popped a pimple on his chin. Some white stuff came out of that, too, but so did some blood. "Fuck me," he said as he tried wiping it off. "Who's on makeup here?"

"She did me awhile ago," I said.

"You mind calling to your mom? I can't go out like this."

I said no problem, and I opened the door and saw Jane talking to what must have been Tyler's manager, who was this guy in his early thirties in a nice suit and glasses with thick black frames. Now, he *definitely* wasn't good-looking, but something about the suit and the glasses and his neat haircut made it seem like this guy never messed up and got whatever he wanted. "Jane, Tyler needs makeup," I said.

"Hundred-to-one he's popping his zits again," the manager said. "These are the pitfalls of managing a seventeen-year-old. Jane, when the time comes, go with Accutane, it'll save you tons of grief."

"I've already been talking about that with his dermatologist," Jane said, which she hadn't told me.

The manager found the show's makeup woman and she came into the tent and cleaned up Tyler's popped zit and caked on concealer and a new coat of foundation. It's always like that when you see celebrities up close. They have all the same zits and blackheads and scars normal people do, only they've got better products and experts to cover them up.

We had some time to kill before we went on, so I asked if he wanted to do a dry run of "Guys vs. Girls" real quick, and he said he was cool, he knew it as well as one of his own songs, and that was maybe the biggest compliment I could ever get from another singer unless MJ came back to life and told me he'd gotten into my music after he departed the realm. If I invited him to play Zenon, he might think that was unprofessional to do preshow. It didn't matter, though, since he said he was going to stretch and do warm-ups in the greenroom. He walked out the door to the right. "The greenroom's the other way," I said.

"Oh, they give me my own here," he said. "From being on the show so much. I'm sure you'll get one next time you come back." That was cool of him to say. But they might not bring me back. Maybe they were only having me on now because I was bundled with Tyler.

So I played Zenon till the show coordinator told me to get ready, and I met Tyler backstage and we got miked up. After a commercial break, the host said they had two of the brightest young stars in music performing one of their own songs each and a duet. "First up is Jonny Valentine," he said, and the audience cheered. "And then we have Tyler Beats," he finished, and you almost couldn't hear him through the applause. I didn't have to vomit, but I also didn't feel great. Late-night

TV audiences are less friendly than morning-show crowds. I guess people who go to sleep late are more hostile than people who get up early in the morning. They're waiting to laugh at you if you mess up. Tyler didn't seem nervous at all.

The house guitarist played the G chord to "RSVP (To My Heart)," which was my cue to go onstage. The rest of the house band was tight. When we rehearsed preshow, they looked like regular guys who joke around with each other, like the Latchkeys, except they're not young and famous even though they're on TV every night. It's only a job to them. They come into work, do their thing, and go home.

My performance was an A and the audience was into it and gave me a warm ovation when it was done and I went into the holding area backstage. Then the opening bass line for "Beats Me" kicked in, and the crowd was like, This is what we *really* came for, and the monitors were showing everyone dancing in the seats even before Tyler sang his first line. I'd like to make music like that someday, not just diarrhea pop for little girls to cry to, but something that hits *everyone* and moves them.

They went wild when he finished, and it was so loud the band had to wait before they could begin "Guys vs. Girls" and I could come back onstage. Finally they started up, and the crowd came alive every time Tyler sang backup, which was way better than my real backups.

I got so distracted over how Tyler was outshining me that when the third verse came along, I couldn't remember the first line. I froze up on something I'd sung ten thousand times. I let a whole sixteen beats go by and did some trademark spin moves to pretend like I was doing a dance break, but I still couldn't remember it, and at one point I made eye contact with Tyler, and he must have seen in my face that my memory was like, Fuck you, Jonny, this is what you get for popping all that zolpidem. So he sang the verse himself:

> *Saw a lady walking down the street*
> *Looking so good with her golden curls*
> *Yellin' and screamin' at some loser dude*
> *Just another case of guys versus girls*

It was like the crowd had an Eric for me but comed for him. Tyler was the better singer. Even the lay listener could hear that. He had more range, more texture, more charisma, more vocal control. Jane was lying, or wrong, when she kept saying I was more talented than Tyler. I was a talented freak, but he was a freak even compared to other freaks. The only way I could ever beat him was to work twice as hard. And Jane said he had the best work ethic already. I'm not even sure I could beat him if I *did* work that hard.

We sang the last verse together, I think because Tyler was afraid I'd forget the words again:

> *Pay attention, fellas, I got something to say*
> *Listen up, ladies, all around the world*
> *We'll never get nowhere if we keep this silly war up*
> *You know what it is: guys versus girls*

We did our bows at the same time, which I was happy about, because the cheers would've been way louder for him than for me. They arranged it so I sat closer to the desk on the couch, but I wished Tyler had taken the seat. The host asked me about my concert on Valentine's Day, and I said all the things Jane had coached me on, like how I was super-excited to perform for the first time in front of my fans in New York and for the whole world on the Internet for just $19.95.

"For just $19.95?" he said. "If they act now, do you throw in a set of steak knives?"

I didn't get the joke but I knew he was making fun of me. I fake-laughed along with the audience, though. Laugh all the way to glossy coverage, Jane says whenever a comedian makes fun of me. "And Tyler, what are you plugging?" he asked.

"I've got absolutely nothing going on," Tyler said. "It's a sad, empty existence. Thank you for letting me come here and be around other human beings." The crowd loved it. He gave good interview.

The host turned back to me. "Now, you've had quite an eventful last few weeks."

"It's been a lot of work and a lot of concerts, but I'm grateful for the opportunity to get to play in front of so many fans," I said.

"Uh, I meant more what's been happening *after* the concerts," he said. More hostile laughter. I knew Jane was watching on a monitor, getting ready to bitch someone out for letting him ask about this and going off-script from the mock-interview.

"People like to talk about me," I said. "I don't listen to them. I just try to stay positive."

"I stay positive, too," Tyler said.

"Oh, yeah?" the host said, smiling, like he was passing him the ball for an easy assist.

"Yeah, I'm positive I'm miserable," Tyler said. Even with a joke I'd heard in fourth grade and knew was coming, the audience lapped it up.

The host got serious. "But why is that? Why are people so utterly fascinated with you?"

This was different from, "What's your best feature?" I didn't have an answer besides that the creative department of my label had *made* people get fascinated with me. If there was another kid who was cute enough and sang good enough, they'd be fascinated with him. You can't say that stuff, though, since people get pissed when they realize they don't choose most things in life they think they're choosing, that it's all picked for them by someone who controls the purse strings.

"I don't know," I said. "I'm only a kid."

"But an *utterly fascinating* kid," Tyler said, and the audience whooped. He was trying to help out and change the subject, but the host wouldn't let it go.

"That's just it," he said. "You're a kid, yet everyone wants to know what's happening in your life. And you're, what, all of four feet tall?"

The sheep laughed again. But they're the ones who waited in line three hours to see me when they had nothing better to do with their stupid vacations from the Midwest. Except they probably really came to see Tyler.

"People like to think about celebrities," I said. "Sometimes they're a little happier from watching us sing or act or play sports, because we take them away from everything."

This was the standard line I'd seen other celebrities give, and pretty close to an answer I'd given a few times before. I was going to stop, but the host said, "Hey, he learned to talk!" and the crowd laughed *again,* and something flipped inside me and I started saying stuff I hadn't said before, or maybe even thought before.

"But when things go bad for us, it really makes them happier about their own lives," I said. "And when they make fun of my mother, it makes them feel better about how they raise their own normal kids. So even when they think they love you for not being like a normal person, underneath it they actually hate you, because that's the part that hates themselves for not being special, and for knowing they couldn't handle the pressure of being famous anyway."

This shut the crowd up, and even the host. I was afraid to say anything else. It was tense until Tyler said, "I paid him to say that." Everyone cheered, and he took his wallet out and handed me a twenty-dollar bill and stuffed it into my track sweater pocket, which made them cheer even louder. I don't even *own* a wallet. Tyler wasn't only a better performer, he was a triple-threat entertainer: singing, dancing, and personality, which meant he could act. And I got the sense he didn't even *care* about it all that much, but he could turn it on at any moment and think fast and always win over the audience, and he knew it. Me, I needed dialogue coaching and an allied interviewer and a receptive crowd, and even if I won them over the last twenty times in a row, I wasn't sure I could do it on the twenty-first.

The host thanked us both and plugged my concert again, and the show was over. The band kicked in, and he pretended to be talking to us, but he was mouthing words, and when the producer said we were clear, he walked offstage without saying good-bye. It was only a job to him, too, and it ended the second his show was over. It must be nice not to have to kiss anyone's ass.

Someone led me and Tyler backstage, and Jane was waiting right there. She congratulated both of us and waited till he walked down the hall and around the corner to his private greenroom.

"That was a *really* bad answer," she said. "But it's not your fault. They explicitly promised me there'd be nothing like that. I'm going to yell at someone." The shadow of a body was on the wall by the corner Tyler had walked around. I got all hot, even though the studio was like fifty-five degrees, thinking about him listening to Jane criticize me post-performance. His manager wouldn't do that.

She told me to eat in the greenroom and she'd be over soon. The guests who were on earlier had already left the greenroom, so it was only me in there with the whole buffet to myself. I wondered if Jane had even fully heard what I'd said on the show. She probably agreed with me, too, but didn't want to admit it, since she used to be one of those regular people who worshiped celebrities, and even though she *is* one now herself, she still does, at least the ones who are more famous than her.

In a couple minutes Tyler came in. "Hey," he said. "The spread in my greenroom was shitty. Mind if I crash yours?" I said that was cool. He scooped up nearly *everything* on the buffet line.

Once he sat down, I said, "Thanks." He nodded as he stuffed his face. We didn't need to say any more. Musicians are like athletes. They all know who the MVP is.

"Starving," he said between bites. "You not allowed to eat before a show, either?"

"Sort of."

"I get sixteen hundred calories a day. You're lucky. My metabolism is slow as hell. But I'm on break now, except for this. So, fuck it."

I picked at some salad. I didn't want Jane coming in and catching me scarfing down crap and thinking this was why I was less successful than Tyler, even though he was the one eating like an elephant. She did come in a minute later and said how great he was, and told me she was still talking to the producer and she'd be back in a few.

Tyler tossed a piece of sushi into his mouth like it was popcorn. "Your mom's always been your manager?"

"Yeah."

"Who produces you?"

"We've had a couple. Jane always thinks they didn't do a good enough job and finds someone new."

"You should work with my guy. I can set it up." I thanked him, and he added, "Then maybe *I'll* produce you."

"You produce?"

"Not yet," he said. "But the plan is to start in a couple years."

"You're still going to sing, right?"

He shrugged his shoulders as he poured barbecue sauce over his filet mignon. For such a small guy, he could seriously pack it away.

"A little, to keep up a profile," he said. "But performing is for amateurs. The people with real power are always behind the scenes. Talent gets chewed up and used. Better to be the one chewing." He yanked off a huge chunk of the filet mignon with his teeth and gnashed it loudly as a joke.

It made sense. You didn't want to be the cow. Because even if you were filet mignon, the best meat, you got chewed up. You didn't really want to be the human who *ate* the cow, either, since he was just like another farm animal. You wanted to be the human who *sold* the cow to that guy. And compared to Tyler, I wasn't even filet mignon. I was the roast beef sandwich you ate when you were trapped in your airplane seat. Plus I wasn't the kind of person who could ever chew anyone else up. Tyler wouldn't have thought that when he was eleven, either. He blew up when he was thirteen, so he didn't have exactly the same career trajectory, but it was close. Maybe Jane would let me call him when we got back to L.A. I'd tell her it was to ask him questions about his career, and I really would ask him about it. But he also knew what it was like to be someone like us. Zack was a different type of musician, and he didn't seem interested in talking to me anymore. Lisa Pinto was an actress first, and she *definitely* wasn't interested in talking to me. Tyler was like me, the same kind of meat. Just a better cut.

CHAPTER 21

New York (Second Day)

I was so amped up for the Garden show that I woke up way early, even before Jane. I grabbed the *USA Today* outside my door to kill time and to see if they mentioned anything about us or my show.

I had zero real estate, but there *was* an interview with Zack. The intro explained how he'd been kicked off our tour and out of the label after the Memphis incident:

Q: What are the Latchkeys' plans now?

A: We are in the process of inking a deal with a small label, and believe we will be well taken care of in our new home, which respects our independence and provides artistic, not merely financial, support. And lower-back support.

Do you regret signing with a major label?

Well, they did help put us on the map, which resulted in interviews in august publications like your own, but on their terms, both musically and presentation-wise. Complete control.

If you could do it again, would you have toured with Jonny Valentine?

That was a decision made for us, so we went along with it. But you can't regret your actions, even when they're regrettable. Hey, how about that: the world's worst needlepoint sampler.

What's Jonny like offstage?

He's a good kid.

And his mother, Jane Valentine?

I would prefer to talk about the Latchkeys and our exciting musical future.

You have nothing to say about the situation?

This is my final statement on the matter: It's an environment I wouldn't subject my own child to. Not that I have a child born out of wedlock I've been keeping in hiding in Raleigh, North Carolina, for seven years, whom I see only on layovers. Wait a minute, is this why you interviewed me, simply to ask about these items of lurid interest to the entire nation, and not because you like my limited body of work beloved by a small coterie of music consumers? God, I feel so used.

If Zack liked me so much, and if it was an environment he wouldn't raise his own child in, how come he hung up so quickly and didn't ask if I wanted to hang out in L.A.? He pretended to be so concerned about me, but he just rode me and my fan base to develop the Latchkeys' brand. He could say it was a decision made by the label, but I'm sure the band loved it. They'd never sell that many seats on their own. And Dana was right. He tried so hard to be clever.

I bet the interviewer didn't get the reference to "Complete Control," though. I'd have to find a way to listen to that song again some-time.

The phone rang as I read a preview of the baseball season and their fantasy-baseball picks. If there was a fantasy-pop-star draft, Tyler would go first overall, and I'd probably drop to the third round now.

I picked up the phone and said, "Hi, Jane."

"Hi, Jonny. This is Stacy Palter, from creative."

"Oh, hi," I said. This was the first time anyone from the label had ever called me on tour without going through Jane.

"I hope I didn't wake you? It's five-thirty here, so I figured you'd be up by now."

"I'm up. Did you want to talk to Jane? She's in room 1812."

I was hoping she'd say, "Eighteen twelve, good year," because even I knew there was a war then, but she said, "No, I actually wanted to talk to you." She paused like she was about to drop bad news. "I saw the show last night. Your performance was great. And your interview was fine until that part at the end."

"Uh-huh." I was glad she didn't mention my fuckup on "Guys vs. Girls." Even professional talent evaluators don't know what's going on a lot of times.

"We don't want to tell you how to conduct yourself in interviews," she said. That's how they talked at the label about business decisions no one wanted to take responsibility for. They always said *we,* even if it was only one person in the room or on the phone. "But we'd love for you to be more professional in the future. This has been a rocky tour, and we've had to devote a lot of PR resources to deflection. We want to be promoting you, not defending you from gaffes."

"Uh-huh," I said again, but I was thinking, How about *you* go onstage four nights a week for a month and a half, and on top of that do a bunch of interviews including with a TV host who's making fun of you in front of a national audience, and everyone's attacking your mother, and your best friends keep disappearing, and see if you can avoid any gaffes.

"And if this continues, it's something we'll have to take into account when your contract sunsets."

Oh. All the times Jane said our career really was in jeopardy, I didn't totally believe her. But if Stacy was calling me at 5:30 in the morning L.A. time, this was serious. Now I had to do really good tonight, to rack up a ton of live-stream sales, first so that my career trajectory pointed up again, and also so that Stacy would apologize, and when they wanted to re-up my contract, I could say, "Sorry, I didn't feel you respected my independence, I want to go with a label that provides artistic, not merely financial, support." Or even that I was through with this cut-throat industry and going back to school, or going to Australia where I could really have an adventure, and it was too bad they threw away millions in future revenue. Except they'd just find someone else. Besides freaks like MJ and Tyler Beats, even top-shelf talent can be replaced.

"I understand," I said. "It won't happen again."

"Great!" she said. "I'm so happy we could have this dialogue. And there's no need to talk to your mom about this. We just wanted to reach out to you."

Right, I thought after we hung up. You know Jane would be seriously pissed you didn't consult with her, and you went over her head to put a real scare into me. Still, though, I wanted to handle it on my own. And I guess Jane agreed with Stacy on this. Maybe she really *would* have been promoted at her marketing firm if she hadn't had me.

If I kept this up, it wouldn't be long before they'd have me and Lisa Pinto do a fake breakup, and since she'd be higher up the label's food chain, they'd make it seem like she ended it. Her statement to the press would be like, "While I have decided that I will no longer 'be his girl today,' I remain dear friends with Jonathan and wish him the best in his professional and social lives." Only they wouldn't do it just yet, not with her album dropping and me getting tons of publicity lately, even if it was all negative.

Now I was even more wound up about my concert, but I was afraid to use the glossy again because Jane had access to my hotel room and she'd sit me down like they do on sitcoms and say, "We need to have a talk about the birds and bees," and I'd have to say something like, "Jane, I have a song *called* 'This Bird Will Always Bee There for You,' I get it."

She wouldn't be the one to have the dialogue with me, though. She'd ask Nadine to do it. Or maybe Walter.

Jane gave me a personal wake-up call at nine. "Make hay while the sun shines," she said. "You have an estimated twenty-three thousand, three hundred and thirty-five days left on earth. Make this one worth it."

The way she said it, I could tell she was thinking, This is the biggest day of your career, you're about to be watched by tens of thousands of paying customers worldwide, but she was trying to sound like, Hey, time to get up, it's just a regular morning.

She gave me the itinerary for the day. She was going to Madison Square Garden early to run through some logistical issues, but she wanted me to get a workout in with Walter without pushing myself too much, and to play Zenon and do whatever I wanted to help me rest and relax before sound check. I didn't tell her that there was no way I could have relaxed normally, but especially not after Stacy's call, plus I didn't know if my father was showing up and how I'd even meet him if he did.

Me and Walter hit the executive hotel gym that was reserved for celebrities and super-rich people. That's the good thing about New York, they have everything set up separately already for celebrities and rich people. They have it like that in L.A., too, but so many people are celebrities in L.A. it's harder to divide them, so instead it's more like keeping the A-listers from the B-listers and down. Jane had to remind Walter to run me through my cross-training cardio routine, though she didn't say what we were all thinking, which is that Rog usually does it. I know all the routines by heart anyway.

Walter wanted to shower in the executive locker room instead of his hotel room since he didn't like the water pressure there, and there was security for the gym so it was okay for me to be alone for a couple minutes. I waited there for him all sweaty because I'm never ever supposed to shower in a public place. A computer terminal for guests was near the door. Now at least I'd know if my father was coming, and if he couldn't afford it, I could ask Walter for help. Walter would do it. He owed me still.

My pulse jumped like it always did when I saw there was an email from him from two days ago.

At your invitation I got a ticket for the concert. How do I
meet you?

He left his cell number. So he really was coming. If I asked Walter to call him, he'd know something was up and would tell Jane because he was afraid of getting fired again. And even if I used my room phone and reached him, I'd have to get away from Jane somehow and he'd have to convince security that Jonny Valentine had asked to see him privately, and they'd probably be like, Certainly, sir, please get in line behind all the other child predators who want to molest him. I wrote

I am figuring it out. I can't check this again before tonight.

At lunch I ate soup and nothing else that would make me throw up and drank tons of Throat Coat with honey. Even though I was near the end of the game, I didn't play Zenon like Jane said I should, since I wanted to stretch more. I did vocal warm-ups on the way to the Garden the most carefully I'd done them in a long time. Walter didn't even talk to me in the car like he usually does to calm me down. He could see how serious I looked. I might not have the raw and refined talents of Tyler Beats, but no one can get into the Jonny Zone like I can.

When we pulled up to the Garden for sound check there was a crowd of security guys waiting for me. That's one thing New York is worse for than L.A., everyone still has to go through the same streets and entrances. But the car we took wasn't flashy and it was early enough in the day that no one really noticed me, except having five huge security guys with headsets huddled around me *made* people stop and stare on the street since they knew someone important must be around, and that made more people stare. Sometimes I think if I walked around normally by myself for a day in regular clothes and my hair not in The Jonny, no one would pay any attention.

I looked for my father in case he was hanging around outside the Garden, but there were a million guys who could've been him from a distance, and besides, obviously he wasn't, and even if he was, Jane was with me.

The star/talent room was the best one I'd had on my entire tour. It was the size of our entire living room at home, and there was a big-screen TV set up with an eight-speaker sound system.

I was on Level 100 of Zenon, so I could've even finished the game before the concert started, but I also didn't want to distract myself when I was in the Jonny Zone. Jane came in and told me I had an hour to kill and I should just relax. Her telling me to relax so much made me *not* relaxed. Someday before a concert she should tell me to get super-nervous, and then I'd probably feel totally relaxed. She was wound up, too, because I could tell she wasn't looking up presale numbers today on purpose. They had to be low still, or else Stacy wouldn't have cared about my late-show interview. The label doesn't mind what you do as long as you're moving product.

So I walked around the Garden tunnels with Walter, and barely anyone was in them yet. There were a lot of tunnels, but with maps everywhere telling you where you were so you didn't get lost. Walter didn't talk while we walked. In the middle we found a side entrance opening to a path to the stage, and I poked my head out for a second to take it in. It was the same size as any regular arena, but it seemed a lot bigger. Empty preshow arenas always look huge, though. In my head I ran through the set list for the night at first, but then I tuned out and didn't think of anything besides my breathing, except every few minutes my brain would be like, I wonder if I'll see my father tonight, or if he's actually coming, or if it's all a prank, or what I'll say if I see him, and I'd notice I wasn't breathing too good. I kind of wished we could keep walking around like that in the tunnels forever. Most of the time on tour, I went in cars from hotels to venues to the bus. I never got to explore.

I was lucky that so much more of my life now was recorded than a normal kid's, so in the future, if I ever wanted to think back on something, I could find footage or an article about it. But there were some moments that no one was recording, and it was up to me to remember them, and maybe sometimes you had to *tell* yourself to freeze a moment in your brain or else it would just file it away with all the others. Most people would remember how it felt when they were about to debut at Madison Square Garden, but I told myself, Remember what it's like to walk around these tunnels with Walter when no one else knows you're there. When you're not Jonny Valentine the singer. When you're not even regular Jonathan Valentino. You're not anyone, in a way.

And this could've been my last big show, if the label dumped me or I went back to school. Then I'd be not anyone again, in a different way. It could be nice, like walking in the tunnels the rest of my life.

I was happy Walter was with me, though. It'd be scary down there if I was on my own.

After what I guess was an hour, Walter told me we were due back. If I didn't have my show, I bet he wouldn't have minded walking around for a lot longer. I know he's paid to hang out with me, and if I wanted to keep hanging out he basically had to until a certain point, but you never worried about wearing out your welcome with Walter. If he didn't feel like talking, he said he was tired, brother, but he never needed to go away for alone time.

It took us a little time to find our way back to the star/talent room, and we ended up on the opposite side of the entrance in another hallway and I thought we had to go all the way around, but Walter noticed there was a back door into it, and he found a maintenance guy to unlock it. That's something Walter's good at, figuring out what to do when your first option doesn't work, especially for building entrances and exits to avoid crowd interference. I should do those walks before all my shows, but not every venue has an underground level that's hidden away like that.

My sound check was strong, and even Jane, who usually doesn't say a sound check went good because she doesn't want me to get lazy, said it was my best one yet. Before I went back to the star/talent room, she bent her knees to talk in my face.

"I know this has been a rough tour," she said. "I want you to know I'm very proud of what you've done on it. And no matter what happens tonight, that's what matters." Her voice cracked at the end and her eyes crinkled up.

"I know," I said, and I hustled away to the star/talent room before she might cry. That was the last thing I wanted to see before the most important night of my life.

On the hundredth level of Zenon, every character I met told me how the Emperor was on this level and was this invincible tyrant that no one could defeat. It was only a game, but it *was* sort of intimidating, the way they talked about it. I had a few hours until my start time, and if I didn't play I'd get worried about if my father had made it and how I'd see him, which I still hadn't figured out, since Jane was popping into my room every twenty minutes to make sure I had everything I needed, so I got into the Jonny Zone for Zenon. The Jonny Zenone, where you're in a Zenon zone because you're no one. I'd tell that one to Nadine for a Creative Stroke credit if she wasn't already in Paris with her boyfriend.

Soon I'd worked my way through the level and up to the entrance to this dungeon where the narrator announced that the Emperor lived, which surprised me. First of all, I hadn't found the level's gem yet, but maybe the protocol was different since it was the last level, and second, I expected it to be a huge dungeon that takes days to find your way through, but it wasn't. After you climbed down into the dungeon, there was a door right there, and when you walked a few feet in, the Emperor was in the middle of a room. He was just a normal-size soldier with a giant halberd in his hands and covered everywhere in armor. I couldn't believe they'd make the Emperor this easy to get to. It's funny how the tunnels under the Garden were more complicated than the final dungeon in Zenon.

But I soon figured out why. The second I ran up to the Emperor, he deflected my two-handed-sword attack, and with one swing from a halberd damaged me enough to depart the realm. I started over from my saved game and tried again, but the same thing happened. I tried casting spells, using invincibility potions, everything. He blocked my attacks or they didn't affect him, my potions didn't do anything, and he damaged me to zero percent with a single halberd stroke. Not everyone had a Major Vulnerability, but everyone had at least a Minor Vulner-ability, except this guy. He was like Tyler Beats is as a performer, only Tyler *does* have a Minor Vulnerability, which is food and his metabo-lism, and also picking at his acne.

Before I could get too worked up about it, Walter knocked and told me 3 Days Dead was finishing up and it was time. I was sort of glad the Emperor was so tough, because it really did distract me, but once I remembered I had to give a show on live-stream to a ton of people, including maybe my father who I was somehow supposed to meet with-out Jane interfering, and if it wasn't a ton of people then that was even worse, my stomach got queasy again and my legs shook like they were postcardio. Walter walked me to backstage, and he must have noticed, since before Jane came over, he said, "Who gives a fuck, right?"

Walter had a way of saying the opposite of what I was thinking and getting me to believe it. "Right," I said.

Jane brought me over to Bill, who handed me the mike and had me do the last-minute microphone check. I was saying, "Microphone check one-two-one-two," over and over as he fiddled with the sound device. Jane went to talk to the guy helping with the heart-shaped swing, like she did every show now. I quietly said into the mike, "Microphone check you like being my little slut."

Bill jerked his head up, with his eyes narrow and wide at the same time. "What's that?"

"Microphone check one-two-one-two."

He stared at some equipment a couple seconds and chuckled and made some final adjustments and said I was all set. "Break a leg," he added.

"If the swing messes up again, maybe I will," I said, which was stupid, because he probably *could* screw the swing up if he wanted and make it look like an accident, but it wasn't worth him getting sued and losing his job and ending up in jail and getting raped by adult predators who were more muscular than him. Maybe he didn't leak Jane doing cocaine to the press, either. It was probably just some lower-tier staff. People will sell anyone out for money, whether they work for them or not.

I could tell the house lights dimmed as the countdown timer ticked to zero and I heard the announcer go, "Now, what you've all been waiting for—"

The crowd buzzed and the tech guys backstage were more worked up than usual since it was the Garden and it was going to be seen everywhere, and I bet even that asshole Bill was getting excited and wanted the show to go perfect.

"—on his last concert for his *Valentine Days* tour, singing tonight on the day of the year dedicated to love and romance, please welcome . . ."

"Go!" Bill said, like we'd practiced, and I ran out through the entrance.

"Jonny Valentine!" the announcer boomed, but I hardly heard it because my fans were already chanting my name and the piano of "Guys vs. Girls" was louder than usual since the audio engineers expected the ambient noise to be so high. It's got a strong instrumental buildup, eight bars where the crowd gets more and more amped to hear my voice, and by the time I get to the first verse, they're insane. Musical foreplay, Rog used to say. Stroke the crowd. It's easier live, when you can dance and use your charisma, but the best songs find a way to drive the listener wild with anticipation in the studio version, too.

So I danced in place while waiting for the lyrical explosion, and sniffed the candy in the air mixing with that sweaty arena smell, and thought about the iconic concerts that were held here and now I was part of that, and felt the hot spotlights on just me that were saying, You're the most talented singer and dancer in the world, everyone loves you, and I unleashed my instrument:

> *Girls and guys, burgers and fries*
> *All gets ruined with a coupla lies*

They couldn't even hear me sing, I'm sure, but it didn't matter. My blood was pumping hard and I was as excited as I was on my first tour, not the nervous excitement I normally get but the kind where you're like, I can't believe three years ago I was busking in the Central West End and now I'm singing at Madison Square Garden. A few things can still do that.

The same way I wanted Zack to somehow see me with that girl Dana, I wanted my father to be there to see this. Even if we didn't meet, I hoped he saw what I'd become, and not just on the Internet, but in person.

When it was time for my banter interlude, they'd written me some stupid lines I really didn't want to say, so instead I was like, "New York City! Will you be my valentine?" They all said yes, and I got down on one knee, like I was proposing to the crowd, and said, "I'm so in love with all of you, but it'll break my heart if you're not in love with me. Are you?" They hollered yes again, louder this time, so I said, "Then let me know . . . by sending an—"

I held out the mike and together we all went, "'RSVP (To My Heart)'!"

A lot of times when I told girls I picked out in the crowd that I loved them, I'd get caught up in the moment and convince myself I did, but I never believed it when I told a whole stadium that I loved them. This time, I sort of did. Like, for a few seconds I had this crazy idea of what it would be like to be in love with twenty thousand people and have them love you, if we all lived together in this stadium and ate the vendor food inside it and wore the clothing merch and every night I'd sing to them and we'd all sleep out here wrapped up in Jonny Valentine beach blankets. We'd never have to leave the stadium.

I kept telling the crowd how I loved them during the interludes and that I'd dreamed about performing here since I was a little kid, which was a lie because I only heard about the Garden before my first national tour when Jane was trying to book it, and I almost told them about the fantasy of us all living there together, but I checked myself. Even my most rabid fans would probably be like, Um, Jonny, we can't spend *all* our time with you, we have to go to school and see our families.

If it wasn't my best work of the tour, it was close to it. But about halfway through, I realized for the first time that every single one of my songs makes me sound like a real loser. In all of them I'm either asking a girl if she likes me or sad that a girl turned me down. Even on "Summa Fling," it's a fling because the girl wants it that way, not me, and she dumps me at the end when school starts. It's never me telling a girl I can't be with her anymore or saying I'm sorry for breaking up with her. I guess most songs are like that, and it helps craft my one-girl image for my fans, but still, it'd be nice if in *one* song I sounded like a cool guy who was fighting off girls and kept moving on to the next one. That's what every song is like in Mi$ter $mith's library. I didn't want my father to go from thinking his son was this famous singer at the beginning to a lame whiner whose songs were all about girls telling me I got served.

I was getting near the end of the show and I had no clue, even if he *was* there, how I'd be able to meet him. Just saying "Al" again wouldn't work, because there was no way he'd have gotten a front-row seat at the Garden. It was such a stupid idea, emailing him. It could've been a child predator who made a fake ID on his computer, or anyone else faking it, and if it was my father, we could be breaking the law by writing to each other. And it was all Jane's fault. If she'd let him see me, or even *talk* to me, I wouldn't have to do this way. I could just meet him, like taking a regular business meeting.

Then I knew how to do it. It would mean Jane would figure out I'd been in contact with him, but it was the only way. And I realized I didn't even care anymore if she knew. Stacy wouldn't like it, either, but who gives a fuck. I was just another client to her.

When it was time for the final medley, right before I stepped in the heart-shaped swing to sing "U R Kewt," I ignored the interlude banter I was supposed to say as the swing descended. "I'm looking for someone," I said, which was a mistake, because a line in "Summa Fling" is "I'm looking for someone, someone I can crush on," so the crowd sang, "Someone I can crush on!" even though I already sang "Summa Fling" earlier in the show. But crowds love repetition, the way really young kids do.

"No, seriously, I am," I said. "I'm looking for Albert Valentino. If your name is Al Valentino, please show your ID to security and come onstage."

Everyone in the Garden started talking and looking around. Not everyone would know or piece together that Al Valentino was my father's name, so that was a smart move. Except Jane would be pissed. If my father was there, he could get onstage at least while I sang the medley.

I scanned for him, but it was too dark and the lights were all on me. The swing lifted me up and I had to focus. I got through "U R Kewt," but I kept worrying that if my father was trying to get up onstage, Jane would intercept him. Or if he was there, I bet he was in the cheap seats and it would take him forever even to reach the floor.

So after "U R Kewt," to buy some more time and to make sure the security people knew what to do, I forced an interlude, which I'm not supposed to do to keep the momentum going, and said again that security should let a guy named Al Valentino onstage. I sang "Roses for Rosie," and I threw all the petals down. Some of them could have been falling on my father's head as he walked toward the stage.

There was still no sign that he was coming when I finished it. I switched to "Guys vs. Girls," and I was looking down the whole time to see if anyone was coming up onstage. No one was, not even any impostors pretending they were named Al Valentino, though there weren't many guys at the show anyway, and the ones who were were probably child predators and the last thing they'd want to do is offer themselves up to security. I got annoyed, which constricts your vocal cords, that he'd made me all worked up for this and hadn't figured out a way for us to meet. I was eleven years old, it shouldn't have been up to me and I definitely shouldn't have had to interrupt the biggest concert of my career, he should've just called Jane and worked it out with her instead of making me sneak around on computers.

The swing set me down with no sign of my father. The dancers and singers and I took our bows, but instead of going offstage with them before coming back for my encore, I stayed where I was and let them go, because I didn't want to run into Jane. "I'm gonna sing an a cappella song to y'all," I told the crowd, even though the set list called for me to do "Love Is Evol" and "Kali Kool" as encores, so that the band wasn't with me and I could sing as long as I wanted in case he showed up. I launched the first verse of "Crushed":

Like an empty can of pop
Like snow and sleet and slush
Girl, with you I can't stop
From feeling like I'm crushed

And when I was about to switch to the chorus, four security guys walked as a group in the darkness of the stands toward the stage. They got closer, and I waited a few seconds as they came down an aisle, but I couldn't make anything out. My breathing and heartbeat sped up, which was bad since this song had slow pacing and I could feel myself rushing the lyrics. I sang the chorus:

I got a crush on you, it ain't funny
Got a crush on you, under your pinkie
You do what you want, girl, it's plain to see
I'm not on your mind, but you're crushing me

People think good singers are just born with strong pipes, but the best singers are creative interpreters, too. Like with the last line of the chorus, I emphasize the hard *c* in *crushing,* like *ka*-rushing, so it's like the pain when you first get hurt, then I soften and draw out and deamplify the rest of the word, *ruuusssshing,* like, This is what's left of me, this gooey inside that you've beaten up, and so I whisper *me* where you can't hardly hear it, because you've destroyed me and you probably don't even think about me anymore.

By the time I finished it, they were at the base of the floor, where all the other security guys were lined up, and one of the four new guys discussed something with one of the guards who was lined up. There was a person in the middle of them, and just enough light from the stage that I could make out the purple bags under his eyes. Our purple bags.

I stopped singing. "Let him come up," I said into the mike.

My father's face was still in the shadows. One of the guards put his hands on his back and walked him around the stage to the little stairs and past a set of security guys, over to my elevated stage and through another line of security, up a last short flight of stairs, and finally over to me. The Garden has top-shelf security.

"I have to stay here between you," the guard said to me. I nodded. I don't think I could have spoken right then if I'd tried.

The crowd was talking now, and I was in danger of losing them if I didn't sing again soon. But I couldn't do it yet. I had to look at the guy standing four feet away on the other side of the security guard.

He was better-looking than he was in his driver's license, which most people are. His chestnut hair was thin but he had all of it, which was good for me even though Jane says what matters most is what her father had, and he went bald young, so we'll explore medication for me eventually. And he dressed kind of cool, with these beat-up black boots and a brown leather jacket that was sort of like Zack's except more rugged and warmer and not as stylish. He looked like someone who could hitchhike anywhere and be fine.

I got nervous over how bad it'd be if Jane interrupted the show and how not only was my father watching me perform, but he was *in* the performance. I blocked it out the best I could and picked up the second verse of "Crushed" as if nothing major had happened and I hadn't met my father for the first time in years and an entire stadium plus an Internet live-stream audience had watched it happen. It was almost like doing it in front of thousands of people was easier than if we'd met one-on-one in a room for face time by ourselves.

For a second, even with what had just gone down, I found myself wondering how many last-minute and in-progress Internet viewers we had. We needed about seventy-five thousand total to break even, after all the marketing and advertising expenses. Over ninety thousand would be considered a triumph.

And when I wrapped up the final chorus, I realized this would be the last song on the tour, and I wanted to draw it out. So I pulled out the melismatics on the words *you're crushing me* so long, the audience kept cheering and clapping for me to go on, and my lungs felt like they were inhaling the applause and they could roll with it forever. Dr. Henson did a test on me once, and I have the lung capacity of a marathon runner. My father was smiling the same way he might if he was watching me sing in a concert at school, like those dads who used to videotape our crap chorus.

The set list called for one more encore, but I'd already switched it up, and if I did another it might give Jane the chance to interfere, so I told the crowd I loved them and would see them again soon, but didn't say we hadn't figured out when or where my next tour would be, or if I'd even still do one.

"This way," I said away from the mike while the crowd cheered. My father followed me. He was still smiling.

I didn't go to the main entrance, though. I went to the side one that I'd found with Walter earlier, on the opposite side of the stage. There was one security guard behind the door there now, and I walked fast in case Jane had told security to grab me before I went off. He didn't stop us, probably since I looked like I knew what I was doing. Support staff is always afraid of losing their jobs.

We were back in the tunnels again. There were so many, it would be a long time until Jane could find us.

Then I got really scared, because what if after all this time he was a child predator who looked enough like what I remembered my father looked like and had made a fake driver's license? Or what if he was my father and was *also* a child predator? I couldn't straight up ask him if he was one. Not many would be like, Yeah, I'm glad you asked, I actually *am* a child predator. Instead I said, "So, you're Al."

"I am," he said. "Thanks for inviting me. You were incredible."

He put out his hand for a high five. It didn't feel dorky the way it did with Dr. Henson. It felt like the way a baseball player congratulates his teammate at home plate on a homer, like, I'm not surprised you did this, but it's still cool.

His voice was baritone and gravelly. It sounded like the narrator in Zenon if you lowered the treble and some of the frequencies. I thought he might have a Kansas or St. Louis or even an Australian accent, but he didn't have much of one. He sounded like he was from nowhere, really. Maybe he spent a lot of time in tunnels, too. "Let's keep walking," I said, though I didn't mention it was so Jane wouldn't find us.

I stayed a few feet ahead of him as we turned through the tunnels. A few more Garden workers were moving around now, but I don't think they knew who I was, because they were mostly Mexican guys. Mexican guys never know who I am. They're too busy working to follow celebrities. And celebrities are too busy being celebrities to pay attention to Mexican guys. It's like neither one knows the other exists.

"How did you get a ticket?" I asked.

"I bought one off the Internet," he said. "They were hard to find. You're a hot ticket."

"I can pay you back."

I pictured him going on the Internet and refreshing the site until a ticket was available and buying it right away. The tunnels were cold, but I felt warm inside, thinking of that.

"No way," he said. "I would've paid a thousand bucks to see you. I bet scalpers can sell them for that much, too."

The most I'd heard of anyone paying for a regular single ticket was around six hundred dollars, and there were some charity seats that went for more, but that didn't count. "Not that much."

"Well, they should. You'd be worth every penny."

I wondered again if he had another family now, or at least a girl-friend. If he'd had a kid in Pittsburgh, maybe the kid and his mother moved to New York, which is why he came back. And I had the same thought about him playing catch with his kid, in Central Park, because you couldn't do it anywhere else in New York. The strange thing is, I suddenly really hoped he did and that he brought them and I could meet them. I'd have a half-brother, or a half-sister. "Did you come with anyone?" I asked without looking back at him.

"Nope. Just me. Some of my friends wanted to come, but I didn't want to ruin your concert with a group of rowdy construction workers."

I was a little disappointed I wouldn't meet this family I'd invented for him. Then I got happier that he might not have one, but I was even more disappointed he hadn't brought his rowdy construction-worker friends. It would be much cooler to have them at my show than a crowd full of tween girls. "You want to play a video game?" I asked. "I have this game, The Secret Land of Zenon, and I'm close to finishing it. It's in the star/talent room."

He looked behind us and ahead of us, but there were only a few Mexican guys moving stuff around. "You sure that's all right?"

"Yeah. They always put a game system in my room. It's in my rider."

I told him we had to use the wall maps. We studied the first one to figure out where we were, and I was about to head one way, but he said, "Hold on. It's the other direction." He walked ahead of me, and I followed behind. I liked how he figured it out so quickly and wasn't like, "I *think* it's the other direction," but was just, "It's the other direction." Jane's always getting lost, even in L.A. and with the GPS. Maybe I'd get his sense of direction. I don't know how mine worked in cities yet, because when I was in St. Louis I was too young to go out on my own, and I can't do it now.

"Do you have a good sense of direction?" I asked.

"Usually," he said.

"When you went on that hiking trip, did you use a map?"

"Hiking trip?"

"In Australia. With your friend Dave."

"Oh, sure," he said. "You shouldn't hike without a map."

"When was that?"

"With Dave? I guess about a year ago. But I used to hike in Kansas growing up, and we never had maps."

I imagined him hiking a year ago in Australia with the guy in that picture, being attacked by kangaroos and meeting a tribe of those Australian black guys who gave him and Dave food and water. A year ago, I was in L.A., gearing up to record *Valentine Days*, probably getting spray-tanned and drinking sugarless pink lemonade.

We turned into the next tunnel and looked at the new YOU ARE HERE sign on the map. We were going in the right direction, and I let him lead us.

"Is it true that toilets flush in the opposite direction there?" I asked in one of the tunnels.

"Where?" he asked as he checked out another map.

"In Australia. I read that they flush opposite how they flush here."

"I never really noticed. But summer and winter are reversed. When it's hot here, it's cold there."

"That's like in Zenon," I said. "A lot of times, the opposite of what you think you should do works best."

He asked me more about the game, and I told him how to play and what it was like as we got closer to the star/talent room. It felt like when you're in a party of adventurers in Zenon, which happens a couple times on certain levels, and you each have a specific skill. My father would be the cartographer, even though he didn't bring maps when he hiked in Kansas. I'd be the bard, I guess, which wasn't really a skill, but sometimes you did meet bards in Zenon, only I didn't play any instruments. It reminded me of that time we were in the car after Richard's birthday party, when we drove on the highway, except this time we knew where we were going. And it also was like when me and Zack ran through the hallways in the Memphis hotel. But Zack was only using me to get into the nightclub, just like he used my Walmart fans to broaden his base. Me and my father were on a real adventure together. And hiding from Jane and venue security in the Garden tunnels was way more like the Underground Railroad than the Memphis hotel was.

"Maybe we could go there someday," I said. "I don't have a foothold in the Australian market yet, but we'd probably still bring along my bodyguard, Walter, for security. You'd like him."

"That would be nice," he said.

When we got close to the star/talent room, I realized that Jane might be waiting outside for me. So I told my father that we had to go around to the rear. I don't think he knew why I said that. We found our way to it, and the hallway was empty. I listened in at the door for a second, since I didn't want him noticing it and asking me why I was being so careful.

I didn't hear anything, so I turned the knob and cracked it open. Me and Walter had forgotten to lock it, which was stupid because anyone could've come in when I was playing Zenon and kidnapped or killed or molested me. It was empty and the front door was closed. "Stay here a second," I said.

I went inside and ran to the front door and locked it, and opened the back door for my father. "Are you inviting me in?" he asked.

I didn't know why he was asking such an obvious question, and why he kept using the word *inviting*, like I was going to say, No, I'm just opening the door to show you how cool the star/talent room is and then I'm closing it on you. But I said yes, and after he did, I locked the back door.

Man, if he *was* a child predator, this was like hitting the jackpot: Jonny Valentine locking himself in a room with you without a security presence.

He looked awkward in the star/talent room, sizing up the buffet table and beanbag chairs and flat-screen like he'd never seen anything like it before. I went over to the buffet and grabbed a plate. "You want some food?"

"Are you having any?"

I wasn't even hungry, but I could tell he'd feel weird about eating if I didn't, so I piled some pasta on my plate. It didn't matter anymore now that the tour was over. I could gain ten pounds of chub and then me and Jane would go on a maple-syrup-and-cayenne master cleanse for two weeks. "Yeah. They'll throw it out if I don't."

"Then I'll have a little."

He started with a small serving of the pasta, but then, just like Tyler, he took some of just about *everything*, the steak and salmon and quiche and all the rest. Even Walter didn't eat this much at my concerts, and that includes days he'd lifted when he needed to replenish with carbs and protein. My father didn't look like he lifted, but like he had lean muscle from his construction work, which probably toned specific zones, like how Peter's forearms were so defined from cooking. Maybe me and him and Walter could squeeze in a session at the hotel gym together.

He looked around the room again. "I used to think you were special, the way you'd sing around the house," he said. "But I figured all fathers think that about their kids. I had no idea how right I was."

In some ways that was better than hearing we'd broken ninety thousand in Internet sales.

We were chewing while standing, so I booted up Zenon and plopped down on one of the two beanbags in front of the TV, and he sat on the other. I explained how I was finally at the Emperor but I couldn't beat him. I put the TV on mute so no one would hear me playing.

The same thing as before happened when I went into the Emperor's lair. I attacked, he deflected, and he fully damaged me with one cut from his halberd. My father kept saying things, like "Whoa!" and "Watch out!" and "Nice try!" Before my fourth try he suggested, "How about letting him attack you first and wear himself out?" which was a smart idea, but I still got damaged with the first hit. I kept trying and getting damaged to zero percent and restarting from my saved game.

"Did you do construction in St. Louis, too?" I asked.

"Yeah. Most of the time. Don't you remember?"

"No."

"And your mother never told you?" I shook my head. "Did you tell her I was coming tonight?"

"Do you remember that time I went to this kid Richard's birthday party?" I asked. "You picked me up and drove on the highway for a few hours and we went to a diner?"

"I'm not sure," he said. "But did you tell Jane I was coming?"

I didn't answer his question again. "They lived in this super-nice house with a huge lawn. I was the last one at the party. You let me order French toast for dinner."

"There's a lot I don't remember from those years," he said. "It's nothing personal. I'm sure we had a good time." He watched me get damaged again by the Emperor. "Aw, I thought you had him!"

As my character was departing the realm for like the seventh time in a row and my ghost slipped up into the air, I said, "Why'd you have to go."

I didn't say it like a question. I just said it like it was too bad we couldn't restart our life from then, from that time at the diner, and he could know I'd become famous and rich later on, and he'd stick around. I didn't turn to watch his reaction, but I could tell he didn't know how to respond, even though he'd probably practiced answering it. He didn't say anything while my saved game restarted.

Finally he said, "It's very complicated, Jonathan."

It was the first time he'd said my name. Plus *Jonathan* sounded super-strange out of his mouth and not Jane's, even if he'd called me it in emails and probably called me it when I was little. "Why?"

We both watched my character run into the dungeon and get damaged again. I didn't know how I was ever going to beat this Emperor. "We had problems."

"Like what?"

"Like money problems, for instance."

"I thought you said you had a job."

"You can have money problems even when you have a job."

"What else?"

"I don't know. It was a long time ago." He put his hand on my shoulder. "I'm very sorry. You deserved better. Every day I've been gone I've thought that." He pulled an envelope out of his jacket. "I brought you something. I know it's not your birthday for about a month, but in case I don't see you then."

He took out a four-by-six photo of me as a little kid in front of the Cardinals' old stadium, wearing a Cardinals hat way too big for my head, sitting on top of his shoulders like I was at the riverfront concert. Maybe he always did that after the concert so I couldn't get lost in crowds. "Remember this? The first game I took you to?"

"No. I only remember watching a game once on TV with you while it was raining." I didn't ask if *he* remembered the riverfront concert.

"Well, we went. A couple times, even." I couldn't remember going with him the other times, either, probably because I went with Michael Carns's family on their season tickets all the time after he left.

He handed it to me. I had a big smile in the picture, and he did, too, like he was excited to show his son a real baseball game for the first time. "If I get to see you again for your birthday, I'll buy you something nicer."

I wanted to tell him to visit for my birthday, that I could take him to the fanciest restaurants in L.A. and get him brand-new clothes and we could drive around in whatever car he wanted. But I couldn't say it. I guess it was like what asking a normal girl out might be like. Even if you know she's going to say yes, there's a part of you that's probably afraid she'll turn you down.

I put the picture down next to the beanbag chair and returned to Zenon. Right as I opened the door to the Emperor's lair, I looked at it again. It was the only picture I had of him except for his old driver's license. Maybe he was right. People make mistakes. In life, you can't restart from a saved game to undo them.

I dropped the controller in my lap and threw my arms around my father's body and buried my head in his chest. His leather jacket smelled like Zack's, without the cigarettes. He didn't react for a second. Then he curled one arm around my back and the other over my head. His heart thumped lightly against my forehead in a one-two-one-two rhythm and his chest moved in and out from his breathing like a metronome.

But because I'd already opened the door to the Emperor's lair, he'd run up to the edge of the room and attacked me, and my ghost departed the realm for like the *twelfth* time. I squirmed out of my father's arms and yelled, "Fuck you, you fucking Emperor!"

That was a mistake. A few seconds later the front doorknob tried to turn but couldn't and there was loud banging and Jane's voice was all high-pitched shouting, "Jonathan? Jonathan, are you in there?"

My father stood up. "Don't let her in," I said.

"I have to."

"No, you don't."

"If I don't, it's considered—" He took a step toward the door. "I just do."

"She'll make you go away," I said. "I saw the letter from her lawyers."

He seemed kind of surprised. "I know. But it's worse if I don't talk to her now." He unlocked the door while the knob was jittering from the outside. When he opened it she looked at him like she was about to smack him.

"Get out," she said, calm and low.

"Jane," my father said, "let me explain—"

"Let's not make this ugly. I can have security here in two seconds." I could tell part of the reason she didn't want to make it ugly was she didn't need another tabloid story.

His body shifted. It looked like he might leave. If he did, I didn't know how I'd ever see him again. "Let him stay," I said. "He's not doing anything bad."

Jane stepped out into the hall and swiveled her head in both directions. She came back in and closed the door. "What are you doing here?"

"I wanted to talk to you both," he said. "This was the only way."

"How'd he know you were here?"

I answered before he could. "I emailed him," I said. "I found him on the Internet and emailed him, and I told him to come to the show."

The side of Jane's lips twisted like she'd been punched but was trying not to show it. "And what do you want out of this?"

"I don't want anything except a chance to see my son."

"Oh, I'm sure," Jane said.

"It's true," I said. "He was in Australia the last few years. That's why he wasn't in touch."

Jane looked at my father first, then at me. He didn't look at either of us.

"Jonathan," she said slowly. "He's a drug addict. He's been one for years. I didn't tell you because you didn't need to know what a lowlife you have for a father. He hasn't been to Australia. I bet he doesn't even have a passport."

My father didn't say anything.

"Is that the truth?" I asked.

He took a few seconds. "I've been clean six months," he said. "I didn't want to reach out while I was still using. But I swear to you, I haven't touched anything in six months. Here." He dug into his pocket and pulled out a big copper coin. Inside a triangle it said "6 Month Recovery."

"I wouldn't be surprised if he bought that off some junkie he's friends with," Jane said.

I ignored her. "What about Australia? Didn't you live there? To have an adventure?"

"No," he said. "A friend did." He put the coin back in his pocket. "I guess I wanted to impress you. You've got this life, and I didn't want you knowing I was strung out on drugs, living in halfway houses, and that's why I was ashamed to get in touch all these years. All I wanted was to see you."

Jane laughed a mean laugh. "Just like you did when you left after Michael."

I thought she meant Michael Carns, which didn't make sense. But the way Jane's face looked, ready to break apart like an egg even though she was angry, and the way my father's face fell down to the ground for the millionth time like he'd done something really bad, I could tell it wasn't.

So his name was Michael, too. And he really was my little brother. I must've been too young to understand what was happening and they never discussed it and I wasn't old enough to really remember anything.

He said, "I'm sorry, Jane. I'm very sorry."

I thought about me and my father in that diner again, and him telling me to order whatever I wanted, he didn't care.

Jane kept staring right at him like she was either going to cry or punch him. "Six years later, and I finally get an apology," she said.

"People change, Jane."

"Right," Jane said. "Jonathan changed a lot, so now you conveniently want to see him."

And Jane in her hospital bed, holding the baby with my face.

"I'd want to see him no matter what," he said. "I don't like what happened any more than you do. My life's back on track."

Everything happens for a reason.

"Anything else you have to say, you can say it to my lawyer," Jane said. "If you don't leave immediately, I'm calling security and putting you in jail." She took her phone out of her purse like it was a weapon.

"Janie," he said.

She dialed. "Don't you dare sweet-talk me. It doesn't work anymore."

The Lord giveth and the Lord taketh away.

"Now, wait a minute." He pulled a crumpled piece of paper out of his jacket pocket, the same pocket that had my photo. "First of all, the restraining order hasn't been approved yet. I'm well within my rights to talk to Jonathan, especially if he's invited me, which he has, to the concert and on the stage and into this room." He smoothed it out and gave it to her. "Your lawyers are receiving this tonight."

Jane's eyes bulged out like after I'd fainted as she got further down the page, but she kept her cool. When she finished, she folded it crisply in half, like it was just any old piece of paper. Complete control.

"If you believe you're financially entitled to all this, you're very mistaken. You owe thousands in child support. You probably think coming here and charming Jonny is going to make it easier than if you'd gone through your lawyers, but you're wrong." She handed the paper back to him. "He's mine, Al. Not yours."

"We'll see," my father said. "We'll be releasing a statement to the press this week if your lawyers don't talk with us."

He really did look a lot like me in the face. If he had my talent he could've been a star. Except maybe not, because a lot of being a star was about sacrifice and work ethic. There was something about my father you could pick up that made him look like someone who did what Rog called the bare minimum. The bare-minimum singers who were lucky were one-hit wonders. The ones who were less lucky never made it at all, they only played small clubs and were bitter and eventually burned out of the industry. The real stars didn't kill themselves only when they liked the work, which anyone can do. They killed themselves when they hated it, when they'd rather be anywhere else. You don't get to ten thousand hours just by having fun.

Jane finally cracked, getting up in my father's face and calling him an asshole and a bunch of other curses, much angrier than when she'd yelled at Kevin the TV producer after the morning-show concert, and he took it without saying anything.

They were about a foot away from each other, near the door, and I was still on the beanbag chair in front of the TV. I could slip out the back door and they wouldn't even notice. They were arguing over me and they'd totally forgotten about me at the same time.

After half a minute the front door opened again. Walter.

"Calm down, calm down," he said as he wedged himself between them with his hands out, like they were paparazzi hounding me post-show, but they wouldn't, or at least Jane wouldn't.

Walter looked over at me while he was in the middle of them like, Should I kick him out? and I shook my head no real quick. But another part of him was looking at me more like, Sorry about this, brother. It could be all right to live with Walter. He didn't know how to take care of me or understand anything about the industry, but at least he was savvy about protection. It was a stupid idea, though, because if he was going to take care of anyone, it would be his own daughters, just like Nadine had her own boyfriend and she'd marry him and have her own kids soon.

Jane was all I really had. And I was the only thing she had. Just the two of us.

"Stop it," I said, and no one heard me, so I used my diaphragm more but without shouting and said, "Please stop it." This time they all shut up like they'd finally remembered I was there.

My father's eyebrows were pinched together, waiting for me to say something. "Show me the paper," I said.

"You don't need to see this, Jonathan," he said.

"Show it to me."

He unfolded the paper and held it out like it was a bad report card. I didn't understand any of it. Except for a dollar amount at the end. It was a lot of money, more than my father could make in a hundred lifetimes doing construction. But I'd seen the figures from my record deals, gate receipts, and merchandising. We could afford it.

And in a funny way, maybe I wouldn't have had a career at all if things had been okay with Michael and if my father hadn't left. Jane wouldn't have needed to make me busk for extra money, wouldn't have put my videos up on YouTube, wouldn't have pulled me out of school and moved us to L.A. I would've just been some kid in school who lived in Dogtown and was a super-talented singer who joined a rock band in high school like his father did. And I would've had a younger brother around I could play Zenon with and teach how the double switch works in baseball.

"I'll make sure her lawyers talk to yours," I said. "We'll work out a deal. You'll get enough money to last you a long time."

"You don't know what you're doing," Jane said to me. She looked at Al. "He has no idea what he's talking about. I'm in charge of all the finances."

"You might be in charge of it," I said. "But I can walk away from all this if I want. This can be my last show."

That shut her up. I'd never said anything like that before. She looked afraid of me, even.

That time we watched the Cardinals game on TV, my father was all sweaty and talking fast. Now he was calm, and he didn't look like he was a drug addict, at least not like the ones in movies. He looked like if you cleaned him up and had him lift for a few months, you could put him in a catalog for men's clothes. Like a guy who got a lot of girls when he was young and women could sense that so he still got a bunch of them.

Jane was an addict, too. Not to drugs, because she couldn't do as much as she did if she was. That was the difference between addicts like Jane and addicts like my father. Some addicts could still turn their son into a pop star in L.A. and be a successful music manager. Other ones got in fights outside bars in Pittsburgh and stayed in halfway houses and lied about living in Australia.

What my father said was true. People *did* change. But there was some part of them they could never get away from, no matter how hard they wanted to. He was a bare-minimum worker, then and now. He'd probably always say his friend was guilty and he was innocent, in a logic test and in real life. And he still looked like the type of guy who left his wife after her baby died to raise their other son on her own.

"And whatever's in this thing sunsets." I handed him back his legal letter. "Deal?"

He seemed scared, like this was the last thing he expected and he didn't know what to do. It was the first time I'd ever proposed a business deal, so I should've been the one who was scared. Only I wasn't. I felt like I knew exactly what I was doing. I guess I'd learned from Jane. I bet she was kind of proud, even.

"Yeah. If this doesn't happen, my lawyer talks to the press about how you're shutting me out."

"It will happen." I thought it would be a lot harder to say the next sentence out loud. It wasn't, though. "But the deal is going to be that I don't want to see you anymore."

You could see him turning it over in his mind.

"No," said my father. "I want to see you. That's more important to me than the money. I didn't come back to charm you so I could get the money, I came back because all I want is to have you in my life so we can do all the things we never did together. I want to take you to Cardinals games again and play video games and travel to Australia and drive you to diners and order French toast for dinner."

Except that's not what he really said. I could restart from a game saved right there a million times and he'd never say that. He nodded once. That was it.

"Please leave," I said, without any diaphragm this time.

He put his lawyer's letter back in his pocket and stared at the floor and shuffled out. His boots didn't make a sound on the floor as he left, like he was a ghost in Zenon. I'd waited half my life to meet my father, and after I'd spent half an hour with him, I was never going to see him again. And I'm the one who'd made the deal.

Me and Jane and Walter stood there for a few seconds. Then Walter did something he never did, probably because he was afraid someone would call him a child predator, but he came over and put one of his meaty arms around my shoulders and palmed the top of my head and patted it once.

"I'll be outside if you need me," he said.

He left, and Jane moved for the first time in two minutes. She took a while to talk, and when she did, her throat sounded froggy. "I wish you didn't have to hear all that."

I shrugged. If she'd just told me everything about my father before, I never would have had to hear all of it right now.

"I know I'm not the perfect mother, but your father . . ." She wasn't crying, but her eyes were a little watery. "I'm sorry, baby," she said, the same way she'd said it in the hospital, and she clutched me to her chest and hugged me and I let her do it but didn't hug back. I closed my eyes. What I was thinking about instead was the picture in my bedroom in L.A. of us on the seesaw in St. Louis. I imagined us going up and down on it a few times, then her slamming down hard and me flying off into the sky, up past the clouds and airplanes and into space and floating away in all the blackness, with Jane holding her arms out to reach for my body but me departing the realm away from her.

"It's okay, Jane." I slid out of her arms and moved back a couple feet. "I think I want to be by myself for a little while."

She swallowed and rubbed her eyes even though there still weren't any tears coming out and told me to get her when I was ready. Her phone pinged on the way out, and she looked at it. She started to talk, stopped, and started again.

"We got over a hundred thousand live-stream purchases. Nearly a third bought in at the very end," she said softly, without turning to me. "Ronald says congratulations."

I didn't say anything, but we were both thinking the same thing, that all the bad press the last couple weeks had helped out, and me bringing my father onstage made us go viral. Sex sells, but controversy really sells.

I went to close the door, but before I did I leaned out in the hallway and said, "Jane."

She spun around on her black high heels. I was with her when she bought them in L.A. But she didn't buy them, she got them free, because I was with her and the boutique loved the publicity. She really did dress like a serious businesswoman. You'd never know she once bagged groceries in St. Louis with Mary Ann Hilford.

If I was going to do this, I was going to do it right. I'd work twice as hard. I'd sacrifice everything in my life that held me back. We'd get the best choreographer, the best producer, the best publicist, the best fake romances, the best scandals. And I already had the best manager. I was the only client she'd ever have.

"I want to do the tour," I said. "You can start planning it now."

I wasn't just going to be the next Tyler Beats. I was going to be the next MJ.

A smile curled up on her face like she'd forgotten everything that happened the last few minutes, and I went back inside my room and swung the door shut, harder than I meant to.

I fell down onto the beanbag chair like standing another minute would kill me, and restarted Zenon and plugged my iPod into the portable speaker and set it to shuffle. I tried a few new weapons and spells, but got damaged by the Emperor each time. After a few songs, the lullaby came on the speakers. I don't listen to it much on my iPod, so I can save it for when Jane sings it.

I went into the Emperor's room and was thinking of what I could do and if there was another angle I could attack him from and how nothing worked against him. The lullaby was playing, but for some reason, in my head I heard that song "Stay," and hummed its melody, and I remembered what I'd just told my father, how in Zenon you sometimes have to do the opposite of what you think you should do. And I thought, What if I *don't stay* in the room with the Emperor, but just *run away*?

So, before I could attack him, I ran back out the way I came in and closed the door behind me.

And in the tunnel leading up to the room was a gem, the last gem I needed.

I picked it up and my experience points kept climbing, which is different from normal where they go up a set amount, and soon the screen turned black and then white, and the narrator's voice and screen said, "You have gained sufficient experience points. All other living beings have departed the realm. You can no longer be damaged. The Secret Land of Zenon is yours entire." The screen flashed back to normal and I was on the first level again, except no one else was around, no people or animals or enemies.

The lullaby finished. I took the iPod off shuffle and went back to the song and put it on repeat and whispered along with the last verse while I played.

> *Go to sleep*
> *Don't you cry*
> *Rest your head upon the clover*
> *Rest your head upon the clover*
> *In your dreams*
> *You shall ride*
> *Whilst your Mammy's watching over*

My character walked all around the first level of Zenon, and I could instantly transport myself to any level. I didn't need gems or experience points. If I chose to go somewhere, I could.

Then I knew what I wanted to say for my final exam for Nadine. Normally I have a tough time outlining my essays. For this one, though, I could already see the beginning, middle, and end, and what my supporting evidence would be. I only hoped it would fit in a thousand words. But I could articulate it now.

The picture of me and my father at the baseball game was on the floor. I turned up the volume on my iPod and set it on top of the picture. It covered his body, right up to me sitting on his shoulders. The part you could still see with me had just my father's head poking out between my legs, like I was a mother giving birth to a grown man. The opposite of a premature infant.

I jumped to a new level in Zenon. The land was mine to explore, all mine. I could go wherever I wanted, do whatever I wanted, no one stopping me, nobody else around, over the tall mountains and through the deep forests and into the dark dungeons. Just me.

I could no longer be damaged.

Acknowledgments

THE MRS. GILES WHITING Foundation and the National Endowment for the Arts provided generous financial support that enabled me to complete this novel. Several people in other fields shared their expertise with me: for medical matters, Clara Boyd, Andrew Epstein, and Andrew Gassman; in the law, Josh Gradinger; and about the music industry, Morgan O'Malley and Matt Paget. Dr. Jane O'Connor's *The Cultural Significance of the Child Star*, along with an article she sent me before its publication, proved to be my most fertile research resources. I am grateful to Kathryn Davis, Joshua Henkin, Marshall Klimasewiski, and Kellie Wells for their continued guidance and help. A cohort of selfless readers improved this novel substantially: Sarah Bruni, Maura Kelly, Eric Lundgren, Diana Spechler, John Warner, Paul Whitlatch, and my beloved retired agent, Rosalie Siegel. Jim Rutman's unwavering confidence and sagacity would make him, in an alternate universe, a superior manager for Jonny Valentine. I am deeply indebted to Millicent Bennett for her brilliant editing, passionate advocacy, and consummate professionalism; her assistant, Chloe Perkins; Sarah Nalle; publisher Martha Levin and editor in chief Dominick Anfuso; Meg Cassidy, Jill Siegel, Carisa Hays, Nicole Judge, Suzanne Donahue, Jackie Jou, Erin Reback, Stuart Smith, Karen Fink, Wendy Sheanin, Nina Pajak, and the rest of the robust sales and marketing departments; Carly Sommerstein, Ellen Sasahara, and Beth Maglione in production; the innovative video team at Studio 4; Jonathan Karp; and everyone else at Free Press and Simon & Schuster for their enthusiasm and faith. Thank you, Jenna McKnight, for being a good kid. And, lastly, my ongoing gratitude to my parents.

The Love Song of Jonny Valentine
Reading Group Guide

O NSTAGE AND OFFSTAGE, FROM swanky hotels to celebrity greenrooms, Teddy Wayne's novel pulls back the curtain of pop stardom to reveal the alternately glittering and grueling reality of eleven-year-old megastar Jonny Valentine's life. The novel follows Jonny, his hard-charging mother, Jane (who is also his manager), and his entourage as he tours for his second album—a tour that will either catapult him into the stratosphere or leave him fumbling for a new record label. As if the pressures of preadolescence weren't enough, Jonny must navigate marketing schemes, fans, elaborately staged performances, and the growing awareness that his life is not his own, all while he is faced with a startling revelation from his past. *The Love Song of Jonny Valentine* is a funny, moving, and unsettling coming-of-age story and a perceptive take on our obsessive and exploitative celebrity culture.

Discussion Questions

1. What do you think makes the first-person narration in the novel ring so true as an eleven-year-old's voice? When does Jonny display knowledge beyond his years and when does he reveal his inexperience and naïveté?

2. How does Jonny regard his pre-music-career life in St. Louis? Is he nostalgic, or conflicted? Does this change after his tour stop in St. Louis?

3. Why does Jane offer Jonny the choice between continuing to tour and going to school? Do you think he's equipped to choose well? How do you feel about Jonny's decision, in the end?

4. How do marketing and promotional concerns circumscribe Jonny's life? How do you think his life would have been different if Jane had not chosen to be his manager? Do you think he would have more freedom to be a kid, or not?

5. Though they are employees, Walter and Nadine both care for Jonny and he cares for them. Why are these relationships so important to him? Why do you think Jonny has an easier time relating to adults than to his peers?

6. What attracts Jonny to the Latchkeys, especially to the lead singer, Zack? In your opinion, were they using him, as Jonny comes to suspect, or was Zack's big-brotherly interest in him genuine?

7. Jane tells Jonny, "The top person is never simply the most talented, or the smartest, or the best looking. They sacrifice anything in their

lives that might hold them back" (page 37). Do you agree? After his appearance with Tyler Beats, how does Jonny's perception of his own talent and work ethic change? Do you think this is a healthy change, or not? Would Jonny have been able to see himself this way at the beginning of the book?

8. How would you characterize Jonny's feelings about his fans and celebrity? At one point he says, "A celeb is only a celeb if you remember them. It's like we disappear if no one is paying attention" (page 96). Do you think he'd prefer to disappear? Or to be loved unconditionally by his fans? If you could choose, would you want to have Jonny's level of fame?

9. Toward the end of his tour, before his Detroit concert, Jonny thinks: "So screw them. If this is what they were giving me, I wasn't just going to do a bad job. I was going to make it my worst show ever" (page 236). What is making him feel this way? Does he deserve to be so angry? Why is he unable to follow through on his intention to deliver a poor show?

10. How does the author use the video game Zenon as a metaphor throughout the book? Does Jonny gain something valuable from the game or does the fictional world of Zenon obstruct his understanding of the real world?

11. Over the course of the book we learn that Jane has concealed from Jonny information both personal and music-related. In your opinion, are her decisions motivated more by protecting Jonny or herself, or by keeping him career-focused? Is she really the bad mother the press claims she is?

12. By the time Jonny finally gets a chance to meet his father, he has built up a number of expectations throughout the course of their correspondence. Discuss how this plays out, and what the result of this meeting means for both Jonny and the novel.

13. Throughout the book, Nadine and Jonny are studying slavery in their history lessons; Jonny's final essay question is "What does it mean to be the property of another person and what does it mean to be free?" (page 223). Talk about how this theme ties into the book's larger message. When Jonny claims at the end that he knows how to answer the essay question, do you think he's right? What does his answer tell you about the journey he's taken over the course of the book?

14. After reading this novel did your feelings about celebrity culture or the music industry change? Do you think one can have both celebrity and normalcy, or are they mutually exclusive?

Enhance Your Book Club

1. Have you ever read a musician's autobiography? If so, were there any similarities to *The Love Song of Jonny Valentine*? What about the autobiographies of some current pop stars, such as Justin Bieber or Miley Cyrus? Ask several members of your group to bring autobiographies to compare to the novel.

2. Set the mood for your book club by preparing a music playlist. What current hits remind your group most of Jonny's songs? Ask group members to suggest songs for the playlist.

3. Ask each member of the group to recall their favorite musicians when they were tweens or teens. Did any of those bands or singers achieve longevity? Discuss how tastes change and whether stars like Jonny can have lasting careers.

Author Q and A

How did you come to write this novel? What inspired you?
I wrote a now-defunct weekly column for *The New York Times* periodically over a span of two years. The focus was on marketing and media, and for nearly every article I would interview an expert in the field, who tended to overuse branding and marketing jargon unironically. Just as my experience editing MBA application essays filled with financial terminology informed the narrator's voice in my first novel, *Kapitoil*, I found this a worthwhile source to plunder for Jonny's vocabulary; it seemed like an apposite metaphor for our culture of self-promotion.

My other interest in writing this book comes from my own tepid flirtation with fame after *Kapitoil* came out in 2010. I was far from a household name, and literary renown is a pale imitation, but my limited exposure to the public showed me how uncomfortable the process made me (at times; it was also often gratifying)— and how incapable of functioning I would be if I ever had, say, Justin Bieber's level of celebrity. That, coupled with my lifelong fascination with both gifted children and child celebrities, inspired this novel.

Did you do any research for the novel? How did you create such an accurate representation of the music industry?
I read a number of child-celebrity autobiographies and biographies, as well as critical literature on the phenomenon. And I immersed myself in the shallower end of the pool, soaking up celebrity tabloids, concert documentaries and footage, and Internet fan sites. I knew a bit about the inner workings of the music industry from being a longtime fan and about the commercial side of media from my own experiences as a writer, but whenever possible I read up on

the behind-the-scenes music details, from recording to tour buses to song analysis.

Did you listen to pop music while writing? Any favorite artists or songs, now or from your teen years?

I expressly listened to more contemporary pop than I do normally to write this book; typically, I encounter it only through osmosis in public spaces. So while I recognize that such songs can occasionally be fun and energizing, my own tastes run (huge surprise) counter to Top 40 paradigms. When writing, I frequently listen to Bob Dylan, since I know the words well enough that they don't distract me, and for help in exploring Jonny's nascent rebellion, reconnected with my teenage musical love, the Clash.

The songs in the book are spot-on—how did you come up with them? Was it fun?

I'm an intermediate guitarist and singer—I wish I were better, but I don't have the chops. Over the years I've written my own, mostly jokey songs, often in the manner of Zack Ford improvising lyrics for the benefit of friends (mine are likely less appreciative). For this novel, though, I didn't want to satirize pop lyrics; I wanted to write realistic embodiments of them. If the effect is comic, it should be because they sound like the real thing, which provides enough comedy without embellishment. They were very fun to write, and I have recorded my own version of "Guys vs. Girls" on acoustic guitar. Record labels, I await your call.

On the one hand, the novel can be read as a dark, ironic send-up of tween pop stars, but on the other hand it's a very affecting coming-of-age story. How did you balance that duality?

Although I write a lot of short-form satire for magazines, I don't enjoy writing or, really, reading caustically satirical novels; I need to feel there's real heart and lives at stake. The key for any novel is crafting a voice, whether it's the author's or a character's, that makes the reader feel like what he or she is reading matters. Once you do that, a novel set on Mars in the year 2400 can seem more authentic than a warmed-over depiction of a failing marriage in contemporary America.

Is there any of your preadolescent experience in Jonny?

Were you not a fan of my 1990 smash hit, "Teddy Time (featuring Tone Lōc)"? Most of the novel draws from my and Tone's now-legendary North American tour as the short-lived T+T Music Factory. Otherwise, Jonny's preoccupations and anxieties are closer to my current state of mind than to my more unfettered pre-teen self. Ultimately, the question shouldn't be how I got into the head of an eleven-year-old boy for this novel, but how do I get *out* of it in my daily life? Every day is a struggle.

What inspired the video game The Secret Land of Zenon? Why is it so integral to Jonny's story?

Admitting to this childhood hobby will make me sound very cool: When I was around Jonny's age, I was a fan of Ultima, a role-playing computer-game series. What appealed to me about it was its completist rendering of an autonomous world. If you chose, you could simply live—one could bake bread, sell it for money, buy food, sleep, ad infinitum—as opposed to trying to win the game. Other characters went about their daily lives, too, as if your presence were irrelevant. It was the first time I saw a gaming world constructed in this profoundly nonlinear fashion. I modeled The Secret Land of Zenon off Ultima, as it makes sense why the career-focused, gaffe-fearing Jonny would want to escape into another world in which he can merely exist as a relatively anonymous character, and where he gains "experience points" by exploring different actions, though he doesn't know what their consequences will be. It's a metaphor for the kind of childhood that expects little of its participants other than that they should figure out who they are and learn from their experiences, for better or worse—precisely what Jonny's own upbringing prohibits.

Both your first novel and *The Love Song of Jonny Valentine* are written in the first person. What draws you to first-person narratives? What are the particular challenges or pleasures of creating a character's voice?

Although third-person novels afford a more epic scale, I have found that first-person novels speak most intimately to me and sustain the strongest illusion that I am inside someone else's head. As a writer, it is similarly pleasurable to escape my own self through another narrator's—and, in the process, end up ventriloquizing what is most important to me. I also prefer novels that take big ideas or settings (9/11 and Wall Street, pop stardom and the gilded cages of a corporate music tour) and funnel them down, quietly, to a highly specific character and viewpoint, as opposed to rendering them in equally sprawling terms (or aiming for a completely hushed story). The challenge is in justifying the first-person voice. If it is a voice that could just as easily be transposed to third person, then it doesn't necessarily warrant the more limited perspective. Both *Kapitoil* and this novel employ idiosyncratic voices that draw heavily from professional idioms while cutting them against mathematical and preteen grammars, respectively. It's difficult to maintain consistency in the writing at first—but then it becomes addictive.

Literary novelists don't command the sort of fame that pop stars do, but being a writer does involve publicity, marketing, and interacting with audiences. How do you balance writing and promoting?

Compared to my experiences promoting even the pre-Internet-age "Teddy Time (featuring Tone Lōc)," you're correct, this is a lot easier. But unless you're a globally celebrated writer, the publicity demands aren't that taxing, and to complain about them is a First World problem among First World problems. The real complaint should be when *no one* wants to hear from you, a condition that has afflicted me for lengthy periods (such as last week). So I'm grateful when the public shows any interest in me, and though I'm on various social media platforms, I don't do it so much that it takes over my life, both out of principle and laziness.

Do you see any similarities between the publishing industry and the music industry, though the scale may be different?

While the literary-publishing industry has more integrity than the pop-music industry (and likely an equal amount to the indie-music industry), and privileges intelligence and originality over image and derivative appeal, and sometimes makes knowingly unprofitable decisions, it is nonetheless a business, and functions the way any business must, even one dealing with ostensibly high art: trafficking in promotion and marketing and hype and packaging and positioning. Just as the majority of music hits are fulfilling expectations from their labels, most "big" books are preordained as such, their fates nearly sealed before publication (although there is always room for sleepers, and, of course, many of these fated bestsellers flop). Had I self-published this novel, there is little chance you would be reading it now, and even less chance it would be reviewed anywhere, though it would be the same text, minus my supremely talented editor's ministrations. It helps to have a polished presentation and a team of dedicated professionals whose job is to disseminate your book to the public. Nevertheless, everyone I've encountered in the field of publishing, to a person, believes deeply in what he or she is doing and could probably be making more money elsewhere; I'm not sure I'd be able to say the same about all music-industry professionals. While *Valentine Days* is Jonny's second album and *The Love Song of Jonny Valentine* is my second novel, I'm happy to have a less cynical relationship with my own industry, though it is still fair to use the word "industry."

Mostly I'm just glad they never make authors do the equivalent of liner notes.

About the Author

Teddy Wayne is the author of *Kapitoil* (Harper Perennial, 2010), for which he was the winner of a 2011 Whiting Writers' Award and a finalist for the New York Public Library Young Lions Fiction Award, the PEN/Robert W. Bingham Prize, and the Dayton Literary Peace Prize. His work regularly appears in *The New Yorker*, *The New York Times*, *Vanity Fair*, *McSweeney's*, and elsewhere. A graduate of Harvard and Washington University in St. Louis and the recipient of an NEA Creative Writing Fellowship, he lives in New York.